CALL DOWN
THE HAWK

CALL DOWN THE HAWK

MAGGIE STIEFVATER

SCHOLASTIC PRESS · NEW YORK

All rights reserved. Published by Scholastic Press, an imprint of Scholastic Inc., *Publishers since 1920*. SCHOLASTIC, SCHOLASTIC PRESS, and associated logos are trademarks and/or registered trademarks of Scholastic Inc.

The publisher does not have any control over and does not assume any responsibility for author or third-party websites or their content.

Library of Congress Cataloging-in-Publication Data available

ISBN 978-1-338-18832-5

10 9 8 7 6 5 4 3 2 1   19 20 21 22 23

Printed in the U.S.A.   23
First edition, November 2019

Book design by Christopher Stengel

*to the magicians who woke me from
my thousand-year sleep*

I will not be clapped in a hood,
Nor a cage, nor alight upon wrist,
Now I have learnt to be proud
Hovering over the wood
In the broken mist
Or tumbling cloud.

—WILLIAM BUTLER YEATS,
"THE HAWK"

If a little dreaming is dangerous, the cure for it is not
to dream less but to dream more, to dream all the time.

—MARCEL PROUST, *IN SEARCH OF*
LOST TIME, VOL. II

Are you sure that a floor cannot also be a ceiling?

—M. C. ESCHER, "ON BEING
A GRAPHIC ARTIST"

PROLOGUE

This is going to be a story about the Lynch brothers.

There were three of them, and if you didn't like one, try another, because the Lynch brother others found too sour or too sweet might be just to your taste. The Lynch brothers, the orphans Lynch. All of them had been made by dreams, one way or another. They were handsome devils, down to the last one.

They looked after themselves. Their mother, Aurora, had died the way some dreams did, gruesomely, blamelessly, unexpectedly. Their father, Niall, had been killed or murdered, depending on how human you considered him. Were there other Lynches? It seemed unlikely. Lynches appeared to be very good at dying.

Dreams are not the safest thing to build a life on.

Because the Lynch brothers had been in danger for so much of their lives, they'd each developed methods of mitigating threats. Declan, the eldest, courted safety by being as dull as possible. He was very good at it. In all things—school, extracurriculars, dating—he invariably chose the dullest option. He had a real gift for it; some forms of boring suggest that the wearer, deep down inside, might actually be a person of whimsy and nuance, but Declan made certain to practice a form of boring that suggested that, deep down inside, there was an even more boring version of him. Declan was not invisible, because invisible had its own charm, its own mystery. He was simply *dull*. Technically he was a college student, a political intern, a twenty-one-year-old with his whole life ahead of him, but it was hard to remember that. It was hard to remember him at all.

Matthew, the youngest, floated in safety by being as kind as possible. He was sweet humored, pliable, and gentle. He *liked* things, and not in an ironic way. He laughed at puns. He swore like a greeting card. He looked kindly, too, growing from a cherubic, golden-haired child to an Adonic, golden-haired seventeen-year-old. All of this treacly, tousled goodness might have been insufferable had not Matthew also been an excruciatingly messy eater, a decidedly lazy student, and not very bright. Everyone wanted to hug Matthew Lynch, and he wanted to let them.

Ronan, the middle brother, defended his safety by being as frightening as possible. Like the other Lynch brothers, he was a regular churchgoer, but most people assumed he played for the other team. He dressed in funereal black and had a raven as a pet. He shaved his hair close to his skull and his back was inked with a clawed and toothed tattoo. He wore an acidic expression and said little. What words he did unsheathe turned out to be knives, glinting and edged and unpleasant to have stuck into you. He had blue eyes. People generally think blue eyes are pretty, but his were not. They were not cornflower, sky, baby, indigo, azure. His were iceberg, squall, hypothermia, eventual death. Everything about him suggested he might take your wallet or drop your baby. He was proud of the family name, and it suited him. His mouth was always shaped like he'd just finished saying it.

The Lynch brothers had many secrets.

Declan was a collector of beautiful, specific phrases that

he would not let himself use in public, and the possessor of an illuminated, specific smile no one would ever see. Matthew had a forged birth certificate and no fingerprints. Sometimes, if he let his mind wander, he found himself walking in a perfectly straight line. Toward something? Away from something? This was a secret even to himself.

Ronan had the most dangerous of the secrets. Like many significant secrets, it was passed down through the family—in this case, from father to son. This was the good and bad of Ronan Lynch: The good was that sometimes, when he fell asleep and dreamt, he woke with that dream. The bad was that sometimes, when he fell asleep and dreamt, he woke with that dream. Monsters and machines, weather and wishes, fears and forests.

Dreams are not the safest thing to build a life on.

After their parents died, the Lynch brothers kept their heads down. Declan removed himself from the business of dreams and went to school for the dullest possible degree in political science. Ronan kept his nightmare games confined to the family farm in rural Virginia as best as he could. And Matthew—well, Matthew only had to keep on making sure he didn't accidentally walk away.

Declan grew more boring and Ronan grew more bored. Matthew tried not to let his feet take him someplace he didn't understand.

They all wanted more.

One of them had to break, eventually. Niall had been a wild Belfast dreamer with fire biting at his heels, and Aurora had been a golden dream with the borderless sky reflected in her eyes. Their sons were built for chaos.

It was a sharp October, a wild October, one of those fretful spans of time that climbs into your skin and flits around. It was two months after the fall semester had begun. The trees were all brittle and grasping. The drying leaves were skittish. Winter yowled round the doorways at night until wood fires drove it away for another few hours.

There was something else afoot that October, something else stretching and straining and panting, but it was mostly as of yet unseen. Later it would have a name, but for now, it simply agitated everything uncanny it touched, and the Lynch brothers were no exception.

Declan broke first.

While the youngest brother was in school and the middle brother malingered at the family farm, Declan opened a drawer in his bedroom and removed a piece of paper with a telephone number on it. His heart beat faster just to look at it. He should have destroyed it, but instead, he entered it into his phone.

"The Lynch boy?" said the voice on the other side of the line.

"Yes," he said simply, "I want the key." Then he hung up.

He told no one else about the call, not even his brothers. What was one more tiny secret, he thought, in a life full of them.

Boredom and secrets: an explosive combination.

Something was going to burn.

I

Creatures of all kinds had begun to fall asleep.

The cat was the most dramatic. It was a beautiful animal, if you liked cats, with a dainty face and long, cottony fur, the kind that seemed like it would melt away into liquid sugar. It was a calico, which under normal circumstances would mean it was certainly not an *it*, but rather a *she*. Calico had to be inherited from two X chromosomes. Perhaps that rule didn't apply here, though, in this comely rural cottage nearly no one knew about. Forces other than science held domain in this place. The calico might not even be a cat at all. It was cat-shaped, but so were some birthday cakes.

It had watched them kill him.

Caomhán Browne had been his name. Was still his name, really. Like good boots, identities outlived those who wore them. They had been told he was dangerous, but he'd thrown everything but what they'd feared at them. A tiny end table. A plump and faded floral recliner. A stack of design magazines. A flat-screen television of modest size. He'd actually stabbed Ramsay with the crucifix from the hallway wall, which Ramsay found funny even during the act of it. *Holy smokes*, he'd said.

One of the women wore lambskin dress-for-success heeled boots, and there was now an unbelievable amount of blood on them. One of the men was prone to migraines, and he could feel the dreamy magic of the place sparking the lights of an aura at the edges of his vision.

In the end, Lock, Ramsay, Nikolenko, and Farooq-Lane had cornered both Browne and the cat in the low-ceilinged kitchen of the Irish holiday cottage, nothing within Browne's reach but a decorative dried broom on the wall and the cat. The broom wasn't good for anything, even sweeping, but the cat might have been used to good effect if thrown properly. Few have the constitution to throw a cat properly, however, and Browne was not one of them. One could see the moment he realized he didn't have it in him and gave up.

"Please don't kill the trees," he said.

They shot him. A few times. Mistakes were expensive and bullets were cheap.

The calico was lucky it hadn't gotten shot, too, crouched behind Browne as it was. Bullets go through things; that's their job. Instead it merely got splattered with blood. It let out an uncanny howl full of rage. It bottle-brushed its tail and puffed its cotton coat. Then it hurled itself straight at them, because you can trust that the Venn diagram of cats and folks willing to throw cats is a circle.

There was a very brief moment where it seemed quite possible that one of them was about to be wearing a cat with every claw extended.

But then Browne gave a final shiver and went still.

The cat dropped.

A body hits the floor with a sound like no other; the multi-faceted *fhlomp* of an unconscious bag of bones can't be replicated in any other way. The calico made this sound and then was also still. Unlike Browne, however, its chest continued to rise and fall, rise and fall, rise and fall.

It was impossibly, unnaturally, entirely asleep.

"Truly fucked up," remarked Ramsay.

There was a window over the little white sink, and through it one could see a deep green field and, closer, three shaggy ponies standing in the churned-up mud by the gate. They sagged to their knees, tipping against each other like drowsy fellows. A pair of goats bleated a confused question before slumping like the ponies. There were chickens, too, but they had already fallen asleep, soft multicolored mounds littered across the green.

Caomhán Browne had been what the Moderators called a Zed. This is what it meant to be a Zed: Sometimes, when they dreamt, they woke up with a thing they'd been dreaming about in their hands. The cat, as suspected, was not a cat. It was a cat-shaped thing drawn out of Browne's head. And like all of Browne's living dreams, it could not stay awake if Browne was dead.

"Note time of death for the record," said Nikolenko.

They all cast their attention back to their prey—or their victim, depending on how human one found him. Farooq-Lane checked her phone and tapped a message into it.

Then they went to find the other Zed.

Overhead, the clouds were dark, eclipsing the tops of the slanting hills. The little Kerry farm was edged by a tiny, mossy wood. It was beautiful, but in between the trees, the air hummed even more than in the cottage. It was not exactly that they couldn't breathe in this atmosphere. It was more like they couldn't think, or like they could think too much. They were all getting a little nervous; the threats seemed truer out here.

The other Zed wasn't even trying to hide. Lock found him sat in the crook of a mossy tree with a disturbingly blank expression.

"You killed him, didn't you?" the Zed asked. Then, when Farooq-Lane joined Lock, he said, "Oh, you."

Complicated familiarity coursed between the Zed and Farooq-Lane.

"It doesn't have to be this way," Farooq-Lane said. She was shivering a little. Not a cold shiver. Not a frightened shiver. One of those *rabbits running over your grave* numbers. "All you have to do is stop dreaming."

Lock cleared his throat as if he felt the bargain wasn't quite as simple as that, but he said nothing.

"Really?" The Zed peered up at Farooq-Lane. His attention was fully on her, as if the others weren't there. Fair enough; her attention was entirely on him, too. "That kills me either way. I expected more complexity from you, Carmen."

Lock raised his gun. He did not say it out loud, but he found this Zed a particularly creepy son of a bitch, and that was even without taking into account what he'd done. "Then you've made your choice."

During all of this, Ramsay had fetched his gas cans from the back of the rental car; he'd been dying to use them all day. *Petrol*, he'd smirked, as if variations in English usage were sufficient material for a joke. Now the small copse had begun to stink of the sweet, carcinogenic perfume of gasoline as Ramsay drop-kicked the last of the gas cans in the direction of the cottage. He was probably the sort of person who would throw a cat.

"We'll need to watch the road while it burns," said Lock. "Let's make this quick."

The Zed looked at them with detached interest. "I under-stand *me*, guys, but why Browne? He was a kitten. What are you afraid of?"

Lock said, "Someone is coming. Someone is coming to end the world."

In this humming wood, dramatic phrases like *end the world* felt not only plausible but probable.

The Zed quirked a gallows smile. "Is it you?"

Lock shot him. Several times. It was pretty clear the first one had done the job, but Lock kept going until he stopped feeling so creeped out. As the shots finished echoing through the wood, something deeper in the copse thudded to the ground with the same distinctive sound as the cat in the kitchen. It had some weight to it. All of them were glad that this dream had fallen asleep before they'd had a chance to meet it.

Now that the woods were silent, everyone left alive looked at Carmen Farooq-Lane.

Her eyes were squeezed tightly shut and her face was turned away, like she'd been bracing for a bullet herself. Her mouth worked but she didn't cry. She did appear younger. Ordinarily she presented herself with such corporate sophistication—linen suits, lovely updos—that it was difficult to guess her age: one saw only a successful, self-possessed businesswoman. But this moment stripped away the glamour and revealed her as the twenty-something she was. It was not a comfortable sensation; there was the strong urge to wrap a blanket around her to return her dignity. But at least they couldn't doubt her dedication. She'd been in this as deep as any of them and had seen it through to the end.

Lock put a paternal hand on her shoulder. In his deep voice, he rumbled, "Fucked-up situation."

It was difficult to tell if this offered Farooq-Lane any comfort.

He told the others, "Let's finish this up and get out of here."

Ramsay lit a match. He used it first to light a cigarette for Nikolenko, and next to light a cigarette for himself. Then he dropped it into the gasoline-soaked undergrowth just before the flame bit his fingertips.

The forest began to burn.

Farooq-Lane turned away.

Releasing a puff of cigarette smoke in the direction of the dead Zed's body, Ramsay asked, "Have we saved the world?"

Lock tapped the time of Nathan Farooq-Lane's death into his phone. "Too soon to say."

2

Ronan Lynch was about to end the world.

His world, anyway. He was ending one and starting another. At the beginning of this road trip would be one Ronan Lynch, and at the end, there would be another.

"Here's the situation," Declan said. This was a classic Declan way to start a conversation. Other hits included *Let's focus on the real action item* and *This is what it's going to take to close this deal* and *In the interest of clearing the air*. "I would have no problem with you driving my car if you would keep it under ninety."

"And I'd have no problem with riding in your car if you'd keep it over *geriatric*," Ronan replied.

It was early November; the trees were handsome; the sky was clear; excitement was in the air. The three brothers debated in a Goodwill parking lot; those entering and leaving stared. They were an eye-catchingly mismatched threesome: Ronan, with his ominous boots and ominous expression; Declan, with his perfectly controlled curls and dutiful gray suit; Matthew, with his outstandingly ugly checked pants and cheerfully blue puffer coat.

Ronan continued, "There are stains that spread faster than you drive. If you drive, it'll take fourteen years to get there. Seventeen. Forty. One hundred. We'll be driving to your funeral by the end."

The Lynch brothers were on the first road trip they'd been on since their parents died. They'd made it fifteen minutes from

Declan's home before Declan had received a call he refused to take in the car. Now they continued to be delayed by negotiations for the driver's seat. Ronan had driven this far; opinions were divided on whether he should get the privilege again. In the Goodwill lot, the brothers presented the facts: It was Declan's car, Ronan's trip, Matthew's vacation. Declan had a letter from the insurance company offering him better rates for his exceptional driving record. Ronan had a letter from the state advising him to change his driving habits lest he lose his license. Matthew had no interest in driving; he said if he didn't have enough friends to drive him anywhere he wanted to go, he was living his life wrong. In any case, he'd failed his driver's test three times.

"Ultimately the decision is mine," Declan said, "as it's my car."

He didn't add *and also because I'm the oldest*, although it hung in the air. Epic battles had been waged between the brothers over this understood sentiment. It represented considerable progress in their relationship that it remained unspoken this time.

"Thank Jesus," Ronan said. "No one else wants it."

"It's very safe," Declan murmured, eyes on his phone. Time burned as he replied to a text or email in the peculiar way he always did, typing with his left thumb and his right index finger.

Ronan kicked one of the Volvo's tires. He wanted to be on the road. He *needed to* be on the road.

"We'll swap every two hours," Declan finally said in his bland way. "That's fair, right? You're happy. I'm happy. Everyone's happy."

That was untrue. Only Matthew was perfectly happy, because Matthew was always perfectly happy. He looked pleased as a pig in slop as he slid into the backseat with his headphones.

He said cheerily, "I'm gonna need snacks before this rig gets to where it's goin'."

Declan put the keys in Ronan's hands. "If you get pulled over, you're never driving my car again."

Then they were off, properly off, Washington, DC, in the rearview mirror.

Ronan couldn't quite believe that Declan had agreed to the premise of the road trip. This excursion, designed for Ronan to tour three rental properties in an entirely different state, seemed to fall solidly under activities Declan would've frowned upon in the past. Ronan, with his dangerous dreams, sleeping someplace other than the Barns or Declan's town house? Dubious. *Moving* someplace other than the Barns or Declan's town house? Never.

Ronan didn't know why Declan was entertaining it. What he did know was that they were an eight-hour drive from finding out if Ronan got to start a whole new life. Aside from a miserable period just after their father, Niall, had died, he'd never lived anywhere but the Barns, the family farm. He loved the Barns, he was bored of the Barns, he wanted to leave, he wanted to stay. At the Barns, Ronan was two seconds from his childhood memories and two hours' drive from his brothers. He knew he could dream safely there, surrounded by nothing but other dreams. He knew who he was there.

Who would Ronan Lynch be in Cambridge?

He had no idea.

In Maryland, they swapped and obtained gas station snacks for Matthew. He ate them in the backseat, noisily, with audible enjoyment. As Declan pulled back onto the interstate, he ordered

Matthew to close his mouth while eating; a fruitless exhortation, as people had been saying this to Matthew for seventeen years.

"Just get him soft food," Ronan advised. "That's the solution. No one hears gummy snacks go down the hatch."

Matthew laughed again. The only thing he enjoyed more than jokes about Declan were jokes about himself.

After they had been on the road for several minutes, Declan asked Ronan in a low voice, "How long has it been since you dreamt?"

Matthew wasn't listening, lost in the pleasures of his headphones and the game on his phone, but it wouldn't have mattered anyway. Ronan's dreaming wasn't a secret to Matthew. Declan just liked everything better if it was a secret.

"Recently."

"Recently enough?"

"I don't know, let me check my dreamer schedule. It'll tell me precisely how recently is recently enough." Ronan emptied a bag of chocolate-covered peanuts into his mouth in the hopes that it would end the conversation. He didn't want to talk about it, but he didn't want to sound like he didn't want to talk about it. He choked a little bit on the peanuts but otherwise managed to look diffident. Unconcerned. It would be fine, his peanut-eating added. Let's talk about something else, his peanut-eating suggested. You're being unreasonable to even ask, the peanut-eating concluded.

Declan held a protein bar against the steering wheel but didn't open it. "Don't act like I'm being unreasonable to ask."

There were two major reasons why overnight traveling was fraught for a dreamer. The first, and most obvious, was that Ronan could never be one hundred percent certain that he wasn't going to accidentally manifest one of his dreams when he woke up. Sometimes the dreams were harmless—a feather, perhaps, or a dead aquarium fish, or a potted plant. But sometimes they were formless songs that made the listener feel physically sick, or lizards with insatiable appetites, or two thousand Oxford shoes, all lefts, all size 9. When these things appeared in waking life at the Lynch family's remote Barns, they were annoyances, sometimes a little more (lizard bites could be very painful). But when they appeared in waking life at Declan's town house or in a hotel room or next to the car Ronan slept in at a rest area—well.

"Can I open your unhappy yuppie candy bar for you?" Ronan asked.

"Don't deflect," Declan chided. But after a moment, he handed over the protein bar.

Ronan peeled the wrapper open and took an experimental bite before handing it back. It felt precisely like he'd fallen face-first into wet, dirty sand.

"Classy, Ronan." Declan blew lightly on the bitten end of the bar as if his breath would lift the Ronan-germs from it. "I just don't know if you're taking this seriously."

The second reason why traveling as a dreamer was fraught was the nightwash: a sexy word Ronan had invented for an unsexy phenomenon. It was a fairly new consequence for him, and all he knew was that if he waited too long between manifesting dreams or spent too long away from the western Virginia foothills where he was born, black ooze began to run from his nose. Then his eyes. Then his ears. If it went unchecked, he could feel it filling his chest, his brain, his body. Killing him. Maybe there was a way to stop it, but Ronan didn't know any other living dreamers to ask. He'd only known two in his life—his father and a now-dead student at his high school—and they'd never talked about it. How well would he tolerate staying in Cambridge, Massachusetts, instead of at the Barns for any length of time? He wouldn't know until he tried.

"It's my turn to pick the music," Matthew said.

"*No*," Declan and Ronan agreed at once.

Declan's phone fussed for attention in the center console. Ronan started to pick it up, but Declan snatched it out of his hands with such speed that he nearly ran off the road. Ronan just had time to see the beginning of the incoming text: *The key is—*

"Whoa there, outlaw," said Ronan. "I wasn't gonna touch your girl."

Declan shoved the phone into the driver side pocket.

"New personal trainer?" Ronan suggested. "New protein bar supplier? Hot lead on some high-tread carpet for the home and garden?"

Declan didn't reply. Matthew hummed along happily to his headphones.

Neither of his brothers had said anything about how they felt about Ronan moving, and he couldn't decide if it was because it didn't make a difference to them or because they didn't really think it would work.

He didn't know which one he'd rather it was.

New York: They pulled over at a service area. Matthew sprinted lightly for the toilets. Declan took another call. Ronan paced. The wind felt crafty and inventive as it worked under his collar, and his pulse felt as fast and streaky as the thin November clouds above.

The little trees bordering the service area were sparse

and shapeless, gathered sticks rather than a forest. They were foreign trees. Strangers. Fragile citizens of an urban zip code. Somehow the sight of them drove home the truth of what Ronan was attempting. For so many years, nothing had changed. He'd dropped out of high school, which he didn't regret, not exactly, and his friends had graduated. Two of them, Gansey and Blue, had invited him on their gap year cross-country road trip, but he hadn't wanted to go anywhere then. Not when he had just gotten entirely wrapped up in—

". . . Adam yet?" Matthew had asked a question, but Ronan had missed it. Matthew had returned with a bag of gummies, and he monched them quietly. "See, I take constructive cristicism. Criticist. Criticism. Gol darn it."

Adam.

Adam Parrish was the destination of this road trip.

Is there any version of you that could come with me to Cambridge? Adam had asked the day he left.

Maybe. Ronan had visited him once since the semester began, but it had been spontaneous—he'd gotten in his car in the middle of the night, spent the day with Adam, and then left the city without closing his eyes for a second. He hadn't really wanted to test himself.

Plausible deniability. Ronan Lynch could make it in Cambridge until proven otherwise.

Adam.

Ronan missed him like a lung.

Declan reappeared, looking at his watch with the expression of a man used to it disappointing him. He opened the driver side door.

"Hey, it's my turn," Ronan protested. If he wasn't driving,

he knew his thoughts would race for the final two hours of the drive. Adam knew Ronan was coming this weekend, but he didn't know Ronan had appointments to see rentals. Ronan couldn't decide how he'd react. "We had a deal."

"A deal full of Goodwill," Matthew said. "That's a joke."

"You aren't driving my car among those Massholes." Declan shut the door as punctuation. Matthew shrugged. Ronan spat.

In the car, Matthew leaned forward to triumphantly claim the AUX cable. A dubstep remix of a pop song oompahed over the speakers.

It was going to be a long two hours to Cambridge.

Ronan put his jacket over his head to drown out the sound and muffle his building nerves. He could feel his pulse thudding in his jaw. He could hear it in his ears. It sounded like everyone else's heartbeat, he thought. Just like Adam's heart when his head was resting on his chest. Ronan wasn't that different. Well, he could seem not that different. He could move to follow the guy he loved, like anyone else. He could live in a city, like anyone else. It could work.

He began to dream.

3

There was a voice in Ronan's dream.

You know this isn't how the world is supposed to be.

It was everywhere and nowhere.

At night, we used to see stars. You could see by starlight back then, after the sun went down. Hundreds of headlights chained together in the sky, good enough to eat, good enough to write legends about, good enough to launch men at.

You don't remember because you were born too late.

The voice was unavoidable and natural, like air, like weather.

Maybe I underestimate you. Your head's full of dreams. They must remember.

Does any part of you still look at the sky and hurt?

Ronan was lying in the middle of an interstate. Three lanes each direction, no cars, just Ronan. In the way of dreams, he understood that the road began at the Barns and ended at Harvard and that he was somewhere in between. Little strangled trees struggled through the thin grass by the road. The sky was the same color as the worn asphalt.

We used to hear the stars, too. When people stopped talking, there was silence. Now you could shut every mouth on the planet and there'd still be a hum. Air-conditioning groaning from the vent beside you. Semi trucks hissing on a highway miles away. A plane complaining ten thousand feet above you.

Silence is an extinct word.

It bothers you, doesn't it?

But the dream was perfectly silent, except for the voice. Ronan hadn't thought about how long it had been since he'd experienced perfect silence until that moment. He wasn't sure he *had* experienced perfect silence before that moment. It was peaceful, not dead. Like putting down a weight he hadn't realized he was carrying, the weight of noise, the weight of every-one else.

Magic. It's a cheap word now. Put a quarter in the slot and get a magic trick for you and your friends. Most people don't remember what it is. It is not cutting a person in half and pulling a rabbit out. It is not sliding a card from your sleeve. It's not are you watching closely?

If you've ever looked into a fire and been unable to look away, it's that. If you've ever looked at the mountains and found you're not breathing, it's that. If you've ever looked at the moon and felt tears in your eyes, it's that.

It's the stuff between stars, the space between roots, the thing that makes electricity get up in the morning.

It fucking hates us.

Ronan wasn't sure what the voice belonged to, or if it belonged to anything. In a dream, physical truths were unimportant. Maybe the voice belonged to this road beneath him. The sky. Someone standing just out of sight.

The opposite of magical *is not* ordinary. *The opposite of* magical is mankind. *The world is a neon sign; it says* HUMANITY *but everything's burnt out except* MAN.

Are you understanding what I'm trying to tell you?

Ronan felt rumbling against his skull: distant trucks roaring toward him where he lay in the center lane.
He refused to let the dream be a nightmare.
Be music, he told the dream.
The rumbling of approaching trucks turned into the thudding of Matthew's dubstep.

The world's killing you, but They'll kill you faster. Capital-T They. Them. You don't know Them yet, but you will.

Bryde. The voice's name suddenly dropped into Ronan's thoughts in the way the knowledge about the interstate had, presented as an understood truth: The sky was blue; the asphalt

was warm; the voice belonged to someone whose name was
Bryde.

*There are two sides to the battle in front of us, and on one side is Black
Friday discount, Wi-Fi hotspot, this year's model, subscription only,
now with more stretch, noise-canceling-noise-creating headphones, one
car to every green, this lane ends.*

The other side is magic.

With effort, Ronan recalled where his physical body was,
riding in a car with his brothers, on his way to Adam and a new
life with his dreams firmly under control.

Don't bring anything back, Ronan told himself. Don't bring back
a truck, or a road sign, or dubstep that can never be shut off, only
buried in a yard somewhere. Keep your dreams in your head.
Prove to Declan you can do it.

Bryde whispered:

You are made of dreams and this world is not for you.

Ronan woke up.

4

"W ake up, Waaaaaashington, DC! Authorities should be notified," laughed TJ Sharma, the host of the party. "Someone tell them a young woman with superpowers is on the loose."

All eyes in the DC-suburb McMansion were on Jordan, a young woman with eyes like a miracle and a smile like a nuclear accident. The other partygoers wore relaxed casual; Jordan didn't believe in either relaxing or being casual. She wore a leather jacket and lace bustier, her natural hair pulled into an enormous kinky ponytail. The floral tattoos on her neck and fingers glowed bright against her dark skin and her enthusiasm glowed bright against the suburban night.

"Shhh, shhh," Jordan said. "Superpowers are like children, mate—"

"Two-point-five for every American family?" TJ asked.

"Better seen than heard," Jordan corrected.

In the background, a nineties band whined frantically about their youth. The microwave dinged—more cheap popcorn. The party's mood was equally ironic and nostalgic; TJ had joked the theme was delayed development. There was a punch bowl full of Cinnamon Toast Crunch, and *SpongeBob* played on the flat screen next to a pile of PS2 games. The partygoers were all mostly whiter than her, older than her, safer than her. She didn't know what they'd be doing at this party if she wasn't performing for them.

"Push in, punters—queuing is for rule followers," she said. She indicated the scratch paper TJ had provided. "Homework time. No partial credit. Write 'the quick brown fox jumps over the lazy dog' and then put your name to it in your best school signature."

Jordan was attending this party as Hennessy. No one here knew the real Hennessy, so there was no one to say she wasn't. Even TJ knew her as Hennessy. Jordan was accustomed to wearing identities that weren't hers—it would've felt stranger, in fact, for someone to know her by her actual name.

"You're gonna love this," TJ told the others, voice invested with high excitement. Jordan liked him well enough—he was the young vice president of an area bank, a slender-boned Peter Pan, a boy in a grown-up world, or vice versa. He still bought himself toys and waited for his phone to tell him when to go to bed. He lived in this mass-produced mansion with roommates, not because he couldn't afford to live alone, but because he hadn't yet learned how to.

They'd met on the streets of DC just a few weeks after Hennessy and Jordan had first arrived in the area. One a.m., nothing but anticipation and mercury vapor lighting the night. Jordan was on her way to return a stolen car before it got them all shot, and TJ was returning from a bored midnight Walmart run.

His: a souped-up Toyota Supra he'd bought off eBay after seeing one in a YouTube series.

Hers: a souped-up old Challenger Hennessy had stolen a few hours before.

He'd challenged her to a grudge match at a gas station. Winner took the other's car. Jordan wasn't ordinarily a fool, but she was just enough like Hennessy to get sucked into such a game.

The short version of the story was that Jordan now drove a Supra everywhere. She'd driven TJ for a little while, too, but Jordan didn't date anyone for long. They were still friends, though. Or at least as close as people could be when one of them was pretending to be someone else.

"The key to proper forgery," Jordan told the partygoers, "is to remember you can't copy it, the signature. The curves and the flourishes will look stilted, everything will end in hard stops instead of trailing off prettily. *Okay*, I hear you say, *so I'll trace it.* No way. Trace it, the lines'll wobble their way from bed to pub and back. Any amateur who looks close can tell if a signature's been traced. *But, Hennessy*, I hear you say, *what else is there?* You have to internalize the organic structure of it, don't you? You have to get the architecture in your hand, you have to have the system of shapes memorized. Intuition, not logic."

As she spoke, she rapidly drew signatures and random letter combinations over and over. She barely looked at her work as she did, her eyes entirely on the partygoers' handwriting. "You have to become that person for a little bit."

Jordan had homed in on just one of the handwriting samples. *The quick brown fox jumps over the lazy dog*, signed with the unusual name *Breck Myrtle.* It was an angular signature, which was easier than a fluid one, and he had a few really good specific tics in his handwriting that would make the trick satisfying for onlookers.

Flipping the paper over to hide her scratchings, she confidently wrote one last set of words on the blank expanse: *I deed over all my possessions on this day in November to the most fabulous Hennessy.* Then she signed it flawlessly: *Breck Myrtle.*

Jordan pushed the paper to the partygoers for their assessment.

There were delighted noises. Laughs. A few sounds of mock dismay.

Breck Myrtle, the partygoer in question, had a complicated reaction to this. "How did you . . . ?"

"She's got you, Breck," said one of the other women. "That's perfect."

"Isn't she scary?" asked TJ.

None of them had seen the scariest bits of her—not by a long shot. If Breck Myrtle kept talking, Jordan could've learned to predict his way of using language, too, and she could use that knowledge to compose personal letters and emails and texts instead of having to hide in formal contractual language. Forgery was a skill transferrable to many media, even if she generally used them more in her personal than business life.

"You're so young for crime," laughed one of the other women.

"She's just coming into her powers," TJ said.

But Jordan had been pretty well into her powers for a while. Both she and the real Hennessy were art forgers. The other girls in their house dabbled in it, but they were more properly copyists. Jordan found there was a tendency to misunderstand—to conflate—art forgers with copyists. The art world had plenty of artists who could replicate famous paintings down to every last fold in a sleeve. *Copies*, Hennessy would say contemptuously, *are not art*. A true forgery was a new painting made *in the style* of the original artist. To copy an existing Matisse was nothing: All one needed was a grid system and a good understanding of color and technique. To forge a new Matisse, one must not only paint like Matisse, but one must also *think* like Matisse. *That*, Hennessy would say, *is art*.

And Jordan would agree.

A doorbell ring cut through the nineties music.

Jordan's heart flopped with anticipation.

"Bernie!" TJ said. "You don't have to ring the bell like a stranger! Come in, straggler!"

Jordan was still friendly with TJ, but she wouldn't have partied with his more boring friends without an ulterior motive. And here the motive was: a woman in a smart, purple pantsuit and tinted round glasses. Bernadette Feinman. With her silver hair gripped tight in a glinting pearl claw, Feinman looked like the only adult in the room. She looked not only like an adult but also like an adult ready to make a coat out of one hundred and one Dalmatians. Unknown to probably everyone else in the room, Feinman was also one of the gatekeepers for the DC Fairy Market, a rotating, global, underground black market that traded in all sorts of prestigious illegal goods and services. Emphasis on *prestigious*.

Not just any old criminal could display wares at the Market. You had to be a high-class criminal.

Jordan wanted in. She *needed* in.

Bernadette Feinman would decide.

Feinman stepped deeper into the house. She had a creaky, particular way of walking, like a mantis, but when she spoke, her voice was soft and melodic. "I would say I didn't mean to be late, but I think we should be honest with each other."

TJ pressed a drink into her hand, looking like a little boy cautiously making sure a respected grandmother had everything she needed. Everyone else got beer, Jordan noted, but Feinman got a stem glass with a leggy white wine for one hand and a clove cigarette for the other.

"This is Bernie, guys. She's my Yoda, my mentor, so let's drink to our elders!" TJ said. He kissed her cheek. The party-goers drank to their elders, and then they turned on the PS2.

Feinman leaned over the table to look at the signatures. She raised her gaze to Jordan. "So you're Hennessy. Surely this isn't all you've got."

Jordan flashed a huge grin at her. Her world-eating grin, full of confidence and goodwill. No sign of nerves or how important this was to her.

TJ frowned a little. "What, Bernie?"

"Hennessy's interviewing for a spot at the agency." Feinman lied so swiftly that Jordan wondered if she'd had the lie prepared before she got there.

"Doing biz at my party?" TJ said. "You're supposed to pay the daily rate for my living room conference room if it's for business purposes."

Feinman handed him her still-full glass. "Go find me some more wine, Tej."

TJ went away, silent and obedient as a child.

Clacking silver-painted nails on Breck's forged signature, Feinman cut through the bullshit. "I trust I'll be looking at more than party tricks."

"These are candy bars at the cashier," Jordan said. "Don't mistake them for an entrée."

Feinman's teeth were a little line of pearls hidden behind tight lips. "Fetch me the meal, then."

"Back in a tick."

Jordan's grin vanished the moment she wound out into the cold November. For a moment she steadied herself by looking at the Supra on the curb she'd won it from, at the way the suburban houses behind it were lit by washes of porch and garage lights, the way the cars slept quietly in the half-light beneath skeletal fall trees. She thought about how she'd paint this neighborhood, where she'd place the focal point, what she would emphasize, what she would push back into obscurity. She thought of how she'd make it art.

Then she pulled six paintings from the car and rejoined the party.

Inside, she laid her goods on the dining room table for Feinman to examine them, wine glass held in mantis grip. They were copies. Demonstrations of power. A Mary Cassatt, a Hockney, a Waterhouse, a Whistler, and a *Mona Lisa* with Jordan's tattoos, because Jordan liked a joke as well as anyone.

If the partygoers had been amused before, now they were properly impressed. Even forged Breck Myrtle had returned to look closely.

"You're scary," TJ said. "You can really look like anyone, can't you?"

Feinman leaned close to study the important parts: the edges of canvases and boards, marks on backs, textures, brushwork, pigments used, accuracy of the supports. She wasn't going to find a fault.

"What does your own art look like?" Feinman asked.

Jordan didn't know. She spent all her time painting other people's. "A lady never tells."

"I think it must be pretty spectacular." Feinman and her clove cigarette moved close to the parody *Mona Lisa*. The paint was aged and cracked and looked precisely like a museum find, but the anachronistic tattoos proved its etymology. "Although these games have their pleasures."

Jordan held her breath.

She needed this. They needed this.

TJ said, "So is she getting the job?"

Feinman turned her mantis body toward Jordan and peered with the same intense gaze she'd previously used on the copies, her eyes unblinking behind her tinted glasses. She was, Jordan thought, someone who was used to her word being god—her word being god both to someone like TJ and to someone like Jordan. It seemed to Jordan that if you could hold dominion over both those worlds—both day and night—you had quite a lot of power indeed.

"Sometimes," Feinman said, "you have to turn someone down because they're too qualified. You don't want to hold them back from who they're meant to be."

It took Jordan a beat to realize that she was being told no.

"Oh, but—"

"I'm doing you a favor," Feinman said. She cast a last look at the *Mona Lisa*. "You might not know it yet, but you're meant for originals, Hennessy."

If only any part of that sentence had ever been true.

5

Adam Parrish.

This was how it had begun: Ronan had been in the passenger seat of Richard Campbell Gansey III's bright orange '73 Camaro, hanging out the window because walls couldn't hold him. Little historic Henrietta, Virginia, curled close, trees and streetlights alike leaning in as if to catch the conversation down below. What a pair the two of them were. Gansey, searching desperately for meaning, Ronan, sure that he wouldn't find any. Voted most and least likely to succeed, respectively, at Aglionby Academy, their shared high school. Those days, Gansey was the hunter and Ronan the hawkish best friend kept hooded and belled to prevent him tearing himself to shreds with his own talons.

This was how it had begun: a student walking his bike up the last hill into town, clearly headed the same place they were. He wore the Aglionby uniform, although as they grew closer Ronan saw it was threadbare in a way school uniforms couldn't manage in a single year's use—secondhand. His sleeves were pushed up and his forearms were wiry, the thin muscles picked out in stark relief. Ronan's attention stuck on his hands. Lovely boyish hands with prominent knuckles, gaunt and long like his unfamiliar face.

"Who's that?" Gansey had asked, and Ronan hadn't answered, just kept hanging out the window. As they passed,

Adam's expression was all contradictions: intense and wary, resigned and resilient, defeated and defiant.

Ronan hadn't known anything about who Adam was then and, if possible, he'd known even less about who he himself was, but as they drove away from the boy with the bicycle, this was how it had begun: Ronan leaning back against his seat and closing his eyes and sending up a simple, inexplicable, desperate prayer to God:

Please.

And now Ronan had followed Adam to Harvard. After Declan dropped him off at the gate ("Don't do anything stupid. Text me in the morning."), he just stood inside the Yard's iron perimeter, regarding the fine, handsome buildings and the fine, handsome trees. Everything was russet: brick dorms and brick paths, November leaves and November grass, autumnal scarves round students' throats as they idled past. The campus felt unfamiliar, transformed by the seasons. Funny how quickly a handful of weeks could render something unrecognizable.

Six thousand seven hundred undergraduate students. Legacy students: twenty-nine percent. Receiving financial aid: sixty percent. Average financial award: forty thousand. Yearly tuition: sixty-seven thousand dollars. Median annual salary of Harvard grad after ten years: seventy thousand. Acceptance rate: four-point-seven percent.

Ronan knew all the Harvard statistics. After Adam had been accepted, he'd spent evening after evening at the Barns pulling apart every detail and fact he could find about the school. Ronan had spent weeks with two Adams: one certain he had earned his place at an Ivy and one certain the school would soon discover how worthless he truly was. Ronan endured it with as much grace as he could manage. Who else did Adam have to crow to, after all? His mother was a disconnected wraith and if his father had gotten his way, Adam might have been dead before he'd graduated high school. So Ronan absorbed the data and the anxiety and the anticipation and tried not to think about how he and Adam were stepping onto differing paths. He tried not to think about all the shining, educated, straightforward faces in the brochures that Adam Parrish might fall in love with instead of him. Sometimes Ronan thought about what might have happened if he'd finished high school and gone off to college this fall, too. But that was as impossible as imagining an Adam who had dropped out of high school and stayed in Henrietta. They knew who they were. Adam, a scholar. Ronan, a dreamer.

Is there any version of you that could come with me to Cambridge?
Maybe. Maybe.

It took Ronan several moments of digging through his phone to find the name of Adam's dorm—Thayer—and then several more to find a campus map. He could have texted Adam to tell him he was there, but he liked the idea of the soft surprise of it, of Adam knowing he was coming today but not knowing when. Ronan was well versed in comings and goings, in the tidal rhythm of a lover washing out to sea and returning under favorable winds. This was his father, after all, leaving the Barns with a trunk full of dreams and returning some months later with a trunk full of money and gifts. This was his mother, after all, sending him off and then welcoming him home. Ronan remembered the reunions well. The way Aurora's smile got unwrapped along with the rest of the parcels in Niall's trunk, the way Niall's was dusted off from a high shelf where Aurora kept it.

Over the past few days, Ronan had played his reunion with Adam over in his head many times, trying to imagine what shape it would take. Stunned quiet before an embrace on the stairs outside Adam's dorm? Slowly growing grins before a kiss in a hallway? *Ronan,* said this imaginary Adam as his dorm room door fell open.

But it wasn't any of those.

It was Ronan finally figuring out how to point himself toward Thayer, Ronan stalking through the students and tourists, Ronan hearing, surprised, "Ronan?"

It was him, turning, and realizing they'd passed each other on the walkway.

He'd walked right by Adam.

Even looking at him now, properly, the two of them an arm's length away as others were forced to make a berth around them, he realized why he had. Adam looked like himself but also not. His gaunt face had not changed in the weeks since Ronan had last seen him—he was still that boy with the bicycle. His dusty hair was still as Ronan recalled, charmingly and unevenly cropped short as if by self-piloted scissors in a bathroom mirror.

All the car grease and sweat and grit Ronan remembered was gone, though.

Adam was impeccably dressed: collared shirt, sleeves rolled just so, vintage tweed vest, perfect brown slacks cuffed above stylish shoes. He held himself in that precise, reticent way he always had, but it looked even more remote and proper now. He looked as if he belonged here in Cambridge.

"I didn't recognize you," they both said at the same time.

Ronan thought this was a ridiculous sentiment. *He* was

unchanged. Completely unchanged. He couldn't change if he wanted to.

"I walked right by you," Adam said, with wonder.

He even *sounded* different. There was no trace at all of his subtle Virginia accent. He'd endlessly practiced erasing it in high school but never pulled it off. Now it was completely hidden. A stranger's voice.

Ronan felt a little unsteady. There had been no room for this experience in his daydreams.

Adam glanced at his watch, and Ronan saw then that it was *his* watch, the elegant timepiece Ronan had dreamt him for Christmas, the watch that told the correct time for wherever Ronan was in the world. The ground steadied a little beneath him.

Adam said, "I thought you wouldn't be here for hours. I thought you—I should've known how you drive. I thought . . ."

He was staring at Ronan in an unfamiliar way, and after a moment, Ronan realized that Adam was staring at him in exactly the same way Ronan was staring at Adam.

"This is fucking weird," Ronan said, and Adam laughed in a haggard, relieved way. They hugged, hard.

This was as Ronan remembered it. Adam's ribs fit against his ribs just as they had before. His arms wrapped around Adam's narrow frame the same way they had before. His hand still pressed against the back of Ronan's skull the way it always did when they hugged. His voice was missing his accent, but now it sounded properly like him as he murmured into Ronan's skin: "You smell like home."

Home.

Ronan felt even steadier. It was going to be all right. He was with Adam, and Adam still loved him, and this was going to work.

They stepped back from each other. Adam said, "Do you want to meet my friends?"

Friends were serious business for Ronan Lynch. He was slow to acquire them, slower to lose them. The list was small, both because secrets made relationships complicated and because friends, for Ronan, were time-consuming. They got all of him. You could not, Ronan thought, give all of yourself away to many people, or there would be nothing left. So there was burnished Gansey, who might not have saved Ronan's life in high school, but at the very least kept it mostly out of Ronan's reach so that he could not take it down and break it. There was pocket-sized Blue Sargent, the psychic's daughter, with her ferocious sense of right and wrong; they'd learned each other so slowly, peeling back layers and only truly figuring each other out just in time for high school to end. There was Adam, and there were Ronan's brothers. That was it. Ronan could have had more casual friends, but he didn't see the point.

"Repo! You're supposed to say Repo."

"What?" Ronan was playing a card game. It was a confusing card game, with a lot of rules, an elaborate setup, and an unclear time frame for completing gameplay. He was fairly certain it had been developed by students at Harvard. He was fairly certain, in fact, that it had been developed by the students at Harvard he currently sat with: Fletcher, Eliot, Gillian, and Benjy. Adam sat beside him, hearing ear closest (he was deaf in one).

Beneath the table, Adam's shoe was pressed hard up against Ronan's.

Eliot explained, "To notify the other players."

"Of what?"

Eliot flinched at his tone, although Ronan hadn't thought he'd been any more terse than usual. Possibly his usual was enough. The first thing breezy Eliot had said when they met Ronan was "Oh, you're scarier than I expected!"

Fucking nice to meet you, too, Ronan had thought.

The game unrolled at a table in the basement common room of Thayer. Other students played pool, gathered around TVs and laptops, and listened to music. It smelled like garlic and take-out food. The brick arches holding up the ceiling gave the entire space the vibe of either a wine cellar or catacombs. It all felt like a secret club.

Gillian, who wore a tie knotted with more certainty and polish than Ronan ever had, shook her cards at him. "You say 'Repo' unto them so they can assess the suit and color of your lot and form a strategy to hopefully stop you from repo'ing the last card you need to win."

Ronan looked at the cards he'd already laid out on the table. "I only need one more?"

"He's a savant," said Fletcher, whose great, round expanse was held in by a snazzy sweater vest. He seemed as if he ought to be smoking a cigar or backing slowly into the black-and-white photo he had emerged from. "He's a savant and he doesn't know it. The beautiful girl who doesn't know her beauty. The brute who doesn't know his strength. Twenty's what you need. Twenty in your lot, and you're the boss, game over. And you, my friend, have nineteen."

"H-E-double boomerang," said Benjy softly, with feeling. He had only two cards in his lot.

"But you could be put off," Gillian explained. "Adam, for instance, could pay his bill with his spades. He could put them all in the bank, and then you wouldn't be able to complete the spades in your lot with his cards."

Beneath the table, Adam pressed the rest of his leg up against Ronan's, his expression unchanging as he did.

This card game, Ronan thought, was going on forever.

"But if Adam pays spades, then he wouldn't be able to complete his own lot with spades," Fletcher interjected in his plummy voice. "Technically, yes, but not practically. Paying spades would be on his record for ten more turns, so he couldn't play spades until after that. At this stage in the game, someone else will have won before he frees up spades for himself again."

"That's heavy," Ronan said.

"Poverty sucks," Fletcher mused, smoothing his sweater.

"Anecdotally," Gillian said wryly.

Ronan shot a glance at Adam. Adam, who'd grown up in a trailer; Adam, who even now wore that secondhand tweed vest Gansey's father had given him years ago; Adam, who had never spared words about the entitled students at the private school he'd worked three jobs to attend.

But Adam just tilted his cards toward his chest so the others couldn't see his hand anymore.

"Well, fucking Repo, then," Ronan said.

Gillian played a joker next to Ronan's lot. "I'm parking you in."

"Noble," whispered Benjy.

"Write it on my grave," she said.

As the others took another round of turns, skipping both Ronan and Gillian because of her sacrificial move, Ronan stared around the common room and tried to imagine spending time here regularly. He hadn't told Adam about the appointments yet. It wasn't a conversation he wanted to have in front of everyone here; they wouldn't understand why it was even a decision. To the outside eye, there was no reason why Ronan shouldn't move: his parents were dead, he had no job, he wasn't going to college, and the Barns could run wild and unattended until he returned to visit his brothers for holidays.

To the outside eye, Ronan Lynch was a loser.

"Hey, Scary," said Eliot. "Scary Spice."

"Lynch, it's your turn," added Adam.

Ronan cast an appraising look over the table. Picking up Gillian's joker, he added the four other jokers he'd collected over the course of the game, and put the five matching cards down in the center of the table.

"This is how this works, right?" he asked as he plucked a king of hearts out of Fletcher's lot to add to his own lot of nineteen cards he'd assembled in front of him, making it an even twenty.

"God, it is, God, I hate you," Fletcher moaned operatically.

"Who are you to come to our lands and take our women," murmured Gillian.

"We don't like your boyfriend, Adam," Benjy said.

Adam just smiled a private smile as he deftly swept his cards into a stack. "I'm taking the winner away, you guys."

"Wait," Gillian said. "You and I should talk to Yanbin before you go."

"Just a second," Adam told Ronan. Leaning in close, he added, "Don't kill anyone." The words were only an excuse to breathe in Ronan's ear; it made a marvel of his nerve endings.

Ronan was left facing Adam's remaining friends. He didn't know how good of friends they were. Not good enough to come up in phone conversations more than Gansey and Blue, but good enough that they could claim a game of Repo before Ronan got Adam to himself. They weren't what he expected. Aglionby had been a private boarding school, and he'd expected Harvard kids to be some unpleasant variation of the Aglionbros. But Adam's friends were not remotely the same species. They were not even the same species as each other; they were peculiar, distinct individuals. They were also more openly and gleefully queer than any Aglionby student Ronan had ever met. Ronan, who'd spent most of his high school years assuming other people were rich assholes and being the only gay person he knew, found these developments somewhat unsettling.

It was not that he thought Adam would replace him. It was just that now he saw precisely what Adam *could* replace him with.

"So where'd he find you crying?" Benjy murmured.

Ronan thought he'd misheard him. "What?"

Eliot said, "When you met. Where were you crying?"

Their words clarified nothing. Ronan couldn't imagine why they would have thought him a crier, period. The last time Ronan had cried had been over the memory of his dreamed mother, who had been eviscerated while a magical forest he adored was similarly dismantled around her. It seemed unlikely Adam would have told strangers any part of that, but the idea of it nonetheless sent an unpleasant warmth through his chest. Maybe Adam had told an untrue story of how they'd met. Also unpleasant to consider.

Fletcher seemed to read Ronan's face, because he patted his

ample tummy fondly before rumbling, "So he didn't always collect criers, then. You're pre-crying."

"Maybe he doesn't date criers," Eliot pointed out.

"You're going to have to back this truck up," Ronan said.

"We're the Crying Club," Benjy explained. "We were all criers."

"Adam Parrish and the Crying Club, like a band," Fletcher said. "He has a nose for us. Like a superhero. Somewhere on the Harvard campus someone is hidden in a stairwell crying right now, and Adam is on his way to find them and comfort them and give them someone to play cards with on a Friday night."

Ronan spent a fraught few seconds trying to reconcile the standoffish Adam he knew with this description. The Adam he knew was a silent observer. A cataloguer of the human experience. A look don't touch. The idea of him being something else, something Ronan didn't know, felt as unsettling as realizing that Adam's new friends weren't awful. He and Adam had been making the same memories for so long that he'd forgotten that it didn't always have to be like that. Adam was here having a new life, becoming a new person, growing from something beaten down into whoever he was meant to be. And Ronan was . . . Ronan. Still hidden away in the foothills of Virginia. Dropped out of school. Living in the place he'd been born. Keeping his head down so he could stay alive. Making the same memories he'd been making for months.

Adam was changing. Ronan couldn't.

He was moving here, he thought. It would work.

Ronan snarled, "Yeah, he's always been a regular Florence Nightingale."

"They say opposites attract," Eliot said. They took a photo

of Ronan's winning lot and put their head down to text it to someone.

"That's me," Ronan said. "He saves people; I take their lunch money."

Benjy had stopped collecting cards and instead pensively eyed the stack he'd made. In his small voice, he said, "I envy him. I wish I had his family."

Eliot's fingers paused in their texting. "Yeah. I wish my dad could meet his dad. I hate my father."

Record scratch, freeze-frame, stop the press.

"He has such wonderful Southern family stories," Fletcher said grandly. "He's like Twain without the racism. His words, the gravy, our ears, the biscuits."

Once upon a time, Ronan Lynch had punched Adam Parrish's father in front of the Parrish trailer. Once upon a time, Ronan Lynch had been there when Adam Parrish's father had beaten the hearing out of his left ear for good. Once upon a time, Ronan Lynch had helped move Adam Parrish's stuff into a shitty rented room so that he wouldn't have to live with his parents ever again.

Ronan felt as if he was blinking around in a dream. Everything subtly incorrect.

He was still staring at the Crying Club when Adam reappeared.

"You ready?" Adam asked.

"It was nice to meet you, Ronan Lynch." Fletcher held his hand out across the table.

Ronan hesitated, still off balance. Then he knocked Fletcher's hand sideways so he could bump knuckles instead. "Yeah."

"Don't be a stranger," Eliot said.

"Buh-bye," added Benjy.

"Fuck off," Gillian said kindly.

As they walked away, Ronan heard Fletcher say, "That man is very fetch."

They pushed out of the common room; Adam reached between them to take Ronan's hand. They climbed the stairs; Ronan disentangled their fingers and instead put his arm round Adam so that they climbed hip-to-hip. They stepped into Adam's room; they made it no farther. In the dark, they tangled in each other for several minutes, and finally broke off when stubble had made lips sore.

"I missed you," Adam said, voice muffled, face pressed against Ronan's neck.

For a long moment, Ronan didn't reply. It was too ideal; he didn't want to ruin it. The bed was right there; Adam felt warm and familiar; he longed for him even while holding him.

But then he said, "Why did you lie to them?"

It was difficult to ascertain how he knew Adam reacted, since he didn't reply or move, but Ronan nonetheless felt it.

"The Crying Club," Ronan added. "Don't tell me you didn't."

Adam stepped away. Even in the dark, Ronan could see that his expression looked more like the Adam that Ronan had known for years. Guarded.

"I didn't really," Adam said.

"Like hell you didn't. They think your father—I don't even want to fucking *call* him that—is some kind of saint."

Adam just held his gaze.

"What are you playing at, Adam?" Ronan asked. "You sitting there at that table with a bunch of rich kids playing a card game where the punch line's poverty, pretending you left some Brady Bunch bull back home?"

He could remember it like it had happened yesterday. No, like it had happened minutes ago. No, like it was still happening, always happening, kept fresh in a perfect, savage memory: Adam on his hands and knees outside the trailer, swaying, disoriented, broken, the light from the porch cut into fragments by his strange shadow. His father standing over him, trying to convince Adam it was his fault, always his fault. At the time it had only flooded Ronan with boiling, bursting, non-negotiable rage. But now it made him feel sick.

"Is it so bad?" Adam asked. "Is it so bad to start over? Nobody knows me here. I don't have to be the kid from the trailer park or the kid whose dad beats him. Nobody has to feel sorry for me or judge me. I can just be me."

"That's some pretty fucked-up shit." As Ronan's eyes got used to the dark, he saw Adam's profile clearly against the dull blue Cambridge night outside the dorm windows. Furrowed brow, lips tight. Pained. Old Adam. Adam from before graduation, before summer. Perfectly and depressingly recognizable, unlike that elegantly coiffed one on the walkway.

"You wouldn't get it."

This was too much; Adam wasn't allowed ownership of hardship. Ronan growled, "I'm gonna start telling people my parents are still alive. I don't want everyone to think of me as that orphan from now on."

"This is what I got. You have your brothers. I've got no one, okay?" Adam said. "Leave me alone, because you have no idea."

His voice hitched on *because.*

And like that, the fight was over. It had never been a fight between them, anyway. For Adam, it was what it always was: a fight between Adam and himself, between Adam and the world.

For Ronan, it was what it always was, too: a fight between truth and compromise, between the black and white he saw and the reality everyone else experienced.

They knotted back together and stood there, eyes closed. Ronan put his lips on Adam's deaf ear, and he hated Adam's father, and then he said it out loud: "I'm looking at apartments. Tomorrow."

For a breath, he was worried Adam no longer wanted a version of Ronan who could come stay with him in Cambridge, but then Adam said, "Don't just say that. Don't just throw it out. I can't . . ."

"I'm not just saying it. Declan's here. Matthew. They drove me up. I had to be in the Volvo for, like, eight hours. We have— I've got—appointments and shit. Tours. To see them. To pick one. You can come with if you aren't doing your Harvard parade. It's all set up."

Adam pulled away again, but this time his expression was quite different. This was neither old-old Adam nor new-polished Adam. This was the Adam who'd spent the last year at the Barns, a complicated Adam who didn't try to hide or reconcile all the complex truths inside himself, who just *was*. "How would that work?"

"I can control it."

"Can you?"

"I stay at Declan's all the time." Ronan didn't get much sleep there, but the statement was still true.

"And what about your face? The . . . nightwash. What about that?"

"I'll go out of town every weekend to dream. I'll find someplace safe."

Adam said, "What about . . ." but he didn't add anything

else. He just frowned more deeply than he had during the entire exchange, his mouth all crumpled with consternation.

"What's the face for?"

"I want it too much," Adam said.

That sentence, Ronan thought, was enough to undo all bad feeling he might have had meeting Adam's Harvard friends, all bad feeling about looking like a loser, all bad feeling about feeling stuck, all bad feeling, ever. Adam Parrish wanted him, and he wanted Adam Parrish.

"It'll work," Ronan told him. "It'll work."

6

It looked as if the apocalypse was still a go.

Carmen Farooq-Lane stood in one of London Heathrow's infernally busy terminals, her head tilted back to look at the gate announcements. People flowed around her in the stop-start way humans did in airports and train stations, their journeys more stream of consciousness than logic. Most people didn't care for airports; they were in survival mode. Id mode. They became the purest, most unfiltered versions of themselves. Panicked, rambling, erratic. But Farooq-Lane liked them. She liked schedules, systems, things in their place, holidays with specific celebratory rituals, games where people took turns. Before the Moderators, airports had represented the pleasant thrill of plans coming to fruition. New places seen. New foods eaten, new people met.

She was good at airports.

Now she was a vision of professional loveliness as she waited, poised in a diffuse spotlight, her pale linen suit impeccable; her small, expensive, wheeled suitcase spotless; her long, dark hair pulled into a softly braided updo; her absurdly long eyelashes lowered over her dark eyes. Her boots were new; she'd bought them from an airport store and thrown out the bloodstained pair in the ladies' room. She looked flawless.

Inside her, however, a smaller Carmen Farooq-Lane screamed and beat against the doors.

Nathan was dead.

Nathan was dead.

She'd had him killed.

Of course, the Moderators hadn't said they were going to kill him, but she'd known there wasn't a prison for people like Nathan. The only way to securely imprison Zeds was to never let them sleep—never let them dream. Impossible, of course.

I expected more complexity from you, Carmen.

Her brother had earned his death sentence, several times over. But still. She grieved the memory of who she'd thought he was, before she'd found out what he'd done. The heart was so foolish, she thought. Her head knew so much better.

If only it had actually stopped the apocalypse.

A flight to Berlin appeared on the board; she'd be up next. Chicago. It was morning here. Middle of the night there. Ten hours from now, she'd be climbing the stairs to her row house, groceries in hand, bag slung over her shoulder, steeling herself for the long task of trying to insert herself back in her old life. Back to her own bed, to a commute and a day job, her friends and what was left of her family. She'd done what she'd promised the Moderators she'd do, and now she'd earned her freedom.

But how was she supposed to manage clients' financial futures if she knew there might not *be* a future? How was she supposed to go back to her old life when she was no longer the Carmen Farooq-Lane who'd been living it?

Beside her, a man sneezed gustily. He searched his pockets unsuccessfully for a tissue. Farooq-Lane had been using plenty and had just restocked for another tumultuous day. She produced one from her bag; he accepted it gratefully. He seemed about to use it as an excuse for conversation, but her phone rang, and she turned away to answer.

"Are you still in the terminal?" Lock asked.

"Just about to board," Farooq-Lane said.

"Going home."

Farooq-Lane didn't answer this one.

"Look," he rumbled, "I'll cut right to it. I know you've done what we asked, I know you're finished, but you're good at this like no one else is."

"I don't know about that."

"Not the breaking-things part. The finding-things part. People like you. That's important. We need you. Do you think you could help us with one more?"

One more. Was it really one more? Did it matter? It was as if some part of her had been hoping or anticipating that he would ask, because she heard herself say yes before she even really considered. That heart-head dissonance again. She wanted to be done, but she just couldn't be until the world was safe.

"I was hoping you might say that," Lock said. "Nikolenko is there with a package for you and new flight information. Meet her at the Costa."

As her gate information appeared on the board, Farooq-Lane left it behind and navigated through the throngs of people until she found Nikolenko, a short, stone-faced woman with short, stone-colored hair. Nikolenko waited beside an angular young man in a T-shirt, suit coat, and tiny round glasses. He was extraordinarily tall and extraordinarily hunched. Elbows, knees, and Adam's apple were all prominent. His shoulder-length blond hair was tucked behind his ears. He looked a little like a young undertaker or, with those skeletal features, like one of the cadavers.

Nikolenko handed him some money. "Go get a coffee."

He looked at it as if he did not want a coffee, but people did what Nikolenko said, so off he shuffled.

Nikolenko handed Farooq-Lane an envelope. "That's your ticket and the address of where you're staying."

"Lock said there'd be a package?"

"He's the package," Nikolenko said, jerking her chin to where the kid stood in line.

Farooq-Lane didn't understand.

"He's the Visionary," Nikolenko said. "He's going with you."

Oh.

The Visionary was why they knew the world was going to end. The Visionar*ies*. This kid was only the most recent of them, the second Visionary the Moderators had worked with since Farooq-Lane had started up with them. She didn't know how many there had been before. Each of the Visionaries experienced intensely vivid and detailed premonitions, specifically focused on Zeds and other Visionaries.

Also, specifically focused on the end of the world.

Each of the Visionaries spoke of an apocalypse brought about in the same way, with starving, unquenchable fire. *Dreamed* unquenchable fire. Farooq-Lane didn't know exactly how long the Moderators had been looking for the Zed who would dream this fire into being, but she knew that at some point an intergovernmental entity had been quietly formed. Moderators came from all corners of the world. Some of them were convinced by one of the Visionary's predictions. Some of them were convinced by knowing a Zed and what they could do firsthand. And one of them was convinced by a need to prove to the other Moderators that she wasn't complicit in her brother's crimes.

Nathan had been their best lead so far. They already knew he wanted to see the world burn.

But his death hadn't stopped the Visionary's fiery prophecies.

Farooq-Lane eyed the Visionary as he counted out money at the cashier. "Just flying on an ordinary plane?" she asked Nikolenko. "Is that safe?"

"He's been in control for months."

Farooq-Lane couldn't identify the feeling inside herself, but it wasn't one of the good ones.

"I didn't know I was going to have to take care of a teenager," Farooq-Lane said. She hadn't even known the Visionary *was* a teenager; she'd only ever seen descriptions of his visions. Farooq-Lane wasn't very maternal. Life was messy until you were in your twenties, she felt, and she preferred to forget all her previous ages.

"He's not difficult to handle," Nikolenko assured her. "He just does what you tell him."

That didn't make it any better. "Why is he coming with me? I did fine with the descriptions before."

"He's close to done. He's getting fragmented. It'll be easier for you to talk the visions out with him."

Close to done? Farooq-Lane didn't know much about the life spans of the Visionaries, but she knew the end was nothing you wanted to be around for. "I—"

"Look, princess," Nikolenko interrupted, "you have the easiest assignment here. Take Lurch there and find the Zed he's seeing. Be on the lookout for another Visionary to replace him. Call us when you find something. Then the grown-ups will fly in and take care of it so you don't have to get your shoes dirty again."

Farooq-Lane would not be made to feel bad for being a reluctant killer. She and Nikolenko glared at each other until the Visionary returned with a coffee.

"I won't drink this," he told Nikolenko. He had an accent. German, maybe. "Do you want it?"

Without hesitation, Nikolenko took it from his hand and dropped it into the trash can beside her, one smooth motion. "Problem solved. Check in with Lock when you get there, Farooq-Lane."

Without another word, she departed. The Visionary eyed the trash can where the coffee had just met its end, and then he eyed Farooq-Lane.

Farooq-Lane held out a hand and introduced herself to her new charge. "Carmen Farooq-Lane."

He shook her hand, then repeated her name carefully before introducing himself to his new keeper. "Parsifal Bauer."

When she opened the envelope, two tickets for them slid out right into her hands, eager to be out of confinement. "I guess we're going to be spending a lot of time together in . . . Washington, DC."

As good a place to save the world as any.

7

The voice was back.

You're wondering if this is real.

You want proof this is an actual encounter and not just a bit of sub-conscious mindfuckery.

What is real? Listen: You fall asleep, dream of feathers, and wake with a raven in your hands, and you're still asking, What is real?

Ronan was dreaming of Bryde's voice, but he was also dreaming of Lindenmere.

Lindenmere, Lindenmere.

It was a name out of a poem that had never existed. It didn't sound dangerous.

Lindenmere, Lindenmere. It was a forest, or rather, it was a thing that was forest-shaped for now. Ronan had an idea that it had existed somewhere else for a very long time, and only now whispered its way into the world this time in the shape of a forest. It knew him, and he knew it, insofar that they could be known, both of them full of mysteries, even to themselves.

He was in love with it, and it with him.

As he walked between Lindenmere's trees, he heard Bryde's voice from somewhere beyond them. Perhaps Bryde was one of these massive gnarled oak trees. Perhaps he was one of the small specks flying overhead. Perhaps he was the flowers that curled around the brambles. Perhaps he was only Ronan's subconscious.

"Lindenmere," Ronan said out loud. "What is Bryde? Is he real?"

The leaves in the trees murmured. They put together words: *You know.*

And beyond them, Bryde's voice continued.

You are bigger than that, bigger than what is real. You have been raised among wolves and now you've forgotten you have thumbs. Real was a word invented for other people. Scrub it from your vocabulary. I don't want to hear you say it again. If you dream a fiction and wake with that fiction in your hands, it becomes fact.

Do you understand? For you, reality is not an external condition. For you, reality is a decision.

Still you long for what reality means to everyone else, even if it makes your world smaller. Maybe because it makes your world smaller.

Ronan climbed a mossy incline. The light here was shimmery, lush, golden, tangible. He skimmed his fingers through it and it clung to his skin, both feeling and sight. He repeated, "I wouldn't have asked if I did."

The trees murmured again. *Dreamer.*

Another dreamer? Here? A tiny cloud of luminous gnats parted around Ronan as he walked, scanning the feral undergrowth for signs of another human. He knew it was possible for a dreamer to meet him in dreamspace, but only one ever had, and that other dreamer had known Ronan in the waking world before he'd tried to find him in this otherworld.

Plus, he was dead now.

No one else knew Ronan was a dreamer.

Or they shouldn't.

"I don't believe you," he said out loud. "I have trust issues."

There's a game children play with chalk and asphalt. Snail—that's what it's called. Chalk a spiral on the ground, a snail's shell, and section it into ever-shrinking squares. Toss a pebble; wherever it lands, that box is off-limits. Now jump on one foot in a tightening spiral, careful not to land in the box with the pebble. You see how the game gets harder the more pebbles are thrown. The tighter the spiral twists. The goal is to get to the middle without falling over.

That's the game we're going to play, you and I.

"Maybe I don't want to play a game," Ronan said. His dreamy walking, which covered at the same time much ground and little, took him to a clearing bisected by a deep black stream. A floating plank served as a bridge, and parked on top of it was a vintage-looking motorbike that thrummed with life, the exhaust visible in a delicate shuddering breath behind it.

Adam was always talking about how he would trade his car for a motorcycle if he could. *He'd like this bike,* Ronan thought. It reminded him a little bit of Adam, in fact. Elegant and rough and ready at once.

When Ronan stepped up onto the hovering board-bridge, it quivered, but held. Below, the stream was an emotional truth rather than a physical one, the water present but not yet wet, not unless he turned his attention to it: This was the way of dreams.

He laid a hand on the cool leather seat of the bike. It already had Adam's name stitched on the edge of it. Ronan ran his fingers along the dimpled constellation of embroidery. It felt real.

Every box will be a task.

I will be in the center at the end of it all.

First box—

"I don't know if you're real or a figment of my imagination," Ronan said. "But I'm trying to work here."

Let's deal with that, first. An object lesson in real *or not. I'm doing sums in my head, you want me to demonstrate my work on the margin. Fine.*

First box: What is real.

First box: Ask your brother about the Fairy Market.

First box: They'll be whispering my name.

Proof? It will have to do. You make reality.

Ronan rolled the motorcycle to shore. Behind him, the floating bridge bobbed up several inches, relieved of the weight of the bike. As it did, he suddenly discovered that the stream below it was filled not with black water, but with animals.

They seethed.

"Shit," Ronan said.

Jump, skip, throw a pebble, next turn.

See you on the other side.

He woke up.

8

It was morning.

Ronan could hear all sorts of morning sounds. An electric shaver humming across the hall, music nattering away in another room, feet slap-shuffling up and down aged stairs. Outside he heard asthmatic leaf blowers, percussive car doors, garrulous students, grumbling delivery trucks, petulant horns.

He'd spent the night in Cambridge.

Ronan looked at himself from above.

It was as if he were an angel haunting his own body. A spirit. Ghost of Christmas Past. Whatever it was that floated above you and watched you sleep. Ronan Lynch's thoughts gazed down upon Ronan Lynch's body.

He saw a young man in the narrow dorm bed below, motionless but nonetheless looking as if he spoiled for a fight. Between his brows, two knitted lines formed the universal symbol for *I'll fuck you up.* His eyes were open, looking at nothing. Adam was slotted between him and the wall, mouth parted with abandon, hair wild against the pillow.

They were completely covered with monsters.

Their bodies were weighted with peculiar creatures that looked sort of like horseshoe crabs at first blush. A closer look revealed that instead of hard shells, they had dramatic masks, with little mouths snapping open and shut hungrily on their backs. Perfectly shaped cow teeth filled each mouth.

The crabs looked nightmarish and wrong, because they *were* nightmarish and wrong. They were a species that hadn't existed until Ronan woke up. They were a species that only existed because Ronan *had* woken up.

This was what it meant to be Ronan Lynch.

Dream to reality.

They seethed and milled slowly, pulling the sheets into swirly patterns with their small, rigid legs.

Adam didn't move because his hearing ear was buried in the pillow and his perpetually exhausted body was lost to sleep.

Ronan couldn't move. He was always paralyzed for a few minutes after he successfully brought something back from a dream. It was as if he swapped those minutes of wakeful capability in his dreams for a few minutes of somnolent uselessness. There was no way to speed it up, either, no matter how threatening the circumstances were when he woke. He could only float like this, outside his body, watching the dreams do whatever they wanted to do without his interference.

Adam, he thought, but couldn't say it.

Sclack, sclack. The crabs' monstrous little mouths sounded wet as they opened and closed, just as they had when he saw them beneath the bridge in his dream. Dream things didn't change their stripes in the waking world. If they disobeyed the laws of physics in the dream, like a piece of wood that hovered just above the ground, they continued to disobey them when brought into real life. If they were an abstract concept made flesh in the dream, like a song that could somehow be scooped up in your hands, the peculiar, brain-bending quality of the thing persisted into waking.

If they were murder crabs that wanted to eat you in the

dream, they kept on wanting to eat you in waking life.

Sclack, sclack.

Ronan attempted to wiggle his toes. Nothing. All he could do was float over his own body and wait. Fortunately, the crabs' mask-mouths were on their backs, so for the moment, Ronan and Adam were safe.

For the moment.

Adam.

He willed Adam to wake.

A few crabs fell from the bed with a clatter, their little legs tapping away on the floorboards. It was an off-putting sound that perfectly matched their appearance. *Sclack, sclack, skitter, skitter.*

Shit, and now Ronan saw that he had not brought back only the crabs. The floating bridge had come back as well, hovering right beside the bed like a rustic skateboard. And the pretty little motorcycle sat in the middle of the room between the two dorm beds. It was running, just as it had been in the dream, a little intense puff of exhaust twirling behind it.

He'd brought every single damn thing in sight.

How had he fucked up so badly?

Sclack, sclack.

That other dreamer—Bryde—had put him off his game.

The other dreamer. Other *dreamer.* Ronan had nearly forgotten. It seemed impossible to forget something of such magnitude, but that was the way of dreams, wasn't it? Even the best and worst of them could dissipate from memory immediately. Now it flooded back to him.

Ronan needed another dreamer like he needed a shit-ton of murder crabs in his bed.

The only mercy was that the other dorm bed was still empty.

Ronan didn't know if Adam had arranged for his roommate to be gone overnight or if it was a fortunate coincidence, but he was grateful. Now he just needed to be able to *move*.

One of the murder crabs scuttled up Adam's body toward his deaf ear.

Wake up, Adam, wake up.

Ronan had the hideous thought that they'd already killed Adam and that was why he didn't rise, because he was already dead and cooling, murdered by Ronan's dreams while he floated helplessly overhead—

One of the murder crabs scuttled onto Ronan's face, each crisp leg an unpleasant pressure point. Quite suddenly, he saw it from his physical body instead of from above, so control was returning to his body. There was a barcode on the crab's belly, and in small letters above it TCP MIXED NUTS 1101, and below that, a set of blinking blue eyes with really full eyelashes. The 1101 was for his birthday, which was nigh, the big old one-nine, but God knew why the rest was there. Ronan Lynch's subconscious was a jungle.

Another crab collided into the first, flipping one of the terrors onto its back. Mouth side down. It went for his eye.

Fuckity fuck.

For a brief moment, he could imagine the next few minutes laid out: the crab snapping through his eye, his mouth unable to shout or even whimper, him silently losing half his sight as Adam lay beside him, sleeping or dead.

But then he could move, he could move, his whole body was his again.

Kicking off the blankets, he tipped as many of the crabs as he could off him and Adam. The little horrors rolled and skittled off the bed, some of them landing on the hovering board beside it. The force of the movement sent the board rocketing across the room, a floating crab taxi, before it hit the wall and dislodged them all.

"Oh God," Adam said.

He had been sleeping, not dead, and now his face reflected the truth: that he'd woken to a hell-room of crustacean roommates.

"God, Ronan, God! What did you *do*?"

"I'm fixing it." Ronan slid out of bed.

Slam.

As Ronan cast for a weapon, he saw that Adam had smashed one against the wall with a biology text. Its insides shot out— yellow glop like the inside of a squashed caterpillar.

This worked the rest of the creatures to frenzy.

"Fix it *faster*," Adam said.

The hoverboard bobbed close; Ronan leapt on it. The momentum sent him rocketing to the corner of the dorm room, slamming up against the wall, but he kept his balance. Giving the wall a shove, he shot to the other corner instead, where a flag was leaned. He lifted it high, wielding it like a gallant Irish hero of old.

Slam. Adam smashed another, and another.

Ronan stabbed a crab with his makeshift lance. It pierced right through the barcode.

"Gotcha, you hungry bastards," Ronan told them.

Another crab landed on his arm; he smashed it against the wall and impaled it just as quick. Another flipped onto its back; he stabbed it through the barcode. Stomp, stomp, flick. More slime. *Slam. Slam.* Adam was killing the ones by the bed. It had a certain gruesome satisfaction.

There was a knocking on the door.

It was unclear how long it had been going on. Only now with all the crabs dead was it quiet enough to hear.

Adam looked at Ronan, horrified.

"The bed," Ronan hissed. "Put them under the covers for now."

The knocking continued.

"Just a second!" Adam said.

The two of them furiously scraped a mound of gloppy crab corpses under the comforter. Ronan shoved the hoverboard beneath the bed, where it pressed up tightly against the mattress, desperate for flight.

Adam went to the door. Out of breath, he opened it a crack. "Yeah?"

"Adam Parrish," Fletcher's plummy voice said. "What the hell is going on? They're gonna call the proctor."

"Fletcher, look, I . . ." Adam said.

Fletcher pushed open the door.

He stood with his glorious breadth in the door, his hair oiled, books under one arm.

The room was a compelling contemporary painting, a textural experiment of disembodied crab legs, bright liquid guts, and a little bit of Adam's and Ronan's blood. It was beginning to stink of exhaust.

Fletcher's eyes roved over all this. His eyes landed on Ronan's makeshift lance.

"My flag," Fletcher said.

Adam shut the door hurriedly behind him.

"The walls," Fletcher said.

The crab guts were peeling the paint off them and the hoverboard had left several large dents in the plaster.

"The beds," Fletcher said.

The sheets were torn and ruined.

"The window," Fletcher said.

One of the panes had somehow gotten broken.

"A motorcycle," Fletcher said.

It occurred to Ronan that the latter was the most likely to kill him right now, if Adam didn't, so he turned it off. It took him a second to figure it out because it didn't have a key, but eventually he found a toggle switch labeled *YES/NO.*

There was nothing overtly supernatural about the picture without seeing the crabs beneath the covers or the hoverboard beneath the bed.

There was only several thousand dollars' worth of damage to a Harvard dorm, Ronan's choking guilt, and a proctor on the way.

Adam said, very simply, "Help me."

9

Even though Breck Myrtle was technically the number one on this whole thing, he had Jeff Pick break the window to get into the house. That made Pick the guy who started it. Silly, but it made Myrtle feel better about being involved.

Burglary was not Myrtle's usual modus operandi. His siblings were into that sort of crime, the breaking and entering, the writing of bad checks, the taking of handbags out of unlocked Nissan Sentras. Their mother had taught them all this sort of low-impact criminality. Not taught-taught, not like flash cards. In a lead-by-example way. She was a Walmart greeter now and had urged her prodigy to go legit, but Myrtle had decided to rise above this. He sold art out of a shop in Takoma Park and also on eBay. The online component worked the best, as people trusted him more when they couldn't see his face. All of the Myrtles had long faces with tiny eyes, and even when at their most benevolent, they had the look of something that might creep out of the dark to eat your body after you died. But that didn't matter when he was selling art online; it wasn't about him, it was about the work. Most of it was real, some of it was fake. He didn't feel bad about the fake stuff; it was barely criminal. People only believed in fake art because they wanted to, so really he was just giving them what they wanted.

He was not a burglar.

But he was making an exception this time for Hennessy. She

was already a criminal. Stealing from criminals was like multiplying negative numbers. It turned out positive in the end.

The McLean mansion they had just broken into sprawled at just under twenty thousand square feet, about the same size as the sculpted lot it sat on. If you don't live in a twenty-thousand-square-foot house, it's a hard size to wrap your head around. It is about the size of one hundred parking spots, or just under half the size of an NFL-regulation football field, or twice the size of the average American strip mall built between 1980 and today. The mansion had eight bedrooms and ten bathrooms and one ballroom and a pool and a fountain with mermaid statues in it and a movie room and a library full of books with only white spines and a kitchen with two ovens in it. The front room was the size of most New York apartments and was completely empty apart from a chandelier large enough to gain sentience and two sweeping staircases up to the second floor, just in case you wanted to go up one and come down another. Things that you didn't expect to be coated in gold were coated in gold. Floors were made from marble that had once been someplace famous or covered in wood from trees that were now endangered.

It was hard to say how long Hennessy had been squatting there. Properties like these, owned by Saudi investors or princelings or something, they could sit empty for years.

They—Myrtle, Pick, and another Jeff, Jeff Robinson— had come in via the glass-walled poolroom. Pick, who seemed well versed in the art of breaking and entering, had brought a large, lightly adhesive window decal advertising specials on chainsaws. He'd affixed this to one of the large panes of glass and then punched it. The sound had been remarkable mostly in its unremarkableness—just a dull, sandy sound, nothing that warned of home invasion.

"See," Pick whispered as he peeled off the decal with its new shattered-glass crust, "I told you, no alarms. Hennessy don't want the police here."

They took stock in something that seemed to be an enormous and grand living room. A wall of French doors overlooked a stone patio where a bronze woman shot an arrow straight into the sky. The room was decorated with a delicate tufted couch and two chairs pointed at the carved fireplace, a priceless Persian rug, several abstract paintings, a ten-foot-tall potted schefflera, and a brilliant yellow Lexus supercar parked askance as if it had driven in from the patio to enjoy a fire. A paper plate with a congealed half-slice of pizza sat on the car's hood; a cigarette was extinguished in the extra cheese. These final three objects provided the bulk of the room's odor of exhaust, smoke, and marinara sauce.

Despite all this excess, the real focal point was a perfect copy of Sargent's masterpiece *Madame X* that leaned on a substantial easel. The white-and-black marble floor beneath it was a universe of paint constellations and comet streaks. It was a showstopper. The woman in the portrait was nearly as tall as Myrtle and stood gracefully, one hand gathering the bulk of her black satin dress. Her hair was deep red, her skin so pale it was nearly blue. A signature was painted in the bottom right corner: *JOHN S. SARGENT 1884.*

The painting was absolutely perfect except for the puckered bullet holes over the delicate eyebrow and flushed ear.

"What a head case," Pick said.

Myrtle had heard of Hennessy before the party at TJ Sharma's. Hennessy was supposed to be the best forger on the East Coast. Too expensive for run-of-the-mill copies, but, as evidenced by the perfect copy of *Madame X*, the person you wanted if you were going to try to sell a fake high-end work to a gullible and moneyed overseas buyer outfitting their new mansion. And there she—*she*, that would teach him to make assumptions—was at that Sharma party. Small world. Guess word of when Feinman was going to leave her coffin to walk among the mortals got around. He was surprised Feinman turned down Hennessy's request to get into the Fairy Market; Hennessy was clearly more than qualified for the job. He'd gotten an invite, after all, and what was he but a dealer?

It was easy enough to follow her home and case the joint. He'd have no problem getting good price for her forgeries at the market she couldn't get into.

When life handed out lemons, it just made good sense for *someone* to make lemonade.

"Let's spread out," Myrtle said in a low voice. "Look for the high-ticket things."

"Electronics?" Pick asked.

This was what came from hanging out with criminals. "If that's what you want to do. Meet back at the pool."

Robinson peered inside the Lexus. He asked, "And if Hennessy shows up?"

"A car left this morning," Myrtle said. "Hennessy was in it."

Pick produced a plastic jar of zip ties from the same bag that had produced the adhesive decal. "And if there's anybody else, just tie 'em up."

Myrtle was again impressed with his criminal credentials.

"Right. Right. Nobody's calling the cops, so just keep 'em quiet."

They spread out.

Every room was full of paintings. Hard to tell if they were Hennessys or originals. Some of them he recognized—Mondrian, Waterhouse, Ruysch, Hockney, Sandys, Stanhope. Forgeries? High-end prints? Originals? In a house like this, they could be.

He began to take everything he saw, making multiple trips to stack the frames by the door.

Myrtle discovered Hennessy's workspace in one of the wings. The light was turned on, though it was empty. The ceiling was high and crowned with another massive chandelier. A headboard and footboard leaned against the wall behind rolls of canvas, empty gilt frames, and canvas stretchers. Government paperwork, checkbooks, passports, and envelopes covered a rollback desk. A computer sat on the floor beside it, the keyboard pulled far enough into the room to be in danger of being stepped on. Everywhere else was paint, pencils, paper, books, paintings, drawings. He saw Sargent's *The Daughters of Edward Darley Boit*, Abbott Thayer's *The Sisters*, William Orpen's *To the Unknown British Soldier in France*—but they were surely for Hennessy's own satisfaction, being too well-known to ever be passed off as originals.

A striking portrait took center stage. The subject was a lovely golden-haired woman in a man's jacket; she peered warily at the viewer. He wasn't ordinarily into figurative art, but it made him feel things in his parts. Which parts he hadn't worked out yet. Multi-part feelings.

"The trick is to buy as many shitty old paintings as you can find, then you work over the top of them. You're fucked if they x-ray, of course, but to the casual eye, the unprofessional beauty, all the punter sees is the beat-up old panel, and they're right there with you. Give the people what they want, that's all it's about."

Myrtle slowly turned.

Hennessy stood in the doorway to the room.

She had changed since she'd left in the car. Her kinky hair was now pulled up in a ragged black topknot. She wore tinted glasses, a rabbit fur coat, a lace bralette white against her dark skin, and leather leggings that exposed a fish-scale tattoo on her lower calf. More pastel tattoos covered her knuckles, which were also smeared with paint. He still couldn't tell how old she was. She could be twenty-five. She could be seventeen.

"The most successful forgeries change as little as possible," Hennessy said, lighting a cigarette. She had a face that looked like it was smiling even if she wasn't smiling. "You follow the rules ninety-nine percent of the time, people won't notice the one percent you don't. A thousand little lies, pal, that's the way to do it, not a big lie. A new Van Gogh? No one believes. But they'll buy a mislaid Henry Tonks. A new Monet water lily? Fat chance. But a minor Philip Guston? Money for dinner. Piece of advice? No one's gonna buy that Degas you're holding."

Myrtle had not prepared himself for this scene. He searched for a reply inside himself and found only anger. It was the way she was unafraid. It was the way she hadn't screamed. It made him furious. His mother had always warned him he was an angry person and maybe it was true, because he felt his rage multiplying. Tripling, quadrupling, abillioning.

He put down the Degas and took out a knife. "You little bitch. You don't just talk to me like that."

Hennessy tapped ash onto the floor. "You don't just creep

into people's houses like some mission impossible motherfucker, either, and yet here we are."

A scream came from elsewhere in the mansion. It was hard to tell what age or gender of person had produced it. It did not appear to concern Hennessy.

Myrtle threw himself at her. He was not bad with a knife, and his nuclear rage lent him superpowers. Hennessy ducked out of the way as his shoes lost traction on the loose rug. As he slid onto his ass, anger ignited to white-hot hatred. He hadn't hurt anyone in several years, but now he could only imagine how it would feel to crush his fingernails through her skin.

There was another scream. Unknown victim, unknown crime scene.

He scrambled to his feet to lunge for her again as she stood there smoking next to a half-finished nude.

"Hold it," said a voice behind him. Something cold and blunt tickled the skin beneath his ear. "Unless you want to be licking up the mess of your brains."

He held it.

"Why don't you hand that knife to Hennessy?"

He handed it to Hennessy, who dropped it into an open jug of paint.

"Jordan," Hennessy said, "it took you forever to get here."

The voice attached to the gun replied, "Accident on 495."

The newcomer stepped into his view. The first thing he saw was the gun, now pointing at his face, a Walther with the word *D!PLOMACY* sharpie-d on the barrel. The second thing he saw was the person holding it.

She was a twin; she had to be. She looked just like Hennessy—

same hair, same face, same nose ring, same tattoos. She moved like her, too, kinetic, confident, taking up room where there was no room to be had, all muscle and power and teeth-flashing challenge.

He also hated her.

"Now who's the little bitch?" Hennessy asked him, in that same lazy, mild way.

He called her an offensive word that started with a *C* and was not *crunk*.

"Don't be a stereotype," Hennessy said. She extinguished her cigarette on his bald spot, and when he was done yelling, the twin with the gun said, "We're going to take a little walk to the door, and then I never want to see you again."

Together, the three of them walked down the long hallway, past the collection of paintings he'd been gathering, and then to the door with the broken glass.

Pick stood by it, shivering and holding himself. Blood covered one half of his face, although it was hard to tell where it was coming from. Robinson crouched with an assortment of teeth, presumably his own, cupped in his palm.

Three other girls stood in the gray morning shadows. The light was poor, but to Myrtle, it seemed that they, too, looked very similar to Hennessy. At the very least they all stood like her, like they would fuck you or fuck you up.

The one called Jordan went through Myrtle's pockets and got his wallet.

"My mind's like a sieve," she said. The bright friendliness of her voice as she snapped a cell photo of his ID was one of the more threatening things he'd ever heard. "Wouldn't want to forget. Oh, hey now."

She'd taken his Fairy Market invite out of his wallet.

"It's got my name on it," he said.

Hennessy laughed, as if that was the least important detail.

"You'll be sorry," he said as Jordan handed it off to one of the other girls and vanished it away.

"I don't think I will be, friend," replied Jordan.

Hennessy smiled widely at Myrtle, her mouth wide enough to swallow the planet. "Thanks for the dance."

10

Ronan walked for hours.

At first he walked nowhere, just one foot in front of the other, eyes on boots, boots on leaves, leaves from foreign trees that didn't know him and didn't care to. He changed courses only when a walkway turned, when a building loomed, when the wall of Harvard Yard forbiddingly turned him back. Eventually, he found himself walking a labyrinth in an isolated courtyard outside the Divinity School. Some labyrinths had walls of stone or shrubbery; this one was just a brain-like pattern inlaid in the courtyard stones. One could step off the path from outermost circle to innermost at any time. The only thing that kept one in this maze was one's own feet.

He walked the labyrinth in to its center, and then he walked it back out, and then he walked it in, and then he walked it back out. He didn't think, because if he did, he'd think about how somewhere, Adam was explaining himself to his proctor and God knew who else.

He just walked.

He just walked.

He just walked.

If he'd had a car, he would have gotten in it and driven. Where? Anywhere. As fast as possible.

You see how the game gets harder the more pebbles are thrown. The tighter the spiral twists.

Declan called at some point. "I told you to text in the morning. The rules of this were very simple."

Ronan tested his voice, found it wanting, and then tried it again. It worked this time, even though he did not think it sounded particularly like his own. It said to Declan, "I ruined his dorm."

There was silence, and then Declan said, "I'm going to call Adam."

Ronan kept walking the labyrinth. Somewhere someone was playing a single poignant French horn very, very well. It was far more audible than the murmured sounds of the day's traffic.

He sat in the center of the labyrinth. Put his head down on his legs. Folded his hands over the back of his neck. This was how Adam found him some time later. He sat down behind Ronan so that they were back to back in the center of the maze.

"Declan took the crabs," Adam said.

Ronan didn't say anything.

"He told me to blame everything on you," Adam said.

Ronan didn't say anything.

"I told them . . ." Adam hesitated. "I told them you got drunk. I'm sorry, I—"

"Good," Ronan said. *Drunken loser trashes dorm.* "Good. It was my fault. I don't care what they think about me. It's not fucking important what they think about me. Are you in trouble?"

"Of course." It was impossible to tell how Adam felt about this without seeing his face. He was at his most precise and remote. "I have to fix it. Fletcher had to vouch that it was you instead of me. And I'm not allowed to have you over again. They made me sign something saying you wouldn't come on campus."

The French horn player mourned downward before spiraling up again.

"I'll pay for it," Ronan said. His father had left him some money, and he never touched it. What would he spend money on when he could dream anything he needed?

Everything except a life here.

Adam turned around. Ronan turned, too, and they sat facing each other in the center of the labyrinth. Adam wiped one tear from Ronan's right eye. He showed the finger to Ronan. It glistened damply with the single tear. Then he reached out and wiped the tear from Ronan's left eye. He showed this finger to Ronan, too.

It was smeared darkly with black.

Nightwash.

"This won't work, Ronan," Adam said.

Ronan already knew this. He knew this because he knew it was late enough that he was supposed to be seeing one of the apartments and Declan hadn't called him again. He knew that meant Declan had canceled the appointments. He knew it was over because Adam had signed a piece of paper saying Ronan wouldn't visit him on campus. He knew that meant Ronan would return to waiting at the Barns for him.

It felt like sadness was like radiation, like the amount of time between exposures was irrelevant, like you got a badge that eventually got filled up from a lifetime of it, and then it just killed you.

Adam Parrish and the Crying Club.

"*We're* still okay," Adam said. "This isn't about that."

Is there any version of you that could come with me to Cambridge?

No.

Adam went on. "I'm not trapped here on campus. I can still come to you on break."

Ronan watched a leaf skitter along the labyrinth, scuttling effortlessly from outer ring to inner before being joined by several others. They huddled together and shivered in the breeze for a moment before hurrying off somewhere together.

"Tell me to go to school closer to you and I will," Adam said in a rush, the words piled together. "Just say it."

Ronan pressed the heel of his hand against his eye, checking for nightwash, but it wasn't bad yet. "I'm not that big of an asshole."

"Oh, you are," Adam said, trying for humor. Failing. "Just not about that."

The French horn had gone silent and all that was left was the sound of the city that would slowly kill Ronan if he let it. He stood up.

It was over.

You are made of dreams and this world is not for you.

11

7:07 A.M.: WAKE UP, ASSHOLE. YOU'RE ALIVE.

Ronan was awake.

He stared at a list written in dark, cramped hand-writing and taped on the slanted plaster wall above his childhood bed at the Barns. After he had failed to answer any texts or calls for four days post-Cambridge, Declan had paid a surprise visit and found the middle Lynch brother in bed eating expired baked beans in the same jeans he'd been wearing on the road trip.

You need a routine, Declan had demanded.

I have a routine.

I thought you said you never lied.

7:15 A.M.: GET DRESSED AND SHAVE THAT BEAUTIFUL BALD HEAD.

It had been a long time since Ronan had gotten a proper Declan lecture. After their father died, Declan had become legally responsible for his brothers until they hit eighteen. He'd hectored Ronan constantly: Don't skip class, Ronan. Don't get another ticket, Ronan. Don't stay out late with Gansey, Ronan. Don't wear dirty socks twice in a row, Ronan. Don't swear, Ronan. Don't drink yourself into oblivion, Ronan. Don't hang out with those using losers, Ronan. Don't kill yourself, Ronan. Don't use a double Windsor knot with that collar, Ronan.

Write your routine, Ronan. Now. While I watch. I want to see it.

7:45 A.M.: THE MOST IMPORTANT MEAL OF THE DAY.

8:00 A.M.: FEED ANIMALS.

9:30 A.M.: REPAIR BARNS OR HOUSE.

12:00 P.M.: LUNCH @ THAT WEIRD GAS STATION.

1:30 P.M.: RONAN LYNCH'S MARVELOUS DREAM EMPORIUM.

What does this one mean, Ronan?

It meant practice makes perfect. It meant ten thousand hours to mastery, if at first you don't succeed, there is no try only do. Ronan had spent hours over the last year dreaming ever more complex and precise objects into being, culminating in an intricate security system that rendered the Barns largely impossible to find unless you knew exactly where you were going. After Cambridge, though, it felt like all the fun had run out of the game.

I don't ask what you do *at work, Declan.*

6:00 P.M.: DRIVE AROUND.

7:15 P.M.: NUKE SOME DINNER, YO.

7:30 P.M.: MOVIE TIME.

11:00 P.M.: TEXT PARRISH.

Adam's most recent text said simply: *$4200.*

It was the amount Ronan had to send to cover the dorm room repairs.

*11:30 P.M.: Go to bed.
*Saturday/Sunday: Church/DC.
*Monday: Laundry & Grocery.
*Tuesday: Text or call Gansey.

These last items on the list were in Declan's handwriting, his addendums subtly suggesting all the components of a fulfilling grown-up life Ronan had missed when crafting it. They only served to depress Ronan more. Look how each week was the same, the routine announced. Look how you can predict the next forty-eight hours, seventy-two hours, ninety-six hours, look how you can predict the rest of your life. The entire word *routine* depressed Ronan. The sameness. Fuck everything.

Gansey texted: *Declan told me to tell you to get out of bed.*

Ronan texted back: *why*

He watched the morning light move over the varied black-gray shapes in his bedroom. Shelves of model cars; an open Uilleann pipes case; an old scuffed desk with a stuffed whale on it; a metal tree with wondrously intricate branches; heaps of laundry curled around beet-red wood shavings.

Gansey texted back: *don't make me get on a plane I'm currently chained to one of the largest black walnut trees in Oregon*

With a sigh, Ronan took a photo of his elbow bent to make it look like a butt, texted it over, and got up. This late in the year, the mornings were dim, but he didn't bother turning on the lights as he made himself breakfast and got his work supplies. He could navigate the farmhouse in pitch-black. His fingers knew the shape of the walls and his feet knew the creak of the floorboards and his nose knew the woodsmoke or long-ago lemon scents of the rooms, all of it memorized like a tune on an instrument. The house contained most of his childhood memories, which might have made it a miserable place for others. But for Ronan, the Barns had always felt like one of his few surviving family members.

If he was imprisoned by circumstance, he thought, at least there were worse places than the Barns.

Outside, the mist lay thick and sluggish across the burnished fields. Long purple shadows fell behind the multiple outbuildings, but the sun-sides of them were lit so bright he had to blink away. As he walked across the slanted fields, dew soaking his legs, he felt his mood lifting. Funny, Ronan thought, how sad an empty house felt and how preferable an empty landscape was.

As he picked his way, creatures that defied existence crept through the tall grass behind him, some more worrisome in proportion than others. He loved his odd menagerie: his stags and his fireflies, his morning monsters and his shadow birds, his pale mice and small furred dragons. Ethically, he wasn't sure if they were allowed. If you could dream a life out of nothing, should you? On weekdays, he gave in to the impulse of adding to his strange herds. On weekends, he spent Mass regretfully apologizing to God for his hubris.

That morning, he was making his way to someone else's dream creatures, however. His father's handsomely colored cattle were permanent residents of the Barns, dew-covered mounds of chocolate, dun, black, gold, bone, chestnut, granite. Like all living dream things, they couldn't stay awake without their dreamer, and so they had been sleeping since Niall died. It was a fate Ronan had to accept would eventually befall all his own creatures, too.

Suddenly, Ronan was enveloped in a rank-smelling charcoal cloud. Muscles coiled and shot him in the air before he realized what it was.

"Gasoline," he snapped, angrier than he might have been because he knew he'd looked stupid, "you better not go far."

Gasoline was a dream creature that was cooler in theory than in practice—an enormous, minivan-sized boar, with small, intelligent eyes and wiry, metallic hair. If it galloped on hard surfaces, sparks came up from its hooves. If it was surprised, it dissipated into a cloud of smoke. When it cried out, it sounded like a bird. It also had no genitalia. This didn't seem like a memorable livestock feature, but once you noticed its absence, you couldn't stop.

The foul-smelling smoke let out a distinctly avian trill before dissipating.

Ronan waved the rest of it away as he knelt beside one of his father's sleeping cows, a delicate speckled gray specimen with one crooked horn. He patted her smooth, warm shoulder. "I've booked your flight. You get a window and an aisle."

He unfolded a dream object he'd brought from the house— a blanket that appeared to be knit out of fall leaves, as large as a tablecloth—and spread it across her shoulders, standing on his toes to toss it over. He searched the edge until he found the hidden drawstring he remembered from the dream it had come from. It was tucked underneath in a way that hurt his logical mind to think about too hard, so he didn't think. He just tugged it out and down, and watched the blanket *tighten* until he couldn't stand to look at it anymore because its movement made no logical sense. It was best not to look straight at some of the dreamfuckery. There were a lot of folktales about wizards and seers going mad from magic, and it was true that some of the dreams felt more brain-breaking than others. The leaf blanket was one of them.

Ronan gave the drawstring three little twitches and, just as in the dream that had created it, the blanket began to float, taking the cow with it. Now Ronan had a cow on a string. A cow balloon. A bovine blimp. In the back of his head he'd thought he might spend the winter trying again to dream something that would rouse a dead sleeper's dreams, a task that would be more pleasant in the climate-controlled long barn. He'd just needed a cow transportation device.

He was pleased the cow transportation device worked, even if he was unconvinced that he would have any more luck waking the cows than he had over the past several months.

He wondered suddenly if this other dreamer, Bryde, might know how to wake another dreamer's dreams.

That would be a thing that made Bryde's game worth playing.

"*Kerah!*" A cry came from overhead. He tilted his head back just as a murder-black bird swooped down to him.

It was Chainsaw, one of his oldest dream creatures. She was a raven and, like Ronan, all the parts that made her interesting were hidden from the casual glance.

He reached a hand out to her, but she just barked and shat a few inches from his shoulder as she circled the floating cow.

"Brat!"

"*Krek!*" Chainsaw spat. Her invented vocabulary mostly had room for extremes: stuff she liked a lot (*kerah*, which was Ronan) or stuff she hated (*krek-krek*, an emphatic form of *krek*, her word for *dreamthing*, referred to a specific and hated dreamthing named Opal, Ronan's other psychopomp). *Snack* was a good word, too, already raven-shaped. So was *Atom*, which was nearly recognizable as *Adam* if you were listening hard.

"Yeah," Ronan said. "Come on if you're coming."

He began to walk his cow balloon to the long barn, keeping a good hold on it. He didn't think the leaf blanket would ever stop going up if he let go, and he wasn't thrilled with the idea of the cow heading out to space.

As he got to the barn, his phone buzzed. He ignored it as he did a little whistle at the door until it obligingly unlocked. He had a bad moment when he realized the cow was never going to fit through his ordinary entrance, and he had to tie her to the doorknob in order to go inside to open the bigger sliding door.

His phone buzzed again. He ignored it.

Inside, the barn was piled with his dream creations— clawsome machines, gearish creatures, supernatural weather stored under tarps, and heartbeats contained in glass bulbs— the mess adhering to no system but his own. He hastily cleared a cow-sized area in front of the sliding door.

His phone buzzed again. He ignored it.

Ronan towed the still-floating cow in, careful not to knock her head on the doorway. He wrinkled his nose. Something smelled rank around here.

His phone buzzed, buzzed, buzzed.

"Goddamn it," Ronan remarked to Chainsaw, who flew skillfully into the barn without touching a feather against any of the clutter. Gripping the cow-leash with one hand, he answered the phone. "What, Declan? I'm trying to fucking tow a cow."

"I just had a very troubling parent-teacher conference. I need you up here."

This didn't immediately make sense to Ronan, as he had neither parents nor teachers in his life. Then he worked it out as he backed another careful step into the barn, the cow bobbing after. "Matthew?"

"Who else?" Declan said. "Do you have another brother you dreamed who's fucking up?"

A dreamer, a dream, and Declan: that was the brothers Lynch.

Chainsaw was an old dream of Ronan's, but Matthew was older. An accident. Ronan had been a toddler. He hadn't even realized it at the time; he'd just accepted the new presence of a surprise baby brother who, unlike Declan, was nearly always happy. He'd loved him at once. Everyone loved Matthew at once. Ronan didn't like to think about it, but it was possible that this lovability had been dreamt into him.

Here was the reason why Bryde's game would be worth the hassle if he knew how to wake dead dreamer's dreams: Matthew would go to sleep with the rest of Ronan's dreams if Ronan died.

There wasn't enough confession time in the Catholic Church to make Ronan feel good about the weight of dreaming another human into being.

Matthew didn't know that he was a dream.

"Okay," Ronan said. The awful smell was building; it was nearly to the breathe-through-your-mouth place. "I—"

Abruptly, the unpleasant smell took concrete form as Gasoline, the minivan-sized boar, rematerialized. Ronan was knocked from his feet. His phone skirled merrily across the gravel and dirt. The cow flitted into the air, rope flapping like a kite tail.

Ronan spewed every single swear he'd ever learned. The cow, eyes closed, oblivious, innocent, gently drifted toward the sun.

"Chainsaw!" Ronan shouted, although he wasn't immediately

sure what words he thought would follow that one. "The—
the—*krek!*"

Chainsaw winged out of the barn, circling him and barking
gleefully, *"Kerah!"*

"No!" He pointed at the cow, which had now floated to the
level of the barn roof. "The *krek!*"

Chainsaw flapped upward to circle the cow ascendant,
looking at it curiously. What a fun game, her body language
suggested. What an excellent cow, what strong decisions it had
made this morning, how delightful that it had taken to the air
like she had. With several cheerful barks, she swirled close before
wheeling back playfully.

"Bring me the *krek!* There's a cookie in it for you! Snack!
Beef!" Ronan offered everything in his potential treat arsenal.
"Cake! Cheese!"

Cow and raven appeared ever smaller as they ascended.

"Trash!" Ronan offered desperately, the one thing Chainsaw
always desperately wanted and was not allowed to have.

Chainsaw clamped claws onto the drawstring.

For a second, Ronan was worried the leaf blanket's levita-
tion would be weightier than the raven. But then Chainsaw made
headway, flapping just a little more strenuously than usual as she
towed steadily. He stretched a hand out to her supportively. At
the end, there were another few fraught moments as he worried
that she'd let go of the string right before he could reach it—
Chainsaw could be a quitter—but then the drawstring was in his
hand and he had towed the cow inside the barn.

Flicking out his pocketknife, he sliced the blanket off the
cow. She dropped the final few inches to the dirt floor.

Finally he allowed himself to be relieved.

Out of breath, he kicked the lid off the metal trash can to fulfill his promise to Chainsaw, and then he stalked over to his fallen phone. The caller ID still showed an active call with DBAG LYNCH.

Ronan put it on his shoulder. "You still there? I was —"

"I don't want to know," Declan said. "Get here when you can."

12

Declan Lynch was a liar.

He'd been a liar his entire life. Lies came to him fluidly, easily, instinctively. What does your father do for a living? He sells high-end sports cars in the summer, life insurance in the winter. He's an anesthesiologist. He does financial consulting for divorcees. He does advertising work for international companies in English-speaking markets. He's in the FBI. Where did he meet your mother? They were on yearbook together in high school. They were set up by friends. She took his picture at the county fair, said she wanted to keep his smile forever. Why can't Ronan come to a sleepover? He sleepwalks. Once he walked out to the road and my father had to convince a trucker who'd stopped before hitting him he was really his son. How did your mother die? Brain bleed. Rare. Genetic. Passes from mother to daughter, which is the only good thing, 'cause she only had sons. How are you doing? Fine. Good. Great.

At a certain point, the truth felt worse. Truth was a closed-casket funeral attended by its estranged living relatives, Lies, Safety, and Secrets.

He lied to everyone. He lied to his lovers, his friends, his brothers.

Well.

More often he simply didn't tell his brothers the truth.

"It's always so nice here," Matthew said as he got out of the car, shoes crunching on gravel.

The three brothers were on the Virginia side of Great Falls, a densely wooded national park only miles away from Declan's town house. The attraction featured both a pleasant walk along a historical canal and the opportunity to witness the Potomac holding its nose and jumping over a seventy-foot ledge as it churned busily from West Virginia to the Atlantic. The sky hung down low and shaggy and gray, intensifying the late fall colors. Everything smelled of the nostalgic, smoky scent of dead oak leaves. It was pleasant, particularly if you had never been there.

Declan had been there many, many times.

"I always like coming," Declan lied.

"It's a regular carnival," Ronan said, slamming the passenger door. *Why shut anything*, seemed to be his motto, *when you can slam it.* The Harvard debacle had shoved him deep into a black mood. It was not always easy to tell how bad it was with him, but Declan had become somewhat of a connoisseur of Ronan's moods. Slamming meant the heart was still pumping blood. Silence meant danger moldered slowly in his veins. Declan had been afraid of the idea of a Ronan who moved to Cambridge. Now he was afraid of a Ronan who couldn't.

There were, Declan thought, so many damn things to be afraid of.

"My car didn't do anything to you," Declan said blandly, easing his own door shut. "Matthew, the bag."

Matthew retrieved the take-out bag of burritos. He was in a great mood. He was always in fine spirits, of course—that was what it meant to be Matthew—but he was in even better spirits when allowed to come to Great Falls. He would come every day if he could, a fact Declan had found out earlier that summer. He took his role as substitute parent seriously. He read articles on discipline, motivation, support. He established curfews, enforced consequences, and served as adviser rather than friend. His promotion to legal guardian meant he could no longer be just a brother. He had to be Law. It meant he'd been quite strict with Ronan after their parents died. With Matthew, however— well, Matthew was so happy that Declan found he would do anything to keep him that way. That summer, however, he'd requested to come day after day until eventually Declan, for the first time, had to turn him down.

Declan thought he still felt worse about that conversation than Matthew did.

"Give me my burrito," Ronan said. "I'm so hungry I could eat it twice."

It was clear to Declan that Ronan wasn't remotely in the mood to joke, but he, too, would do anything to make Matthew happy.

And it worked. Matthew burst into his easy, infectious laugh as he slapped on an ugly hat. He had ghastly fashion sense. The kid was the entire reason why school uniforms had been invented.

"My hiking hat," he said, as if the manicured, flat trail could possibly be construed as anything more severe than a stroll.

They walked. They ate—well, Ronan and Matthew did. Ronan, in big wolfing bites. Matthew, with the barely checked delight of a child at Christmas. Declan left his untouched because he hadn't brought an antacid and his stomach was a ruin as usual. The only sounds were their footfalls and the continuous rush of the falls. Damp yellow leaves sometimes fell here or there, deeper in the trees. Puddles on the walk sometimes trembled as if rain had fallen in them, though there was no sign of rain. It felt wild. Hidden.

Declan cautiously stepped onto the topic at hand. "Your teachers say you've been sitting on the roof."

"Yup," Matthew said cheerfully.

"Ronan, Mary mother of *God*, chew some of that before you choke." To Matthew, Declan persisted, "They said you were looking at the river."

"Yup," Matthew said.

Ronan tuned in. "You can't *see* the river from the school, Matthew."

Matthew laughed at this, as if Ronan had cracked a joke. "Yup."

Declan couldn't probe the motivations of Matthew's mysterious pull toward the river too hard, because that might tip Matthew off to his dreamt origin. Why did Declan withhold this bit of truth? Because Matthew had been raised as human by their parents and it felt cruel to take it from him now. Because Declan could only handle one brother in crisis. Because he was so thoroughly trained in secrets that everything was one until proven otherwise or stolen from him.

"They said you keep leaving class," Declan said. "Without explanation."

Matthew's teachers had said that and a lot more. They'd explained that they loved Matthew (an unnecessary statement; how could they not?), but they worried he was losing his way. Papers were turned in late, art assignments forgotten. He lost focus during class discussion. He asked to use the restroom in the middle of the period and then never returned. He had been discovered in the unused stairwells, empty rooms, on the roof.

On the roof? Declan had echoed, tasting bile. He felt he'd lived one thousand years, every one of them hell.

Oh, not like that, the teachers had hurried to explain. *Just sitting. Just looking. At the river, he said.*

"Whatdya gonna do?" Matthew said, with an amiable shrug, as if his behavior were something puzzling even to him. And probably it was. It was not that he was stupid. It was more that he had a deliberate absence of intellectual skepticism. Byproduct of being a dream? Deliberately dreamt into him?

Declan hated that he loved someone who wasn't real.

Mostly he hated Niall. If he'd bothered teaching Ronan a damn thing about the dreaming, life would look very different right now.

Matthew seemed to have clued in to the idea, at the very least, that he was troubling his brothers, because he asked, "Whatdya want me to do?"

Declan exchanged a look with Ronan behind Matthew's head. Ronan's look said, *What the hell do you want me to do?* and Declan's look back meant, *This is far more your territory than mine.*

Ronan said, "Mom would've wanted you to do a good job."

For a brief moment a cloud passed over Matthew's expression. Ronan was allowed to invoke Aurora because they all knew Ronan loved her as much as Matthew had. Declan, whose skeptical love was imperfect, could not.

"I'm not untrying," Matthew said.

Ronan's phone buzzed. He swept it up at once, which meant it could be only one person: Adam Parrish. For a few minutes, he listened to it very hard, and then, in a very quiet, very small, very un-Ronan voice, he said, *"Alter idem"* and hung up.

Declan found it all worrisome, but Matthew just asked with breezy curiosity, "Why don't you just say 'I love you'?"

Ronan snarled, "Why do you wear your burrito on your shirt instead of in your mouth?"

Matthew, unbothered by his tone, flapped some of the lettuce from his clothing with a hand.

Declan had complicated feelings on the topic of Adam Parrish. There was no way Declan would ever tell a significant other the truth of the Lynch family; it was too dangerous for someone disposable to know. But Adam knew everything, both because he'd been there when certain things had gone down, and because Ronan shared everything with him. So theoretically the relationship was a weak link.

But Adam Parrish was also cautious, calculating, ambitious, intensely focused on the long game, so therefore a good influence. And one only had to spend a minute with the two of them to see that he was deeply invested in Ronan. So theoretically Adam was more positive than negative in the safety department.

Unless he left Ronan.

Declan didn't know how much complication was too much complication for Adam Parrish.

It wasn't like Adam was the most straightforward of people, either, even if he was pretending he was at the moment.

The Lynch brothers had reached Matthew's favorite vantage point, Overlook I. The sturdy, complex decking jutted out toward the falls, cleverly fit around boulders larger than men. If one was less nimble, one could observe from the railing. If one was more nimble, one could scramble up the boulders for a higher view. Matthew always preferred scrambling.

Today was the same as all the others. Matthew pressed his

burrito wrapper into Declan's hands. His ugly hat tumbled from his head, but he didn't seem to notice it as he clambered across the rocks, getting as high as he could get, as close as he could get.

He was transfixed.

The Potomac was unsettled and fast and wide through here as it clawed over the rocks. Leaning on the railing, Matthew closed his eyes and sucked in huge breaths of air, as if he'd been suffocating until now. His brows released until-then-unnoticed tension. His Adonis locks lifted in the wind off the river, revealing not a kid's profile, but a young man's.

"Matthew——" Declan began, but stopped. Matthew had not heard him. The falls had him in their grip.

After many minutes, Ronan simply breathed *fuck*.

It was true that it was eerie—their normally ebullient brother transformed into this enchanted prince. Matthew was not prone to introspection; it was bizarre to see his eyes closed and his mind elsewhere. And it got worse the longer the minutes dragged on. Five minutes, ten, fifteen—that felt long to stand around waiting for him, but not uncanny. One hour, two, three—that was something else. That raised the hairs on the back of your neck. It was, Declan thought, becoming more obvious what he truly was, his existence reliant on Ronan and perhaps on something beyond even that. What powered Ronan? What had powered Niall? Something related to this surging water.

It seemed like only a matter of time before Matthew figured it out.

Ronan sucked air in through his mouth and released it slowly out his nose, such a familiar Ronan gesture that Declan could have identified him just by the sound of it. Then Ronan asked, "What's the Fairy Market?"

Declan's stomach heard the question before his brain did. It seized up in hot anxiety.

Damn it.

His thoughts rapidly followed the flowchart of secrets, of lies. How did Ronan even know to ask that question? Had he found something of Niall's at the Barns; had someone approached him; was their secrecy in question; what had Declan triggered when he made that phone call, when he picked up that key, when he went to that house in Boston while Ronan met up with Adam—

Declan said blandly, "The what?"

"Don't lie," Ronan said. "I'm too pissed off for bullshit."

Declan looked at his younger brother. The more natural brother of the two, but not by much. He had grown up to look exactly like their father. He was missing Niall's long curls and Niall's effervescent charm, but the nose, the mouth, the eyebrows, the stance, the simmering restlessness in the eyes, everything else was the same, as if Aurora had had no part in the transaction at all. Ronan was no longer a boy, or a teen. He was turning into a man, or a mature version of whatever he was. A dreamer.

Stop protecting him, Declan told himself. *Tell him the truth.*

But a lie felt safer.

He knew Ronan was failing alone at the Barns. The farm he adored wasn't enough for him. His brothers weren't enough for him. Adam wasn't really enough for him, either, but Declan knew he hadn't gotten that far yet. There was something strange and yawning and hungry inside Ronan, and Declan knew that he could either feed it or risk losing Ronan to a far more mundane ending and, by extension, lose his other brother, too. His entire family.

Declan clenched his teeth, and then he gazed at the river as it threw itself over the rocks. "Want to come with me?"

13

Sometimes Hennessy imagined flinging herself off the roof. She imagined how, for just a collection of seconds, she would be ascending as her initial jump brought her a few feet above the roof level, before the sucking sensation of gravity wrapped itself around her body. Only then would she be officially falling. Nine point eight one meters per second squared, that was the speed of a fall, all other variables taken out of the picture. Air resistance, friction, balanced and unbalanced forces, six other girls leaning over the edge of the roof shouting *Hennessy come back.*

The French had a term for it. *L'appel du vide,* the call of the void. The urge even non-suicidal people felt to jump when confronted with a high place. Fifty percent of people thought about hurling themselves from heights, much to their shock. One in two. So it wasn't only Hennessy who would imagine her body plummeting into the junipers three stories below.

Hennessy stood on the concrete balcony at the McLean mansion's roof, the toes of her boots poking over the edge, looking at the yard far below. Music spat in the background, something murmuring and sensual and restless. One of the girls sang along with the song even though it was in a language Hennessy didn't speak—had to be Jordan or June. Conversation spiked and lulled. Glasses and bottles clinked. Somewhere, a gun went off, once, twice, three times, distant and percussive in the house, sounding like distant cue balls on a pool table. It was a trash party. A secret party. A party for people who had so much dirty laundry they could be trusted to not air anyone else's.

"You scream, I scream, we all scream for ice cream," said a voice beside her.

It was Hennessy's voice, but out of a different body. Not a different body. A *distinct* body. Hennessy had to look to tell which of the girls it was, and even then, she wasn't sure. Trinity, maybe. Or Madox. The newer ones were harder to place. They were like looking in a mirror.

The girl eyed Hennessy's body language and continued, "You jump, I jump, we all jump."

Everyone at this secret party thought Hennessy's big reveal was that she was one of the most prolific art forgers on the East Coast. The real secret was this: Hennessy, Jordan, June, Brooklyn, Madox, Trinity. Six girls with one face.

Hennessy had dreamt them all.

Only two of the girls were allowed to be seen at the same time. Twins were understandable. Triplets a little more novel. Quadruplets, quintuplets—any number above three became increasingly noteworthy.

Hennessy's life was shit-complicated enough. She had no desire to be extorted further by someone who knew the real truth about her.

"This place was landscaped by a drunk Italian Tim Burton fanboy," Hennessy said, looking down at the intricately hard-scaped backyard. It had not been kept up, but the geometry of it had not yet been lost to untamed growth. Frantically intricate planters and boxwood labyrinths and moss growing between delicately tiled paths. Then, to hide that she couldn't tell which copy the girl beside her was, she asked, "What do you want, bitch?"

"Madox, asshole," said Madox; she could tell Hennessy's tricks right off because she *was* Hennessy. "The vodka. Where did it get to?"

"It's not in the Porsche?"

Madox shook her head.

"Which devils got into it, one wonders?" Hennessy said lightly. "You go spin and spoil in these mortal pleasures on my behalf and I'll look. Which rooms are already overflowing with me?"

"Only the kitchen," Madox said. "I think June and Trinity are in there."

Hennessy stepped off the ledge and rejoined her own party. As she glittered through the house, people she'd forged for and people she'd gotten cash from and people she'd hidden bodies with and people she'd slept with nodded at her or touched her elbow or kissed her on the mouth. She was not looking for the vodka. Madox didn't care about the vodka. It probably was still in the Porsche. Madox had gone up there to get her off the ledge. Been sent, more likely.

Hennessy stalked into one of the side hallways, stepping over broken glass and blood from Breck's break-in until she got to the room Jordan used for most of her forgery. Jordan, like Hennessy, liked to work after dark, which meant she didn't need a room with windows; she needed a room with power outlets so she could sit close to the canvas with her OttLites as brilliant as stage lights. She always double-checked her colors by natural light later. Hennessy wasn't sure why they both preferred to work at night; it was bad art practice, surely. But the sun had never felt like a friend.

"I wasn't going to," Hennessy said as she walked into the windowless studio.

Sure enough, Jordan was installed there among the big, dark canvases and the turpentine and the rags and the brushes stored bristle side up with paint dripping in rich luxurious colors down their handles. She was working on their invite for the Fairy Market. Beneath the microscope on the desk was Breck's original invitation, a delicate, peculiar square of linen, like an arcane handkerchief. Several discarded drafts were strewn about it. Jordan currently had her fingers gripped round a very small Copic marker as she tested yet another spare textile.

"I don't know what you're talking about," Jordan said, not looking up from her work.

Hennessy stepped up on a chair to view the desk from above. "Well, that looks like absolute horseshit."

Jordan used a handheld microscope to assess the bleed of the mark she had just made. "I've nearly got it."

Jordan had been the first of the copies Jordan Hennessy had dreamt into being many years before. She kept *Hennessy* for herself. She gave away *Jordan* to this new girl. Because she was the first copy, and the oldest, Jordan was the most complex of all of the copies—even if Hennessy had dreamt the other girls with as much complexity as she had dreamt her, Jordan had over a decade of her own memories and experience.

Sometimes Hennessy forgot that Jordan was actually her.

Sometimes she thought Jordan forgot, too.

"Your undying optimism should be bronzed," Hennessy said. "It should be displayed in a museum someplace where schoolchildren can see it, read the plaque, and learn from it. It should be cut into smaller pieces and placed in rich soil with plenty of sunlight so that each piece might grow into new opti-mism ready to be harvested by—"

Jordan turned her linen and made a mark with a different pen. "How long do you think we have?"

Once upon a time, Hennessy had wondered if she'd share this face—this life—with two dozen girls. Fifty. One hundred. One thousand. Now she knew that would never happen. Every time Hennessy dreamt a copy of herself into being, it physically cost her something, and it was getting worse.

But she couldn't stop. Neither dreaming, nor dreaming herself.

Every night was divided into twenty-minute segments, her alarm jolting her out of sleep before she could begin to dream. Every day was spent waiting for the black blood to signal that she couldn't put off dreaming forever.

She knew it would kill her soon.

Unless Jordan's Fairy Market plan worked.

Instead of answering Jordan's question, Hennessy said, "You should stretch that linen."

If you stared at puzzles long enough, you started solving them even when you hadn't set your brain on them. This whole time, she'd been looking at that Fairy Market invite and looking at Jordan's efforts and trying to reconcile the difference. Pull that linen taut, ink it, release it, and the ink would have the same amount of bleed as Breck's original.

"Of course," Jordan said. She shook her head at herself, already rising to find the equipment she'd need. "This is why you should've been doing this."

She was wrong, of course. Jordan had to do this because she gave a shit. That was the rule: If you gave a shit about the job, the job was yours. Hennessy gave a shit about surviving, of course, but the bottom line was that she just didn't think this Fairy Market plan was going to launch.

Jordan seemed to read her mind—easier, of course, when the minds were so similar—because she said, "It'll work, Hennessy." At the end of the day, this was the difference between Hennessy and Jordan. While Hennessy imagined flinging herself from a roof and falling, Jordan imagined flinging herself from a roof and flying.

14

It had only taken Farooq-Lane a day to discover that Nikolenko had been entirely wrong about Parsifal Bauer. He was not *easy*, he was passive, which was another thing entirely. He did not do anything he didn't particularly want to do, but it was often hard to tell he'd managed to avoid it or subvert it. When Farooq-Lane had been young, they'd had a family dog who behaved the same way. Muna, a beautiful sort of shepherd mix with lush tufted black hair around her throat, like a fox. She seemed perfectly pliable until asked to do something she didn't want to do—go out in the rain, come into a room for company to admire her. Then she would flop to the ground, a boneless rag doll, and have to be dragged, which was never worth it.

This was Parsifal Bauer.

For starters, he was an infernally picky eater. Farooq-Lane was an excellent cook (what was cooking but a delicious system?) and believed in good food treated well, but Parsifal Bauer made her look like an indiscriminate hog. He would sooner not eat than consume a meal that violated his secret inner rules. Soups and sauces were treated with distrust, meat could not be left pink in the center, crusts on baked goods could not be tolerated. Carbonated drinks were an outrage. He enjoyed a specific sort of yellow sponge cake but not frosting. Strawberry jam but not strawberries. Getting him to eat at the hotel that first night in Washington, DC, had been an absolute failure. It had been late enough that little was open and Farooq-Lane had felt virtuous to have found sandwiches for them both. Parsifal had not said he wouldn't eat his, but he looked at the sandwich on the plate until midnight and then midnight thirty and then eventually she gave up on him.

He had rules for other parts of life, too. He had to sit by a window. He would not be the first through a door. He did not like to be seen without shoes. He would not allow others to carry his bag. He needed to have a pen on his person at all times. He wanted to listen to opera or silence. He had to brush his teeth three times a day. He preferred to not sleep in a full-sized bed. He would not sleep with the windows closed. He would not drink tap water. Bathroom stalls had to have doors that went all the way to the floor if he was to do anything of consequence. He would not go out in public without showering first.

He was most flexible first thing in the morning, and then he slowly became worse as he grew more tired. By night, he was an impossibility of caged rules and desires, his mood secretive and gloomy. The moods were so intractable and thorough that Farooq-Lane went straight through sympathy to aggravation.

The first fight they had was when Parsifal discovered they were sharing a room, Moderators' orders. It was a suite, so he had a pullout bed in the sitting area, and she had a door she could close, but the bathroom was only accessible through Farooq-Lane's room—impossible!—and he insisted the window be open while he slept. It was freezing, Farooq-Lane pointed out, and she didn't think either of them getting flu would serve the situation. Parsifal, in the process of piling sofa pillows onto one side of his bed in order to make it seem more like a twin than a full, argued that she could keep the door to her room shut.

Farooq-Lane countered that the in-room thermostat would respond to the open window and pump up the heat to intolerable levels. She thought the conversation was over. Decided. They went to bed.

After her door was closed, he opened the window.

She roasted. The window was closed by the time she got up, but she knew he'd closed it right before she came out. She confronted him. He was unapologetic, unresponsive. The window was closed now, wasn't it?

This was Parsifal Bauer.

"I am not going," Parsifal told her, his tall form perched on the edge of his sofa bed with its barricade of pillows.

It was evening on day four—no, day five, she thought. Day six? When you were traveling, time got mixed up. It stretched and pinched to create unexpected shapes. Farooq-Lane and Parsifal had been together in the hotel for several sweltering nights, battling over secretively open windows and take-out food against a backdrop of generic hotel carpet and deep-cut German opera. Parsifal had not yet had another vision, so she was operating on the data from his last one. It had taken her and the others days of arduous research to discover that his vision was presenting something called the Fairy Market, a rotating black market that only began after dark. It was hard to say what they would find there, but if Parsifal was having a vision about it, it had to involve either a Zed or a Visionary.

Lock had just sent her an entry pass via courier. There weren't any other Moderators in the city, but Farooq-Lane had a number to call for backup from local agency staffers if she found something that needed to be acted on immediately. This meant if someone needed to be killed. Some*thing* needed to be killed. A Zed.

"You have to come with," Farooq-Lane told Parsifal. "That's not coming from me. That's coming from above."

Parsifal didn't reply. He merely began to fold his laundry, which she'd just had washed by the hotel.

"I'm going to be gone for hours," Farooq-Lane said. She should have been gone already. The night was fully black behind the hotel's ugly gray drapes. "It's unacceptable for us to be apart that long. What if you have a vision?"

He tucked two very long black socks together, fastidiously plucking some lint off one before pressing it flat on top of his already folded clothing. He didn't bother to argue with her; he simply failed to get up. What was she going to do, drag him?

Farooq-Lane never lost her temper. As a child, she'd been famous for this unflappability—both her mother and Nathan had wild tempers. Her mother could be trusted to lose her patience over anything that began with the word *invoice*, while Nathan would be sanguine for days, weeks, before suddenly bursting into surprising fury over triggers no one else could identify. Farooq-Lane, however, could be neither needled nor frustrated. She'd been born with a head for plans. Making them, keeping them, revising them, executing them. As long as there was a plan, a system, she was serene.

Parsifal Bauer was making her lose her temper.

"Food," Farooq-Lane said, hating herself first for not being any more eloquent and then because she had been reduced to bribery. "Come with me and we'll find whatever food you want."

"Nothing will be open," Parsifal said reasonably.

"Grocery stores will be," she said. "Dark chocolate can be had. Seventy percent. Ninety, even. We'll get more bottled water."

He kept folding as if she hadn't spoken. She could feel her

temperature continuing to rise. Was this what Nathan had felt like before he killed people? This swelling grim urgency?

She pushed that away.

"You can wait in the car," she said. "With your phone. You can text me if you begin to have a vision, and I'll come out of the hotel."

Lock would be steamed by this wretched compromise, but Parsifal didn't seem to realize what a stretch she was making. He carefully tucked the arms of a sweater with elbow patches into a perfectly geometric shape.

Farooq-Lane had absolutely no idea how to make a teen boy do anything he didn't want to do.

But to her relief, Parsifal was now standing up. Selecting a few of the items of clothing. Heading toward the bedroom.

"What are you doing?" she asked.

He turned, his expression unfathomable behind his tiny glasses. "If I'm going out, I have to shower first."

The door closed behind him. She could hear music begin to play from his phone speaker. Two women richly cooed at each other with the trembling drama only possible in old opera. The shower began to run.

Farooq-Lane closed her eyes and counted to ten.

She hoped they found these Zeds soon.

15

*A*sk your brother about the Fairy Market.

It really existed.

It really existed, and that meant Bryde did, too.

They'll be whispering my name.

It was black outside, black, black, black, and Ronan's mood was electric. He and Declan were at the Fairy Market, which Declan knew because Niall Lynch had frequented it and Ronan knew because a stranger had whispered it to him in a dream. Things were changing. His head didn't know if it was for better or for worse yet, but his heart didn't care. It was pumping pure night through him.

The Carter Hotel, the site of the Fairy Market, was a big, older building, perfectly square, with lots of small windows and intricate carving at the roofline, formal and tatty as a grandpa dressed for church. It was the kind of hotel one used as a landmark when giving directions, not a hotel one checked into. The parking lot was full of cars and vans. Lots of vans. Ronan wondered what they'd brought. Guns? Drugs? Dreamers? Was Bryde here tonight?

"He wouldn't have been happy I was bringing you to this," Declan said, glancing in the dark rearview mirror. For what, who knew. "He wouldn't have wanted anything bad to happen to you."

He did not quite emphasize the *to you,* but it was understood.

Nothing bad to happen to *you*, something bad could happen to *me*. Sons and fathers, fathers and sons. Of all the things Niall Lynch had dreamt into being, his family was the most marvelous. Of course, he had only technically dreamt part of it—his gentle wife, the boys' adoring mother, Aurora Lynch. A creature of fairy tales by nearly every measure: the bride with a mysterious past, the woman who'd never been a girl, the lady with the golden hair, the lover with the lovely voice. He hadn't dreamt his sons, but they couldn't help but be shaped by his dreams. His dreams both populated and paid for the Barns. His dreams taught the boys secrecy, the importance of being hidden, the value of the unspoken. His dreams made them an island: Niall had no forbearers that were ever spoken of—there was an aunt and an uncle in New York, but even as children, the brothers understood that these were pet names, not true titles—and Aurora of course had no other family. Her pedigree began with Niall Lynch's imagination, and that wasn't a thing you could visit at Christmas.

The Lynch brothers were not Niall Lynch's dreams, but they grew into the shape of them anyway.

And who more than Ronan, a son with his father's face and father's dreaming?

"He's welcome to come back to stop me," Ronan said.

"Don't make it a dare, or he just might," Declan said as he backed into a spot, scrutinizing his automotive neighbors, assessing their desire and aptitude for opening their doors into the side of his car.

"We're at an illegal black market and you're worried about some Honda opening their door into you?" His brother's Declanisms never ceased to amaze Ronan; just when he felt he had reached peak Declan, he always dug deep and found another gear.

"Not that Honda—they keep it clean. Are you carrying anything that might be construed as a weapon? Sometimes they search."

"I have this." Ronan slid what looked like a pocketknife out of his pocket and flicked the button that would normally release the blade. Instead, an explosion of wings and talons surged out. They shredded the air, a flock of terror contained in a small handle.

"Mother Mary," Declan snapped. "Don't ruin my dashboard."

Ronan released the button. Immediately, the wings folded back inside. Declan leaned over to brush a speck of feather dust off his dash and then shot his brother a cutting look.

Outside, the asphalt glistened darkly. Red taillights ignited puddles here and there. The air smelled like shawarma and exhaust. The sky was the dull black of a cloudy night, the storm of the past few days still persisting. On the news they had said this was climate change, this was what storms did now, they moved to a place and camped there, they lavished attention on one place instead of many, until the objects of their affection could no longer stand all the love and washed away. *We have flooding*, the anchor noted, *but think of Ohio, think of their drought*, as if thinking would change any of it. It all made Ronan feel itchy. It was worse to think it wasn't only his personal world that was askew.

Declan peered up at the old sign with its block letters: CARTER HOTEL. It could have been from this decade, from four decades ago. It felt like they had time-traveled. "The last one I went to with Dad was in Tokyo. First one was LA, I think. Maybe Berlin. Memories are liars."

Ronan had to fit this into his recollection of his own childhood. When had Declan nipped off to Tokyo? Was it passed off as a school sports trip? How many times had he been rawly jealous of Declan for being permitted a sleepover when really Declan was yawning and stepping off a plane in Berlin? Ronan knew Declan was made of secrets, but he still managed to be shocked by the reveal of a new one.

A doorman waited at the entrance. It was a good doorway, intricately carved, a solid portal to adventure, and he was a proper doorman, dressed like a drawing of a doorman, in a suit with gold piping. Younger guy, with a sort of messy, too-red mouth.

He looked at Ronan expectantly.

It took Ronan a moment to realize the doorman had assessed the two brothers—Declan in his bland gray suit and clean shoes, Ronan with his tats and boots and murder-crab-scratched face—and thought Ronan was the one leading this show.

That was a weird feeling.

Declan silently recaptured the doorman's attention, offering him a linen handkerchief from his pocket. It had unusual marks printed on it above Declan's name. The doorman studied the marks for just a moment before returning it to Declan, along with a slender printed card, like a menu, from within his jacket.

He handed Ronan an unmarked keycard.

"Ink on your skin means you're hiding things," he told Ronan.

"That's what breathing means," Ronan replied.

The doorman's face hemorrhaged into a smile, and he opened the door.

The Carter's massive lobby was lined with blood-red carpets and lit by dated brass fixtures with long, uneven curls, like rib bones. Ronan could feel the plush of the rug even under his boot soles. It smelled like a burned-out matchstick and lemon. It all had a classy, run-down look, like a place to be aesthetically killed by a really famous poltergeist. It also seemed to be empty. There was no one behind the polished reception desk, and the leather armchairs were unoccupied.

"Sure this is the right place?"

"Everyone's in the rooms," Declan said. He tilted the printed card so that Ronan could read it with him. Floor and room numbers filled one column. In another were short alphanumeric combinations. "Each of those codes stands for something. Art, animals, weapons, drugs. Services."

"Cleaning," Ronan said. "Accounting. Childcare."

"Probably yes, actually," Declan said, "but not in the way you're thinking." He traced a finger down the card. "I don't know all the codes as well as I should. But I think it'll be in an eighty-four room, or a twelve. Maybe a Z-twelve."

"What are we looking for?" Ronan asked.

Declan put the card in his jacket. "*You* aren't looking for anything. You're just looking. And sticking with me. Do you understand? Some of these codes—you go in that room, and you're not coming out."

Everything about this felt false, heightened, unpredictable. Everything about this felt like a dream.

"Say you copy," Declan said.

"I copy, asshole."

"Dad would've hated this," Declan breathed again, more to himself than to Ronan.

"Declan? Declan Lynch?"

Smoothly, Declan turned on his heel. The lobby was no longer empty. A woman stood behind the reception desk. She was dark-haired and voluptuous, wearing a dress or blouse with a collar that looked like the top of a drawstring tote bag. She made an uncomfortable amount of eye contact with both brothers. Her eyebrows had been drawn into very surprised shapes.

"Angie," Declan said. Impossible to tell how he felt about her.

"It's been so long, honey," she said.

She was staring at Ronan, so Declan led him over and said, "This is my brother."

Angie was still making an uncomfortable amount of eye contact. Ronan was a champion at staring, but she might have had him beat for sheer intensity. "He looks—"

"I know," Declan said.

"You talk?" Angie asked Ronan.

Ronan bared his teeth. Her eyebrows continued looking surprised.

"Where you boys keeping yourselves?" Angie asked. "Your daddy was always telling me to come over for dinner if I was in the area, and here we are. It always sounded like a paradise. The Lynch farm. I feel like I could draw that farmhouse if I had to, he was such a good storyteller."

Ronan felt a twinge of betrayal. The Barns was the Lynch family's secret, not something to be given away over a pint or two. He'd idolized Niall before he died; maybe he didn't want to know more about this side of him.

"It burned down," Declan lied smoothly, without a pause. "Vandals, while we were away at school."

Angie's face turned tragic. "You boys have had more than your fair share of bad news. You're like a podcast. Look at you. Tragedy. What brings you back? You here like everyone else, to see if you can catch a glimpse of him before they bring him in?"

"Him?"

She leaned across the counter, all of her spilling against the drawstring closure. In a stage whisper, she said, "He's breaking the rules, they said. On the wrong side of everything. Doesn't care about the rules out there or the rules in here. Just does what he wants. They say he's here because there's law here and we all know how we feel about that."

Declan said, "Who?"

Angie patted his cheek. "You always did want answers."

Annoyance briefly broke through Declan's features before being replaced with his neutral expression again. "We'd better go. Time's money."

It was always a good time, Ronan thought, to trot out a Declanism.

"Watch out for the po-po," Angie said.

Declan was already turning away. "I'll do that."

As the Lynch brothers retreated down a long red hallway, Ronan asked, "Does she help run this?"

"Angie? Why would you think that?"

"She was behind the desk."

"She was probably seeing if she could get cash from the drawers. Do you have the keycard? We'll need it to get into the elevator."

This was dreamlike, too, this casual admission of her criminality, said in the same bland tone Declan said everything. But this used to be Declan's world, Ronan reminded himself. Before the gray town house, before the gray suit, before gray tone of voice, before invisibility, before their father's murder, Declan Lynch came to these often enough to be recognized.

Sometimes Ronan wasn't sure he knew any of his family.

The elevator doors at the end of the hall were like a gateway to an otherworld: brass and glimmering and surrounded by an elaborately carved frame, set like a jewel in the blood-red wall.

Declan swiped the keycard in the elevator's reader and the doors hissed open, revealing mirrored sides. The brothers, outside, looked at the brothers, inside. Declan, with his good boring suit and Niall Lynch's nose and curled dark hair. Ronan, with his shaved head and his tattoo creeping out of his collar and Niall Lynch's mouth and nose and eyes and chin and build and dream ability and everything else. Unmistakably Niall Lynch's sons, unmistakably brothers.

They stepped in.

"Up we go," said Declan.

16

Jordan sat in her car in the Carter parking lot. It was only dumb luck that she'd found a spot there, one last circle round through the cars, telling herself that if she was meant to find a spot there would be one, and there it was.

She was late, but she took a moment anyway, because she was having one of her episodes.

Jordan didn't dream when she slept—she didn't think any of Hennessy's dreamed girls did—but when this feeling started, she thought she knew what it must feel like. Her thoughts pulsed with slightly wrong memories and places she had never been and people she had never met. If she didn't stay focused, those daydreams would seem as important as reality. She'd find herself breathing in time with a pulse outside herself. If she didn't focus, she'd find herself heading toward the Potomac, or just due west. Once she'd come back to herself and found she'd driven two hours to the Blue Ridge Mountains.

It had taken all of her concentration to get to the Carter.

Please pass, she thought. *Not tonight. Tonight's not a good time.*

She forced herself to be in the moment by considering how she would re-create the view before her on canvas. The big, square Carter Hotel looked like a dollhouse made out of a moving box, its tiny windows alight with a yellow glow, silhouettes moving festively in them. It would be easy to render the scene charming, but really, everything here had an edge. Dark, dead leaves heaved restlessly in front of the exterior lights. The sidewalks were apocalyptically empty. For every cozily lit window was a shrouded window. Statistically, someone behind one of them was getting hurt.

She felt a little more grounded—or at least the real world felt truer than the hazy ghost world of the episode. As she finally climbed out, her phone rang.

"Where are you, bitch?" Hennessy's amiable voice was distorted on the other end of the line.

"Just parked."

As Jordan opened the Supra's tailgate, Hennessy launched into a profane pep talk. Jordan gathered her supplies. Three canvases, her sealed palette, her brushes, her turp. Two of the canvases meant nothing to her—they were just another day at the office. The third, which she would be handing off to one of the girls as soon as she got inside, was everything. It was *everything*.

How good are we? she asked herself.

She slid it all out.

The best.

She shut the tailgate on her doubts.

Stepped away.

". . . shell game where every shell is turned over at the same time," Hennessy concluded.

"I was just thinking *shell game*," Jordan said.

"Great minds."

"Okay, mate. I'm headed in."

"Balls out." Hennessy hung up.

The doorman, smoking, watched her cross the lot to him. Not rudely, not salaciously. Just with interest. Even with large parcels tucked under one arm, she had a walk that seemed like there should be a slow-motion explosion occurring behind her. She would watch herself, too, if she wasn't herself.

But it probably had less to do with that and more to do with the fact that he would have seen several other versions of her already that night, all dressed exactly the same, down to the last hair on their heads. One to keep watch. One to distract. One to steal. One to replace. One to be an alibi. Only June waited somewhere in the lot. She had to be the getaway driver— she'd straightened her hair to get that bank job and couldn't look convincingly like Hennessy anymore without a hat. Jordan appreciated the sentiment, the small gesture of individuality, but it sure was a pain in the ass.

Jordan stepped up to the doorman. She hoped none of the other girls had chatted him up or made small talk that she would need to remember. They were good at this, she reminded herself, being each other, being forgeries of Hennessy. They would have texted her if she needed to know something to be convincing. *Be casual. Be Hennessy.* "What's cooking, friend?"

He offered her his cigarette in response. She accepted it, took an inhale as he watched her, and breathed it out into the cold night. She wanted another mouthful, but she had quit six months ago, so she handed it back to him. Hennessy had informed Jordan that she had an *addictive personality*, and maybe she did.

"Thanks, mate," she said.

"Forgot something?" he asked.

"Needed a top up on the ol' victuals. Supplies ran low. The troops were hungry."

"You know I have to ask."

"You know I've got an answer." She reached into her jacket—*casual, be casual*—and handed him the linen handkerchief.

She'd forged four copies of Breck's invite with JORDAN HENNESSY. It had taken ages. Her hand was aching by the end, so Hennessy had stepped in and done the last one. It was impossible to know which of the girls had Hennessy's forgery and which had Jordan's. Even Jordan couldn't tell.

He studied it.

She held her breath.

He was looking at the edge of the handkerchief, which she had carefully frayed to match all the others he had seen the girls use.

Now he eyed her. The septum ring; the scrubby ponytail; the floral tattoo ringing her throat; the crocheted corset beneath the leather jacket; the fingers covered with rings and more floral tattoos; the wide and perfect smile that almost certainly was amused at your expense. Hennessy's style. Which made it Jordan's, too.

Both the invite and Jordan were flawless copies.

The doorman handed the handkerchief back to her.

He said, "Welcome back."

She was in.

17

When Ronan was young and didn't know any better, he thought everyone was like him. He made rules for humanity based upon observation, his idea of the truth only as broad as his world was. Everyone must sleep and eat. Everyone has hands, feet. Everyone's skin is sensitive; no one's hair is. Everyone whispers to hide and shouts to be heard. Everyone has pale skin and blue eyes, every man has long dark hair, every woman has long golden hair. Every child knows the stories of Irish heroes, every mother knows songs about weaver women and lonely boatmen. Every house is surrounded by secret fields and ancient barns, every pasture is watched by blue mountains, every narrow drive leads to a hidden world. Everyone sometimes wakes with their dreams still gripped in their hands.

Then he crept out of childhood, and suddenly the uniqueness of experience unveiled itself. Not all fathers are wild, charming schemers, wiry, far-eyed gods; and not all mothers are dulcet, soft-spoken friends, patient as buds in spring. There are people who don't care about cars and there are people who like to live in cities. Some families do not have older and younger brothers; some families don't have brothers at all. Most men do not go to Mass every Sunday and most men do not fall in love with other men. And no one brings dreams to life. No one brings dreams to life. No one brings dreams to life.

These were the things that made Ronan Lynch himself, but he didn't realize it until he met the rest of the world.

The Fairy Market didn't truly begin for Ronan until the brothers stepped out of the elevator and into another red hallway. They passed a very tall black man who looked as if he was talking into a phone but whose mouth was making no sound. A very old white woman, buckled around a rolling suitcase that dripped liquid as she went. A pair of deeply bronzed women who seemed like they ought to be selling makeup strolling with arms linked, laughing. None of them bothered to hide their stares.

This was so like a dream. All this time, places like this had existed, and Ronan had been shuffling across tidily paved parking lots and blinking underneath a suburban sun. He didn't know if he belonged here, but he suspected he belonged here more than in the world where he'd been hiding. Declan must've known it, too, but he hadn't told him. His father must have known it, but he hadn't told him, either.

Ronan had been raised in an ordinary nest and made to feel like he had no kin.

"Don't talk to anyone about Dad," Declan said to Ronan in a low voice. "People knew him here. As a collector, not as a dreamer. They thought he found all the stuff he sold. Don't give them any other ideas. Don't—"

"Do I look like I'm gonna chitchat?" Ronan asked.

Declan eyed himself in a mirror as they passed. Ronan looked at him, too. He watched his brother's reflection square his shoulders. He watched his brother's reflection mouth: *Don't make me regret this.*

They came to the first door. Declan swiped the keycard; the door hummed.

Ronan remembered, all of a sudden, one of the first things Bryde had told him:

You are made of dreams and this world is not for you.

They plunged into the arcane.

Room one: textiles. It was a typical hotel room: two queen beds, high-sheen comforters, big mirror on one wall, flat screen on the other. But it was also a bazaar, a shop stall. Rugs were draped over the beds and curled into Fibonacci spirals on the floor. Sheer scarves hung from the golden curtain rods. A tattered wall-hanging covered most of the flat screen. Two men with deeply lined skin eyed the brothers as they entered. One was eating bright yellow rice from a take-out container. The other was playing on his phone.

Ronan wasn't sure what he expected of a mythological underground market, but it wasn't *rugs*.

One of the men said, "Declan."

Declan shook hands with him, familiarly, like bros. "Heydar."

How many people here knew Declan?

As the two of them conversed in low murmurs, the other guy offered Ronan some kind of patterned cookie. Ronan shook his head.

"For a hot moment I thought they were talking about your father," Heydar was saying. "Everyone's talking about it."

"Who?" Declan asked.

"'Him,' 'him,' all this talk about a man with incredible things, leading them on a merry chase after that thing in Ireland."

Declan said again, "Who?"

Heydar shrugged. He looked past Declan at Ronan. "Your brother is Niall's son for sure."

Declan's expression changed. From one blank expression to another, blanker one. He'd always seemed annoyed that Ronan looked so much like their father. "I want eighty-four for paintings, right?"

"Eighty-four or two-Y," Heydar said. He was still looking at Ronan. "Makes you miss the bastard, doesn't it?"

"I'm used to it," Declan said. "Hey, give me a call when you're in town next."

In the hall, Ronan waited until the door fell closed and then demanded, "Rugs?"

"Stolen," Declan said. "Or looted from archaeological sites."

"Is it all going to be this boring?"

Declan said, "I hope so."

Room two: mechanical masks. Most of the light came from a collection of candles flickering in front of the black TV. The masks each had glass eyeballs fixed into them and what looked like real animal fur attached to human facial structures. Dozens of empty eyeholes gazed at nothing. Animal skins were stretched on tenterhooks on the walls between them, shaped like agony. Zebra stripes, endangered spots, ivory white and sharkskin gray; the whole place smelled like things that had been alive recently. This room was busy; they had to shoulder in to fit among the lookers.

Declan made a beeline for a collection of frames in the corner. Ronan stayed put; he didn't want to get any closer to the masks. It all reminded him unpleasantly of the murder crabs, which reminded him unpleasantly of Harvard. He held his breath to keep from taking in any more of the dead animal stench.

A hand gripped his upper arm.

A tall white woman with a dopamine tremor looked down at

him. She seemed like she should be teaching arithmetic instead of standing in a room of masks, her hair stretched into a bun, tight as those skins on their tenterhooks, her blouse buttoned all the way up to her chin, a bow tie knotted at her throat.

"Back again?" she asked.

Ronan attempted to pull himself free, but her fingers were long enough to wrap all the way around his bicep. He could've forced the issue, but she was strong enough that he'd knock into the assembled people behind him if he jerked harder. "Uh, wrong number, lady. Please hang up and dial again."

"She doesn't make mistakes," said another woman, turning from the masks. Ronan blinked—she looked the same as the woman holding his arm. Then he realized there were subtle differences: longer nose, more pronounced crow's-feet, deeper eye sockets. Sisters, one older than the other. She leaned in to Ronan. "Do any of these masks look back at you? If they look back at you, they're meant to be yours."

"You wouldn't have come back if they didn't look at you," said the first woman.

He twisted his arm again. "I didn't *come* back."

"So you're already wearing a mask, then," said the second woman. "Who are you really?"

This felt like a dream, too, only in a dream, he'd be able to change the contents. Here he was only as powerful as his physical waking body.

Ronan wrenched himself free. The sisters laughed as he backed away.

When Declan took his arm a moment later, he flinched.

"Stop horsing around," Declan said, turning him to propel

him through the crowd. Before Ronan could protest this, Declan added in a low voice, "They're talking about that guy in here, too. The one Angie and Heydar were talking about. *Him.*"

Say it, Ronan thought. *Say Bryde.*

Room three, room four, room five. Room six, seven, eight, nine: They saw stolen art, jeweled dresses, rooms striped with blood, more endangered species hanging on walls, jewelry from dead people's collections. Guns. Lots of guns. Poisons, too, and drugs. They swiped one door open and on the other side of it a man had his hands around a woman's throat. The woman's eyes were wide and veins bulging, but when she saw the brothers watching she mouthed *GO AWAY.* There was something terrible about the scene, in the complicity of it, in the way the woman was not saving herself, in the way they couldn't tell if she was the client or the product. Ronan let the door fall shut, but he knew from experience when he'd seen an image that would haunt him again in dreams.

As they passed through one room, a fortune-teller with a visible third eye tattooed over her invisible third eye said to Ronan, "Twenty dollars, final offer, your future," as if Ronan had already begun a negotiation with her.

"I've already got one," Ronan said.

"Do you?"

"Ronan," Declan said. "Come on."

"Lynch boy!" A man leaning on a cane beside a box of other boxes recognized Declan. "Have you seen him? Have you seen him run?"

Declan, all business, just twitched his fingers dismissively as he passed, but Ronan paused.

"Who?" Ronan asked. "Tell me. Don't play."

The old man gestured him closer in order to whisper in his ear. He smelled of garlic and something sweeter and something fouler, reminiscent of the odor of Gasoline the vanishing boar.

Declan had stopped, looking over his shoulder at Ronan, eyes narrowed. He didn't know what was going on, but he didn't like it, probably *because* he didn't know what was going on.

"I want his name," Ronan said.

You're wondering if this is real.

Say it, thought Ronan.

The old man whispered, "Bryde."

Room ten: This was a top-floor library, a holdover from a far earlier era. The room was very long and very thin, dark and close, one side lined with dark bookshelves, the other with deeply red-and-gold wallpaper that matched the deeply red-and-gold carpet. Dusty crystals gleamed dimly in low-hanging chandeliers, like insects caught in spiderwebs. Art was everywhere: hanging on the walls, piled against harpsichords and pianos in the middle of the room. Music played from somewhere, some sort of sloping, uncanny reed instrument.

A man in a purple slicker on his way out asked Declan, "Do you have the time?"

"Not today," Declan replied, as if answering an entirely different question. The purple slicker turned toward Ronan, and Declan put a hand on his chest firmly. "He doesn't, either."

The man sighed and moved on.

Declan stopped before a pairing of two abstract pieces, one of them violent or passionate, depending on your point of view, and one of them complexly black. On either side of the paintings hung antique violins, their bodies spindly and fragile with age. Ronan didn't care for the first painting, but the second was alluring in the way it could be so many different things at once while still being entirely black. He could *feel* it as well as see it.

"Dreamed?" Ronan asked.

Declan said, "That one's a Soulages. The other's de Kooning. Several million dollars between the two of them. You like them?"

Ronan jerked his chin toward the Soulages. "That one's all right."

"'All right.' Figures. Everything in black, right?" Declan said ruefully. "There's a thing Soulages said. 'A window looks outside, but a painting should do the opposite—it should look inside of us.'" He recited it carefully, perfectly. Like their father, he had an ear and a desire for a cunning turn of phrase, but unlike Niall, he rarely demonstrated it.

"Do you like them?" Ronan asked.

Declan said, "They make me want to goddamn cry."

Ronan had never seen his older brother goddamn cry and could not remotely begin to picture it. Declan had already moved on to rummage through a pile of canvases leaned against each other in a temporary booth. They were dull so Ronan left him there to prowl in ever-widening circles. Canvases, pastels behind glass, paper rolled into uneven scrolls, sculpture reaching toward the lights, boards leaned akimbo like someone starting a house of cards. He wanted to take a photo of all this to show Adam, but he had an idea this was the kind of place that wouldn't take kindly to photos.

Then Ronan saw it.

It. It. *Her.*

"Declan," Ronan said.

Declan kept digging through paintings.

"Declan."

His brother turned at the tone in his voice. Ronan didn't point. He just looked, and let his brother look with him.

It was fifty feet away and it was through cluttered booths and the light was dim, but it didn't matter. Ronan would recognize his dead mother anywhere.

18

*B*ryde, they said.

Everyone was saying it, all over the hotel. Farooq-Lane felt as if she heard the end of the word the moment she walked into a room and heard the beginning of it the moment she walked out.

Bryde. Bryde. Bryde.

Maybe a Zed. Definitely someone of note. Whoever he was, he had everyone in this strange place under his spell. Who was he? Someone to keep your eye on.

And if he had the attention of people at a place like this, he had to be something strange indeed.

Unfortunately, she could tell at once that she was in over her head. This wasn't Carmen Farooq-Lane standing in a group of armed Moderators facing down a Zed or two. This was Carmen Farooq-Lane, a previously quiet citizen hurriedly turned specialized operative, in a building full of people who existed outside the bounds of most of the world. She felt like they could see it on her the moment she walked into a room. Glancing at her and away, their attention spotted just out of the corner of her eye. Just like that name. *Bryde. Bryde. Bryde.* She hadn't thought her usual linen suit and long coat would be an inappropriate choice, but it was. She appeared too clean, too straight-edge, too at home in the world as it was currently constructed.

"They don't like law there," Lock had told her on the phone. "They've got an understanding."

"An understanding?" she'd echoed. "Like a no-fly zone? A no-go zone? A . . ."

She had heard about places like this on the news but couldn't remember the name for them in the moment. Places where cops didn't go, places with their own local law. She supposed she hadn't really believed in them.

"Outside our pay grade, Carmen. Save the world," Lock said, "and then you can go back into the Fairy Markets and clean up."

She was supposed to be looking for signs of Zeds, which generally meant anything unusual. But everything here was unusual. Uncomfortable. Weapons. Stolen art. A room of demure young men and women displayed as wares. Dogs clipped to look like lions. Electronics with product numbers rubbed off them. Boxes of driver's licenses, passports. These masks? Were they dreamt? This ivory?

She didn't know how to tell.

As the stares increased, Farooq-Lane found herself losing her temper at Parsifal once more. Unbelievable, considering he hadn't even come in with her. Nonetheless, he managed. If his vision had been more specific, she would have known what she was looking for.

Her cover, if anyone asked, was that she was a buyer. She had thirty thousand dollars in cash to go along with her linen handkerchief invite. PADMA MARK. She didn't think she looked like a Padma. Parsifal had an invite, too, not that he was using it; it was in his own name. When she'd asked Lock why he got to be PARSIFAL BAUER when she had to be Padma, he said it was because Parsifal had a properly disruptive history if anyone bothered to look it up. Parsifal looked like someone who would come to one of these things.

Parsifal Bauer? Disruptive?

Bryde. Bryde. Bryde.

They were all looking at her. She thought: *Buy something.* They would all stop looking at her if she bought something.

But she didn't want to buy anything illegal; it would make her feel complicit. Her world operated on a system she mostly believed in, a system of laws designed to promote ethics and fairness and sustainability of resources.

There were only so many of her principles she was willing to let slip, even to save the world.

There. A fortune-teller. Fortune-telling was dubious in value but not in legality. Farooq-Lane waited until a knot of men who seemed to be priests moved out of her way, and then drew close. The woman behind the table had a third eye tattooed between her eyebrows and odd silvery curls all over her head, so tightly formed that they seemed to be metal. Maybe she was dreamt, Farooq-Lane thought, and nearly laughed.

She realized she was very frightened.

"How much?" she asked the woman. She didn't sound frightened. She sounded like Carmen Farooq-Lane, young professional who you could trust with your future.

The curls didn't bob as the woman looked up. Maybe they were a wig. "Two thousand."

"Dollars?" This was the wrong question, somehow. Farooq-Lane felt it draw attention. Four women in garb that looked as if it was formal attire somewhere that wasn't corporate America glanced over their shoulders at her. The priests seemed to move in slow motion. A tall man put his hand inside his bomber jacket in a worrisome way. Hurriedly, she dug out the bills and sat at the chair the woman indicated.

She felt quite woozy once she was off her feet. The air was richly scented; maybe she was high. Maybe it was just her racing heart, her too-fast breaths. Were they still looking? She didn't want to check.

Bryde, Bryde. They were still whispering it even now. Maybe she was imagining it now.

"Give me your hand," the fortune-teller instructed.

Reluctantly, Farooq-Lane slid her palm over; the fortune-teller gathered all her fingers together as if collecting a bundle of sticks. She would feel Farooq-Lane's flapping pulse, she thought.

But the fortune-teller just said in an old New Jersey accent, "Smooth. What do you use?"

Farooq-Lane blinked. "Oh. Uh. Oatmeal and argan oil?"

"Very beautiful," the fortune-teller said. "Like you. Beautiful woman on the outside. Let us see the inside."

Farooq-Lane risked a glance around as the fortune-teller closed her eyes. The gazes had turned away from her, but she nonetheless felt watched. She wondered how upset Lock would be if she emerged from this experience with only a name: *Bryde.*

Suddenly, she was overwhelmed with the smells of mist, of damp, of warm blood freshly spilled. She was back in Ireland, and Nathan's body was accepting bullets from Lock's gun without protest. Farooq-Lane's mind reeled, and the fortune-teller's eyes opened again. Her pupils were enormous, her eyes all black. Her mouth was somehow arranged differently than it had been before. Her grip was tight on Farooq-Lane's fingers.

She smiled cannily.

"Bryde . . ." the fortune-teller started, and the hair on the back of Farooq-Lane's head tingled. "Beautiful lady, Bryde says if you want to kill someone and keep it a secret, don't do it where the trees can see you."

Farooq-Lane felt the words before she heard them.

Her lips parted in shock.

She jerked her hand out of the fortune-teller's fingers.

The fortune-teller blinked. She looked at Farooq-Lane with her ordinary eyes, her face arranged as it had been before. Just a woman. Just a woman with silver curls, looking at Farooq-Lane as she had when she'd first stopped in front of her table.

But then the fortune-teller's expression hardened. She said, loudly and clearly, *"Who wants a piece of the law?"*

Every single head nearby turned to look at Farooq-Lane.

Farooq-Lane didn't wait.

She ran.

19

Declan hadn't told anyone that he knew Aurora Lynch was dreamt.

It was a secret, after all, and he knew how to handle secrets. It was a lie, too, because Niall expected them to believe that she was as real as the rest of them, but Declan knew how to handle lies.

It was a little heavier to carry than Declan's other secrets and lies.

Not heavier.

Lonelier.

Aurora didn't fall asleep right away after Niall died. She should have. On the day of his murder, the cows fell asleep. The cat. The family of finches that nested outside the farmhouse. The coffee machine that had always felt warm must have been technically alive, because even as other dreamt contraptions continued working, it stopped. Every other dreamt creature of his was fast asleep within seconds of his death, but not Aurora.

It was a Wednesday. Declan remembered that, because for years he'd considered Wednesdays days of bad news. Maybe he still did. He wouldn't schedule something on a Wednesday if he could help it. Magical thinking, probably, but it felt like mid-week still soured things.

On Thursday, Aurora was still awake. Awake? Sleepless. She stayed awake all night, pacing, restless, like those animals sensing an impending natural disaster. Declan knew she was awake, because he was, too. On Thursday, the Lynch brothers were not yet orphans.

Friday, a dead-eyed Ronan took Matthew out for a walk in the hayfield, leaving Declan alone in the still house with the dreamt thing called Aurora Lynch. Declan was relieved. He couldn't bear looking at Ronan right now. Something foul and dark had nested inside Ronan the moment he'd found their father's body; it was as if it woke up as everything else fell asleep. It was the most terrifying aspect of the situation so far—proof, it felt like, that things would never be the same.

Aurora was slow by Friday. Bewildered. She kept starting in one direction and then being distracted by things that ordinarily wouldn't have drawn her attention. Mirrors. Sinks. Glass. She shied away from metal, coming suddenly alert when she nearly touched a doorknob or a faucet, before falling dazed once more.

Declan found her fumbling in the hall closet. She was moving the same three coats back and forth and gasping a little, as if the space was airless. Her eyes were glazed, half-lidded. He watched her for several long minutes, dread icing his heart. Dread and anticipation.

By then, he felt sure he was the only one in this house who knew the truth about her. The only one who knew what was coming.

Ah, Ronan, ah, Matthew. The brothers Lynch. They didn't think their hearts would break more.

Aurora noticed him, finally, and wafted away from the coats to him.

"Declan," she said. "I was going to walk. I was going to find . . ."

He stood motionless and stiff as she hugged him, thoroughly, messily, her face pressed against his hair. He felt her swaying. He felt her heartbeat. Or maybe it was him. Maybe he was swaying. Maybe it was his heart. She might not even have a heart. Dreams didn't have rules like men did.

He was going to be alone, he thought, he was going to be alone and it was going to be just him and that new terrifying Ronan, and Matthew whose life depended on him, and somewhere out there was something that killed Lynches.

"The will is in the cedar box in our bedroom closet," she said into his hair.

Declan closed his eyes. He whispered, "I hate him."

"My dauntless Declan," Aurora said, and then she slid softly to the floor.

The orphans Lynch.

Now Declan watched Ronan stare at a painting that looked very, very much like Aurora Lynch. It was called *The Dark Lady*, and it was the reason Declan had come to the Fairy Market.

The subject of the painting was a woman with golden hair pinned to bob around her chin and a particular, puerile way of standing, head and neck jutted forward, hands defiant on hips. She wore a diaphanous periwinkle-blue dress and had a man's suit jacket across her shoulders, as if it had been offered against a chill. Her head was turned to stare at the viewer, but the meaning of her expression was difficult to discern because the hollows of her eyes were cast in deep, almost skull-like shadow. Every color in the painting was black or blue or brown or gray. The entire image was subtly imbued with desire in a way observers probably thought was good art but Declan understood was part of the dream object's magic. It was signed in familiar handwriting.

Niall Lynch.

"It's one of Dad's," Declan said.

"I can fucking see that." Ronan sounded furious, which told Declan little about what he was really feeling. Every emotion that wasn't happiness in Ronan usually presented itself as anger. "This is what you came for? I didn't think you were sentimental about Dad's stuff."

Declan wasn't, but he wanted this painting.

He *needed* it.

For years it had been in a collection in Boston, having been sold to Colin Greenmantle, the crooked collector who'd eventually had their father killed. Several months ago, Greenmantle had died himself—through equally shady circumstances—and one of the dealers who'd known both him and Niall had gotten in touch with Declan. He'd offered him the key to Greenmantle's odd collection.

Take anything you want of your father's before I sell it, he'd said. *You earned it with blood.*

A generous offer. Very generous. Generosity on a scale of tens of thousands of dollars.

I don't want it, Declan had said.

He was going to keep his head down. Be invisible. Pretend that part of his life had never happened.

I don't want any of it, and even as he said it, he knew it was a lie.

But what was Declan Lynch but a liar?

"She has a legend," Declan told Ronan, who eyed it where it sat, one of several paintings leaned against a temporary booth's walls. "Whoever sleeps in the same room as her will dream of the ocean."

Apparently it drove people crazy. While Ronan was destroying a Harvard dorm room, Declan had been looking through what was left of Greenmantle's collection in Boston. He'd discovered that *The Dark Lady* had been sold shortly after Greenmantle's death and then changed hands dozens of times, no one keeping her for longer than a few weeks. And she was to be sold again, this time at the Fairy Market in Washington, DC.

It was like it was meant to be.

"I'm going to buy it, if I can afford it," Declan said. The Lynch brothers were rich, but conditionally so. Niall had left each of them a piece of property—the Barns to his favorite son, an empty field in Armagh, Northern Ireland, to Aurora'a favorite son, and a sterile town house in Alexandria to the son left over—and a sum of money that would keep them in middle-class comfort for most of their lives as long as they didn't make many splashy spends like car purchases, hospital stays, or deals for supernatural paintings. "Play it cool."

"Play it cool," mocked Ronan softly, but he arranged his face into indifference as they headed over to the booth.

The man who ran this booth didn't look like he should be selling art. He looked like he should be running a gym, smiling on a billboard for the weight-lifting program he'd developed, promoting protein shakes, losing it all when he was busted for steroid use. His hair was greased into spikes nearly as strong as the rest of him.

"How much for that one?" Declan asked. "Of the blond woman?"

"Twenty thousand for that little lady," said the man standing among the canvases. "Look at her spirit. What a gal. You can tell she's got a giggle in her somewhere."

Declan assessed his tone and posture and the placement of the painting in the booth, analyzing how invested the man was and how valuable he felt it was. And part of him tucked away the way the man spoke, too. Declan's private collection of words and phrases was free and forever secret, a perfect hobby.

He said, "For a painting by a nobody?"

Ronan's gaze bored holes in the side of his head. It wouldn't have hurt Ronan a bit if he made his peace with lying for good cause, Declan thought.

"She'll make you dream of the shore," the man said. "My little daughter said it made her dream of the seaside. I had to try it out myself. Shuck and darn if it didn't. There was the seaside, every night she was under my roof. Like a free vacation! That's a guar-an-tee."

"I don't need a parlor trick," Declan said. "I just need something to hang over my dining room table. Three-five."

"Twenty thousand is firm."

The pricing of uncanny objects was always subjective. How much was it worth, the feeling that you owned something that shouldn't exist, or something that touched a supernatural realm you didn't otherwise have access to, or something that made you believe that there was more to the world than what you'd been given? The answer was usually *a lot*. Declan didn't know how much he could really talk the guy down. But twenty thousand was a big ding out of his carefully hoarded savings. An unwise sum for an already unwise decision. "Four thousand."

"Nineteen."

Declan said blandly, "I don't want to leave this on the table, but I'm not going another round. Fifteen is my final."

The man relented and accepted the bills. "I'll get some wrapping paper."

You're really doing this, Declan thought. *Down the rabbit hole.*

Beside Declan, Ronan knelt by the painting. His hand

hovered over the woman's face but didn't touch the surface. It wasn't difficult to tell that it meant a lot to him to see Aurora again; Ronan couldn't lie even with his body language. Somehow, objectively troubling truths about their parents had been unable to mar Ronan's feelings for them. Declan envied him. His love and his grief both.

The seller returned with the wrapping paper and a fat, tattered ledger.

Declan eyed this second object. "What's that?"

"I'll need your name and zip. This piece is registered," the seller said. "Her sales are tracked."

This was unusual in a market that was defined by discretion. Tracked objects were dangerous, absurdly valuable, or tied to organized crime of one brand or another.

Declan felt a burst of misgiving. "By who?"

"Boudicca," the seller said.

The word meant nothing to Declan, but he didn't like it anyway. He didn't do strings-attached. "I'll give you nineteen for it, unregistered."

The big muscle-bound man shook his head regretfully. "Can't do that, buddy."

"Twenty-five."

"Can't. Not for Boudicca. Not worth it."

Declan weighed this. It was bad enough to come to this place where people would know him and buy one of his father's old dreams. It was something else to come here and be on the record about it. He didn't like how the guy said Boudicca, either. It sounded like power. It sounded like malice. He didn't like it one bit.

He'd already given out his business card once that evening and that felt dangerous enough.

"Then that's a no from me," Declan said. He held out his hand to get his cash back. "Sorry."

"Come on," the guy said. "The deal's almost closed."

"Sorry."

The guy kept holding out the ledger. "It's not an address. Just name and zip. Easy. You give that at the Starbucks drive-through. You write that on the bathroom wall."

Declan kept holding his hand out for his money.

In the background, the sounds of the Fairy Market continued. There was some kind of kerfuffle happening on the other side of the room. People scuffling. Voices raised. It was dangerous tonight; it was always dangerous at these places. Declan had known that and he'd come anyway. He'd brought Ronan. He'd edged out on this limb and reached for this painting from his past. He knew better than this.

The Dark Lady stared at him mistrustfully.

"Lynch," Ronan said abruptly.

Both Declan and the guy looked at Ronan. For a moment, Declan couldn't decide if Ronan had actually said something, or if Declan had merely imagined it.

"Ronan Lynch, 22740."

Declan could kill him. He could absolutely kill him.

The man wrote it down. Declan could feel his skin prickling all over when he saw the words in ink. Ronan. Lynch. A truth, given away. A truth, transcribed forever. He hated it. So much softer to lie. So much easier to just put down the painting and what it promised and walk away.

The man lifted the painting of the golden-haired woman into Ronan's arms.

"Enjoy the ocean."

20

Jordan was performing again.

Tonight was not entirely unlike the party at TJ's, except that the audience was made up of criminals, Jordan was very much hoping Feinman *wouldn't* show up, and the stakes were even higher because if their plan failed tonight, she couldn't think of what a fallback plan might look like.

Jordan was copying John Singer Sargent's *Street in Venice* in the middle of the Fairy Market. She'd copied this particular painting many, many times before, but familiarity made it soothing rather than boring, like rewatching a favorite movie. In it, a girl clutched her shawl as she walked briskly down an alley. Two men, loosely depicted in dark colors, stared at her as she passed. The girl's eyes were cut low to the side, furtively watching them watch her. A couple sat at a café as well, but Jordan hadn't even noticed them the first few times she'd seen the painting. Just the wary girl, darkly observed, and the city creeping in close.

Like all Sargents, the key to copying it was painting without hesitation. He had broad, free, effortless-looking strokes, and if the artist approached the work with timidity, the resulting copy looked fussy and forced.

Jordan didn't hesitate.

Not long after she'd set up, Hennessy called. "All eyes on you?"

"Green light go."

"Got my fortune told. Lady said our house was going to get broken into again."

Jordan breathed out. "We don't have a house."

"Too right, we have a home," Hennessy said. "I'm gonna go see a man about a dog."

She hung up.

Jordan turned her attention back to the canvas in front of her. Art, art, think of the art. If she thought of the art, she wouldn't think about everything that could go wrong. Art was a solid part of Jordan. Not art like *take up a brush and let your soul pour out through pigments,* but rather art as an object in the trunk of your car, art as a physical proof of cultural identity, art as a commodity. She had scars, stains, and blisters from art. Probably it was inevitable, given her pedigree. Hennessy's father had collected art, including her mother, and her mother had painted portraits right up until she'd died. Her mother's portraits had been a little famous before her death and now they were very famous. This was, Jordan discovered, because art always lasted longer when mingled with blood.

"I wish I could say I was surprised," a familiar voice said.

Feinman. Bernadette Feinman looked even more hectic and dramatic in this environment, adding a long fur coat to the rose-tinted glasses Jordan had seen her in before. She looked like a poised older lady who'd seen some things in the past and was open to seeing more things in the present. She still had her clove cigarette; she smoked it now in a long holder. Jordan appreciated the commitment to the aesthetic even as she felt her heart sink.

"Crumbs," said Jordan. Rapidly, she tried to think of how the plan would change if Feinman had her thrown out.

"Calm down and paint on," Feinman said. "I'm not ratting you out. I knew who you were when I turned you down at Tej's. I knew you could just forge your way in here. Sometimes, you just have to be a conscientious objector. I wanted it on the record that I feel you could do more with yourself."

"Absolutely. Explore my full potential. A benevolent big E. I appreciate it. One always wants to be more," Jordan said. "So this is just a neighborly visit?"

Feinman peered at Jordan in a complicated way, as if thinking that Jordan's reasons for choosing a life of criminality might surface if she looked hard enough. Finally, she just said, "Keep that smile. It's an original."

After she had gone, Jordan let out a long, long, long breath of relief. Belatedly, Trinity texted her: *I think I saw Feinman headed your way.*

Jordan texted back: *Hot tip. What's going on with H?*

Trinity: *Still mum*

No word was good. Or at least it was not bad.

Usually Hennessy and Jordan were art forgers.

Tonight they were thieves.

Hennessy had gotten in earlier to suss out where the intended target was. With this many floors and rooms, and with none of the vendors neatly catalogued, that was quite a feat. After she'd discovered where the painting was, Jordan had arrived with her precious wrapped decoy and her painting supplies. She'd set up in the most public place possible to demonstrate her trade. *Look at me,* her presence shouted. *Look at me being Hennessy, sitting here painting a copy of a Sargent, definitely not somewhere else stealing a painting. Look at me and my alibi.* It was to be the perfect crime: Jordan had spent weeks working on a flawless copy of the painting they meant to steal, and Hennessy's job was to swap them while the owner wasn't looking.

They needed it.

Jordan went back to work. She tried not to think about what Hennessy was doing. She got some commissions. She heard the word *Bryde* whispered back and forth; she didn't know what it meant. She smiled for her small, shifting crowd of watchers. Most only paused for a few seconds unless they were placing a commission.

Except for one.

He stayed long enough that Jordan glanced up. Conservative, expensive gray suit. Conservative, expensive black watch. Conservative, expensive silk black tie. All behaving so well in concert that they were utterly forgettable.

"They say ten percent of works in museums are fakes," he observed.

Jordan glanced up at him. He was young and handsome in a way so in line with cultural expectations that his appearance passed through attraction straight into boredom. His hair was carefully tousled and curled, his facial hair carefully allowed to shadow his chin in an orderly fashion. He had good teeth, good skin. Very blue eyes. He was inoffensive in every way. She said, "And, what, another forty percent misattributed without any malicious intent?"

He replied blandly, "That makes at least half of art appreciation the cultivation of a willing suspension of disbelief."

"Fun for all ages."

He laughed. It was a smooth and easy laugh. It did not imply that it was laughing at her. It implied it might be laughing at him, if that was what she wanted. Or it might just be laughing, if she preferred that. He observed, "You're incredibly good."

"Yes," agreed Jordan.

"I can't draw a stick figure," he said. "I've got no—"

"Don't be boring," she interrupted. "Just say you never tried. People are always saying *talent* when they mean *practice*."

"I never tried," he concurred. "I practiced other skills."

"Such as? Provide an itemized list."

He glanced off into the crowd. Not quite skittish, because skittish didn't seem to be his style. But something else was asking for his attention. "You remind me of my brother."

"Congratulations," she said.

"On what?"

"On having such a beautiful brother."

Now he laughed for real, a considerably less even sound, and he looked away from her as he did, as if he might muffle the truth of it by so doing. This was obviously not a sound he meant to hand out to people. She wondered how deep he was in this world. He didn't seem to have that edge one required to survive. He seemed more likely to sell annuities or bonds.

She returned to her work. "Can I ask what you're doing here tonight?"

"No," he said.

She looked up at him. He smiled that bland smile but didn't back down from that *no*. It was a *no* that wasn't malicious or rude. It was simply a fact. *No. You're not allowed to know.*

Suddenly, she saw how he might survive in this world.

"Declan," someone said, and his eyes narrowed. It was a far more memorable expression than any he'd worn to that point. He shifted, and as he did, she noticed his shoes. They were also surprising. Excellent, buttery brogues with smart tooling. Not bland. Not forgettable.

"Is that you?" Jordan asked.

Instead of replying, he tucked a business card just behind the edge of her canvas. There was one word above the telephone number, printed in silver: LYNCH.

Lynch.

Now there was a coincidental name. She enjoyed it; it felt like it meant things were going to go right.

"If you want to know more," he said, "call me."

"Smooth," she said. "Well done."

He smiled his straight-teeth corporate smile at her again.

"Declan."

He was gone. Other viewers came to take his place, but Jordan found she kept looking at that business card. LYNCH.

Get your head in the game, Jordan, she told herself. *Tonight's about something bigger than that.*

The phone rang. It was Hennessy. Jordan's heart revved way up as she picked it up.

"Someone bought it," Hennessy said. "Just now."

"What?"

"Someone bought it. Right before I got there. It's gone."

Of all the paintings for sale under this roof. After all this time tracking it. Someone else had gotten to *The Dark Lady* first. Jordan's stomach dropped out. "Do we know who?"

"It's not like we could roll up and ask that fucking bum nugget," Hennessy said. "But Brooklyn saw the mark. We're gonna see if we can find him before he leaves. Then, like, assess the goddamn situation."

Jordan was already scraping her tubes of paint into her bag

and looking around for someone holding a parcel of the correct size. "What's the buyer look like?"

"Young. Twenties. Dark hair, blue eyes. Brooklyn said he had full on blue eyes."

Dark hair. Blue eyes. Jordan looked at that business card: LYNCH.

Crumbs.

She jumped to her feet, but Declan Lynch was long gone.

21

The brothers Lynch were back in the mirrored elevator, the sounds of the library left behind, replaced with the dead-air silence of the descending elevator car. The quiet was punctuated only by the muffled *ding* of it marking off floors. Ronan's body still felt revved up from the truth of Bryde, the shock of seeing his mother's face, the charge of the completed deal, the heat of Declan's anger. His older brother still looked pissed. More pissed than he'd been in months.

"I can't believe you," Declan said. "I brought you here. I trusted you."

"What's the big deal?" Ronan demanded. *Ding.* "People recognized your face all over this place."

"They didn't enter my name into a log for some syndicate to monitor," Declan said.

"Is that what Boudicca is?"

Declan shrugged. "Did you see that guy's face when he said it? That's called fear, Ronan, and you might try getting some."

Declan had no idea.

Ding.

"Did you know it was going to be a painting of Mom?" It was a peculiar likeness. Aurora's head, on someone else's body. Aurora would never stand like that, petulant and challenging. Even her face was a little different than Ronan remembered, the features more acute, more spoiling for battle, than Aurora's had ever been in real life. It was possible it wasn't a very good portrait, he supposed. But it was also possible there was a side of his mother he hadn't known.

Before tonight he would've denied that possibility, but at the moment, almost anything felt possible.

Declan had begun to peck at his phone, his peculiar thumb and forefinger technique. "I had a guess."

"What else do you know that you haven't told me?"

Ding.

The elevator door opened. It was not the ground floor. It was the third floor, the one with the masks. A woman waited on the other side, hands in the pockets of a gray bomber jacket. First Ronan saw the way she stood. Tense, coiled, a predator. Then he saw her hair: golden. Then her eyes: pretty, blue.

Cornflower, sky, baby, indigo, azure, sky.

For the second time that night, Ronan found himself looking directly at his dead mother, only this time she was in the flesh.

His brain was rejecting it—*this doesn't happen when you're awake, it's not what you think*—

And she was just looking at him, staring at him, her gaze petulant, spoiling for battle, just like the portrait leaned against Declan's legs. Then she looked at Declan, and she flinched.

None of them moved—not toward, not away—they just looked, looked, *looked*. Transfixed, like Matthew at the falls. Bespelled, lost. The brothers Lynch and their dead mother.

Then the elevator doors closed on Aurora.

Ronan was startled into action. "The door, Declan—"

Both slammed the door open button, but the elevator ignored them, already on its way down. Ronan mashed the second-floor button just in time, and the doors obediently opened. Ronan bolted into the hallway.

"Ronan—" Declan started, but Ronan was already gone.

He pounded down the hallway, leaping over a woman who'd bent to pick up her dropped bag. He swerved around a couple of men stepping out of a room. He hurdled over a tray, noticing in strange, heightened detail as he flew over it that it was set with an ornate, old-fashioned tea service, complete with a tiered sandwich tray.

He had to get to the third floor before that woman caught another elevator, before she moved.

He skidded to slow just before he got to the exit door at the end of the hall. *Don't be locked,* he thought, and it wasn't, and he was through it and hurling himself up the metal stairs in the stairwell. They clanged and roared like a steam machine as he took them two at a time. Here: the door for the third floor. *Don't be locked,* he thought, and this one wasn't, either, and he was through this, too, running back down the hall toward the elevators where she'd been.

He got there just as the doors dinged shut, closing her away. The arrow pointed down, down, down.

He smashed the door button again, but nothing happened.

Gasping for air, he breathed a swear word. He linked his arms behind his head and tried for air, for reality. Damn, damn. He was getting his breath back but not his heart. It was skipping rope and entertaining itself out of rhythm. His *mother.* A ghost.

Three doors down, two women emerged from a room and made their way toward the elevators. They were arm in arm, talking in low voices. The sisters. The sisters from the mask room. They looked at him with curiosity, seeming to find his disarray more interesting than distressing.

"Oh, the man with a mask," said one of them.

The other asked, "Where's your pretty lady?"

He put it together. "The lady, the lady you saw before. Was she blond—was she wearing a jacket—did she—did she have blue eyes?" He pointed at his own.

They both looked at him, lips pursed, schoolmarmish.

"Look, she was dead. I know she was dead. I saw—I need to know what's going on," Ronan said. *Please help. Please help me understand.* "Please. Did you talk to her?"

The sisters scrutinized him. One of them, the older one, reached out to trace Ronan's eye socket lightly, as if she were sizing him for a mask. Her finger was icy cold. He turned his face away.

"She gave us this card," one of the sisters said. "You can have it; we don't want it." She handed over a square tile. There was a block-printed image of a woman on it, with a cross painted on her face.

It didn't mean anything to him, but he took it anyway. "What did she want?"

"What everyone else wanted. To know more about . . ."

He knew what they were about to say, because it was the word that had been concluding nearly every sentence that night. He finished it for them. "Him."

"Yes," said the older sister. "Bryde."

22

Farooq-Lane had never put her physicality to the test. Not a real test. Not a lion-gazelle situation. Not a hurtling down hallways and vaulting through doorways and knee-up-careful-now spiral down a dozen flights of stairs. She had only ever run on the treadmill of her local gym, earbuds spitting beats at her, and sometimes beside the lake on good days, shoes matching shorts matching sports bra matching Fitbit counting up toward health on her wrist, and occasionally in the fitness centers in hotels, bottled water reflecting the up-down of her smoothly toned legs. She had only ever run to look good.

She hadn't ever run for her life.

But that was how she exited the Carter Hotel, trailing an increasing number of antagonists on every floor. She heard things hit the walls behind her, but she didn't look to see what they were. At one point, she felt a hand encircle her ankle, and she slid free of it and poured on more speed.

As she bolted through the lobby, a woman in a drawstring top smiled at her, not in a pleasant way, and said, "Run, cop."

Farooq-Lane skidded out the front doors. She hurtled down the front stairs so quickly that she almost ran into the car parked at the base of them.

It was her car. Her rental.

Parsifal Bauer sat behind the wheel of it, sitting perfectly straight, looking like an undertaker behind the wheel of a hearse.

She heard someone—probably the doorman—coming up behind her.

She threw herself into the backseat. The car was already moving as she dragged the door shut behind her. The doors audibly locked.

A little *thwick* as they pulled away indicated the sound of both a bullet hitting the car and Farooq-Lane being glad she'd gotten full insurance coverage on the rental.

About a mile away, Parsifal pulled over and put the car in park. "I don't want to drive anymore. I don't have a license."

Farooq-Lane was still out of breath, her side pinching with a stitch. She couldn't believe that he'd been right there, waiting for her. Quite possibly he'd just saved her life. "Did you have a vision?"

He shook his head.

"How did you know to be there?"

Parsifal unbuckled his seat belt. "Common sense."

23

We gave the world to them back before we knew any better.

Already they were telling stories about us and we were believing them. The story was this: The trade-off for being a dreamer was emotional infirmity. We could dream, but we couldn't stand being awake. We could dream, but we couldn't smile. We could dream, but we were meant to die young. How they loved us still, despite our weaknesses, our unsuitedness to all things practical.

And we believed them. A benevolent, wicked fairy tale, and we believed it. We couldn't run the world. We couldn't even run ourselves.

We handed them the keys to the goddamn car.

Ronan dreamt of summer, of Adam.

He was in a sun-simmering garden, surrounded by tomato plants as tall as him. Green. So green. Colors in dreams weren't seen with eyes, they were seen with emotion, so there was no limit to their intensity. A radio was skewed in the mulch, playing Bryde's voice, and Adam was there, his gaunt features looking sun-bitten and elegant. He was an adult. Recently, he'd been an adult in all of Ronan's dreams, not just cigarette-legal but properly, truly into adulthood, every bit of him mature, certain, resolved—probably there was some psychological explanation for this, but Ronan couldn't guess at it.

Now they've built the whole thing inside out. Conscious, that's what they call being awake. Unconscious, that's what they call dreaming. Subconscious, that's what they call everything in between. You and I know that's bullshit.

But thus spake Zarathustra or whatever and now they gave us spirituality and took actuality for themselves.

The audacity of it.

In this dream, this confident and powerful older Adam, still boyishly wiry but with jawline brindled with handsome scruff, put a ripe, ripe cherry tomato in Ronan's mouth. Warm from the sun, skin taut against his tongue. Shockingly hot sweet-savory seeds exploded as Ronan crushed the flesh against the roof of his mouth. It tasted like summer felt.

You need to understand this: They need you to be broken. They can't stand it otherwise. If you could do what you do, but without any doubt?

Don't tell me you don't have doubt.

Don't tell me you have it figured out.

Your heebie-jeebie nightmare crabs are on you, not me. It wasn't my birthday printed on their bellies. You don't yet believe in the reality of your dreams. Of you.

I don't want you to think this ever again: It was just a dream.

That's a good way to get yourself killed.

"*Tamquam,*" said Adam.

"Wait," said Ronan.

"*Tamquam,*" he said again, gently.

"*Alter idem,*" Ronan said, and found himself alone. The garden had vanished and now he stood on a ragged shoreline, shivering, bent against the wind. The air was frigid but the ocean was tropical blue. The rocks rising behind him were black and rough but the shore was creamy beige sand. He was filled with desire. The dream was made of longing for things just out of reach. It floated in the air like humidity. It washed up on the shore with the salt water. He sucked in more longing with every inhale, he exhaled some of his happiness on the other side. How miserable.

No. Ronan was not at the mercy of the dream.

"Happy," Ronan said into the air. He said it with intention, so that the dream would hear him. Really hear him. "Fucking dolphins."

Smooth gray backs surfaced joyfully a few yards out from shore. Dolphins squealed. The misery lifted from his chest somewhat.

There you are. You're not without skills. I think you're getting intrigued, aren't you?

"I don't like people who don't show themselves," Ronan said out loud.

You heard how it was last night. Everyone wants a piece of me. You're going to have to come toward me a bit first. Remember our game? Throw the pebble, jump to the next box, closer to the center?

A plastic baggie of teeth washed up on the shore. Ronan snatched it up; he hated news stories about plastic in the ocean. "I don't have time for games."

Life's a game, but only some bother to play.

Next box: You don't know which rabbit to chase right now, me or her.

Next box: Doesn't matter. Either rabbit will take you to the same warren. We're all struggling the same direction these days. Foraging for crumbs.

Next box: Throw a pebble, jump, jump. Jump after the rabbits.

Next box: Happy hunting.

24

The morning after the Fairy Market, Ronan woke in Declan's guest room. Since Cambridge, he'd had to give himself a little talking-to before he convinced himself to get out of bed, but today, he immediately rolled out from under the duvet and got dressed.

For the first time in a long while, he was more interested in being awake than asleep.

Bryde.

Bryde.

Bryde.

Plus a dreamlike underground market, and a stranger with his mother's face. The world felt enormous and extraordinary, and his blood felt warm again through his veins.

Jump after the rabbits.

Ronan even had a clue: the card the mask-woman had given him outside the elevator.

Retrieving it from his jacket pocket, he took a better look at it. It was heavy cardstock, more like a disposable coaster than a business card. It was pleasant to hold. Professionally made, perfectly square, rounded corners. One side featured that image of the woman with a broad cross on her face, striping over her forehead and chin vertically, striping over her eyes and cheekbones horizontally. The other side was flat black. There was no other information on it that he could see, even holding it up to the light.

He snapped a photo of it, typed *do you know what this is?* and texted it off to Gansey in hopes that he was still tied to that black walnut tree or somewhere else with a phone signal. Richard Campbell Gansey III was the most academic and mythic person he knew, and the most likely of any of Ronan's acquaintances to have an idea of what the significance of the image might be. He wanted to send it to Adam, but he didn't want Adam to think he had to devote time to it. He'd already fucked up Adam's life enough at the moment. He didn't think Adam was angry with him, but things had been different since the dorm was destroyed. Quieter, sort of. Ronan didn't know how to make things right again, and he was afraid of making things more wrong.

So he just texted him: *dreamt of you.*

As he headed downstairs and into the kitchen, Declan's voice sounded lecturey. "You aren't even remotely dressed for the recital. I need at least forty extra minutes for traffic. And please stop."

Matthew was cheerfully chanting through a mouth stuffed full of pancakes and jam, accompanying the sound with a small dance. His chant sounded like "Ror a ror a ror a ror." It was hard to tell if it was a phrase he liked the feel of or a fragment of a song, not that it particularly made a difference; he had, on previous occasions, sung phrases he liked the feel of for hours.

Declan looked long-suffering. He ate a handful of antacids and washed them down with coffee, which Ronan suspected was counter-indicated, but hell, everyone had their vices.

"What's he saying?" Ronan asked.

"He's saying he wants to be late for his recital," Declan said sourly.

Matthew, still dancing and chanting, pointed at the now unwrapped *Dark Lady* where it was leaned against the cabinets.

It was quite marvelous to see her in the full, hard light of morning. Last night's dream had been reality, and vice versa. The Fairy Market existed; Bryde existed; the woman they'd seen with Aurora's face existed. The Dark Lady peered at Ronan with her hard look. Aurora had been tender, trusting. There was none of that in this portrait.

Matthew finally swallowed his mouthful and sang, with more clarity: "More oh core-ah, More oh core-ah!"

Joining Ronan, he turned the painting over. The back of the painting was sealed neatly with brown paper, protecting the canvas. Matthew tapped the bottom right corner, where there was an inscription in their father's handwriting. *Mór Ó Corra.*

Ronan said it out loud himself, throwing his back into the Irish *r*'s. "'More oh core-ah.'"

It did have a certain addictive ring to it. A certain nostalgic shape to the vowels that reminded him of his father, of the parts of his childhood that were unsullied by everything that came after. He'd nearly forgotten his father's Northern Irish accent. What a ridiculous thing to forget.

Ronan looked at his older brother. "What's *Mór Ó Corra?*"

Declan said, "Who knows? It's just a dream. Could be anything. Matthew, please for the love of Mary. Get dressed. Let's please grease the wheels."

This Declanism drove Matthew upstairs.

Declan's words—*just a dream*—echoed in Ronan's mind as he recalled how Bryde had forbidden him from ever saying them again. He asked Declan, "Did you dream of the sea?"

"Yes," Declan said. "An Irish one."

"So it performs as advertised."

"Looks that way."

Ronan's phone buzzed with a text: Gansey.

Reached out to a few peers, it said, as if he were sixty instead of the same age as Ronan. *Image you sent confirmed logo for Boudicca. All-lady group involved in the protection and organization of women in business. Henry says his mother thinks they're pretty powerful.*

Another text came in. *Boudicca is actually a very interesting historical figure in her own right.*

Another: *She was a warrior queen of the Celts around 60 CE and she fought against the Romans*

Another: *Blue wants you to know Boudicca is*

Another: *Sorry sent too soon quote is 'Boudicca is the original goth. Ronan Lynch wishes he was that badass'*

Another: *Is badass one word or two*

Ronan's phone displayed ellipses to show that Gansey was about to shoot off another text.

Ronan texted back hurriedly, *If you have to ask you aren't one. Thanks old man. I'll wiki it.*

Declan asked, "Parrish?"

"Gansey," Ronan said. "He knows what Boudicca is. He knows about the card that woman"——he didn't know what to call the woman with his mother's face——"left with the mask-ladies last night."

"Don't go chasing this, Ronan," Declan intoned. Hefting up the painting, he slid it into the nearest closet and closed the door on her. Ronan was no art aficionado, but he wasn't exactly sure that was the display method he would have chosen. "I can see you think it'll be fun, but it won't be." He was always doing that—guessing Ronan's next action correctly, guessing his motivation incorrectly.

"You don't want to know?"

"No." He began to get ready to go: shoving dishes in the sink, stabbing food down the disposal with a spatula, rinsing out his coffee cup and setting it upside down on a towel. "No, I don't. Matthew, come on, hurry up, two minutes! I'm giving up my day for this!"

Ronan snarled, "It's like you checked out of the family at birth."

He knew it was nasty. He knew it was the kind of thing that would've made Gansey say *Ronan* and Adam give him a knowing look. But he couldn't help it. It was as though the less Declan got riled up, the less he seemed to care, the more Ronan wanted to make him break.

But Declan just continued stacking dishes, his voice as even-keeled as if they'd been discussing gardening. "Evolution favors the simplest organism, Ronan, and right now we're the simplest organism."

Ronan made a vow to never be as dull a person, as passionless a person, as dead a person as Declan Lynch.

"A fucking single-celled organism is the simplest organism," Ronan said. "And there are three of us."

Declan looked at him heavily. "As if I don't think about that every single day."

Matthew reappeared, dressed in all black—not the classy black of a funeral, but the rumpled black of either a server at a steakhouse or a student in a high school orchestra.

"Thank God," Declan said, retrieving his car keys.

"You can if you like," Matthew said. "But I dressed myself."

He shot a look at Ronan to make sure his joke had been funny.

Acting like Ronan had not just been foul to him, Declan asked, "Ronan, are you coming to this thing?"

Ronan wasn't one hundred percent sure what kind of recital it was, but he was one hundred percent sure he'd rather be chasing rabbits toward Bryde and Boudicca. He was also fairly sure from Declan's expression that Declan knew this.

"You should totally come," Matthew said, bounding over. "I'm *awful*, it's great. There's this one organ solo that's so bad you'll pee yourself laughing. There's . . . oh. Ronan?"

He broke off and made a little gesture under his own nose, the sort you do when you mean to be a benevolent mirror for someone else.

Ronan mirrored Matthew's gesture, dabbing his knuckle against his nostril. Looked at it. A smear of black, dark as ink, covered his skin.

Nightwash.

He hadn't even felt it coming. He always thought he should be able to feel it coming.

Declan's eyes tightened, as if he were disappointed in Ronan. Like it was his fault.

"Guess you're not coming with us," Matthew said.

25

"Parsifal?" Farooq-Lane said. "I need to get in there eventually."

She'd been waiting for her turn in the bathroom for ages. He'd already been in there when her alarm woke her, having silently made it through her room and into the bathroom at some point in the night. She didn't want to know what was taking him so long. Nathan had been clean and secretive as a teenager, but the cultural idea of teen boys being disgusting had nevertheless fully invaded her subconscious. She didn't ask questions.

She made herself a cup of bad instant coffee, ate an apple, and then, when he still didn't emerge, prepared an egg-white omelet. She curled over her laptop and scoured forums for clues about *Bryde*. It was the only thing she had to go on—the only other thing she'd gotten from the Fairy Market was a workout. What she needed was more visions to work with. She'd never appreciated how difficult this side of the job was. Before, when she was traveling places with the Moderators, someone else had already interpreted the Visionary's information into drawings, locations, or times. Often it was incredibly detailed—they'd basically gotten written instructions for where to find Nathan in Ireland. She hadn't thought about what it had actually been like to get that information: that somewhere a Moderator had to sit in a hotel room with a Visionary who may or may not have been impossible to live with, waiting for visions to appear.

She didn't know if the failing was her or Parsifal.

After a space of time, Farooq-Lane made a second cup of bad coffee and brought it to the bathroom door as a resentful offering, full of badwill. She knocked. "Parsifal."

The only answer was a vague sound from inside, something moving against tile, possibly. She put the mug on the ground.

The phone rang. It was Lock.

"It's okay," he said. "We understand. It happens to all of us. You were on enemy territory. You had no reinforcements. We don't blame you. At least you got a name."

She sighed. "Should I be doing something to make Parsifal have a vision?"

"Nothing you can do," Lock said. "We know he's fragmented. We're searching for another Visionary on our end, so we won't be without when he's finished. But Bauer is still the most likely to find another. Tell him to focus. Get him whatever he needs. Use that budget we sent you. Keep him happy. Keep him productive."

Farooq-Lane wasn't remotely sure that *happy* was a word she'd ever use to describe Parsifal, but she promised to try her best. Hanging up, she returned to the door. "Parsifal?"

No answer. She felt an uncertain pang. She tried the doorknob. Unlocked.

"I'm coming in," she said, and pushed it open.

A reek rolled out.

Inside the bathroom, she found Parsifal lying in the empty bathtub with all his clothing on. He was also wearing her oversized sunglasses (his little round glasses looked sad and vulnerable folded on the edge of the sink). There was vomit down the outside of the tub and all over the floor; it was like he'd climbed inside the tub as a boat against a vomit ocean. His legs were buckled up to fit into the tub, and his face was colorless.

"Oh," Farooq-Lane said, falling back.

He rolled his head toward her, and she thought he would say something, but he just blinked. For the first time she remembered how old he was. Not in an *I can't believe I have to live with a teen boy* way but in a *This is a person who will die before they hit twenty* way.

It was one thing to hear Lock talking in his clinical way about how troubling it was to have to replace Visionaries after they burned out. It was another thing to be looking right at a burning-out Visionary.

Farooq-Lane left the bathroom, put her coat on over her silk pajamas, took her keycard, and went out to the hall. A few doors down she found housekeeping and traded them a twenty-dollar bill from her Padma black market buyer fund for some extra towels and cleaning supplies.

Back in her room, she rolled up her pajama bottoms and sleeves and put on her boots before dropping a lemon in a glass of water and wading across the vomit to set it next to Parsifal's limp hand. Then she put in her earbuds and turned on her music, and as hip-hop barked at her, she silently cleaned the floor and the outside of the tub. Once the bathroom was clean, she put Parsifal's glasses within his reach, bundled up everything dirty, and took it outside to housekeeping again.

"My friend has the flu," she told them, and gave them another twenty dollars because that felt appropriate.

When she came back, the empty water glass with the lemon in it was on the kitchenette counter and Parsifal was sitting straight and proper on the sofa, glasses on, neatly dressed, as if he had never been otherwise. His mouth looked stiff and cranky as it ordinarily did. She was beginning to see that the expression that was always on his face might be pain. She was beginning to understand he might want to control everything he could because of the things he couldn't.

She was beginning to see why the other Moderators had been eager to give this job away.

He didn't thank her for cleaning up his vomit, and she didn't ask him how he was feeling.

"I had a vision," he told her.

26

Ronan didn't go home right away.

He was oozing black slowly from his right nostril, and he really should have begun the two-hour drive back to the Barns to take care of it, but instead, he lingered in the city. He felt less like putting miles between him and the Fairy Market and more like hunting Bryde's rabbits.

He had time, he thought. He could play those odds.

He felt like a hero from one of his parents' old stories. When Niall had been home, he'd spun wild adventure tales of children turned into swans, crones simmering wisdom in cauldrons, and kings felled by powerful knights and poor decision-making skills and lovely daughters. When he was gone, Aurora had retold these stories, but from the points of view of the swans, the crones, the queens, and the daughters. Aurora's stories were kinder, in general. Softer. But she didn't soften the heroes' taboos. Their *geasa*. All the heroes had them. Some were acquired along their journeys; some were given to them by other heroes; some were inherited. All were peculiar. Some heroes couldn't refuse food from a woman, and others couldn't be struck three times in a row without a word spoken in between; some couldn't kill a boar, and others couldn't pass an orphan without helping them. The penalty for defying one's *geis* was deliciously terrible: death.

In Aurora's versions, a poignant, soft-focus death. In Niall's, a complex and several-minute-long finial.

On long car trips, Ronan and Matthew sometimes invented new *geasa* to pass the time. A hero who had to pet every dog he saw. Clap his hands every time he entered a church. Say exactly what he was thinking as he said it. Wear a gray suit every day.

Your father has the geis *of blarney,* Aurora often said. *He has to tell stories or he'll die.*

Geis *of bullshit,* Declan had replied once, and had promptly gotten sent to the cow shed to muck stalls in the cold.

Here was Ronan's *geis,* he thought: Dream things into being, or dissolve into nothing.

He was headed back to the Carter Hotel. He wasn't sure what he was hoping to find there—Inspiration. Evidence. A staff member who remembered something, anything. In the back of his head was a bit of advice Uncle used to say. If you'd lost things, he'd say you should retrace your steps to where you last had them. He'd been a great treasure trove of these clickable bits of potpourri-scented wisdom, searchable apple-cider proverbs, cross-stitched country kitchen words to live by. If you want breakfast in bed, sleep in the kitchen. Why fit in when you were born to stand out? You have to be odd to be number one. Go as far as you can see; when you get there, you'll be able to see a little farther. Make your life a masterpiece; you only get one canvas. He wondered what happened to him and Aunt. As a kid, he'd never thought to ask for their real names. As a kid, he hadn't thought there was any other kind of name.

Declan texted as he got closer to the hotel. *Tell me when you get that taken care of.*

Ronan knew that the real meaning of the text was *Tell me when you are safely installed at the Barns instead of chasing things I told you not to chase.*

He didn't reply. He sat in traffic. He wiped his nose. He

edged close to the hotel. The sun glared down, touching every-thing, brilliant and caustic.

Declan called.

"What?" Ronan demanded. "This is a fucking stick shift."

"You're going home, right?" Declan asked. There was some kind of terrible youthful singing audible in the background.

"Don't harass me just because you're having a bad time."

"Are you?"

Ronan didn't care for lying, but he also didn't care for a lec-ture. He grunted noncommittally.

"Don't do anything stupid," Declan said, and hung up.

Here was Declan's *geis*: to never pull the stick out of his ass.

"You have arrived at your destination," remarked the GPS.

But Ronan hadn't. He had to pull over and roll down the window to get a better look, because he couldn't believe what he was seeing.

The Carter Hotel was gone.

Caution tape lay limply over the entrance to the parking lot like dispirited birthday streamers. Beyond it, the lot was empty except for a single anonymous little white sedan and scudding gray tumbleweeds of ash. The hotel building itself was just a black, flattened ruin.

It was still smoldering in places.

Ronan wiped his nose. He stared. He wiped his nose again. He stared some more.

It was simply *gone*.

He could smell its remains, the complicated, toxic smell of things that melted instead of burned, combined with the appe-tizing, feral scent of burned wood and paper.

Ronan wondered if this was the cost of hosting the Fairy

Market. Perhaps every location was burned to the ground the day after. Perhaps this was yet another thing Declan had known and Ronan hadn't known to ask. Helluva one-night stand.

Well, there went that lead.

He tasted the inky nightwash as it dripped over his lip. It was acrid. The sort of flavor you smelled as well as tasted, the sort of flavor you recoiled from, instantly understanding its toxicity. Impatiently, he fumbled in his glove box for some napkins. He didn't have any; he had gas receipts. He used them to wipe his face and spat nightwash out the window until his mouth no longer puckered. When he straightened up again, he saw two figures picking their way from the wreckage to the white sedan parked in the lot.

As they got in, he just had time to see that one of them had familiar, glinting golden hair.

Uncle had been right.

Already Ronan was negotiating with himself, telling himself all the reasons he was allowed to chase instead of finding a safe place to dream and banish the nightwash again. He didn't have to make it all the way back to the Barns. He could stop somewhere around Warrenton and find a quiet field. It would be good enough.

Happy hunting.

The white sedan would have to come right by the BMW in order to leave the lot. Ronan fumbled to get the car in gear. The gearshift knob was slick with black inkiness. He scuffed his palm against his jeans and got a better grip. He could feel himself bracing for the shock of seeing his mother's face again, tensing in the way one does on a roller coaster so that the stomach doesn't sail up unpleasantly. It didn't entirely work. His guts snarled up again when he saw her face behind the wheel of the sedan.

And that wasn't even the most astonishing part.

When the car pulled out of the lot beside the BMW, for the first time, Ronan got a good look at the passenger seat's occupant.

He sat in the passenger seat. Ronan Lynch.

He was looking at his own face. An uncanny mirror. Not elevator doors opening to reveal a woman who looked eerily like his mother, but *Ronan* looking at *Ronan*.

You're awake, he told himself. *You're awake.*

After the first picosecond of shock, he realized that it wasn't a perfect likeness. The hair was wrong. Ronan's was buzzed, and this other Ronan had curled hair down to his shoulders. This Ronan was smooth shaven, and that Ronan had darkened scruff across his chin. This Ronan was shocked. That other Ronan was not.

The two of them looked at each other.

Then the little white sedan tore off with a howl of its tires.

It was just an unassuming little import, not a sports car, but it nonetheless got the jump on Ronan. It had the advantage of going balls-out from the get.

Ronan had not realized he was going to chase until they ran.

And run they did. Flat-out for a few quiet blocks, straight through stop signs, barely pausing as the intersections got busier.

Ronan didn't realize the stakes until the sedan cut in front of an oncoming car to leap the curb. It rambled up the sidewalk for a few yards before shooting through the corner lot of a gas station to avoid a light.

Horns wailed.

Ronan hadn't thought there was someone less cautious in a car than he, but it turned out there was. He couldn't bring himself to throw the BMW directly in front of an oncoming delivery truck. He sat at the light, agonizingly, counting down the seconds until he was freed, and then shot after them again. They hadn't made enough progress to get out of his sight, so when they pitched off into a neighborhood, he was able to follow a few seconds later.

His mouth tasted like garbage, like rot. He knew if he looked in the mirror and opened his mouth, his tongue would be coated black.

Fuck.

He negotiated with himself again. He could go back to the town house after this. Declan had forbidden him to dream there, but he could dream something small. He could be in control. Declan would never know. He could keep going.

The white sedan rocketed across a four-lane highway, shooting the gap between oncoming cars in a way that, again, Ronan didn't feel he should replicate. Not with all the creatures and brothers who would fall asleep if something happened to him. He made up for it by throttling the BMW as high as he could once he'd crossed; their car had less caution, but his father's dreamt Beemer had more horsepower.

The chase battled through more neighborhoods. With each mile, Ronan crept a little closer to the sedan, and with each mile, he bled a little more black. It was dripping down his neck from his ears and splattering the steering wheel. His body begged him to dream. It was a feeling like no other, a feeling that he didn't have to be taught. When he was tired, he knew he had to sleep. When he was hungry, he knew he had to eat. This feeling—the feeling of being unmade, undone, unstitched in ways that other bodies had never been sewn in the first place—had no name, but he knew it meant he had to dream.

Up ahead, the sedan faltered; it had unknowingly entered a cul-de-sac. The only way out was past Ronan. He'd won.

But Ronan couldn't breathe.

The nightwash was choking him, drowning his heartbeat, filling his lungs with black.

The best *geasa* in Niall and Aurora's stories were the ones that collaborated to agonizingly trap the heroes at the end. Even the most invincible heroes could be trapped by conflicting *geasa*. The mighty Hound of Ulster, one of the boys' favorite heroes, had a *geis* to never eat dog ("Shame," Niall said, "it's very tasty.") and a *geis* to never refuse hospitality, and so when he was offered dog meat by a host, what other choice had he but to spiral into tragedy?

Poignant, ungory tragedy in Aurora's version. Complex, lengthy horror in Niall's.

And here was Ronan, trapped between his two *geasa*: the *geis* that was growing inside him, demanding that he dream, and the *geis* Declan had put on him, the need to stay hidden.

The little white sedan pulled round to face him. It would have been the simplest thing in the world to pull the BMW across the road to block them. They were trapped. At his mercy. He could still do it, but his heart—his—

The BMW coasted to a stop in the middle of the cul-de-sac.

Shit, he thought, *not here*—

27

"You were right," Farooq-Lane said, with wonder.

"Of course I was," Parsifal said stiffly.

The two of them sat in her rental car, looking at the still-smoking ruin of the Carter Hotel. He'd told her that he'd seen the Carter Hotel burned to the ground in his vision, and so he promised, so it was. It seemed unbelievable that there had been enough time for the entire hotel to burn since she'd run from it. There should be chunks, she thought. Columns. Chimneys. Skeletal bones of hotel reaching up toward the blue, blue sky. But there was just a thorough, blackened expanse with tire tracks through it. One could not have done a better job obliterating a building if one had tried. And surely someone had, she thought. This couldn't have been an accident.

"I didn't mean it that way," Farooq-Lane said. "It was more about me than you."

She could feel him watch as she sipped her coffee. She'd asked him if he wanted to stop for coffee ("If you want to." "Will you drink it?" "That seems unlikely.") and then gone out of her way to find a good roaster anyway. She missed her routine of good coffee, good work, good life, and she felt the appearance of a successful vision merited the return of at least one of those things.

Now she had a nice espresso and she was feeling more like herself than she had in ages, and Parsifal had a cocoa and looked like a load of laundry that had been taken out of the dryer before it was done. Nothing about his body language indicated that he was enjoying the beverage in his hand.

She asked, "Did you see how it happened? Was it intentional?"

Parsifal didn't reply. He rolled down his window and sucked in some air. It smelled ashy. Noxious. His sour face matched it.

"Lock asked me if there was anything we could do to make you happy," Farooq-Lane said. "Anything to improve your comfort. Is there something you'd like?"

He turned to the radio and began silently punching buttons.

She refused to let him ruin her good mood and good coffee. "I have a good budget."

"All I would like is a piece of Bienenstich the way my mother made it for me," Parsifal said, managing to sound as if she had somehow maligned his mother. His long fingers constricted from the radio like a dying spider's legs: He had found opera. A chesty man cooed from the rental car's speakers. "And that is not to be had."

Farooq-Lane swiftly googled *Bienenstich*, intent on proving him wrong. This was America, you could Uber Eats or overnight anything in a metropolis if you had a solid credit card and a can-do attitude. It took her only a few minutes, however, to discover that can-do attitudes didn't apply to Bienenstich. It was a kind of a dull-looking German cake that did not seem to have found an audience in the DC area, nor among the kind of bakeries that would drop ship a cake to a hotel room. It didn't seem to have an American counterpart, either.

Why couldn't he just want to drive in a fast car or to get laid or whatever it was that boys were supposed to want, she thought with annoyance.

She furtively texted Lock. *Find me Bienenstich.*

Then she asked, "Can I do something to help you remember what you saw in the vision? Give me some ideas. Let's brainstorm. Jog something loose."

He looked out over the ash. "Why do you do this?"

"The same reason you do," she replied.

Parsifal blinked back at her, his eyes confused and surprised behind his glasses. "What?"

"I said I do it for the same reason you do it," Farooq-Lane replied. "To save the world. Who wouldn't do that?"

He looked perplexed. "What?"

"You can't tell me that you aren't sitting in this car with me because you want to stop the apocalypse from killing all of mankind," Farooq-Lane said.

"*What?*"

"You asked why I did this."

He shook his head, eyeing her warily. "I didn't say anything."

Farooq-Lane put her coffee down in the cup holder a little harder than she needed to. Her hands were wobbly again. She replayed the last minute back in her mind. Had she actually heard Parsifal? Or had it sounded instead like Nathan taunting her, inside her head, just like he had done when he was alive?

"Sorry," she said. "I think I'm a little on edge."

Parsifal gave her an extremely annoying look that indicated that he completely agreed, and then he said, "That's him." He pointed out the window to the tire tracks that dragged ash across the street. "I saw that. I remember that. I saw his car make them. Today. I'm sure it was today."

She felt her heart beat a little faster. This was more like it. This was how it had felt when they were closing in on Nathan. Specific little puzzle pieces that made more and more of a picture as each was revealed. Things that could be checked off a list. Things that might prove to Lock that his faith in her wasn't unfounded. "Good. That's good, Parsifal. What happened after that? Where do we go?"

Parsifal's fingers clawed a little more tightly around his take-away cup. "The vision was not so good after that."

"Try."

"I saw him in a gray car. I . . . I saw him in a white car, too. I think the gray car is correct. A BMW. I think. I don't know. I am more confused than I used to be. I could say before if . . . I could tell if . . ." He trailed off. His mouth made an agitated shape.

"It's all right if it doesn't make sense," Farooq-Lane said. "Just talk it out. That's why I'm here."

"I saw a road that does this." Parsifal did a somewhat rude-looking hand gesture. "I don't know it in English."

"Roundabout?"

"*Sackgasse?*" he suggested.

"Exit ramp?"

He drew an imaginary street on the dashboard. "Here house, here house, here house, here, here, here house, turn around here, house, house, house."

"Cul-de-sac," Farooq-Lane said immediately. He squinted, not understanding. She tried again. "Dead-end street."

He brightened. "Yes, yes."

"Near here?"

"Surely he is close if those tire tracks are still clear on the street," Parsifal said logically. "No one has yet driven through them."

Relieved to have something to do, Farooq-Lane rapidly opened a map app. She zoomed out until she could see the neighborhood streets around her. Worst-case scenario would be if there were no cul-de-sacs nearby. Real-world scenario would be if there were several cul-de-sacs nearby. Best-case scenario would be just one within a few-mile radius.

They were living in the best-case scenario.

Parsifal, who was leaning over her shoulder, mouth-breathing into her ear, pointed, splashing his cocoa onto her screen. She made a soft noise of annoyance. He had a gift.

"Da, there, there," he said. "Andover. That's the word I saw. This street is where your Zed is."

And just like that, they had a destination.

Parsifal rolled up his window and put his cocoa cup securely in the holder behind Farooq-Lane's.

The fortune-teller's words came back to her.

If you want to kill someone and keep it a secret, don't do it where the trees can see you.

Farooq-Lane shivered. She was doing this for the right reason. She was saving the world.

"This Zed," she asked Parsifal as she put the car into gear. "In your vision, was he armed? Was he dangerous?"

I expected more complexity from you, Carmen.

She kept having dreams of Nathan being shot and Nathan being alive again, and she couldn't decide which one was worse.

"No," Parsifal said. "I remember that part well. He is quite helpless."

She said, "Let's go get him, then."

28

B lack.

It's harder when you're far away.

Everything was black.
Not black.
It was whatever you called the absence of light.
Ronan's throat full of it, choking—

You think it's hard for you to hear the dreams when you're far away from your mountains. From our ley line. From your forest. From Lindenmere. That's not right. It's not wrong, but it's only half right. It's hard for the dreams to hear you.

Even in the dream, he was dying of it.

You ever get asked to identify a song playing in a crowded restaurant? There's noise everywhere. That shitty father lecturing his kid in the booth behind you. The waiters singing happy birthday to someone who never wanted to remember the occasion. The song's playing out of speakers bought by the lowest bidder, an afterthought. When people shut the fuck up for a second, you can catch part of the tune here and there. If a lull coincides with the refrain, you have it. Done, shout the title, look clever.

His eyes, wet with it—

Otherwise, it's just a song you heard once but can't place. That's what you are to the ley line, to your forest, when you're far away.

Ronan tried to reach for Lindenmere. He didn't even know which way to reach in the darkness. He just knew he needed to grab something to bring back if he was to end the nightwash. But there was only blackness. The absence of dreams.

It's trying to place you, but you're not making it easy. It's guessing what you want. Auto-filling, and we all know how that goes. That's when shit starts to go wrong.

Please, Ronan thought, but he didn't even know what he was asking.

You shouldn't have waited so long. I'll do what I can, but you're a song in a crowded restaurant and it's so hard to hear with all this shitty noise.

Ronan reached, and the darkness reached back.

Hold on, kid.

29

Ronan woke. Slowly. Stickily. His eyelashes were glued together.

He was frozen, unmoving, looking at himself from above. A gloriously incandescent bar of golden sun burned his eyes, but he couldn't turn his head away from it. A single trail of black tapered thinly from one nostril; the rest of his skin was clear.

His body was in the backseat of the BMW. One of Matthew's school sweatshirts was balled up under his head as a pillow. His hands were folded on his chest in a way that seemed unlike any gesture he would have chosen for them. The quality of light in the car was curious; it seemed like neither day nor night. It was dark, save for that bar of strong light. He couldn't understand it. He couldn't understand how he'd gotten into the backseat. And he couldn't understand what he'd brought back from his dream.

His hands were cupped over something, but the shape under his fingers didn't make sense to him. He didn't *feel* anything moving, but who knew. It could be a murder crab waiting for light to activate it. It could be a disembodied scream. It could be anything. What he recalled of his dream offered no clues. He just remembered a wasteland of many convulsing darknesses, and Bryde's voice breaking gently through.

Ronan could move again.

He gingerly opened his hands. Collected in his palms was

a broken sword hilt, its finish complexly black, just like the Soulages painting from the Fairy Market, the one that made Declan Lynch want to goddamn cry. The matte-black blade was broken off just beneath the guard. On the grip, three words were printed in very small letters, also black, only visible when the hilt was tilted in the light: VEXED TO NIGHTMARE.

He had no recollection of dreaming about it.

It was possible that Bryde had just saved his life.

It was a strange feeling, too big to be labeled with good or bad just yet. It had been overwhelming enough to know that the world was vastly huger and more mysterious than he had given it credit for. It was above and beyond to think that world had his back.

He sat up to get his bearings.

The not-day-not-night quality of light in the car was because it was parked in something like a lean-to or an old shed. The siding was battered and rustic, only as constructed as it needed to be. The slat of light that had burned Ronan's eyes was from a missing board.

The floorboards of the backseat were covered with wadded-up tissues, each of them soaked in black. He hadn't had tissues in the car, had he? No, he'd had receipts to sop up his face. The driver's seat was moved far forward, revealing a cache of trash formerly hidden by the seat, and on the floor mat were two black shoe prints, too small to be his. Someone had laid his car keys on the center console where he would see them.

It was backward to sleep and wake somewhere different rather than falling asleep so that his mind could fly elsewhere. Everything was impossible today.

He let himself out of the car, stumbling a little as he did.

The dried ground was stubbled with hoofprints—this was an animal lean-to. Stepping out of the shed, he shielded his eyes from the long afternoon light, taking stock. Distant horses cropped grass, taking no interest in him as he peered around the sloping long field. He could hear the rush of cars fairly close by. The interstate. A flattened path through the grass led from the lean-to to a distant gate and then, beyond that, to a crumbling two-lane road.

There was no sign of the little white sedan, or any other cars, for that matter.

Taking out his phone, he opened the map. He was forty minutes outside the city. Northwest, not remotely on the way to the Barns.

The truth of the situation was slowly unfolding. One of them—the woman, probably, because the seat was moved so far forward—must have driven him far out of the city to dream, to make sure his two conflicting *geasa* didn't get him into trouble this time. Then hidden his car. Cleaned his face. Left his keys where he could find them. Driven away with the man with a Lynch's face, leaving Ronan with more questions than answers.

They'd saved his body and Bryde had saved his mind, and he was no closer to knowing who any of them were.

Ronan kicked the ground.

One step forward, two steps back.

Hold on, kid.

30

"H ennessy."

It was Hennessy's fault.

That was the beginning and end of most of the girls' problems, really. They couldn't go to college or do anything that required a distinct social security number: Hennessy's fault. Were banned from the Nine O'Clock Club: Hennessy's fault. Had painful wisdom teeth in bad weather: Hennessy's fault. Had to resort to an elaborate plan to forge and nick a painting instead of just liquidating some shit and buying it with a wad of cash: Hennessy's fault.

Everything about *The Dark Lady* situation was Hennessy's fault.

"Hennessy."

Last year, Hennessy had sold a John Everett Millais forgery to Rex Busque, muscle-bound dealer of portraits and Pre-Raphaelite pieces, longtime Fairy Market attendee. It featured a young titian-haired woman holding a single card, its face pressed to her bosom, leaving it up to the viewer to decide if it was a playing card, a tarot card, or something else entirely. Her eyes suggested it was whatever was the most mysterious option. The forgery was a bit more gutsy than Hennessy would have ordinarily done—it would've been safer to "find" some Millais sketches or unfinished works—but Busque had asked for something splashy, as he'd gotten himself into a bit of money trouble and wanted to turn something over for a lot of money in a little time. She'd warned Busque it was too good a find to go without scrutiny and that he should only try to turn it overseas to a private collector.

"Hennessyyyy."

Of course it got busted by the first prestigious gallery Busque had tried to pass it to. Millais worked his compositions directly on the canvas, graphite underdrawing and all, and Hennessy had just winged it, and once the question had been asked, the dominoes fell: the strokes were too big, the varnish was wrong, where did you say you found this?

Hennessy was viciously uncontrite. She'd warned him, she told him; his fault he was a lazy needledick who couldn't be bothered to look up an international country code.

Of course he would be the one who ended up with *The Dark Lady* months later.

"I'd sooner burn a painting than sell it to you," he'd told Hennessy.

Hennessy's fault.

She'd have given up by now if it weren't for the rest of them.

She was so tired.

"Heloise," Jordan said. Hennessy wasn't looking at the girls, but she knew it was Jordan; only Jordan called her that. Hennessy's name was not Heloise. That was the joke. "Your face."

Hennessy knew about her face. Wiping it wouldn't change it. She lay on her back on the tiled kitchen floor, smoking, a small rivulet of black running from her nostril down her cheek.

It had been too long since she'd dreamt.

And since their plan had fallen through, there'd be another

copy of her soon. Another flower on the tattoo encircling her throat. Another step toward dying. Another step toward every girl in this kitchen going to sleep forever.

Hennessy's fault.

"Did that just start?" June asked. Poor June. She mostly tried hard and was the second most likely to show up if you called and was the best at holding down a legal part-time job. Like Hennessy, she drank too much and liked dogs. Unlike Hennessy, she had straightened her hair and also liked cats. She was the second oldest living copy, which meant she was the most complex copy after Jordan.

Poor Jordan. She didn't deserve this. None of them did, but especially not her.

"If you think about it metaphorically," Hennessy said, "has it ever really stopped?"

The girls were cleaning the mansion's white-and-copper kitchen, which was trashed. It was always trashed. It was used by six forgers to form pastels, mix pigments, make glue, stain paper, and reheat pizza, and all of these components were scattered across the floor and counter, along with some hair and teeth from the Breck break-in. Long evening light through the garden windows illuminated paint spattered over marble floor, cobwebs trailing through the copper pots hanging overhead, take-out boxes covering the marble island.

"You know who I hate?" Madox said. She sounded pissed. She always sounded pissed. It was like Hennessy's temper was the main thing that made it to her. "That fucking junk handler Busque."

"You want to run your mouth?" June said. She tended to be

practical. It was like Hennessy's problem-solving was the only thing that had made it to her. "Then fuck off outside. What's the move?"

"The kid has it. The Lynch kid," Hennessy replied.

"He lives here," Madox said. "I saw his swish town house. I still vote we jump him."

"You *are* the stupid one. He works for a senator," June said. "You don't think that won't be headlines on some shock blog? That's a risk."

"June's right," Trinity said pensively. She always sounded pensive, down on herself, like Hennessy's self-hatred was the only thing that had made it over to her. "We'd have to split town, which is only worth it if *The Dark Lady* works."

Hennessy exchanged a look with Jordan, who leaned against the counter with a handful of brushes. It was hard to say what Jordan was thinking. She was looking at the black ink running from Hennessy's face and touching the floral tattoo on her own neck, the one that matched Hennessy's.

Jordan, of all the girls, should have had a life of her own. She wasn't Hennessy. She was Jordan. Her own person, trapped in Hennessy's shit life.

Hennessy's fault.

"I'm tired of naming you girls," Hennessy said.

"Can we buy it off him?" Brooklyn suggested, standing by the sink with a dustpan full of obliterated pastels. This was a shock of a suggestion, but mostly because Brooklyn's suggestions ordinarily tended toward the sexual, the only part of Hennessy that had really rubbed off on her.

"If he doesn't want to sell it, then we've tipped him off, haven't we?" June said.

"Maybe we should just give it up. It might not work anyway," said Madox.

"Bad take, Mad," said June.

"Or at least go into it knowing it's an unpopular opinion," Trinity muttered.

The principle behind acquiring *The Dark Lady* was simple. Her legend was well documented: Whoever slept under the same roof as her would dream of the seaside. Hennessy, therefore, would be forced to dream of the seaside instead of her usual recurring nightmare, and would bring back a gull or sand or some other beach paraphernalia, all of which would cost her less physically than producing a copy of herself.

Jordan finally spoke up. "What if we just swap it again?"

Trinity asked, "What . . . break into his house?"

"Same plan," Jordan said. "Exactly same plan. Nip in, leave our copy, nick the real one."

The girls thought.

"You're round the twist," Madox said.

As if she hadn't said anything, June mused, "Still risks exposure."

Brooklyn chucked the pastel dust into the garbage disposal. "Not if we break a window and then replace the glass when we're done."

"We'd need time," Trinity said. "He'd have to be out of the house for a good long while."

All this fucking trouble, Hennessy thought. All because Hennessy couldn't stop having the same damn dream.

Hennessy's fault.

Jordan crossed the floor and took the cigarette from Hennessy. She took a drag before flicking it into the sink.

That, Hennessy thought, was the biggest difference between the two of them. Like Hennessy, Jordan would try almost anything, but in the end, Jordan could always toss away the stuff that was bad for her before it killed her.

Except for Hennessy. Hennessy was the deadliest habit any of them had, and none of them could quit her.

Jordan said, "I think I know how to do that."

31

No, thank you."

It was one thing to be victimized by Parsifal Bauer's uncompromising, tactless nature. It was yet another thing to watch someone else be victimized by it. Several someones. An entire room of someones. The entire staff of Pfeiffer's German Pastry Shoppe in Alexandria, Virginia, had come from the back room and behind the counter to watch Parsifal Bauer take his first bite of Bienenstich in years. Lock, who'd found the bakery, had apparently laid it on thick when he called to secure the cake. They only made Bienenstich as a seasonal special, but he'd explained that Parsifal Bauer was a very sick young man in the country seeking medical treatment far from his family, who were too unwell to travel themselves, a family who used to make him the treat to encourage him to think of the sweeter things in life.

Pfeiffer's had risen artfully to the challenge. Give us a few hours, they had said gallantly, as we make sure we have the almonds, the pastry cream, the yeast dough, the mettle!

"You don't want a box for the rest of it?" one of the staff members asked.

Parsifal Bauer sat on the edge of a cheap café chair as he always sat, long hair tucked behind his ears, body bolt upright, as if his bones had all been assembled only with much effort and were likely to fall apart if he unbalanced the structure too much. The square of Bienenstich cake sat on a plate in front of him. He was the only customer in the shop. Bakers had come from the back room to watch his first bite. Cashiers had come from behind the pastry case. Cameras were ready for filming. Candles were involved. Something peppy and German played overhead.

Farooq-Lane felt bad for them the moment she stepped in. She already knew how this was going to go.

"We won't take this piece from you," the cashier said, misunderstanding his *no, thank you.* "We mean the rest of the cake! We made a whole cake! For you!"

Parsifal looked at that single square of Bienenstich on the plate again. It looked back at him. He did not move toward the cake or away. He looked as if his head were a glass of water and he was trying very hard not to spill it.

"No, it is not entertaining for me," Parsifal said again, politely.

"Not entertaining?" echoed the second baker.

He reddened a little. "Perhaps that is not the way to say it in English."

One of the other staff members laughed in a jolly way and said, "Oh, son, we have German here! All the German! You've come to the right place!" And he began to speak to Parsifal in a flow of it. All of them pitched in, newly excited, as if this, they knew, would be the true gift for him, hearing his native tongue after so long away from home. They pattered on around him while Parsifal listened motionless.

It had not been a good day. Farooq-Lane and Parsifal had arrived at the lone cul-de-sac in time to see what indeed looked like a charcoal-gray BMW parked in the exact middle of it, but before they could get close enough to get a plate number or see the driver, a little white sedan had backed out of a driveway into the side of their rental car. The apologetic driver had waved frantically, working hard to dislodge his car from theirs, but by the time he'd managed to disentangle himself, the BMW was long gone. He'd babbled on in some foreign language that neither Parsifal nor Farooq-Lane got, but they figured out the gist: He didn't have insurance, he was sorry, he was going now.

Farooq-Lane had just let him go. There was already a bullet hole in the rental. What was one more dent?

She became aware that the bakery staff had fallen silent, waiting for Parsifal to reply. He said a few words in German. Farooq-Lane could tell from their faces that they did not like him any better in German than they liked him in English. Camera phones were being lowered. Bilingual muttering was happening. They were drawing close to Farooq-Lane as if she were his caretaker and might explain him.

"Perhaps he's overtired and will change his mind later," one of the staff members said to her in a low voice, as another staff member began to lower the lights and yet another held up her keys to remotely start her car.

"I think you're probably right," Farooq-Lane lied. "He's so overwhelmed. Tomorrow he'll feel differently. We appreciate all that you did."

A week before she probably would've been mortified, but now she knew him too well. Of course he didn't like it, Farooq-Lane thought. He didn't like most things. She collected the white box of Bee Sting Cake—that was the translation of Bienenstich. Someone had drawn a little cheery bee on it with a thought bubble that read *PARSIFAL! GET WELL!* She thanked them again and took both box and boy to the beleaguered rental.

In the car, he said, "I won't feel differently tomorrow."

She dropped her hand from the ignition and gave him a withering look. "I know you won't, Parsifal. That's a thing that you say to someone to make them feel better about spending a lot of time making something for someone and then having that someone just stare at their food like it's going to give them a disease."

"I did not like it," he said.

"I think they got that."

"I was not trying to offend them."

"I don't think they got that."

"It was not like my mother's," he said. "I knew it wouldn't be. I told you so. I did not ask anyone to do this for me."

"Sometimes," Farooq-Lane said, feeling her temper playing round the edges again, "people still try, even if they don't think a thing will work. Sometimes there are nice surprises in this world, Parsifal."

He sat just as he had in the café, straight up, box on his lap, looking straight ahead at the dark lot. His jaw was set. Eventually, he said, "She would make it every single month on the first day, always from the same recipe, and she would freeze it, so that I could thaw it and have a piece every single day for breakfast."

"Every day?"

"Every day. If something always works, why would you change it?"

They sat in the dimming gray evening there, the car chilly and smelling of toasted almonds and sweet, yeasty cake. She didn't know where they were going to go next. After the cul-de-sac failure, Parsifal had been unwilling to brainstorm about anything else he might have experienced in his vision. Morale was low for everyone involved. Farooq-Lane. Parsifal. The bullet-ridden rental.

"Do you have the recipe?" she asked. "Your mother's? Can I ask her? Or someone who speaks German? Can you ask her?" It occurred to her only after she asked this that she had not seen Parsifal call or text anyone since she had been with him. She hadn't seen him do anything with his phone but use it to play his ever-present opera.

Parsifal looked out the side window at the closed pastry shop, holding very, very still.

"She's dead," he said, in his stiff, affectless way. "I killed them all the first time I saw the end of the world."

32

ost people pretended not to notice the woman at the gas station. The gas station, about thirty minutes west of Washington, DC, was one of those interstate oases common on the eastern corridor, always busy because of strong branding promising sandwiches that didn't smell bad and toilets you wouldn't stick to. The woman was lovely, with pale skin and long red hair, and she was clean, with a nice trench coat over a pretty flowered dress, but she looked lost—not in space, but in time—and that meant that no one could meet her eyes.

Shawna Wells had been watching the woman for the past twenty minutes. Shawna was waiting for her husband, Darren, to stop sulking and return to his new truck, parked beside her, so that they could continue their caravan back home to Gaithersburg. Possibly he was waiting for *her* to stop sulking. She couldn't tell, and in any case, she wasn't going to leave the van to get him. She had two occupied car seats in the back, in case he had forgotten, and she was not about to unbuckle them just to end a quarrel.

She watched the woman instead. At first Shawna thought the woman was asking for money, but the longer she watched, the more she thought that she was instead trying to hitch a ride. *What woman hitches a ride these days?* she wondered. Wasn't every woman told it was dangerous to get into a stranger's car? After a while, though, Shawna realized her question had morphed into a different one—*What kind of woman takes on a hitchhiker?*—and she also realized that she was about to ask the woman which direction she was headed.

The quarrel between Darren and Shawna had been about whether or not Shawna was selfish to be angry about him purchasing the new truck for himself. She'd wanted a new deck for parties. He'd wanted the new Raptor for his commute. She hardly saw how that made her selfish. He said that was the point.

She decided that if the woman asked her before Darren returned, she would say yes.

As minutes dragged on, however, and it seemed increasingly likely that Darren would soon give in, she grew impulsive. She put the van in gear. The children muttered. As she pulled out of the spot, she saw both Darren and the woman look up. The first in confusion, and the woman in something like recognition.

Shawna rolled down the window. The old van didn't always work quite right, so the window stopped halfway, but that was enough to ask, "Are you looking for a ride?"

The woman was very lovely up close, with green-glass eyes and a coral-colored mouth and freckles all across her translucent skin. Sometimes looking at a beautiful woman can make another woman feel self-conscious about her appearance, but Shawna felt the opposite—she was suffused with a new awareness of the things about her body that she found beautiful.

"I'm trying to get to Washington, DC," the woman said.

"I'm going that way." Shawna darted a glance to Darren, who was watching with bewilderment. "Hop in."

The woman smiled then, and Shawna remembered even more things that she liked about herself—her eyes, for instance, always looked like she was happy, even if she wasn't laughing, and Darren sometimes said that just looking at them made him happy, too. He really wasn't a dirtbag, most of the time, shame about that truck.

The woman got in.

Shawna held Darren's gaze for a second (he was making the universal gesture for *What the hell are you doing, Shawna?*) before heading out of the station.

"I'm grateful," the woman said.

"No problem," Shawna replied, as if she did this all the time. Her phone, attached to a holder by the radio, was buzzing rapidly with texts. *What are you doing?* Another buzz. *You have our children in the car.* "What's your name?"'

"Liliana."

They pulled onto the interstate. The old van wasn't fast, but it got to the speed limit eventually. Shawna considered herself a safe driver.

"That's a really pretty name," Shawna said. The woman didn't seem to have an accent, but the way she said *Liliana* seemed to imply that she came from a place that did.

"Thank you. What are your children's names?"

Shawna reached up to click the button on the side of the phone to turn the screen off. She didn't want the woman to see Darren's texts and feel unwelcome. "Jenson and Taylor. They're my babies."

"Bless you, Jenson, and bless you, Taylor," the woman said softly, and Shawna felt as if she could *feel* the words, like a real blessing, as if even though the woman had only just glimpsed her children in the backseat, she truly loved them.

For a while, they drove in silence. Shawna did not normally care for silence, but the fact of the woman, this strange woman, this *hitchhiker*, in the van was so loud that she didn't notice the lack of conversation. Traffic grew heavier and lanes multiplied. The evening sun was bold and golden behind them; the sky before them was darkening with night and with a bank of storm clouds.

"So what's in DC, Liliana?"

"I'm looking for someone." The woman gazed out the window. She had such a lot of long red hair, and Shawna remembered suddenly how full her own hair had gotten when she was pregnant. You didn't lose hair when you were pregnant, and so there had just been a lot of it, big and fantastic and glorious, until the hormones changed and she started shedding again after Taylor was born. Shawna had not thought about having another baby, but now, right now, in this moment, the idea appeared and was compelling. She'd enjoyed pregnancy so much, and Darren loved the babies. She'd felt so purposeful when she was growing life.

She asked the woman, "And this person's in DC?"

The woman shook her head. "But I might discover how to find them there. I hope." When some people say *I hope*, they mean that they have none, but the woman said *I hope* like hope was a holy thing, or an occupation.

What do you do?

I hope.

In the rearview mirror, Shawna saw the profile of Darren's new truck catching up, trapped behind several rows of fast-moving traffic, but there nonetheless. She found that she no longer resented the truck. Yes, she would have preferred the deck, but the truck was evidence that Darren was still volatile, still prone to youthful fits of desire. Wasn't that what she loved about him?

Up ahead, the thunder rumbled, audible even over the sound of the minivan. Lightning jerked from cloud to cloud. Shawna had been afraid of thunderstorms when she was a girl. At first it had been an ungrounded fear, but later, she had been lying in bed when lightning arced through the window to the light switch on her bedroom wall. The new understanding that there was lawless electricity in the world meant that even the slightest cloud cover would send her darting indoors to a windowless room. She had gotten over it a long time ago, but looking at the storm now, she discovered that she was just as afraid of that power as she used to be.

It felt stupid that she and Darren had fought over something so pointless. They were good together, and they were going to have another child.

The lightning darted again, charging the atmosphere, and she looked in her rearview mirror for Darren's truck. She wanted it to be close. She wanted to see his face.

It was close. He'd caught up and was right behind them, making a phone gesture to her in her mirror. She regretted not making up with him before they'd left.

The sound sucked out of the minivan.

It rolled back to nothing, to dead air, like the knob had been spun on reality's volume. The minivan ghosted forward through soundless traffic.

Shawna tried to say *Lord!* but that required noise, and there was none.

Then there was all the sound. A cacophony of every sound of every kind and every volume screamed inside the minivan. It was decades of sounds layered on top of each other.

It was an assault.

The noise bludgeoned the occupants of the car. If there was screaming, it could not be heard amid the rest of the sound. The windshield burst; the windows burst; blood splattered from somewhere. The minivan suddenly stopped moving forward, and the truck careened into it from behind. That sound, too, was absorbed by the howl of sound in the minivan. The two vehicles spun, spun, spun, and were hit again, and again, and again, and still the sound carried on.

Then all the vehicles were motionless in the farthest right lane, and the world resumed its ordinary score.

In the truck, Darren was crumpled over the steering wheel. The minivan seeped antifreeze. Shawna was draped sloppily back against her seat, blood running from her eyes and ears, her body battered. Everything in the interior of the minivan appeared to have been tumbled and crushed—the epicenter of a personal earthquake.

In the backseat of the minivan, Jenson and Taylor wailed. They were soft and unharmed, though the backseat was pounded out of shape and their car seats were compacted and split.

A teen girl climbed out of the passenger seat of the minivan. She was as untouched as the children in the backseat. She had long red hair, freckles all across her skin, and green-glass eyes, and she was quietly crying.

She crouched on the shoulder of the road and rocked with her knuckle pressed against her teeth until she heard the sound of an approaching siren. Then she stood and began to walk toward DC.

It started to rain.

33

It was well after dark when Ronan arrived at the Barns. The driveway was difficult to see, a tunnel of foliage to a hidden warren, but it would've been difficult to find even under the full sun because of the newly dreamt security system. The dream had taken him weeks to perfect, and even though he was normally a slob in his workshop, he'd painstakingly cleaned up after finishing this particular project. He'd destroyed every draft; he didn't want to ever run across one accidentally. It had been designed to work upon waking emotions, a sort of dream object Ronan ordinarily avoided. Fucking with free will felt distinctly uncatholic to him—one of those slippery slopes one is warned about. But he wanted the Barns to be safe, and every other idea he had relied on physical harm. Hurting intruders meant exposure, and killing intruders meant cleanup, so mindfuck it was.

The dreamt security system confused and saddened and obscured, tangling the intruder in nothing more or less poisonous than the terrible truths in their own histories. It didn't precisely block the view of the driveway, but once caught, one simply couldn't remember the present well enough to ever notice the entrance among the trees. It had been monstrous to install; it had taken Ronan the better part of a day to endure stretching it the few yards across the driveway. He'd had to stop every few minutes to put his head in his hands until the dread and regret passed.

That night, even knowing full well that his family home was

on the other side of the driveway threshold, even having spent most of his life here, Ronan still had to give himself a firm talking-to when his GPS reached the coordinates of the house.

"Just get it over with," he told himself.

He charged at the drive. Doubt and unpleasant memories swept through him and then—

The BMW was through and heading down the driveway on the other side. His headlights picked out a motionless cow here or there. Far on the other side of the deeply folded fields, dreamt fireflies winked in the woods.

Then the lights illuminated the old white farmhouse in the gloom, and beyond it, the glinting sides of numerous outbuildings, like silent attendants. Home.

For several long minutes, he sat in the car in the parking area in front of the farmhouse, listening to the night noises of the Barns. The crickets and the dreamt nightbirds and the hush of the wind from the mountains gently rocking the car. Everything about this place was the same as he had left it except for the person who lived inside it: him.

He texted Adam: *you up?*

Adam replied immediately. *Yes.*

Ronan, relieved, called him. "Bryde saved my life."

He had not thought he was going to tell Adam the whole of it. At first he hadn't wanted to call while Adam was in class, and then he hadn't wanted to call when he might be playing cards with the Crying Club because the thought of him telling them *just wait a minute it's Ronan* to take the call after the dorm incident was unbearable. Also, he hadn't been sure how to talk about a thing he didn't understand himself. But once he'd begun to explain the day to Adam, he couldn't stop, not only because he *needed* to hear it said out loud, but because he needed to say it out loud to Adam.

Adam listened quietly while Ronan told him everything that had happened, and then, at the end of it, he was quiet for a long space. Then he said, "I want to know what he gets out of it. Out of saving you. All of them, actually. I want to know why they moved you."

"Why do they have to get something out of it?"

"They have to," Adam said. "That's just the way the world works."

"*You* saved my life." Ronan remembered it freshly because the driveway security system sometimes dredged it up. Not the successful end, but the feelings before: Ronan drowning in an acid lake, hand stretched to his little psychopomp Opal, completely failing to save either her or himself. Adam and his exceptional, rarely used ability swooping in to rescue him, surprising them all.

"That's different."

"How is it different?"

Adam sounded irritable. "I saved your life because I love you and I was scared and I didn't know what else to do. That doesn't sound like Bryde."

This statement simultaneously pleased and aggravated Ronan. His mind stored away the first half for safekeeping, to take out and look at again on a rotten day, and decided to discard the second half because it felt deflating.

"Most people aren't like you, Ronan," Adam went on. "They're too afraid to put their necks out for nothing. There's an element of—what do you call it? Self-defense. Survival. Not doing something risky without a good reason because bodies are fragile."

"You don't know if he had to stick his neck out," Ronan said. He used his car key to dig cracker crumbs out from around the cigarette lighter. "You don't know if they were risking anything to move my car and me in it."

"There's such thing as an emotional cost," Adam said. "Investing in someone else's survival isn't free, and some people's emotional banks are already overdrawn. Anyway, I know what you want me to say."

"What do I want you to say?"

"You want me to tell you it's okay to go after Bryde and those other people, no matter what Declan thinks."

Adam was right. Once Ronan had heard it, he knew that this was, in fact, exactly what he wanted to hear.

Adam continued, "Only problem with that is that I agree with Declan."

"For fuck's sake."

"I didn't say I had the same reasons. I don't think you have to spend your life under a rock, but I don't think you should go chasing tigers until you're sure you have matching stripes."

Now Ronan knew *he* sounded irritable. "Poetic. You're a fucking sage. I'm writing that down."

"I'm just saying. Go slow. If you wait for break, I can help, maybe."

Ronan did not want to go slow. He felt like this was a candle that might burn out if he waited too long.

"I just want to know," Adam said finally, in a slightly different voice from before, "that when I come for break, you'll be there."

"I'll be here." He was always here. Double-sided murder crabs had made sure of it.

"In one piece."

"In one piece."

"I know you," Adam said, but he didn't add anything else, nothing about what knowing Ronan meant.

They sat in the quiet of a phone call with nothing in it for nearly a minute. Ronan could hear the sounds of doors opening and closing on Adam's side of the call, voices murmuring and laughing. He was sure Adam could hear the night noises of the Barns on Ronan's end.

"I have to go paint over some crab blood," Adam said eventually. *"Tamquam—"*

It had been over a year since either had sat in a Latin class, but it lingered as their private language. It had been one of the languages spoken in Ronan's dreams for a very long time, and so Latin had been one of the few classes Ronan had thrown himself into when they were at school. Adam couldn't stand not to be the best at whichever class he was in, so he'd had to throw himself into it with just as much fervor. It was possible that no two students at Aglionby had ever come away with such a thorough understanding of Latin (or, possibly, of each other).

"—*alter idem,*" finished Ronan.

They hung up.

Ronan climbed out of the car in a better mood than he'd climbed into it. Poking Chainsaw the raven where she slept on the farmhouse porch railing, he unlocked the door, and then the two of them went inside. He set himself a fire in the sitting room and started a can of soup on the stove while he showered and cotton swabbed all the black rubbish out of his ears and hair. A curious energy was running through him. Adam had not told him yes but he hadn't told him no, either.

He'd told him *go slow.*

He could go slow, he told himself.

He could go look at photos of his real mother and compare her to the woman he'd seen earlier that day. That was slow. That wouldn't hurt anything. He could do that while eating soup in front of a fire. Surely that would keep both Adam and Declan happy.

He retrieved an old photo box from the storage space in his parents' old bedroom and returned downstairs. With a mug of soup, he sat by his fire in the sitting room. It was a comforting, low-ceilinged space with exposed beams, the fireplace yawning in an unevenly plastered wall, all of it appearing to belong to an older country than the one it had been built in. Like the rest of the house, it felt as organic and alive as Ronan. It was a good friend to look at these photos with.

He really was in a good mood.

"Cracker," Ronan told Chainsaw. He held one out to her where she sat on her pooping-blanket on the couch. She had one eye on the desired saltine and one eye on the fire, which she didn't trust. Every time it popped, she twitched with knowing suspicion.

"Cracker," he said again. He tapped her beak with it so that she'd pay more attention to him and less to the fire.

"*Kreker,*" she croaked.

He stroked the small feathers next to her large beak and let her have it.

Sitting on the floor, he flipped the lid off the box. Inside were haphazardly stacked vintage photos, some in photo books, some not. He saw his mother, his father, aunt and uncle (he pulled that one out to save it for further study), his brothers when much younger, a variety of animals and musical instruments. His mother looked as he remembered her—softer than that portrait. Softer than that woman wearing her face in the little white sedan. He was glad to see that his memory hadn't tricked him, but it didn't really provide an answer for the other woman's existence.

He kept digging, down, down, down, to the bottom of the box, until suddenly, he saw a corner of a photo tucked beneath another that made his fingers draw back. He couldn't see much of the photo, but he recognized the corner. Not truly recognized. Rather, he remembered the way it used to make him feel to look at it. He knew without pulling out the rest of it that it was a photo of Niall Lynch in his youth, not long before he came over from Belfast. He hadn't looked at it in many, many years, and he didn't remember many of the details of it apart from the overwhelming memory of not liking it. It had made a younger Ronan feel bad enough that he had stuffed it right down to the bottom of the photo box, where he wouldn't easily uncover it again in other photo-looking sessions. All he recalled now was his father's ferocious energy in it—he was a wild person, more alive than anyone else Ronan had ever met, more awake than anyone else Ronan had ever met—and his *youth*. Eighteen. Twenty.

Thinking about it now, he thought that the youth was what had engendered Ronan's pronounced dislike. To child Ronan, seeing his father with so much life ahead of him felt retroactively terrifying. Like the Niall in the photo had so many choices left to make, and any one of them might make him never end up their father.

But now Ronan was the same age as the man in the photograph, and in any case, their father had already made all the choices he was ever going to make, all of them leading to him being dead.

He pulled out the photo and studied it again now.

Niall wore a leather jacket, collar popped up. A white V-neck. Leather bands wound round his wrists that he'd stopped wearing before Ronan was born—strange to think that Ronan wore them now without having remembered this detail. This young Niall had long, curly hair nearly down to his shoulders. He had a ferocious, living expression. He was young and alive, alive, oh.

It did not make Ronan feel bad to look at it. It made him feel the opposite. It also gave him something he wasn't expecting: an answer.

It wasn't Ronan's face he'd seen peering out of the car by the burned hotel. It had been his father's.

34

Jordan spent quite a bit of time working in museums. Continuing education. Job security. Sanity check. At least twice a week, she joined the ranks of area art students who went to galleries to learn by imitation. For a few hours, she became a forgery herself: She looked exactly like the other young artists working in the museum while in reality being nothing like them.

DC was spoiled for choice when it came to museums. The pink-hued National Portrait Gallery. The slyly uncomfortable Renwick. The chaotically colorful Museum of African Art. The Art Museum of the Americas and Mexican Cultural Institute with their beautiful Mayan and Pueblo tiles. Dumbarton Oaks' lovely garden. The NMWA, which Hennessy had once gotten thrown out of for an altercation so now none of them could really go back. The Kreeger and the Phillips, the Hillwood and the Hirshhorn. There were so many. The small and chilly Freer was Jordan's favorite, its small collection curated long ago by a man who collected with his heart first and his brain second. She and Hennessy had an agreement: Jordan would not work in the Sackler next door, and Hennessy would not work in the Freer.

One thing, at least, that they didn't share.

But this morning, because she was not giving away real pieces of herself, she headed into the National Gallery of Art. It was a big, handsome building with sky-high ceilings, heavy crown molding, and richly muted walls to show off its gilt-edged treasure. There were always plenty of students and art groups sketching, and several of the rooms already had massive, heavy easels for visiting artists to copy works. A forger could work right in the middle of it without being the center of attention.

She checked the time. She was a little late. Hennessy said that arriving late for a meeting was an act of aggression. It was like reaching into someone's pocket, she said, and thumbing out their wallet. It was leaning against their car and siphoning their fuel, she said, while making eye contact. Or it was just DC traffic, Jordan had replied once, and Hennessy had said they'd have to agree to disagree.

She glimpsed a figure on the other side of the lobby, studying one of the marble statues. His back was to her, and his gray suit was unspecific and anonymous, but nonetheless she felt certain she recognized the posture, the curled dark hair. It was an artful scene with the light filtering in among the columns, everything brown and black and white. It would have been a good painting, if she painted originals.

"I heard," she announced, "you're the son of the Devil."

Declan Lynch did not turn his head as she approached, but she saw his mouth tense in a suppressed smile. He said, "That's true."

It had taken only a few keystrokes to find out that he was the eldest son of Niall Lynch, *The Dark Lady*'s creator. She hadn't been trying to research him. Really she'd just wanted to know what to expect for the dutiful date. In the few photos she found of him—in his private school's website archives, in background shots on political news articles, in posed photos at an art show opening—he looked dull and forgettable. *Portrait of a Dark-Haired Youth*. There was nothing to remind her of what had seemed fleetingly appealing about him at the Fairy Market; it was probably the heightened atmosphere of the night that had lent him charm, she thought. This would be a chore, she decided. An acceptable chore she could bullshit through while they reached into his pocket and thumbed out his wallet, but a chore nonetheless. She was relieved, really. Better that way.

She sidled by him. He was not as dull-looking as the photos and her memory had suggested. Already she had forgotten that he was handsome. It seemed a strange thing to forget. He was scented with something subtly mannish, mild and unfamiliar, an oil rather than a fragrance. Jordan was reminded at a most basic level of all the strangers she had made out with, strangers who smelled pleasantly of scents never again encountered, scents that forever belonged only to them in her memory.

"I did a little reading on you since we last met."

"Coincidentally," Declan said, his gaze still fixed on the statue, "so did I. I hear you grew up in London."

What did one find when one looked up Jordan Hennessy? They found her mother, who possessed a tragic story so familiar it registered less as tragedy than as nodding predictability. The troubled genius artist, the life cut short, the body of work suddenly rendered meaningful and pricey. Hennessy had grown up with her in London; Hennessy had a London accent and so, therefore, did Jordan and all the other girls. "I grew up everywhere. I hear you grew up west of here."

"I was born grown-up," he said blandly.

"I found out about your father. Tragic."

"I found out about your mother. Also tragic."

It was Hennessy's tragedy, though, not Jordan's. She said, "Less tragic than a murder. My mother's was her own fault."

"One could argue," Declan said, "my father's was as well. Mm. Art and violence." He finally turned his head to her; he looked at her mouth. She just had time to see this—to *feel* it, an intense and surprising and agreeable heat—and then he said, "Walk and talk?"

Hennessy would hate him.

Hennessy wasn't here.

They began to stroll through the museum. There was something spare and unusual about it, about the morning-time wander through a museum populated with schoolchildren and retirees and locals. Time worked differently before noon when one ordinarily stayed up all night.

The two of them allowed themselves to get snagged in the net of a line for the traveling Manet exhibition.

Declan said, "I didn't think you'd call."

"Nor I, Mr. Lynch."

"Oh, that reminds me." He reached into his jacket pocket. "I brought you something."

This was uncomfortable. Here he was doing the proper date thing, and at the moment, the other girls were quite certainly breaking into his house. "Not flowers, I hope."

They moved a few steps closer to the entrance to the exhibition.

"Hand," he said as the line stopped again. She put her hand out. He set his gift in the middle of her palm.

She was astonished despite herself.

"Is this really what it says on the label?" she asked.

He gave her that bland smile.

It was a very small glass jar, the size you'd find holding fancy cosmetics. Inside was a mere dusting of purple pigment, so little that it wasn't even visible unless you turned the glass jar a certain way. A handwritten label on the outside read: *Tyrian purple*. A historical pigment, nearly impossible to get. It was made from excreted dye of sea snails such as the *Purpura lapillus*. Snails were ill-motivated pigment makers; it took an enormous number of them to produce even a small amount of Tyrian purple. Jordan couldn't remember the precise number. Thousands. Thousands of snails. It was very expensive.

"I can't—"

"Don't be boring and say 'I can't accept this,'" Declan said. "It took a lot of work to find that at short notice."

Jordan had not expected to feel conflicted about this experience. Everything about this experience was supposed to be disposable. A means to an end. Not a real date, nothing to beg the real question of *would I like this person*.

She hid this all behind her wide smile before slipping the jar into her own pocket. "Crumbs. I won't, then. I'll utter your name when I paint something with it."

"Say it now," he said, and he nearly let himself smile. Nearly.

"Declan," she said, but had to cut her eyes away because she could feel herself grinning, and not the slick grin she normally gave away. *Fuck*, she thought.

"Jordan," he said, trying it, and she blinked up, surprised. But of course he would call her by her first name. He hadn't come to her from the world of forgery, of late-night grudge matches, of her introducing herself as Hennessy. He'd looked her up, and had found the full name: Jordan Hennessy.

Normally this was where she'd correct people. Tell them, no, it's just Hennessy, really, because that's what Hennessy would say, and they were all her.

But she didn't correct him.

The Manet exhibition was choked with people, and as they left it, Declan and Jordan were momentarily trapped in the doorway. Suit coats brushed her hands; purses jostled her back. She was crushed against Declan and he against her. For a moment she looked at him and he back, and she saw bright intrigue in his expression and knew he saw it mirrored. Then they backed out of the room and she assembled her swagger and he drew his dull corporate composure close again.

Eventually they found themselves in Gallery 70, looking at *Street in Venice*, the painting she had copied before so many eyes at the Fairy Market.

Around them people moved like erratic clockwork. Jordan had spent so much time in this room copying *Street in Venice* that all the paintings in it felt like old friends. Eventually, she said, "When I first went looking for Sargent in a museum, I didn't know which wing to look for his stuff in. Born in America, American wing? Lived in England, British wing? You'd think belonging in both worlds would make it easier to find the chap, but really, it was just as when he was alive. Belonging in more than one world means that you end up belonging in none of them."

Who was she? Jordan. Hennessy. Jordan Hennessy. Both and neither.

This was a little more of her than she'd expected to give away before she came here today, but he'd given her the Tyrian purple. It seemed fair that she at least give him a little truth in return.

Declan didn't shift his gaze from the Sargent. He said thoughtfully, "When Sargent was in Venice, he used to stay at the Palazzo Barbaro . . . Supposed to be a very beautiful place.

He was related to the owners. Cousins, I think. Do you know this already? Don't let me bore you if you do."

"Go on."

"They hosted almost continuous art salons with the greatest expatriate Americans of the time. Wharton, James, Whistler, dazzles to think of them under the same roof. But the guy who owned the place, Daniel Sargent Curtis, he wasn't an artist. He was just a family man. He'd been a judge back in Boston. For decades, he lived a very dull, very forgettable life there, until one day, he punched another judge in the face. Wham! Imagine that other judge. Knocked off his feet by a man people barely remembered."

Declan paused as if he was thinking, but Jordan could tell that he was also pausing for the oratorial effect, allowing her to digest the words he'd just given her before he offered her more; this was a man who had been fed stories at some point and remembered how it was done.

Then he concluded: "Once he got out of jail, he moved his entire family to Venice, bought the Palazzo Barbaro, and literally did nothing but live and breathe art for the rest of his life."

He cut his eyes over to her. He was a good storyteller. It was obvious he liked the sound and play of words released into the air.

She sensed he'd given her as much as she'd given him. She wanted to ask him when he was going to punch a judge, but a question like that was basically begging intimacy, and she'd already gotten in too deep for a disposable date. "Art and violence. Is that story true?"

"I'm not as uninformed as you think."

"I don't think you're uninformed," Jordan said. "I think

you're all safe and sorted. Why don't you dress the rest of you like your feet?"

"Why do you only paint what other people have already painted?"

Touché, touché.

Jordan's phone buzzed. It was Hennessy. *Deed's done Trinity will come get you.*

"I . . ." she said, but she didn't know how to finish it.

He smoothly anticipated the cue. "I have to go to class anyway."

It was impossible to imagine him in class. In class for *what*. Probably business school. Whatever the most boring option was. She was beginning to understand his game; it was the same game as hers, played in the exact opposite way.

Declan's fingers found his jacket lapel and assessed it for blemish. A firm pinch reestablished the sharp edge. "Do you want to see me again?"

They regarded each other. It was now impossible to not see the lines of the Dark Lady in his face: his nose, his mouth, her nose, her mouth, those shared blue eyes.

As one-sixth of a person—one-sixth of a person who was currently robbing this guy—Jordan knew now what the real answer was.

But she answered as she would've if her life was her own.

"Yes," Jordan said.

35

Farooq-Lane's morning began with dead ends but finished with fresh leads.

It began quite typically. When she'd told Parsifal they needed to go out and drive until they found some clues, he'd disappeared into the hotel room bathroom and turned on the water. He'd stayed in there so long that Farooq-Lane had finished her coffee and then given in to her curiosity. Guiltily, quietly, she had typed his name into a search engine to find out what had happened to his family. Killed them all, Parsifal had said, and she'd guessed at the generalities. She, like every other Moderator, had been given the same crash course in Visionaries: Visionaries saw the future in dreamlike spurts. Visionaries' visions always had either a Zed or an unschooled Visionary in them. Undirected Visionaries were deadly when they had their episodes, so approach them with as much care as a Zed. Possibly more: They would kill you whether or not they wanted to if you were around when they had a vision. A new Visionary should be advised that the visions didn't have to be deadly to other people if the Visionaries turned them inward, they'd been told. They'll know what this means. Don't tell them it will kill them instead. They'll figure it out eventually.

Twenty-two Killed in Germany; Teen Survivor Under Investigation

In the bathroom, Parsifal let out a little yelp, and then there was a crash.

"Parsifal? You all right in there?" Farooq-Lane slapped her laptop closed.

When he emerged, fully dressed, he nonetheless looked naked and unlike himself. His broken glasses were cradled in the bony cage of his hand.

"Are you all right?" she asked.

"I'm nearly out of toothpaste," he replied.

Later, as he sat rigidly in the waiting area of a same-day eyeglasses shop in a mall, squinting into nothing, he asked her, "What kind of places have many teapots?"

Farooq-Lane looked up from the home and garden magazine she'd been reading. She used to really enjoy those sorts of magazines when she lived in a home and had a garden. "Kitchen stores. Collectors. Novelty shops. What kind of teapots?"

"Colorful." He frowned. He didn't look real, sitting straight up among the banks of frames in the shop. He looked like a very convincing mannequin waiting to model the latest styles. "Ugly."

"Is this about a Zed?"

"Try these on, sweetie." The optometric technician had returned with Parsifal's glasses. He endured her hooking them onto his ears. Everything about his body language silently raged against the contact of her fingers against the side of his head. "How are those for you? You like them?"

Farooq-Lane could tell from Parsifal's face that he did not, he very much did not, but he shot a quick glance at Farooq-Lane and said, "Thank you very much."

Parsifal Bauer had just been polite to another human being because of her.

Miracles never ceased.

"Let's just give them a little fine-tune," the technician said.

"You like them now, just wait till we adjust how they sit!"

Parsifal's mouth worked. He had come to the end of his politeness. He cut his eyes over to Farooq-Lane again.

Farooq-Lane rescued him. "Actually, we're in a hurry. We have to meet someone."

He stood up with immediate relief.

Outside, at the car, as she pulled open the door, she said, "That was very polite of you. We can get them fixed after we find the Zed."

His voice was brusque and impatient as he slid into the passenger seat. He said, "I don't know if there will be time."

Then they scoured the city for teapots. They went from junk shop to junk shop, and then from kitchen supply store to kitchen supply store, and then from craft shop to craft shop. None of them were right, but the ways they were wrong kept jogging Parsifal's memory, giving him more and more clues to follow. It was Springfield. It was near an interstate. It was a neighborhood, not a shopping center.

It was the split-level house they were parked in front of.

It was an unassuming neighborhood, ramblers and split-levels with patchy but mowed lawns and no trees. *MARY'S ODDS 'N' ENDS, COME ON IN* said a hand-painted sign by the driveway, with a little smiling flower painted beside it. It did not seem like the kind of place many people did come on in.

"No BMW," Farooq-Lane said.

"Different person," Parsifal replied.

"Was it dangerous? What you saw? Should we just go on in?"

Parsifal was already unbuckling his seat belt.

At the door, she was about to knock, but he pointed to another sign: *JUST COME IN!* with an illustration of a smiling coffee cup.

Inside, they found a dim, low-ceilinged living room set up as a dowdy little craft shop, unassuming and appealing in its complete lack of ambition. Lumpy, bright teapots in rainbow colors lined the mantel with handwritten price tags. Lumpy, tall mugs gathered on shelves made from old crates. Unevenly knitted blankets in the same psychedelic colors as the pottery were draped over the back of a wicker sofa. The rug was eye-bleedingly bright and hand woven, and also had a price tag. Everything looked unusual, but not in a Zed sense. This was just some old lady's hobby, she thought.

Parsifal let out a small little sigh. He didn't say anything along with it, but nonetheless she felt she could interpret the meaning of it quite well. It was the sound of satisfaction, or rather, of release. Of a job done.

She followed his gaze. He was looking into the kitchen; a sliver of countertop was visible through the living room doorway. Just that sliver was enough to reveal a dream. She knew it was a dream because it broke her brain a little bit. The thing was not even really a dream object, it was just a collection of wild colors sitting on the counter. There were no logical words to describe it. It was not a thing that was wildly colored. It was just the concept of the colors themselves, balled up together on the counter. The colors themselves matched the crafts the Zed had made by ordinary, handcrafted means. They were all obviously a product of the same mind.

Farooq-Lane took a step closer. Beyond the dreamthing were sugar and flour canisters and other ordinary kitchen objects. The dream sat among them, a proud little art piece.

A dreamt art piece.

Both Parsifal and Farooq-Lane jumped as the sliding door from the backyard opened.

"You came on in!" said the newcomer happily.

She was very old. She was a soft, plump lady who'd dyed her white hair pink, and she was wearing very colorful lipstick, too. Her clothing matched the colors of the teapots and the thing on the counter. Farooq-Lane caught a glimpse of something in her mouth but wasn't sur—

She asked, "Did you make all this?"

"Everything in this house," the old lady said. She reached for a bright canister on a bright end table. Farooq-Lane flinched as she removed the lid, but she only tipped the contents toward them in an offer.

"Don't worry, they aren't dog biscuits," she said, and laughed merrily at herself. As she did, Farooq-Lane saw what she had glimpsed before. The woman had a false tooth, a molar way in the back. It was the same swirling collection of rainbows that the thing on the counter was. A dreamt false tooth.

She felt a surge of adrenaline. There was no thought immediately attached to it. Just that bubbling rush of warmth through her limbs. They'd found a Zed.

This was a person who took things from their dreams.

They'd done it.

The Zed shook the canister at Parsifal. "They're biscotti I made yesterday."

To Farooq-Lane's shock, Parsifal accepted one, so she was required to as well.

"Have you seen anything you like?" the Zed asked as Parsifal took an experimental bite of the biscotti.

Farooq-Lane hadn't, but she used some of her buyers' fund from the Fairy Market to buy the rug. She didn't know why she bought something. She panicked, she supposed. She had to do something. She picked the rug. She had half a thought the teapots would be breakable, although she didn't know why that mattered since she didn't intend on keeping whatever she bought.

"Another?" the Zed asked. Parsifal accepted another biscotti, making it officially the most Farooq-Lane had seen him eat in one sitting since they'd met. He didn't say thank you, but the Zed smiled at him as sweetly as if he had, and said, "Better take one for the road."

Back at the car, Parsifal ate the third cookie and watched Farooq-Lane wrestle the rug into the backseat.

Then the two of them sat there in the quiet car.

"She's very old," Parsifal said.

"I know."

"She's not going to end the world," he said.

"I know."

Parsifal watched her taking out her phone. "Then what are you doing?"

"I have to tell them we found one, Parsifal."

He looked at her sharply. "They'll kill her!"

"I'll tell them she's no threat," Farooq-Lane said. "But I have to report her."

"They'll *kill* her!"

He was starting to get agitated. He squeezed his knobby hands into fists and stretched them out again on top of his knobby knees, and rocked a little as he looked back at the house. She wasn't feeling great herself; adrenaline never felt good as it washed back out to sea.

She said, "Parsifal, they already think I might be on the Zeds' side because of my brother. I know they're testing me, and I'm failing. I'll tell them she's just an old lady. They're not going to kill an old lady." He curled a hand on the door handle and gripped it hard enough to turn his knuckles white as exposed bone, not as if he were going to get out, but as if he were keeping himself from floating away. She said, "*You're* being fishy yourself, you know. Why don't you want a Zed reported? They wouldn't like that, either."

She called Lock.

She and Parsifal didn't speak for the rest of the day.

This was, she told herself, the business of the end of the world.

36

It was probably, Hennessy thought, not actually the end of the world.

She had mixed feelings about this.

"People like your mother were born to die young," Hennessy's father had told her once, before it had become obvious that his daughter *was* people like her mother. "I knew that before I married her. Her kind burn fast and hard. Exciting. Dangerous. Gorgeous. Always take the inside line. Push it until they break it. I knew it. Everyone told me that." He hadn't actually told this to Hennessy. He'd told Jordan, who he thought was Hennessy, but Hennessy had been hiding under the dining room table, so she'd heard it. It wasn't a gaspworthy reveal anyway. This was dinner table conversation, old war stories.

"I married her nonetheless," he'd said. "I wouldn't take it back, but she was like a Pontiac. Some cars you only need to drive once."

Hennessy's father was Bill Dower and he was a race-car driver and kit-car fabricator. Everything he said came out as a race-car metaphor. Before one met Bill Dower, it seemed impossible for everything to eventually tie back into racing, but after one met him, it was hard to forget.

Hennessy's mother was J. H. Hennessy, known as Jay to her friends, though it was understood that was not what the *J* stood for, only how the *J* sounded. Hennessy never knew what her real first name was. Art writers never knew, either, despite their best efforts, and theorized that she might not have truly had a *J* name at all. Maybe, they said, the initials were a sort of pseudonym, an invented identity. Maybe, others said, she had never really existed at all. Maybe, they posed, she was a co-op of artists all creating art under the name J. H. Hennessy and that was why she could not be effectively researched posthumously. Perhaps the woman who appeared at events had been hired to be the face of J. H. Hennessy and she was the Banksy of the gallery world.

Oh, she was real all right.

Anyone who had to live with her could never think otherwise.

Hennessy's phone rang. She watched it skip and patter across the concrete stair until it fell to the next, where it lay on its face and hummed morosely. She left it there.

It was afternoon-ish. A crime had recently been committed in a young man's town house in Alexandria; not too long ago, several women had finished breaking a window, stealing a painting, and repairing a broken window. Now Hennessy and *The Dark Lady* sat on the stairs of the National Harbor, alone except for some young professionals and the sun, both jogging through on their way somewhere else. In front of her she could see Seward Johnson's *The Awakening*, a seventy-foot sculpture of a man emerging from the sand. Possibly emerging. Possibly sinking. If one didn't know the piece's title, it was just as likely the clawing hands and desperate face were being sucked back down into the earth.

She was stalling.

Hennessy wiped her nose with the back of her hand and then studied the darkness smeared on her knuckles with detached observation. Recently, she had seen what was considered the blackest paint in the world. Singularity Black, it was called.

They'd coated a dress with it. It was so black that whatever it coated ceased to have any details beyond being black; there were no deeper shadows, no subtle highlights. It became an outline of a dress, all complexity erased. Singularity Black wasn't properly a pigment, it was some kind of nanoshit, tiny bits and bobs that ate ninety-some percent of the light around them. NASA used it to paint astronauts so aliens couldn't see them or something. Hennessy had looked into getting some of it for Jordan for their birthday before she'd found out it had to be applied fifty coats thick, cured at six hundred degrees, and then could still be wiped off with a finger. Only NASA could put up with that shit.

But it *had* been impressively black.

Not as dark, however, as the liquid coming out of Hennessy, because it wasn't truly black. It was less than black. It was not anything. It was nothing. It only seemed black from far away, and when one got close, one could see its supernatural origins.

Was it a side effect of being a dreamer, or a side effect of being Hennessy? There wasn't anyone alive for her to ask.

J. H. Hennessy had been a dreamer. She didn't talk about it with Hennessy except in metaphorical terms, but Hennessy knew what she was. Her mother would fall asleep drunk on the stairs or under the piano, and it didn't take too much observation to discover that she tended to wake with more paints and bottles around her than she'd fallen asleep with. Or maybe it did, because Hennessy was sure that her father had never figured out that Jay could dream things into being.

When he said she was a mess, he just meant the vodka and ecstasy.

Retrospectively, Hennessy could see that he liked that J. H. Hennessy was a mess.

"Are you gonna save me?" Hennessy asked the Dark Lady, wiping her face again. The Dark Lady looked at her mistrustfully, pessimistically. "Us, I meant to say. Thanks for straightening that." The Dark Lady didn't smile. Neither did Hennessy. She didn't know how potent *The Dark Lady*'s power to influence dreams was, but she didn't think there was a chance in hell it was enough to shift Hennessy's recurring nightmare. If it hadn't wavered in sixteen years, it seemed unlikely that it was going to flinch now. Hennessy closed her eyes—there it was. She didn't even have to close her eyes. She stopped thinking—there it was.

She was so tired.

Judging from the dream creations she woke with, Jay's dreams seemed straightforward, uncomplicated. She dreamt of what she had been doing while she was awake. She went to a party, she woke with sequins. She got into a fight with Bill Dower, she woke with divorce papers. He lured her back with flowers and jewelry, she woke with more flowers and jewelry. The only thing she'd ever dreamt that interested Hennessy was Hennessy's ferret, which she'd dreamt the day Hennessy spent all day begging for one.

Cassatt had been a great pet. He didn't smell and ate nothing except prescription drugs.

Until Jay died and he fell asleep forever.

Curled up on the concrete stairs, Hennessy was starting to feel not good. She could tell her ears were starting to fill with the black stuff. The taste of it was awful.

"I'm gonna do it," Hennessy told the Dark Lady, who was beginning to judge her for staying awake for so long. Didn't she care about the other girls? the Dark Lady wondered. Didn't she care that they were all probably starting to stagger around about now, starting to feel the trickle-down effects of the black ooze bubbling up in their creator? Didn't she care that if she died, they'd all sleep? Hennessy resented all of this. The girls were basically the only thing she *did* care about. "I'm just not mad about the idea. Gimme a few to talk myself into it."

It wasn't just hatred of the nightmare that kept her awake. As bad as this felt, the way her body felt after she dreamt a copy of herself was worse.

She just didn't think *The Dark Lady* was going to save her from that.

Hennessy's phone buzzed again. She toed it over to see the caller ID. Jordan. So she was done with her date with Declan Lynch. She'd survived, apparently. Hennessy had googled the guy and it looked like Jordan had definitely drawn the shortest out of all possible straws, and that was including the black ooze among the straws. Hennessy would rather bleed out than date a boring white man in last year's suit.

Jordan texted: *The girls said you mistreated them*

She hadn't mistreated them. She'd just taken the newly stolen painting and told them to go spend the rest of their lives doing end-of-the-world things in case this next dreamt copy was the one to kill her. They hadn't wanted to leave her. She'd repeated the exhortation. Persuasively. Stridently. It's what she would have wanted. Party right up till the end. No warning. Not much in the way of parties to find at noon on a DC weekday, but surely they could think of something. They were Hennessys.

Jordan: *Where are you*

This wouldn't be the copy to kill her anyway, Hennessy

thought. Three more. That's what she thought. Every time she dreamt a copy, a new flower tattoo appeared on her throat, and there was only room for three more.

She wiped some black on the top of her shoe.

"People like me," Hennessy told the Dark Lady, "were born to die young."

Which made it basically murder for J. H. Hennessy to have a kid in the first place.

The Dark Lady's eyes glittered. She thought Hennessy was being melodramatic. Maybe she was. Hennessy shivered and looked out across the water, trying to imagine a dream that had the ocean in it instead of yet another Hennessy.

She couldn't picture it.

She could only imagine the same dream that was already happening behind all of her thoughts. Over and over and over again.

Jordan texted: *You can keep playing silly buggers and I can keep looking for you but it's boring don't you think*

Oh darling, Hennessy texted back, *I don't think boring is something you and I have to worry about.*

37

Declan Lynch knew he was boring.

He'd worked very hard to be that way, after all. It was a magic trick he didn't expect any prize from but survival, even as he looked at other lives and imagined them his. He didn't fool himself. He knew what he was allowed to do and to want and to put in his life.

He knew Jordan Hennessy didn't belong.

But still, when he came back from the National Gallery of Art to his empty town house, he closed the door behind him and for a moment he just leaned against it, eyes closed, pretending—no, not even pretending. He just didn't think. For one second of one minute of the day, he didn't run the probabilities and worst-case scenarios and possibilities and consequences. For one second of one minute of the day, he just let himself feel.

There it was:

Happiness.

Then he let out a deep sigh, and his thoughts came rushing back, and along with them, all the reasons why every relationship before now and after this had to remain disposable.

But joy is a small, tenacious crop, especially in soil that hasn't grown any for a long time, and so it lingered with him as he checked his watch to see when Matthew was due back from soccer and hung up his coat and his keys and toed off his shoes.

Then he did something he hadn't had the guts to do since he'd gotten it.

He turned on the light in the kitchen, clucking his tongue when he saw that Matthew or Ronan had tracked grit in from the back door—was it *so* hard to scuff your feet on the mat if you weren't going to take off your shoes? He pulled open the closet door and there she was, *The Dark Lady*.

Before, looking at *The Dark Lady* had triggered all kinds of complex sensations, most of them shitty.

But today it was just a painting.

He drew it out of the closet and brought it to the dining room table. He set it on its face and looked at the brown backing paper that neatly covered the back of the canvas and sealed the edges of the frame. His eyes glanced off the words *Mór Ó Corra* and away. Then he retrieved a small, sharp knife from the kitchen.

He hesitated.

You can't unsee this, he told himself.

This is not allowed in the life you are living, he told himself.

I want so much more, he told himself.

And he neatly sliced the edge of the brown backing paper. He took his time at first, keeping the cut straight and even and surgical, and then the line grew faster and more ragged and furious as he went, until eventually he was tearing it off with his hands, chanting, *I hate you, I hate you, I hate you.*

Then his fingers were trembling and the paper was removed and he was looking at the back of the canvas.

There was nothing there.

There was nothing there.

There was nothing there.

All of this and there was nothing there.

38

Nothing there. Ronan had been digging through his father's belongings for hours and he'd found jack shit. He had been restless all day. His dreams the night before had been antsy, fractured, Bryde-less. His morning after was antsy, fractured, Adam-less. He spent an hour driving the BMW around and around the muddy skid pad. The growl of the engine was unable to vanquish the thoughts of his father's youthful face and his mother's troubled one, Bryde's compelling voice and Declan's dampening one.

Declan had told him not to chase the rabbit. Bryde had told him to chase the rabbit.

They were tied, and he was not allowed to be the tie-breaker.

Go slow, Adam had said.

Tomorrow Ronan had to drive back to DC for his birthday. He wasn't sentimental over it, but Matthew was a big believer in birthdays and ritual, so he'd return for some level of revelry. Matthew had suggested a picnic to Great Falls. Declan had suggested a nice dinner out. Ronan found both options unbearably *routine*.

Why hadn't Bryde come to him last night?

He knew, though.

Bryde was done with chasing Ronan; it was Ronan's turn now.

And he wanted to chase.

Go slow.

Ronan drove up into the mountains to kill some time. He thought about going farther, about driving all the way to Lindenmere, but it wasn't a good idea to visit the forest in a disordered frame of mind, and Ronan would place his relative disorder at a solid seven on a scale of one to ten. Instead, he returned home, made himself a peanut butter sandwich, and began to tear apart the farmhouse as he had many times before, looking for secrets or dreams he'd overlooked.

Which was when he heard—

Something. An intruder.

An engine fading, possibly. Not right next to the house. That would've been louder. This was more like an engine fading halfway down the drive in order for the driver to come the rest of the way without detection.

Or maybe it was nothing.

Surely no one could have made it through his security system.

Outside, Chainsaw called out. It wasn't her alarmed bark, though, was it? It was just a bark.

He had his little knife filled with talons in his pocket and there was a gun in Declan's old room.

He heard the back door open.

Fuck.

Of course it wasn't locked. Not while he was awake, not while the driveway was protected.

A floorboard in the mudroom creaked.

Ronan was on his feet. Silently. He swiftly moved through the house, avoiding the boards he knew would creak and give him away. He had his knife out. He stopped for the gun.

Thud, thud.

That was just his heart, frustratingly loud in his ears.

Downstairs, the living room was empty. So was the sitting room. The dining room.

Another noise. From the kitchen.

Ronan lifted the gun.

"Jesus, Ronan, it's me!" The kitchen overhead light came on and revealed Adam Parrish, removing a motorcycle helmet. He eyed the gun. "You know how to take a surprise well."

Ronan remained fixed in place, uncertain. It was not that Adam looked wrong at all—he looked marvelously himself, in fact, his hair matted down from being under the helmet, his shoulders lean and fit in a leather jacket Ronan had not seen him in before, his cheeks bright and heightened from the journey. But after the last two days, Ronan could no longer believe someone's face as proof of identity.

"How did you get through the driveway?" he asked suspiciously.

"Horribly," Adam said, rolling the helmet onto the counter and peeling off the jacket and gloves. He threw both next to the helmet and smelled his bare arms. "Is it as bad leaving as it is coming? Because if so I'm staying here forever."

He turned and realized Ronan was still holding the gun. His brows drew together. He didn't look upset. He just looked as if he was trying to understand.

Ronan didn't understand himself, either. Part of his mind was saying, *Of course it's Adam, put the gun down* and another part was saying, *What is real?* He understood why both parts of him existed. What he didn't understand was how evenly they were matched. He hadn't realized that seeing his parents' faces on living bodies had affected him so thoroughly until this moment of seeing someone he loved very much and yet not knowing if he could believe it.

"Tell me what I need to say to prove it," Adam said. He'd worked it out. That alone was nearly enough to convince Ronan even after his face didn't. Adam was the most clever person he knew. "What will make you know it's me?"

Ronan didn't know. "Why are you here?"

"I started thinking about it last night. Then I just got up this morning and thought, I'm going. I'm just going. Gillian found me this jacket at a thrift store. This is Fletcher's helmet—can you imagine him on a scooter? These are my proctor's gardening gloves. I read my sociology notes into my phone and I listened to them the whole way down for my quiz tomorrow. And now I'm here." Then he looked rueful, realizing. He said, "Ronan, I know you."

He said it just the same way he'd said it on the phone the night before. Ronan's adrenaline melted out of him. He discarded all weaponry on a side table. "I'm convinced. Only you would listen to sociology notes on a motorcycle."

They hugged, hard. It was shocking to hold him. The truth of him was right there beneath Ronan's hands, and it still seemed impossible. He smelled like the leather of the thrift store jacket and the woodsmoke he'd ridden through to get here. Things had been the same for so long, and now everything was different, and it was harder to keep up than Ronan had thought.

Adam said, "Happy birthday, by the way."

"My birthday's tomorrow."

"I have a presentation I can't miss tomorrow. I can stay for"—Adam pulled away to check his dreamt watch—"three hours. Sorry I didn't get you a present."

The idea of Adam Parrish on a motorcycle was more than enough birthday present for Ronan; he was senselessly turned on. He couldn't think of anything else to say, so he said, "What the fuck." Normally this was his job, to be impulsive, to be wasteful of time, to visibly *need*. "What the fuck."

"That batshit bike you dreamt doesn't use gas," Adam said. "The tank's wood inside; I put a camera in it to look. Just as well I didn't have to stop for gas anyway because half the time, when I slow down, I dump the bike. You should see the bruises on my legs. I look like I've been fighting bears."

They hugged again, merrily, waltzing messily in the kitchen, and kissed, merrily, waltzing more.

"What do you want to do with your three hours?" Ronan asked.

Adam peered around the kitchen. He always looked at home in it; it was all the same colors as him, washed out and faded and comfortable. "I'm starving. I need to eat. I need to take off your clothes. But first, I want to look at Bryde."

39

Adam Parrish was uncanny.

Perhaps standing next to Ronan Lynch, dreamer of dreams, he looked ordinary, but it was only because everything uncanny about him was turned inside instead of out. He, too, had a connection with the peculiar ley line energy that seemed to power Ronan's dreams, except that Adam's connection happened while he was awake, and only ever produced knowledge instead of objects. He was something like a psychic, if there was such a thing as a psychic whose powers extended more toward the future of the world than the future of people. During the idyllic summer he'd spent at the Barns with Ronan, he'd played with energy nearly every single day. He'd gaze into a bowl of dark liquid and lose himself in the unfathomable pulse that connects all living things. While on the phone with Gansey or Blue, he'd take out his deck of haunted tarot cards and read one or three cards for them. At night, he'd sit on the end of Ronan's childhood bed and meet Ronan in dreamspace—Ronan, asleep, in a dream, Adam, awake, in a trance.

He had put all of that away to go to Harvard.

"If I stop breathing, bring me back," Adam said now. He sat on the end of Ronan's bed with one of Ronan's dreamt lights cupped in his hands. There were all sorts of dreamt lights at the Barns: fireflies in the fields, stars tangled in the trees, orbs hanging in the long barn over his work, eternal wee candles in each of the windows that faced the backyard. The one in Adam's hand was too ferociously bright to look at directly; it was a sun. Gansey had asked Ronan to keep his mint plant alive while he road-tripped, and Ronan, unsure of how to keep plants alive inside, had dreamt the outside in. Now it illuminated the otherwise dim bedroom where the two of them sat knee to knee on the bed.

"If it's longer than fifteen minutes, bring me back," Adam added. He thought about this, then corrected himself. "Ten. I can always go back."

Adam's ability wasn't without its risks. It was a lot like dreaming, but dreaming using the whole world's imagination instead of just his own. There were no limits. No memories to hedge the dreams in, no identity to keep the wandering intimate. Without someone to hold him close within the vast space, Adam's mind could wander into the ether and never return, like the cow floating off into the sun. That was how his deck of tarot cards had become haunted. They were a gift from a dead woman who'd never come back.

"Ten, okay," Ronan said. Reaching out, he twisted the watch on Adam's wrist so that it faced him.

Adam tilted his head back, and Ronan realized he was steeling himself. This was new. Adam had always been cautious, but not intimidated.

"What?" Ronan asked.

"Things have been weird out there."

This was unpleasant to think about; how long would it have taken Ronan to find out if Adam had been found dead in his dorm, his mind lost to the infinite while everyone else's backs were turned? "I didn't know you'd been doing it while you were gone."

"Only twice," Adam said. "In the first week. I know. It was stupid. I haven't done it again. I wouldn't do it again."

"Why did you even do it?"

"Why did you drive after that person who looked like your mother?"

Fair.

"I just have to . . . I have to work myself up to it, is all."

It was truly disconcerting to see him so intimidated by it. "Why?"

"Something's changed. There's something enormous, it feels like, watching us."

"You and I?"

"People. Maybe it's . . . listen to me talking like it's something. Someone. I don't even know what it is. I can't really explore. I don't have any armor out there. It's just my mind floating around."

All of this sounded unpleasant to Ronan. "You don't have to do this now."

Adam muttered, "I do. Me closing my eyes doesn't make the monster go away. I'd rather know. And I don't trust anybody else to spot me. You know what I'm supposed to look like. And I want to know if I can see your guy out there among that something. Or if it *is* your guy."

Ronan narrowed his eyes.

"Don't gimme that look, Ronan. All you know is that he told you he was a dreamer," Adam said. "You can believe him, but nothing says I have to. Earlier today you had a gun on me. I'm just asking you give him the same shake as me."

Again, just as when Ronan had been holding the gun on

Adam, there was no distress, no anger. Adam would never judge someone else for their skepticism. His default setting was mistrust.

"Okay," said Ronan.

Adam went in.

He cast his eyes down to the sun in his hand. For the first few seconds, he blinked, blinked, blinked. He had to. The light was searing; Ronan couldn't look at it for any longer than a stolen glance, and even then, it left green contrails in his vision.

After a few seconds, Adam's blinks grew further and further apart.

And then they were just open.

The sun reflected in his eyes, two fiery miniature suns contained in his pupils.

He was absolutely motionless.

It was an eerie image: this gaunt young man poised over the sun, his gaze unflinching and blank, something about the hang of his shoulders indicating vacancy.

Ronan watched the second hand count off time. He watched Adam's chest rise and fall.

Five minutes. It was unnatural for someone to sit still for a minute, much less two. By five, it became truly unsettling.

Six minutes. The dark had begun to dance with many green orbs from Ronan glancing at the sun and then away as he checked Adam's watch.

Seven minutes.

Eight.

At nine minutes, Ronan began to get antsy. He fidgeted, counting down the seconds.

At nine and a half, Adam began to scream.

It was such an awful sound that, at first, Ronan was pinned in place.

It was not a proper scream, anything that conscious Adam would have done, even in pain. It was a high, thin, reedy sound, like something being torn in two. It didn't waver. It threw back Adam's head and buckled his shoulders and let the sun roll across the comforter.

It was the sound of something that knew it was dying.

The dim walls of the room felt like they absorbed it. Somehow this scream would always be embedded in the plaster, needled into the supports of the house, gasping in the places no one ever saw. Somehow there would always be a thing that would never be happy and whole again.

"Adam," Ronan said.

Adam stopped breathing.

"Adam."

Ronan seized Adam's shoulders and shook. The moment he released him, Adam slumped down and away. An unconscious body has an uncompromising feel to it; it is uninterested in reason and emotion.

"Parrish," Ronan snarled. "You aren't allowed—"

He pulled Adam up and held him close, feeling for breath, for pulse. Nothing, nothing.

The seconds tilted by.

Adam's body didn't breathe. Adam's mind wheeled, untethered, through infinite dreamspace. Wherever it was, it didn't recall Adam Parrish, Harvard student; Adam Parrish, Henrietta-born; Adam Parrish, Ronan Lynch's lover. Adam Parrish, cut loose from his physical body, was fascinated by things so ephemeral and huge that these tiny human concerns didn't even register.

Ronan dug for the little talon knife.

"I'm sorry," Ronan said to him, and then he flicked it open.

The talons winged out, clawing, tearing, a chaos of claws, snarling up Adam's arm.

Blood welled immediately.

Ronan snicked the knife shut and the talons receded, pulling a mighty rasp out of Adam's chest as they did.

"Oh God oh God oh God—" Adam curled down into himself, his eyes closed, rocking.

Ronan fell back in relief. He hurled the talon knife away from the bed and pressed a hand against his own galloping heart.

"What happened?" he demanded.

Adam's chest was still heaving for breath. The rest of him quivered. "Oh God oh God—"

"Adam."

Adam pressed the back of his hand to his forehead, a strange, un-Adam-like gesture, and rolled it back and forth like a child might when tired or anxious. Ronan took it instead, holding it still. Adam's skin was icy cold, as if he had taken his body to outer space. He didn't seem to notice that his arm was bleeding from the talon knife; he still seemed a little unaware of his body. Ronan rubbed Adam's fingers between his hands until they were warm and then kissed them.

"Parrish, that was fucked up," Ronan said. He laid a palm on Adam's pale cheek. It, too, was frigid. Adam turned his face into Ronan's hand, his eyes shuttered.

"It saw me," Adam said. "Oh God."

"What is it?"

Adam didn't answer.

Ronan bundled him close and for several minutes, the two of them stayed like that, tightly wound together, lit by the abandoned dreamt sun, Adam's skin cold as the moon.

"It's not Bryde," Adam said finally. "The something, it's not Bryde."

"How do you know?"

Adam said, "Because whatever it is, it's afraid of him."

40

No one noticed the teen girl who came into the gallery a few minutes before the event. The gallery was a large and modern Arlington establishment called 10Fox, just five miles outside Washington, DC, come to our showroom and consult with our stylists to make your estate a place of art. The front of the house was currently overwhelmed with many dozens of children. Four hundred, the publicist guessed, not counting the parents. Good call on the early start time, go us, go team. You got this, she told her author. Four-hour signing line, everyone's home for late lunch, happy ending.

Jason Morgenthaler did not see anything happy about the situation. He was the owner of 10Fox. He was also a very famous picture-book author. His books were so omnipresent that most children who read them assumed that he must be dead. His most popular work, *Henderson!*, was given to tens of thousands of children by tens of thousands of grandparents each holiday season, and his Skunkboy series had been made into a television series with an extremely annoying theme song. He was currently separated from his wife, who was a famous stand-up comedian. Morgenthaler considered himself a serious artist and a serious art collector and a serious art dealer and he was mostly correct about one of these things.

He did not want to leave the gallery's back room.

Morgenthaler had never liked children, and recently they

had become absolutely repellant to him. Children were tiny anarchists, miniature id-monsters from hell. They did what they wanted whether or not it was a good idea, and whether or not they had permission. When they wanted to eat, they ate; when they wanted to crap, they crapped. They bit, they screamed, they laughed until they puked.

Morgenthaler peered around the corner.

"Oh God," he said. The adults in the room were vastly outnumbered. Two of them were booksellers, standing at attention behind a table set up with picture books. Another two were dressed in enormous full-body mascot costumes, one a skunk and one an enormous-headed girl, terrifying in her proportions.

The publicist patted his arm. She found his pathological burnout droll. She gestured to the other staff behind him.

"Go time," the publicist said.

Morgenthaler finger-combed his colorless brown hair before entering from the back of the gallery, flanked by three more adults in mascot costumes: a green dog, an alarmingly large-headed old man, and something that was supposed to be a squid. One of the children in the front row began to cry, though it was hard to tell if it was from an excess of terror or an excess of excitement.

From the back of the room, Lin Draper, mother of three, watched Morgenthaler's presentation. He had a relentlessly oval-shaped head, she thought, like it had been drawn by someone who'd not seen a real human head for a while. She had expected him to be different, somehow, when she loaded her daughter India into the car to come to the event. More family friendly. He had already sworn twice during his introduction and he seemed a little sweaty. He had dressed himself in a black sport coat and white V-neck T-shirt paired with red Chucks, an outfit that aggressively notified onlookers that he was both collector and artist, both the money and the talent. Morgenthaler was using the sort of jolly voice adults often used on children: "Would you believe I thought I was going to be a famous writer of adult novels? I intended to be a serious painter of representational art. But *no*, my agent said I was better suited to children, and so here I am *still* after ten years—"

"Can I hold your hand?" India whispered.

Lin realized with the ground-swallowing shame only made possible through awkward parenting moments that her little daughter was talking not to *her*, but to a redheaded teen girl.

She admonished India in a low voice and whispered to the redheaded girl, "I'm *so* sorry—"

"It's all right," the girl said. She offered her hand to India without any hesitation. India slid her chubby palm into the teen's and then, impulsively, kissed the back of her hand.

"*India,*" Lin said, horrified. "Let's go have a talk outside."

"Bless you," whispered the teen girl to India as her mother dragged her off, her expression blissful and vague.

"Why don't we just go to a Q and A!" one of the booksellers said with the bright tone that sounded fine and meant *nothing is fine.*

As the booksellers began to solicit questions from the children ("How old are you?" "Is Clancy based on a real person?" "Do you have any dogs?" "What are their names?"), some of the other children cozied up to the teen girl, leaning on her or touching her leg or, like India, clutching her hand. They were far more transfixed by her than by Morgenthaler.

Morgenthaler's voice was rising and getting less jolly. "*Actually,* Maria—did you say your name was Maria? The reason why there are dolls for Henderson and not for Skunkboy is because of a drawn-out legal battle for merchandising rights because it turns out you need to get yourself a lawyer who's not sleeping with your *spouse* if you want good— What, you have something to say about the way I run my events?"

This last statement seemed to be directed toward the old-man costume.

Morgnthaler wound up and punched the head right off the old-man costume.

There was a moment of silence as the old-man head flew off, followed by an equal and opposing measure of sound as it careened into the seated children.

Morgenthaler regarded all of this with a disheveled look before hurling himself at the headless body.

Chaos ensued. More mascots were struck. The stuffed chair managed to gallop into the frontmost row of seated children. A parent was slapped. Picture books flew through the air, pages rustling like injured birds. There was fur stuck to Morgenthaler from one of the costumes. His inner child—a tiny anarchist, a miniature id-monster—was screaming to be free.

Everything was anarchy, except for the redheaded teen girl standing in the back of the crowd.

"Kill your dreams now, children!" Morgenthaler shrilled. "Kill them before New York gets to them and mutates them like . . . like . . ."

The squid suit dragged him into the back.

After they had all gone—the children, the parents, the book-sellers, the publicist, the mascots—Morgenthaler shuffled back out into his gallery and stood in the afternoon light. The gallery was an enormous concrete and glass space now that everyone was gone. His phone was buzzing. He was sure it was his agent. He did not want to talk to his agent.

He looked up and realized he was not alone in the gallery. A teen girl remained. She stood next to a swirling 3-D piece that he had offered to represent because he didn't understand it. She had red hair and looked nothing like his estranged wife, but suddenly he was reminded of what it was like to find one of her hairs on his clothing. It was not a pleasant feeling.

He thought he had locked the door.

"The event's over," he said. "It's all over."

"I'm looking for Hennessy," she said.

"What?"

She didn't repeat herself. "I believe that you can help me."

Morgenthaler couldn't even help himself. He'd tried to open a bottle of sparkling water just five minutes ago to drown his sorrows and had found the lid too difficult to get off.

"I don't know any Hennessy," he said.

The girl pointed to a painting on the wall. "But you must. Hennessy painted that."

She was pointing at a painting called *River Scene*. The artist's name—Joe Jones—was in the corner, as was a date: 1941.

"Kid," Morgenthaler said, "that's a sixty-thousand-dollar painting from, like, a hundred years ago. Joe's dead. I don't know who you're looking for. Ask me something else."

She scrutinized his expression, then rubbed her elbow softly, absently. "Can I . . . stay here?"

"What?"

"Just for tonight." She gestured to the chic couch close to *River Scene*. "Please."

Okay, she was homeless. Things made sense to him now. The publicist had said something about homeless people just the other day, but he couldn't remember what. He wondered if he wasn't a good listener.

"There's shelters," he told the girl. Probably there were shelters. This seemed like a thing that happened in cities, and this was a city.

"I need to stay someplace without people."

She was not crying, but she was twisting her hands fast in the way Morgenthaler knew usually preceded tears. He hoped she didn't actually cry because then he would cry; he had always been both a sympathetic puker and crier.

"You can't," he said. "I'm sorry. It wouldn't be right. There's valuable stuff here."

He expected her to protest again, but she went to the door gently, without another word. When he opened the door, he felt a rush of warm air from the street, strange in this weather. The door closed behind her. He locked it.

She would be all right, he thought. Probably. Right?

He felt strangely bereft as the seconds ticked by. It was not what she had asked for but what she hadn't asked for. It wasn't that she reminded him of his wife; it was that she hadn't. It wasn't that she had made him forget about the frustration of the day; it was that she had made him feel it even more acutely.

Suddenly, he threw back the bolt, pushed open the door, and rushed a few steps down the walk.

"Hey," he shouted. "Hey!"

She had made it several yards already. She stopped on the sidewalk.

"I'll drive you," he said. "To a shelter. To get some food."

She smiled very sweetly and very sadly, then shook her head, her feet already starting to take her away. "I don't want you to get hurt."

She turned and walked away, and both of them began to cry.

41

As night fell, Ronan walked Adam to the end of the driveway, Chainsaw hunched on his shoulder, the dreamt sun tucked into the hood of his sweater to cast some light around their feet. His three hours were up, and now the carriage was to turn back into a pumpkin, the horses back into mice. Adam was trying to ride the dreamt motorcycle at the same pace as Ronan's fast walk, turning the handles this way and that to maintain a wobbly straight line, making the headlight shake its head uncertainly no. It seemed at any moment he would dump it, but he hadn't yet. Ronan didn't know where Adam had learned to ride in the first place. Possibly the mechanic he'd worked for during high school had taught him. Maybe someone at his warehouse job. Adam picked up skills like other people picked up clothing or groceries. He was always in the market.

Now his shadowed face was lost in concentration. One hand rested lightly over the clutch lever and the other over the brake; the one over the brake was wrapped neatly with gauze, the only physical evidence of the scrying session. It was hard to tell what lingered mentally. Ronan knew that scream and the dread that came with it were going to live with him for a long time.

There was something out there so awful that Adam couldn't bear to have it look at him.

But whatever had made him scream was afraid of Bryde.

Ronan's mind turned this over and over and over.

Just before the end of the driveway, Adam tried to stop the bike and dumped it instead, the front wheel buckling suddenly to the left and depositing the bike on top of him. He made a soft, ordinary sound of pain and frustration, and Chainsaw flapped off, looking betrayed. The two of them heaved it back up.

"I always forget . . ." Adam said, but didn't say what he always forgot.

Ronan threw his leg over the bike instead, holding the wheel straight, taking care not to make the same mistake Adam had. Sitting on it felt good, physical, tangible. "Next time you can teach me how to do this the real way, Parrish."

"Return the favor," Adam said, and after a moment, Ronan realized he was talking about the time long ago when Ronan had taught him to drive stick shift. "You don't have to do this for me."

Ronan peered into the darkness, where the dreamy security system hung invisibly over the end of the driveway. "I go in and out of it every day. I'm used to it."

Adam made a dubious sound. But he didn't reject the gift.

"Take the sun thing." Ronan waited until Adam had reached into his hood to retrieve the sun. "That tree over there, the oak with that low branch? Walk around the outside of that one to the road and you'll be clear of it. I'll meet you out there."

It struck Ronan then that he didn't want Adam to go. For many reasons: beginning with the bad feeling of that scream, proceeding through the way his body would miss Adam's when he curled in his bed, and finishing with the knowledge that something big and unknown lurked out there, unseeable to his dreamer's eyes, seeable to Adam's uncanny ones. It seemed incorrect that Adam visiting would have made his loneliness worse, but he missed him acutely even as he was looking at him.

Ronan had not said anything out loud, but Adam said, "I can't miss class in the morning." There was some comfort to seeing that he was stalling as much as Ronan, fidgeting beside the bike, touching a scuff on the tank from his ride down and then a scuff on Ronan's wrist from the murder crabs, turning his head sharply when a night bird came into range of his hearing ear, adjusting the zipper of his jacket. "Say something in Latin."

Ronan thought. *"Inuisus natalis adest, qui rure molesto et sine Adam tristis agendus erit."*

Some ancient poetry bitching about spending one's birthday without a loved one felt apt.

Adam thought it through and then laughed. *"Propertius?* No. *Sulpicia?"*

"Sulpicia. Are you sure I can't drive you?" Eight hours back to Harvard, through the night, on a bike. Ronan was still tired from the nightwash and too many nights of checkered sleep, but he'd stay awake if he was with Adam.

"Matthew wants you for your birthday, and you can't let him down. I'm awake. I promise. I'm very awake. I have a lot to think about."

They both did.

Letting out a breath, Ronan began to walk the bike toward the dreadful security system. Adam patted the tank twice as a *good luck* and headed off to pick through the woods.

Ronan steeled himself as he would steel himself for dreaming. He reminded himself of where his physical body was in the present. He reminded himself that what was about to happen to him was in the past.

Then he headed through the gauzy dreamt security system.

Memories rose up. He expected it to be horror, as it often was. Guts and blood. Bones and hair. Closed-casket funerals. The scream.

Instead it was every time Ronan had been alone.

There was no gore. No shrilling with terror.

There was only the quiet that came after all those things. There was only the quiet that came when you were the only one left. Only the quiet that came when you were something strange enough to outsurvive the things that killed or drove away everyone you loved.

And then Ronan was through and swiping away the tears before Adam joined him by the shoulder, emerging from the dark with the bright dreamt light cupped in his hands.

"Break will be here in just a few days," Adam said. He kissed Ronan's cheek, lightly, and then Ronan's mouth. "I'm coming back. Be here for me."

"*Tamquam*——" Ronan said.

"*——alter idem.*"

They embraced. Adam put on his helmet.

Ronan stood there in the dark long after the taillight had disappeared. Alone.

Then he returned to the house to dream of Bryde.

42

There was a time when Jordan used to fantasize about living on her own. When she turned eighteen, the idea of it was like a crush, an obsession, something that dully ached during the day and frothed her to sleeplessness at night. She'd even gone to look at an apartment one day, telling the others she was going to work at the NGA and then secretly going to the appointment she'd set up.

The property manager had shown her a unit that reeked like chlorine and dog urine, had rooms the size of elevators, had only one parking space, and was a dispiriting fourteen miles from the city.

"I've got a lot of interest in this one," she'd said.

Jordan thought about how she would capture the line of the property manager's heavy-lidded eyes, how they never opened all the way, how that weight was signaled by the skin between her eyebrows, tugged by the longtime burden of staying awake. Her painter's mind catalogued the color gradient between her subtle dye job and her lighter roots. Her fingers twitched by her side, already blocking out the negative space behind the manager's profile.

The manager said, "So if you want to be in consideration, I'd get an application and fee in ASAP. A. SAP."

Jordan didn't like thinking about applications, because she didn't like thinking about prison. She really didn't want to go to prison. It might not have appeared that way—seeing as she spent much of her time doing things that were against laws of all shapes and sizes—but she spent a considerable amount of time thinking of ways to avoid it. For instance, she was careful with what she forged. She forged art, not checks. Lithographs, not money. Paintings, not certificates of authenticity. Historically, the law was kinder to those who forged brushstrokes of all kinds instead of pen marks of any kind.

The manager looked at Jordan. She was standing directly next to a stain on the beige carpet. She had not even bothered to stand in front of or on it in an attempt to hide it. The apartment was not at a price point that required her to. "It'll be just you?"

"Yeah," Jordan lied.

"I've got some one-bedrooms that are cheaper than this, honey."

"I need the extra room for my studio," Jordan said. "I do the old nine to five from home."

The manager tapped on the counter. "You want to look around some more and fill the pre-application out here, honey, you can drop it back off at the office on your way out."

A Post-it note was stuck to the top of the unforgiving application with the appointment time and a name: JORDAN HENNESSY. As if Jordan owned both those names equally. Jordan looked at it for thirty seconds, thinking about how she would re-create the shadow just under the curled edge of the Post-it note, how she would evoke the sense of distance from the paper below, what it would take to replicate the limpid yellow of the note.

Then she had taken a walk around the town house, trying to imagine what it would be like to live there. The little bed-rooms with their flimsy closet doors, their cheap light fixtures overhead—she had to take out her phone to snap a photo of the dead flies caught in the globe of it, because there was something angelic and ephemeral about the way the light came around their bodies in a soft nimbus. She imagined the Supra parked out front, her never having to wonder if one of the other girls had taken it and broken it. She imagined painting here. She imagined painting her own work, not forgeries.

She stood in the tiny bathroom and looked at herself in the mirror. Hennessy's face looked back at her.

She was just playing pretend. No matter how clearly Jordan could paint the picture in her head, she would never be able to replicate it in real life.

She knew the numbers. One thousand, two hundred, seventy-eight. Number of square feet. One thousand, three hundred, ninety-five. Dollars per month for rent. Two thousand, seven hundred, ninety. The first month's rent plus security deposit.

But those weren't the damning numbers.

The damning number was this: six (this was right before Farrah, the fourth copy, had shot herself). The number of girls she lived with: six. The number of girls she shared a face with: six. The number of girls she shared a social security number with: six.

The number of girls she shared an entire life with: six.

The others never found out that she went to look, but Hennessy found out when the property manager called to follow up a week later. Jordan hadn't said anything to explain herself. Hennessy said, "I'd leave me, too."

"Professional beauty," Hennessy said, blowing a smoke ring. She looked disastrous. Black rivulets ran from her eyes. Her ears. Her nostrils. Coated her teeth. She could have passed as ordinary when Jordan found her at the harbor with *The Dark Lady* a little while earlier. She wouldn't be able to now.

Now she bled black and monstrous before the real *Dark Lady*.

Jordan was displeased to find that they'd somehow gotten her wrong when they copied her. Some variation was understandable, given the unideal circumstances they'd been working with—referencing photos and stolen glances at previous public sales. But it wasn't that the brushstrokes or colors were wrong. It was the atmosphere. The original *Dark Lady* had a verve and magnetism that the copy completely lacked. Desire oozed from the original.

Hennessy had said it was because it was a dream.

Jordan didn't know anything about dreams, apart from herself and the other girls. She hadn't realized they could have feeling attached to them. That seemed like a lot of power for one person to have.

Hennessy gestured with her cigarette at the bullet-holed *Madame X*, which leaned next to *The Dark Lady* ("bitches need company," she'd said). "That's what they called hens like her. PBs. Pro. Fessional. Beauties. Everything roses and riches as long as her face was in order. She dusted herself in lavender powder, didn't she, to be that color? Could any of us do what she did? Prepare ourselves for the public eye, ensure that everything about us was ready for no-strings adoration?"

Hennessy had selected one of the mansion's several master bathrooms to try out *The Dark Lady*'s influence. Like every other room in the house, it was outrageous: two hundred square feet, marble floors, tufted armchairs, two toilets, fourteen shower-heads, a bidet. Everything that could be black was black. Everything else was gold. The massive jetted tub was sunk into the floor like a swimming pool, and it was in this empty tub Hennessy reclined, fully dressed in lace, leather, and black ooze. Jordan couldn't figure it out. Hennessy lived a sleep-deprived life, always perched in uncomfortable places, her phone timer carefully set for eighteen or twenty minutes, everything designed to keep her from dreaming. If Jordan had been in the same situation, she would've used this opportunity to luxuriate in sleep for once. Do it right. Bath. Pajamas. Best mattress available, piled high with pillows and duvets. Yes, if she dreamt a copy, it was going to be hell on the other side. But at least she would've gotten wonderful sleep for once. A lemonade/lemons situation.

But Jordan had always seemed more built for lemonade, and Hennessy more for lemons.

"Jordan. Jordan. Jorrrddaaaaaaaan."

"I'm listening," Jordan said. She sat on the edge of the tub, her legs dangling into empty air. She imagined the air was water. She longed for it to be water. One of her strange episodes had begun on the drive from the harbor back here, and now, part of her was once again being made to look at water plunging over rocks, turbulent clouds of smoke rolling over asphalt, moss on rocks, mist ghosting over blue mountains. She felt thirsty for all of it. If she went to the mountains, she thought, she wouldn't feel like this. Starving. Suffocating. Deprived of something she needed to live.

"Read back the last sentence I dictated."

Jordan gave Hennessy the finger.

"Did you like your date with Monsieur Declan Lynch?" Hennessy asked. "You're probably the coolest thing that yob's scored in his life. It'll be the topic of his therapy for decades."

"He gave me a jar of Tyrian purple."

"How'd he score that overnight?" When Jordan didn't speculate, Hennessy continued, "His old man was a dreamer. Or signed his name to someone else's dream. Is that what we're thinking? Is Declan Lynch a dreamer? Did he dream those snails for you? Does that make them real, if he did? Is anything real if you give it a think? Is some maladjusted god fitfully populating his nightmare with us, praying to his own unnamed god that he'll wake up? Is—"

"Hennessy."

She was stalling.

"Jordan."

She knew she was.

Jordan slid down into the tub beside her, inhaling sharply where the tub was cold against her bare skin. The tub was gritty in the bottom. It hadn't been used for its intended purpose for years. Maybe ever. It was impossible to discover the mansion's backstory; squatting here was only possible because the owners and its history were thoroughly absent. It was difficult to imagine it ever being vibrant and loved, vacuumed and lived in. A place like this didn't seem like it had been built for intimacy.

Hennessy put her head down on Jordan's shoulder. Jordan stroked her temples lightly as Hennessy's wide-open brown eyes looked up at the ceiling. Black leaked from the corners. If Jordan looked closely, she could see the darkness leaking into her pupils, too, wicking from the edges like into blotter paper. It wasn't right, she thought. It just wasn't right. It wasn't that it wasn't *fair*. She was sure between the two of them they'd done plenty to deserve anything they had coming to them. But it wasn't *right*. It was *wrong*. It looked corrupt.

"Heloise," she said, "you're getting to where if you don't give it away, the man'll take it from you."

Hennessy's throat moved as she swallowed. The movement sent three tiny rivers of black from her ears down over her neck. She was frightened. She didn't say it, but Jordan knew she was. Not of dying, but of whatever it was she dreamt of every time she let herself sleep for longer than twenty minutes. On many sleepless nights, Jordan had tried to imagine what she herself could possibly dream of that was so terrible she couldn't bear even a minute of it. She couldn't think of a single thing, but what would she know? Dreams didn't dream.

Jordan put her hand over Hennessy's eyes until the feather touch of her eyelashes against her palm told her that Hennessy had finally closed her eyes.

The Dark Lady watched them both with that mistrustful, pessimistic look.

"It's going to work," Jordan said. She wasn't sure if she was addressing the painting or Hennessy. "Take a think about the seaside. All kinds of nice shit there. Portable things. Seashells. Sand toys . . . umbrellas . . ."

"Sharks . . . jellyfish . . ." Hennessy's head was so heavy, but Jordan didn't want to move in case she was the only thing making her sleep. She leaned her chin against her hair. In the mirrors, they looked nearly the same, only Hennessy was ruined and bleeding and Jordan was unmarked and dreamy.

Images flickered at the edges of Jordan's eyes. A waterfall. The mountains. A starving fire.

"I'm so knackered," Hennessy said. "I'm so goddamn knackered."

"I know," whispered Jordan. "I know you are."

They slept.

43

Ronan was dreaming.

He was lucid and electric in this dream, perfectly aware of both his sleeping and his waking forms. Of course he would be. His physical body was close to the ley line and his mountains. Chainsaw, his psychopomp, his dream guide, hunched on the sill of his bedroom's window. He knew what he wanted.

Under these conditions, he was a king.

"Bryde," he said out loud.

In the dream, Ronan stood in Lindenmere, lovely Lindenmere. His forest. His protector and his protected. The trees were massive and shaggy, green and orange lichen scaling their northern sides. Between them, boulders tumbled over one another, moss softening their edges. Mist moved darkly between the trunks, gray, shaggy breath from words just spoken into the air. The sound of water was omnipresent: rivers flowing, waterfalls hushing, rain pattering. Mushrooms and flowers ventured between stumps and fallen logs. In some places, it looked beautiful and ordinary. In other places, it was beautiful and extraordinary.

It was perhaps the purest expression of Ronan's imagination.

"Bryde, are you here?" Ronan called. He climbed through the woods. He could feel the strain of climbing in his calves as well as he would've if he'd been actually doing it.

He didn't know if other dreamers had forests, or whatever

Lindenmere was. Lindenmere was a forest like this: Ronan could close his eyes and get to it in his dreams. Lindenmere was also a forest like this: Ronan could get in the BMW and drive thirty minutes west, up into the mountains, abandon his car on a fire trail, and walk the remaining twenty minutes to the forest where it existed in real life. He could step between those familiar trees and find they knew him and cared for him and manifested his thoughts in the waking world nearly as easily as they did in the dream world. The real-life Lindenmere was a place to dream without closing your eyes.

He had dreamt it into being. One day, there had been nothing but ordinary trees high in the blue mountains. And then the next, he had woken up, and there was Lindenmere hidden among them.

It was perhaps his best dream.

"I suppose you'd say both versions of Lindenmere are equally real," Ronan said into the trees. He reached into the moving air. The mist curled around him. "I can feel you here, Bryde."

Greywaren, murmured Lindenmere, the sound coming from the trees, or the water, or from everywhere. This was Lindenmere's name for him. It knew his real name as well, and sometimes called him that, but Ronan hadn't figured out why it sometimes chose one or another. *Greywaren, he is here.*

He knew Lindenmere was not exactly a forest. Lindenmere seemed to have previously existed somewhere else as . . . something else. And then Ronan, in a dream, had chosen its form in this world. He had not quite dreamt it into being the way he'd dreamt other things into being. He had just opened the door for it and chosen a forest-shaped suit for it to wear.

"You told me to chase," Ronan said. "Here I am."

He found himself looking at a deep creek. A bridge floated

over it. A motorcycle was parked upon it. It was precisely the Harvard dream.

But he wasn't far away from his forest and his ley line now. His thoughts weren't confused and fragmented. This dream was his kingdom and it would do what he bid it.

"No more games," Ronan said impatiently. He lifted his hand. Snapped his fingers. The motorcycle was gone. The bridge was gone. The creek was gone. The dream was exactly as he wanted it.

He had worked hard to be able to control his dreams so well, and it was easy to forget how good he was at it when he was in DC or farther afield, in Cambridge, or half-dead with night-wash. It was easy to forget how much he loved it.

Things begin to fall asleep. Sparrows fall from the sky. Deer canter and jolt to their knees. Trees cease their growing. Children fall into gentle comas. So many creatures sleep that once roamed, imagination trapped in stasis. There are dragons sleeping underground who will never stir again.

"I don't want a monologue," Ronan said.

All around us the world is falling asleep, but no one's looking out their window anymore to mark it. Dreamers are dying. Dreamers are being killed. We are not immortal. And the things we dream . . . What is a dream without its dreamer? It's an animal in a room without air. It's man on a dead planet. It's religion without a god. They sleep without us because they must.

Ronan called, "Why did you save me?"
Bryde said, "Why do I have to get something out of it?"

This

was

different.

Ronan spun in a circle, looking for someone else in the forest. This voice had not been amorphous, coming from everywhere. This voice had weight and timbre. This voice had moved through space to get to him. This voice belonged to a body.

"I'm not going to show myself," Bryde said, his voice sharper, either through reality or circumstance.

"I could make you," Ronan said, and knew it was true. When he felt like this, dreaming on his ley line, dreaming of his forest, he could do nearly anything.

"I believe you," Bryde replied. Ronan turned just in time to see the edge of a shadow, the movement of mist. Something had just been there. "But do you want to see each other or do you want to trust each other?"

Ronan didn't know what he wanted.

Overhead, he heard Chainsaw caw. He knew it was not really his Chainsaw; it was another dream version of her. It didn't matter; he liked hearing her, and he was in no danger of manifesting anything he didn't want when he was dreaming like this.

"Would you save a dying dreamer?" Bryde asked. "Even if you didn't know them?"

"Yes," Ronan answered immediately.

"There are factors affecting that yes. There are costs, you know. Emotional costs. Philanthropy is a hobby for the emotionally rich. "

Rain pattered down on the leaves around him and onto Ronan's shoulders. He could feel its wetness but his clothing remained undampened: dream rules.

"Next box," Bryde said. "Next box. Throw a pebble. Hop. Jump. Closer to the center. There's another dreamer, and she's dying. Or she will be. Will you save her?"

Another dreamer. "Yes."

"Don't just say yes. Think about it. Think about what it means."

This was stupid. Ronan was no hero, but he knew fucking right from fucking wrong. It didn't matter if it was another dreamer. The answer was the same either way. A child knew the answer to this question. "Yes."

"It is not as easy as you think," Bryde said. "It's not pull a lever receive a prize. There are a lot of ways to die."

Ronan was getting impatient.

"You want me to trust you?" Bryde asked. "Save her. Really save her. It's going to mean telling her what you are. It will cost you, emotionally."

"Did it cost you to save me?"

There was a long silence. The mist shimmered darkly in the trees. The rain sighed.

Bryde said finally, "You are the most expensive thing I have ever saved."

An address dropped into Ronan's knowledge. Just like that. McLean, Virginia. He could see the shape of the drive there. He could see the house the address belonged to. He could see a red Supra in the driveway. A garden designed by a frantic and frustrated chess set designer. A back door, unlocked, a back staircase, a long hallway, a room entirely in black and gold.

"Is that where she is?" Ronan asked.

Bryde whispered, "Better drive like the fucking wind, boy."

44

The air in the bathroom was gone.

It was hard to tell how long it had been gone. Long enough that Jordan was already drowning. She had begun dying at some point before she opened her eyes and she was already well into the process now.

Her lungs were howling.

Water was everywhere. The room was full of it, tile to ceiling, complete with it. Towels undulated like sea slugs, toilet paper kelp thrashed in a receding wave. Jordan was just another thing floating in it. Hennessy, too.

Hennessy looked dead.

She was expressionless. Her arms and legs drifting like a corpse.

But she wasn't dead, or Jordan wouldn't be awake. She was paralyzed. She must have brought back a copy.

Focus, Jordan told herself.

Her body screamed for air, but the priority was getting *Hennessy* air. If Hennessy died, it was endgame for both of them.

She swam to Hennessy, kicking off her boots on the way, pushing off the edge of the shower glass to propel herself. When she gripped Hennessy's wrist, her pulse was slow and violent, palpable even in this situation. Dreaming another copy was working its foul consequence on Hennessy, even though the paralysis meant she couldn't react to it yet.

She was dead weight. Jordan had already moved past the lights sparking in her vision part of dying and straight into the darkness shuttering either side of it part. She tried to get some momentum by kicking off the ceiling, but everything was strange and unfamiliar, too hard, too impossible to remember.

Suddenly Hennessy jerked, nearly pulling out of Jordan's grip. Jordan tightened her fingers and was towed. Forward. Down.

Hennessy's legs still drifted, paralyzed.

But still she jerked forward through the gritty water.

Then Jordan saw what was pulling her: another girl with her face, dressed as they all were when they were new: white T-shirt, nice jeans, flowers on the ass pockets.

Another copy.

She had been born into this hell and her first conscious act was doing exactly what Jordan was doing: saving Hennessy.

Together they hauled Hennessy to the door—the bathroom seemed enormous.

The door wouldn't give way.

Was it locked? Was that why this wouldn't work? No, *think*, Jordan, she told herself. It was because the door opened in, and the weight of thousands of pounds of water was keeping it shut.

It seemed impossible that the room was still full of water; it had to be escaping under the door and through the air-conditioning vents and down the drains.

But not fast enough.

Jordan had no more ideas.

Her lungs were a thrashing animal. A dying animal.

Jordan had only one thought: *No one knew I existed.* Her entire life had been spent as Jordan Hennessy, an existence shared with between six and ten other entities at any given time. Same face, same smile, same driver's ID, same career, same boyfriends, same girlfriends. A flowchart where the only choices available were the ones she could crowd-source to the other girls. *Why do you only paint what other people have already painted?* Declan Lynch had asked. Because her brush had already come pre-loaded with someone else's palette.

She'd painted hundreds of paintings with astonishing skill and no one would know she ever existed.

She'd only ever lived someone else's life.

No one knew I existed.

The new copy had released Hennessy and floated off a little bit away. Her eyes were looking at nothing.

Slam.

Slam.

Was it sound or movement? It felt like the water was shaking, or Jordan was shuddering.

She'd spent all this time thinking the end would come with eternal sleep. She hadn't thought she might simply die.

Slam.

Then suddenly the water was draining, feeling as it did like Jordan's skin was peeling from her scalp down.

Jordan sucked in a lungful of air, and then another, and then another. She'd never have enough air again. Beside her, Hennessy was coughing and burbling but making no other movement; Jordan dragged her still-limp body up until she was no longer bubbling. They both were sitting in a few inches of water, but it didn't matter because there was air, air, air.

Oh, the copy, the copy—Jordan splashed through the water to the new girl. She was dead. Jordan tried to revive her, but she stayed dead. She'd only ever lived in a nightmare.

"Crumbs," Jordan said.

The door swung in. It was split unevenly down the middle, splinters jutting inward.

A young man stood in the threshold, lit by weak early morning light. In his hand was the tire iron he'd used to split the door. He had pale skin, a shaved head, sharp eyebrows, sharp mouth, sharp expression. His face was unfamiliar but his eyes were a very, very familiar blue.

Jordan demanded, "Who are you, fuck-arse?"

"I know you're a dreamer," he said.

All the air she thought she'd gotten into her lungs felt like it had vanished.

He paused. His lips were parted to say something else, but he didn't. The words were right there, queued up, but he didn't let them free.

Finally, he said, "And I am, too."

45

Jordan had always known there had to be other dreamers out there. J. H. Hennessy had been a dreamer like her daughter, after all, and like they said about mice, where there was one there was four. There had to be other dreamers out there. Maybe lots of other dreamers. Well, probably not lots. The world would look different, she thought, if there were a lot of other people who could manifest their imagination, even if they were all stifled in ways similar to Hennessy.

She didn't think she'd ever meet another one.

That seemed for the best, really. She figured dreamers were probably like forgers. People forged art for all kinds of reasons. They forged for the money, they forged for the challenge of it, they forged for the lulz. They forged paintings and textiles, drawings and sculpture. What tickled one forger's fancy might leave another entirely cold. It didn't seem like they'd have any more in common with each other than with anyone else. They were also a pretty dysfunctional bunch. Forgers lived at the fringes of the art world, if not society in general. Either situation or personality kept them from swimming along with everyone else. They were neither artist nor criminal.

Jordan didn't see why dreamers should be any different, except with even higher stakes. Might another dreamer have insight into fixing Hennessy? Maybe. Might another dreamer get them all killed? Equally likely.

"Why are you here?" Jordan asked Ronan Lynch. She was sitting, leaned against the wall of the hallway, drenched, dream-logged. Her leggings felt clammy and unpleasant next to her chilly skin. Her brain was drenched, too—she was just as deep into one of her dreamy episodes as antediluvian Jordan had been, struggling to piece together reality from the foggy images of water and talons and fire. The other girls were all frozen in various artful positions in the hall, having arrived just a few seconds after Ronan had busted the door down. They'd been drawn by the sound of the door's destruction, rather than any knowledge of Hennessy's imminent death. If he hadn't arrived, the other girls would've gone to eternal sleep elsewhere in the mansion, never knowing their dreamer had drowned meters away.

Hennessy looked dead, the skin beneath her eyes purpled and her joints loose and unmanned by her consciousness. But she couldn't be, since all her dreams were still awake and coming forward to pull her limp body free from the pooled water.

"That's a funny way of saying *thank you for saving my life*," Ronan said.

He looked like his brother, in a harder way, like Declan Lynch had been inserted into a pencil sharpener and Ronan Lynch had been taken out after. Declan's teeth were even; Ronan's were bared. Declan's eyes were narrow; Ronan's were arrow slits. Declan's hair was curled; Ronan's was obliterated. Declan looked like the kind of person you forgot you'd ever seen. Ronan looked like the kind of person that made you cross to the other side of the street. It was hard to imagine they'd grown up under the same roof; if Jordan had been told they'd been separated as children, she'd have believed it.

Jordan said, "If I showed up on your doorstep, just like that, don't you think you'd ask me the same thing?"

Ronan lifted his feet, one, then the other, watching the way the sodden carpet changed in color as he did. The whole hallway had an unappealing odor now that it was wet; it smelled abandoned, moldy, toxic, not really livable. "No, I think I'd start with a solid 'thanks, man,' first."

"Easy, easy, she's ruined," June hissed as she and Brooklyn propped Hennessy against the wall beside Jordan. As they did, Jordan saw that a brand-new flower marred Hennessy's throat. Room for just two more. Jordan felt sick. Genuinely sick, her stomach heaving and warm. Two was only one less than three, but it felt different. It was no longer really a number. It was *the second to last copy* and then *the last.*

Hennessy's head rolled to the side, but she wasn't entirely passed out; her eyelids fluttered. Even now she battled sleeping. Battled dreaming. Another copy right now would surely be the end of her, no matter what the tattoo on her throat promised.

The Dark Lady hadn't worked.

Jordan had no more ideas.

The mountains flickered in Jordan's thoughts. Fire whispered: *devour.*

Get

it

together.

She was Jordan, and she was the girl who didn't fall apart.

"Well, thanks, mate," Jordan said. "Now, why are you here? Did your brother send you?"

It didn't seem possible that she could feel more bad feeling on top of her current level of bad feeling, but thinking about

Declan Lynch discovering that Jordan had played him managed to deftly add a large amount of shittiness to her situation.

"My brother?" Ronan echoed. "Oh—right. I thought you looked . . . You were the painter at the Market, weren't you? The one he chatted up. Is your name Ashley?"

Jordan said, "What?"

"I'm pretty sure he only dates Ashleys," Ronan said. "The stupider, the better. Just in case you were thinking of calling him back. I wouldn't, personally. It looks like a very boring time. Why are there so fucking many of you? That's messed up. Which of you is the original?"

All of them looked to Hennessy.

Ronan sounded dubious. "Shouldn't she have . . . CPR?"

"If drowning was what ailed her, you'd be right, young man," said Brooklyn. It was the end of the world, but she still spared a moment to check out his body, because she was Brooklyn. Her face said the moment was worth it. "If only it was drowning what ailed us."

"I'm after a blanket," Trinity said, slipping down the hall.

Ronan leaned his head around the corner of the doorway to glance inside the bathroom they'd come from. He made a small *hm* sound, though it was hard to tell from the back of his head if it was over the ridiculousness of the bathroom, the presence of *Madame X*, or the dead copy. He was very lackadaisical about the entire experience. Like it was just another day. Like he expected *them* to also feel like it was just another day. "Bryde told me where to find you. Said you'd be dying and to get my ass moving."

"Fairy Market Bryde?" Madox said. "The one they were all going on about?"

Jordan removed a long, damp hair from inside her mouth. It was stuck to some damp fuzz, too. Almost-drowning came with all kinds of unpredicted small and large miseries. "How does this Bryde know who we are?"

Ronan pushed his toe against a very ugly satin hand towel that must have been in the bathroom before the flood. "How the hell should I know? I don't even know how he knows who *I* am. I've only met him in dreams. Maybe your dreamer met him there."

Jordan had never heard of such a thing, but even if it were possible, it didn't seem possible for Hennessy. She had only dreamt a dozen times in as many years.

Trinity returned with a blanket to gently roll Hennessy onto. After the girls had assembled her on it, Hennessy murmured, "Set . . ." She closed her eyes, wincing. "Set my timer."

"Your phone's fucked," said Trinity. "I'll put it on rice."

"I got you," June said. She set a twenty-minute timer on her phone before resting it on Hennessy's chest. Hennessy gripped it with the neediness of a child handed a favorite toy. As Trinity and Brooklyn picked up either end of the blanket like a stretcher, Ronan ran a hand along his shaved head, looking perplexed. He cast a look around the drenched hallway and the drenched corpse and the drenched décor that had managed to escape the bathroom with Hennessy and Jordan. He remarked, "This is really fucked up."

Jordan agreed. It was really fucked up.

There's always another idea, she told herself. *You have to just open your eyes, there'll be another one. Come on, Jordan.*

She climbed to her feet. She felt wobbly as a new colt, like she'd swum a mile instead of across a bathroom. Her throat was sore as if she'd been screaming instead of drowning. Her mind felt stronger standing to face Ronan, but her body resented it. "Dude, we're grateful. But I mean it in the nicest possible way that I think you ought to tell Bryde to forget he ever knew we existed."

"You—" Ronan broke off as a framed piece of debris caught his eye. Turning the frame over, he found the Dark Lady peering at him bitterly. She was less damaged than any of them by the events; her glossy varnish beaded water but was otherwise unharmed. "I thought I recognized that. What, as the kids say, the fuck? Why would you copy this?"

Jordan, June, and Madox all exchanged looks. Why indeed.

June's expression said, *Well?* Jordan supposed they might as well give it back. There was no point sticking Declan Lynch with a copy when the original wasn't doing them any good. No point trying to keep Declan Lynch from knowing the others had nabbed it while she was out with him. No point to any of this whole damn business now that *The Dark Lady* had failed.

No point to—

Jordan had an idea.

"How good of a dreamer are you?" she asked.

Ronan raised an eyebrow.

"If you are one at all. Maybe we should ask you to prove it."

He grinned. It was a sharp, durable expression, hard-won. "I'm going to need someplace dry to lie down."

46

By the next workday, Declan decided he was glad there hadn't been anything beneath the backing paper of *The Dark Lady*. Thank God, really. It had stopped him from being stupid. He'd gotten an idea in his head and the obsession with it had carried him through several weeks of increasingly risky behavior, late-night phone calls, trips to Boston, the Fairy Market, everything escalating without him quite realizing it, all common sense tased and tied up in the backseat. Who knew how far he would've gone? Far enough for something to get broken, probably. Far enough to throw away everything that he'd done to this point.

He had lawless DNA, after all. Niall was a charming bastard who was always happiest darting in and out of the shadows, and Declan wasn't stupid enough to pretend he didn't like it, too. No, it was good that he'd opened up the back of the painting and found it had been for nothing. Good that he hadn't gotten Jordan's number, that he'd left the ball in her court, so he wasn't tempted.

It was all good. It was all good.

Everything was back to the way it had been before.

"How are those printouts coming, Declan? We gotta get out of here," called Fairlady Banks, the senator's personal assistant, who was not as fair a lady as her name suggested.

Declan interned part time with Senator Jim Rankin, which

meant, practically, that he spent several hours a week making copies in the Hart Senate Office Building, a place of windowless offices and plaques and fluorescent lights and suits and ties and staffers walking without lifting their eyes from their phones and take-out brought up from the lobby by people like Declan.

He was not making copies that morning, but only because he'd already finished them—they were fresh enough from the printer to be still sweet-smelling and warm. He was binding them into handouts, a slightly different menial task. He regarded his watch—God, there was so much more of this day left, it had only just begun—and guessed at the answer Fairlady wanted. "Ten minutes."

"How about eight?"

When he nodded, she moved on to carry two cases of locally sourced organic beverages outside to the hand truck in the hall. The senator was visiting a group of local growers today to discuss how they felt about regulation of farmers' markets, and it was important to show solidarity when feeding and watering them.

Declan didn't hate his job, which was good, because he'd probably be doing some version of it for the rest of his life. There was a point before his father died when he thought he might one day have a word like *Senator* or *Congressman* in front of his name, too, but he knew now that was too much exposure for his family. Still, there were plenty of jobs in government that didn't draw attention. Plenty of jobs that were fine. Livable. He just had to keep performing the delicate, inconspicuous dance of being just good enough to continue being hired, but not good enough to stand out.

Fairlady clicked by him again, making her path to the next

case of drinks cleave close to him, not because it needed to, but to remind him that he had a job to be done in six minutes.

He kept working. When he was finished here, he'd pick up Matthew from school, and then meet Ronan for his birthday. Last year, Ronan had given himself the gift of dropping out of high school for his birthday, throwing away all of Declan's studious efforts to drag him through to a degree. He hoped Ronan wasn't intending on doing anything as stupid for this birthday. Declan had gotten him a membership for the zoo; what did you get for the man who could make himself anything? It would be a nice outing. A quiet afternoon. Ordinary.

Everything back the way it was before.

Declan, said Jordan Hennessy, standing in the museum like a piece of art herself, enigmatic, open to interpretation, unobtainable.

He'd pulled so many strings for that Tyrian purple. Dangerous, complicated strings, a game of criminal telephone until he found someone overnight willing to trade him the pigment for the dreamt clock of Niall's that he'd had hidden in his bedroom closet for ages.

What an idiot. What was he thinking? He hadn't been thinking. He'd just been galloping after his id. That was Ronan's thing, not Declan's.

Last night he'd dreamt of the ocean, but not *The Dark Lady's* ocean. It seemed like he'd broken *The Dark Lady's* spell by tearing the backing paper from the canvas. The ocean he'd dreamt of hadn't been the tattered Irish seashore, not the pure, sandy Kerry beach that he was sure Aurora Lynch had never been to and Niall Lynch had.

No, Declan had dreamt of a tropical beach, his feet buried in the sand. In this paradise, he'd been forever putting sunscreen on his arms, never done putting sunscreen on his arms, an endless loop of squeezing coconut-scented cream onto his fingertips and swiping it onto his skin and squeezing coconut-scented cream onto his fingertips and swiping it onto his skin and squeezing coconut-scented cream onto his fingertips and swiping it onto his skin and . . .

A boring dream.

Better than the dream he'd had before. Better than the dream of him standing on *The Dark Lady*'s sandy Kerry shore and feeling seen, truly seen, truly exposed, watched from the high rocks and from the sky. Better than the dream of him stepping into that aqua water one foot and then another and then another, and then beginning to swim, and then diving, and then swimming so deep that the sunlight stopped piercing the water and he became invisible in the depths.

If he had Ronan's ability, would he have woken up erased?

"*David,*" snapped one of the aides.

Declan looked up. He knew this meant him. "Declan."

"Whichever. Is that your phone? Shut it up—he's on a conference for the next two minutes. Are those things done? We're leaving in three."

Declan's phone was ringing, fussing chaotically on top of a pile of paper clips. Caller ID: Matthew's school.

With an apologetic look at the aide, he picked it up. "Lynch."

"This is Barbara Cody from Thomas Aquinas," said the voice at the other end of the phone. "Your brother seems to have left the school grounds without notifying any of the staff again."

Again.

A half-dozen stories contained in that single word, every

single one of them ending at Great Falls. Declan clenched and unclenched his jaw. In a low voice, he said, "Thank you for letting me know."

"We don't want to start marking him up for it, but . . ."

They should've already; who was allowed to leave school grounds a half-dozen times without consequence? Sunny Matthew, of course, and his benevolently wandering feet.

"I understand. You and I are on the same team here."

"Please tell him that the school counselor would love to talk to him. We want to help."

"Of course." After Declan hung up, he stood there for a moment, feeling as if he was a suit that had been hung up.

"Lynch," barked Fairlady. "It's been nine minutes. The van is double-parked."

Ronan had to already be nearly to DC for his birthday; Declan called him. It rang and rang and rang and rang, then went to voicemail. He called it again. Again. Again. Again. Again. Again.

Calling Ronan was like throwing darts into the ocean. Once in a hundred years a lucky bastard hit a fish and the rest of the time he went hungry.

He texted: *Call me, it's about Matthew.*

"Lynch," Fairlady said.

Declan texted: *I can't leave work*

"Van," Fairlady said.

Declan texted: *Please get him from Great Falls*

"Now," Fairlady said. "Bring the name tags."

Fuck this fuck this fuck this fuck this fuck this fuck

For a brief moment Declan imagined hurling the phone and these collated copies and the pile of paper clips at the wall, trashing this whole place, marching out of his life, diving into the ocean, disappearing.

Then he slid his phone into his suit pocket and balanced a stack of printouts beneath his chin and said, "My youngest brother's having a health issue. I'm seeing about getting my other brother to handle it."

"Why have I never heard of this other brother?" Fairlady said.

Because she hadn't asked, and Declan never gave away a truth unless it was taken from his cold, balled hands. Because the safest shape was being both unknown and unchanging.

Fairlady called over her shoulder, "Odds that you'll have to handle it yourself?"

Declan said, "One hundred percent."

Everything exactly as it was before.

47

Ronan found himself standing on *The Dark Lady*'s seashore once more.

Behind him, tumbled black rocks rose, and under his feet, pale sand stretched in both directions. Before him was the familiar turquoise sea, the one that he'd just let out of the bathroom of the McLean mansion. He shivered. The cold was thorough and damp.

Bryde's voice came from somewhere above, among the rocks. "It used to rain more. The surface of this bare and drying planet used to be billowing with trees. Complicated with trees. These increasingly cloudless skies used to be tangled and alive with rain. Silver and black and purple above. Green and black and blue below. You should have seen it."

Ronan knelt and pushed his fingers into the sand. Feeling it. Really feeling it. The damp abrasion of this coarse sand, the cool pooling of the water when he pushed his fingers down far enough, the itch when the sand had been against the sensitive skin of his wrists for too long. He was far from his forest, but *The Dark Lady*'s spell was strong enough to invoke the seashore clearly.

"I know you feel anxious on sunny days," Bryde remarked. "You haven't said it out loud. You barely think it. *They* love the sunny days, after all. They love a naked sky with a savage white sun set in it like a killer jewel. It doesn't worry them. It's a string of rainy days that makes them grow languid and unsteady. Energy draining, depression eating the marrow out of their bones. Rainy days aren't for them. Do you think a tree hates a rainy day?"

Ronan straightened, looking around himself. Sand, rocks, a little palm leaf cross like a child would make for Palm Sunday wedged between rocks.

"Think of it this way: Fill a swimming pool and throw a fish in it," Bryde said. "You wouldn't do that because no one does. But imagine it. In goes the fish and it swims, swims, swims, all of the pool available to it. Now imagine the same pool without water in it. Throw a fish in it. What happens? You know what the hell happens. This is why there's nothing so ugly as a cloudless day. What will this world be like for us if they stop the rain? Sometimes I fucking weep for all those dead trees."

"Shut up," Ronan said. "I'm trying to work."

He was trying to hold both his sleeping and waking truths in his head at the same time—to stay conscious enough in the dream to shape the events within it, but not become so wakeful that he woke right up.

Bryde sounded amused. "Someone wants to show off."

Ronan ignored this; he wouldn't be goaded by someone who wasn't even visible.

And so what if he wanted to show off.

Bryde was quiet, in any case, as Ronan hunted up and down the beach; there wasn't anything impressive he'd want to take back to the mansion. Sand, rocks, some broken shells when he thrust his hand into the chilly water. He took the little palm leaf cross, but he wanted more.

"This is your world," Bryde said. "Only you limit it."

Only Ronan and *The Dark Lady*, really. Because he could feel how every time he pressed on the contents of the dream, something outside him tried to shape it back to this moment on this seashore.

"I'm too far away," Ronan said.

"I'm not going to help you," Bryde said. "Not when you can do it by yourself. Hop. Skip. Throw the pebble. What's in the next box? Surely you know this game by now."

Ronan thought of his physical body. On the couch, sprawled back, fingers splayed across the gaudy, expensive upholstery. Those paintings leaned up against it—yes.

Bryde laughed.

Bryde *laughed*. He knew what Ronan was going to manifest before he even began.

Ronan began to dig in the sand, imagining, remembering, projecting the truth of what he wanted with all his might, until his fingers felt a hard edge. He pawed with increasing intensity, pausing only to put the palm cross in his shirt where it wouldn't get crushed or forgotten. He could feel it scratching against his skin. Good. Then he'd be sure to remember it.

Then he dug and dug and dug until he'd uncovered his prize.

"Fucking A." He was pleased. Very pleased.

"A king always enjoys his throne," Bryde noted drily.

48

I *don't do drugs,* Salvador Dalí once said. *I am drugs.*

Ronan Lynch was breaking Jordan's brain. In the precise same moment that he woke from his dream in the McLean mansion, Jordan realized that she had never really believed that Hennessy had once dreamt things other than herself. She wasn't sure she'd ever really believed, on a gut level, that Hennessy had dreamt anything, which seemed ridiculous. Of course Jordan knew Hennessy was responsible for the girls with her face. But no one had ever caught her in the act. The only thing they'd ever each been present for was their own creations: coming to life beside a Hennessy paralyzed and agonized from the process. They never saw her go to sleep and wake with anything.

So although they lived this truth every single day, Jordan was astonished to find that she'd never truly believed it.

It was properly morning by now, and the light came in full and colorless through the big, pollen-crusted windows on one side of the room, erasing all shadows, turning the space into a showroom for modern art and urban decay. Above the house, a plane flying into Dulles was audible, the productive roar reminding them all that despite the bizarre night, an ordinary world was continuing for the rest of the greater DC area. The girls were all arrayed in the living room, gathered round the yellow Lexus as if around a warming fire, attention more or less upon Ronan Lynch, who was stretched on the shiny brocade sofa with its bullet holes in the back. He was tall enough that his shaved head wedged up against one corner and his boots crossed over the opposite armrest. While he slept and while Jordan recovered from her dream episode, she'd studied him and imagined how she would paint him. All the dark, angular lines of his clothing, the pale, angular lines of his skin, the coiled restlessness of him apparent even as he slept. What a portrait he and his brother would make, she thought.

Then Ronan woke, bringing his dreams with him.

And it broke Jordan's brain.

It wasn't that he woke, and things appeared suddenly beside him. It wasn't that they faded into existence. It wasn't anything that easy. It was more that he woke, and something about the time around him changed, something about the way everyone experienced the time around him. Because Jordan knew—she *knew*, she knew logically and academically and completely—that Ronan had been sprawled empty-handed on that couch, but now he held a large parcel, and her brain was trying its best to convince her that he had always been holding this new thing. Somehow reality had been edited to allow for the presence of something that hadn't been there before, without allowing her the revelation of seeing it come into being.

Trinity breathed, "Aw, *pants*," which seemed as good a response as any.

He had sand on his knees. Had he had sand on his knees before? Part of Jordan's mind said, *Yes, it's always been like this*, and part of it said, *No, remember, he was soaking wet with the rest of you in the hallway.*

Magic.

Jordan had always thought of Hennessy's dreaming as a terminal diagnosis, but now she realized that it could be magic.

"How long will he be like that, do you think?" Trinity asked, leaning close over him.

Ronan was paralyzed, just like Hennessy always was after a dream, so at least that part was universal. Madox waved a hand back and forth in front of his face.

"Don't be a shitbag," Jordan said.

"Crikey," June said. "Jordan, is that what's supposed to happen? Is that what it's supposed to be like for her? Look." She pressed a finger into Ronan's hand, showing how his skin sprang back, ordinary and healthy.

Jordan didn't have an answer. They only had two data points, which was not enough for even the shoddiest of theses.

"Maybe he could teach her," Trinity said.

"Because if there's a thing Hennessy's good at, it's taking instruction," Madox scoffed.

Jordan said, "Maybe he could dream something just for her. Not like *The Dark Lady*. Something that does the job."

June started to carefully lift the parcel off his chest, and then, unexpectedly, Ronan smacked the back of her palm.

"Fuck you very much," he said, and stretched.

All the girls laughed at him, with both surprise and something else, something less definable. Jordan could tell they were excited. Optimistic. Today, they looked like her, rather than Hennessy.

Jordan was more grateful to Ronan for this than for opening the door on the flooded bathroom. Hope was a thing that died easily in this house these days.

"Welcome back," she said. "What'd you bring for us today? Do I get a prize if I guess?"

Ronan hefted the wrapped parcel to Jordan to open, careful

not to spill June's juice on it as he did. Glancing at him—she definitely already had a guess—she peeled down the brown paper.

Inside was a painting in a very familiar gilt-edged frame.

It was a woman in a periwinkle blue dress, hands defiantly on her hips, a man's jacket thrown across her shoulders. She peered at the viewer defiantly.

Like Jordan's tattooed *Mona Lisa*, this painting was nearly a perfect likeness of the original. It was *The Dark Lady*, the painting that had taken them hours upon hours upon hours to copy for the Fairy Market, but with Hennessy's face and throat and knuckle tattoos.

A perfect and cunning forgery, as good as theirs. No. Better. Because it oozed with the same magnetic, otherworldly desire that the original had and that their copy had missed. This was not a real-world copy of a dream. This was a dream of a dream. Perfect. Beyond perfect.

And he'd done it in half an hour.

Jordan knew the other girls were thinking the same thing, because Trinity said, "That took Jordan forever."

Ronan shrugged.

"You could do anything we do here in a night," June said.

Ronan shrugged.

"What do you even do all day?" Brooklyn asked.

He grinned at her. The arrogance of him. The swaggering arrogance. And why not? What could it possibly be like living like that? He could do anything.

Including, perhaps, saving their lives.

There are some days, Dalí had said, *when I think I'm going to die from an overdose of satisfaction.*

Jordan said, "We need to tell you a story."

49

Parsifal Bauer had reached peak Parsifalness.

He did not like the apples they had for breakfast. They tasted like nothing, he said. Sandy? she asked. No, he replied. Even sand had a flavor. Did he want her to send for more? No, he said, he had lost his appetite. He did not want to read BMW vehicle registrations on Farooq-Lane's laptop anymore. The screen was making his eyes tired. Couldn't he have it in another format? His clothing irritated him. He thought it was the detergent the hotel used when she'd had them do their laundry. He needed it to be washed again, with detergent sourced from elsewhere. Something without dyes, possibly. No, he could not go out with her to pick out new detergent. He was held prisoner in a bathrobe, all other clothing dirty or marred by the hotel's washing.

"This Spring Fresh detergent can be delivered in an hour," Farooq-Lane suggested, tapping through her phone. Guilelessly.

"The fragrance is not the issue," Parsifal replied tersely. "Just without dyes."

Detergent was secured. Clothing was sent off again. The hotel's fan was noisy. Could they switch rooms?

Now Farooq-Lane understood. She was being punished for calling in the old Zed.

Lock called. "Good work. What are you doing now?"

She glared at Parsifal, who sat on the end of his sofa bed in his bathrobe and shoes, face expressionless behind his glasses.

"Waiting for inspiration." It annoyed her too badly to look at him, so she put in her earbuds and went to stand by the window, looking down at the city below.

"Nikolenko or Ramsay will be coming to debrief you about that Zed you've found," said Lock.

"Oh, not Ramsay," Farooq-Lane said. She didn't really want Nikolenko, either, but she knew which she'd prefer of the two.

"Whoever I can pull off the trail over here," Lock said, not seeming to hear her reluctance. "Also I think we're getting some agency help soon, so maybe I'll be able to send both. I've got my eye on a Zed here that seems promising. Ask Bauer to keep an eye on his visions. We want to make sure—"

Something jerked one of her earbuds out of her ear. Farooq-Lane jumped a mile.

"I cannot wear clothing that smells like this," Parsifal said.

"*Parsifal,*" she snapped. Lock was still talking. "Hold on, I'm . . ."

"I can't wear this," Parsifal continued.

This was beyond the pale. "I'm on the phone."

"I can hear you're busy," Lock said. "Ramsay will let you know when he's in town."

With annoyance, Farooq-Lane hung up and faced Parsifal. He didn't smell like anything unusual. Possibly like shampoo and fresh laundry. "You are being absolutely impossible today."

"Did you tell them to not kill her?"

She was losing her temper. She could feel it leaving her. Very soon it would be leaving for good. "You heard exactly what I said. How much power do you think I have in this situation, anyway? You and I both knew that not every Zed we brought to them was going to be the one. Why are you slamming on the brakes now?"

She didn't even know how much of what she was saying she really believed. She felt like she was being forced to be the devil's advocate, and that made her angry, too. What did she believe? She believed something bad was coming to the world, and she believed she knew where it was coming from, generally. She believed most people didn't get a chance to make a difference. She believed that she did. She believed that she didn't know what else she would be doing now if she wasn't doing this.

She believed deep down inside that wasn't really enough to believe in, and that made her even angrier.

Parsifal was very agitated now, twisting his long, knobby hands around each other. He was rolling his shoulders, too, aggravated with his clothing in every way. She remembered Ramsay telling her once that you couldn't trust the Visionaries, not really. They were more on the Zeds' side than the humans', he said, because they had more in common at the end of the day. Plus they spent all day dreaming of the Zeds. Couldn't trust them. She hadn't given it much thought then, but she remembered it now, as Parsifal rubbed his hands over his arms as if he was cold and worked his fingers into many shapes.

"The easiest way to save her is to find the Zed who's actually going to end the world. You can't do that here in your bathrobe. You can either have another vision, or you can come with me in the car and look for things from your last one."

He didn't agree with her. He just didn't disagree.

In the car, they battled again over opera. Parsifal wanted the window rolled down because of the smell of the laundry detergent. He was hungry. None of this looked familiar to him. He was going to be sick. He didn't like the crackers she got him to settle his stomach. She'd gotten the BMW vehicle registrations printed out, but none of the names rang a bell and it was making him sick to read them while they were moving. He didn't want to look out the window for a little bit. These houses still didn't look familiar. No, circling the burned-down hotel again was not going to help. He needed to buy a new shirt. He needed one that was not going to prickle his skin like this one. No, he could not just ignore it. He—

"I've had it," Farooq-Lane said. "You're a terrorist."

She pulled into a florist's empty parking lot and wrenched the car into park. He eyed her mulishly.

"Do you think I want to be doing this?" she demanded. "Don't you think I wanted life to be different than this?"

He just sat that way he always did, tall and rigid.

"My family's dead, too, you know! And I'm not over here making everyone else's life impossible!"

Parsifal's gaze was heavy on her, and for a minute she thought he might actually say something sympathetic, something un-Parsifalish, but he said, "I'm very tired of you."

"*You're* very tired of *me*?"

"I can't think with your driving," he said. "It's making me sick. I can't think with you talking to me. If I'm to recognize anything from my vision, it can't be with you around. It is too much. You're always so you all the time. You have your drink and your hair and your clothing and your voice and the way you sit with your hand on your leg like that and it's too much. I'm getting out."

"You're getting *out*?"

"I'm walking back to the hotel," Parsifal said. He pulled the phone charger out of the bottom of his phone. "Yes. This is better. Goodbye."

"*Goodbye?*"

"For now. *Bis später.*" He let himself out of the car. He used all ten fingers to close the car door with extreme quietude, which felt like another passive-aggressive comment on her noisiness.

Farooq-Lane felt her anger boil.

She hadn't been angry at her family's death. She hadn't been angry about any of Ramsay's stupid comments. She hadn't been angry when Nikolenko treated her like a soft child. She hadn't been angry when she realized they were going to kill that old Zed for nothing. She hadn't been angry over flight delays, ruined shoes, bad food, aggressive drivers, anything.

But she was out of her mind with rage now. She let out a furious sob and laid on the horn. It blared for several long seconds, bringing a staff member momentarily to the large window at the florist's, and then she released it.

The staff member shook their head and vanished.

So did Parsifal.

50

This was how the story began: There would be thirteen Hennessys, and then it would be over. Limited edition, signed by the artist, discontinued.

The thirteenth was the one that would kill her, they told Ronan, and they agreed that seemed fitting. Thirteen was a devilish number for a life lived devilishly. They showed him their throats, their matching tattoos. Count the flowers, they said. Room for thirteen total, they said, thirteen lovely blossoms to create a deadly choker. Room for two more before they died of excess beauty.

Twelve: name to come. Hennessy used to name them, they told Ronan. After Alba, though, she said they could just pick their own names off baby name sites because she wasn't their mother.

Eleven: nameless. Forever nameless. In a way, they said, it was good that Ronan already knew their secret when he arrived, because it spared them having to make up a lie about why there was a dead girl in the bathroom. She'd never had a chance to name herself, or to get frustrated with living the same life as a half-dozen other girls, or to breathe air.

Ten: Trinity. Sweet Trinity, so down on herself you just wanted to hug her or punch the shit out of her. Hennessy had dreamt her in the driveway. She had been so wasted and had waited so long to dream that she'd left a trail of black from the car she fell out of to the patch of driveway she finally passed out in. Trinity had come into being just a few feet away, already smeared in black.

Nine: Octavia. Bitter Octo. She'd hated every single one of the other girls. Hennessy had been alone when she dreamt her, nowhere near any of the other girls, in a stolen souped-up Challenger. Ordinarily, the girls told Ronan, Hennessy let them know when she was going to dream, or it was obvious, because of the what-did-you-call-it? Nightwash. But not this night. Without warning she'd gone off the radar, stolen a car, dreamt a copy—actually, it was hard to tell the order of events, it could have been the other way around—and had only been found after several hours by Jordan and June. If Octo had been friendlier with the other girls, they would've told her which pills you could mix with alcohol.

Eight: Jay. Hennessy had hated Jay. When she'd picked the name Jay, Hennessy had demanded she change it. Because it was Hennessy's mother's name, sort of, the girls explained to Ronan. We don't remember her well. Hennessy doesn't talk much about her. I remember her, one of the girls said. I think. *Don't you have Hennessy's memories?* Ronan asked. Most of them, the girls said. After a massive fight with Hennessy, Jay passed out in the swimming pool and never woke up. Brooklyn thought Hennessy killed her. Jordan said that if Hennessy was capable of killing any of them, she'd be living in a one-bedroom condo with a sugar daddy by now.

Seven: Brooklyn. It sometimes seemed like the girls were colored by whatever Hennessy was feeling when she dreamt them, though they might've been reading too much into it. When Brooklyn came to be, Hennessy was going through a season of joylessly burning her way through partners of every gender, making up for quality with quantity. A trail of exterminated hearts rubbled behind her. Nurture or nature? Brooklyn loved a good make-out session.

Six: Alba. The girls told Ronan they didn't know what the dream was that produced the copies. Hennessy had to be in it, obviously, since that was what she always brought back with her. *She always has the same dream?* he asked. Yes. *And she can't have it without bringing herself back?* Yes. That's why she sleeps in twenty-minute bursts. *I thought,* he said, *that eventually you die if you don't sleep a full night's sleep.* I think, they said, that is true. But it hadn't been sleep deprivation that had killed Alba; she'd totaled one of Bill Dower's cars before they moved out. Official story was that Hennessy had miraculously walked away without a scratch, and in a way, that was true.

Five: Farrah. Stupid Farrah, the girls told Ronan. Stupid Farrah fell in love and he . . . well. *Didn't love her back?* Ronan suggested, and they'd laughed. Stupid Farrah, the girls said. He was, like, forty-five, and married, and Farrah wasn't even Farrah to him, she was Hennessy. Nothing about Hennessy attracted real, uncorrupted affection. It was never going to be white horses and satin, even if Farrah was capable of love, which none of them were; had she looked in the mirror?

Four: Madox. Hennessy had nearly been caught dreaming Madox. They'd still been living at home then. Bob Dower had just gotten his new girlfriend/soon-to-be-new wife and all the girls were pissed about it. They'd been pissed about everything, actually: moving from London to Pennsylvania, going through puberty, being three girls living as one, living as one who was constantly in a bad mood trying to grow boobs on twenty minutes of sleep at a time. Hennessy had gotten the flu, fallen asleep on the couch, bled through her favorite pair of jeans, and manifested Madox in one fell swoop. June had had to smash the urn containing Bob Dower's father's ashes in the kitchen to create a diversion. Madox had been born angry; wouldn't anyone have been?

Three: June. Poor June. She was marred forever in Hennessy's mind by being the girl who proved that the copies weren't a one-time occurrence. It wasn't like Hennessy hadn't known, though, deep down. Because after the first time it happened, she'd started setting that timer every time she closed her eyes. It had taken her years to fuck that up, and June was her punishment.

Two: Jordan. The first would always be a miracle and a curse. The girls didn't know how long it was after Jay died that Jordan came along, but they knew it was within days. Close enough that Hennessy had asked Jordan to go to the funeral for her, and Jordan had. *She didn't want to go to her own mother's funeral?* Ronan asked. You really don't get how Hennessy feels about Jay, the girls said. Anyway, of course Jordan would do it. Jordan would do anything for Hennessy, and vice versa. They were basically the same person, after all.

One: Hennessy. Who was there to say who Jordan Hennessy would have been if she hadn't split? If Jay hadn't died? Maybe there was a version of her in art school now. Maybe there was a version who was too good for art school, maybe there was a version of her who had already stormed out of her classes and was grinning from a London studio dripping with celebrities and cameras. Maybe there was a version of her who believed in love, maybe there was a version of her who gave a toss about anything, maybe there was a version of her who slept eight hours a night. Or maybe not. Look at J. H. Hennessy. Sometimes it was better to just pour a glass of vodka on the grave and accept that the heart had always churned poisoned blood. The girls tapped their drinks together and grudgingly agreed.

Every version of Jordan Hennessy was probably born to die.

After the girls told him their story, Ronan didn't say what he was thinking, which was this: Jordan Hennessy was a liar.

He didn't know why she was, and he didn't know exactly how far down the lie went, but he'd spent enough time with Declan to know one. Liar, liar.

Those copies weren't killing her.

Ronan had dreamt a copy of himself before. It had been an accident. It was long after he had begun to get a handle on dreaming but far before he'd begun to get a handle on his life, and he'd been trying for too much at once. The stakes were high: Ronan had been assembling materials to bury the reputation of the man who'd had Niall Lynch killed and make sure that he never came after the Lynch family again. Ronan had a filthy laundry list to check off in the dream: paperwork, photos, and electronics. The photos were detailed. Distasteful. Some of the materials had been more awful to acquire than others. He'd managed to manifest some with just a nudge of his subconscious, a desire to be holding it in his hand already, but the photos were stubbornly blank. He couldn't make them work without manifesting the hideous scene within the dream, before snapping a photo of it with a phone.

The images were meant to be awful. Breathtakingly awful. Blackmailing someone of Colin Greenmantle's clout required more than standard-issue skin pics. They needed to feature body horror and youth. He needed to bring back a body part in an envelope. He needed premeditation documented in texted photos.

He had to live it to manifest it.

Ronan had felt as if he would never be clean again.

Even in the dream he was disgusted with himself, and with that disgust and shame came his old enemies, the night horrors. Ronan's night horrors were a lot like the things he *liked* to dream about—they had wings, beaks, claws—but with an important difference: They hated him.

They'd come for him just as he'd bundled up all his foul evidence in his arms, prepared to wake with it. He'd been faced with a choice: wake without manifesting anything and know that he would have to try this all over again . . . or give the night horrors something else to aim for while he woke with the goods.

He'd asked the dream to make another Ronan. The dream had manifested one so quickly that it was as if it had been waiting for him to ask.

The night horrors fell upon him.

Ronan remembered seeing himself attacked from the outside, everything about the copy's reactions precisely the same as his would have been. The sounds were the same. His body buckled the same. His hands clawed out the same. His face looked at Ronan and understood why he had done it, the same as Ronan would have for another Ronan.

"Get the fuck out," the other Ronan had snarled, in Ronan's voice. "Don't let it be for noth—"

Ronan had woken.

He'd woken with an armful of disgusting photos, paperwork, and electronics. And on the carpet beside him was another Ronan Lynch. Bloody, bent nearly backward, his spine a horror-bridge, a hand pressed to a neck wound that would never close, gasping.

It had taken him so long to die.

It had been one of the worst things Ronan had ever seen.

But it hadn't taken anything from him physically.

Dreaming copies shouldn't be killing Hennessy. So she was either faking that she was dying, or something else was killing her.

But he didn't say any of this to her dreams. He just told them he had to talk to Hennessy herself. One of them—he couldn't tell any of them apart except for Jordan and June—warned: "She'll just be sleeping or cussing right now."

"I'll take my chances," Ronan said.

The girls had taken her to one of the mansion's many bedrooms, selected, presumably, because it had blinds. They were drawn, and the room was the peculiar gray of a blinkered room in full daylight. It was silent when he let himself in. Like every other room he'd seen in the mansion, it was enormous, ridiculous. Because of his time at Aglionby and his friend Gansey, he'd seen plenty of wealth in his high school years, but it had never looked like this. The windows had satin love seats built into their sills. Three zebra rugs added dimension to the floor, which was otherwise covered with high-piled white carpet. White sculptures of voluptuous women poured urns of water into troughs that led into an en suite bathroom; stagnant water was gray and scummy in them.

The bed itself was on a pedestal accessible by marble steps on three sides. It was barely made: someone had spread two comforters on top of the bare pillow-top mattress.

Hennessy was a small dark smudge in this shapeless nest.

She was neither sleeping nor cussing. She was quietly crying.

Not sorrowful sobs, but small, splintered noises of pain. One hand covered her mouth, as if she didn't want even the empty room to hear her.

He wasn't sure if she'd heard him come in.

"Is that bullshit?" Ronan asked.

The crying stopped.

Her eyes came open. Focused on him. They were dark, intelligent, skeptical.

"It's just me," Ronan said. "Your girls are in the living room. So if it's bullshit, you can cut the act now."

Hennessy sat up. It appeared to take a great deal of effort, particularly to do it without making a sound. Once she had finished it, she took a moment to pull herself together. She didn't look angry about being accused of putting on an act. She looked appraising.

She asked, "Why are we having this conversation?"

Ronan handed her the palm cross he'd taken from *The Dark Lady*'s shore. Hennessy's fingers shook as she held it. Her knuckles were white. She said nothing. She ran her thumb across the papery knot that held the cross together.

"I knew there had to be another one," she said, her voice small and tight. "Statistically. And here you are, aren't you? I killed the latest one, didn't I? I drowned her."

He just held her gaze.

She nodded a little, bitterly. "And you gave them a little run round the showroom. Were they impressed?"

He shrugged a little as if to say, who wouldn't be.

"And you didn't drown any of them with that ocean," Hennessy said. It wasn't a question. "Because you're not a rubbish dreamer. You're good at it."

He shrugged a little again.

"And now they've sent you in here to ask you to save me," Hennessy guessed.

"I know you're lying to them. I just can't figure out why," Ronan said. "Is it that you want them to feel like shit? Do you get off on them feeling guilty?"

"My poor girls," Hennessy said. She put her fingers to the tattoo on her throat, gingerly. She had one more flower there than all the other girls had in their choker, and it was a little brighter than all the others. When she touched it, he saw pinprick bits of blood well up. Not just within the shape of the new flower, like a fresh tattoo, but all across her throat and her cheeks, as if her skin was permeable. Her eyes rolled back.

This wasn't fake.

As she slumped toward the edge of the bed, Ronan vaulted forward to catch her. He propped her against the headboard as the expression returned to her face. He saw now that the comforter beneath her was smeared with blood. Not a lot. But enough.

Her phone was faceup beside her. It ticked down a timer. Eleven minutes.

Even now she'd been keeping herself from dreaming again.

"So it really is hurting you," he said. Maybe he was wrong, he thought. Maybe his experience of dreaming copies wasn't universal. Maybe there was a cost to copying yourself more than once that he hadn't experienced, even if he couldn't think of why it would be true. Maybe—

"That part is true," Hennessy said. "I really am dying."

Ronan left her there in the bed and rummaged in the bathroom for towels. The lights were all burned out and there were no windows, so he had to make do with the roll of toilet paper he could glimpse in the light through the open door.

He returned with it. She took it and dabbed her strange, damaged skin.

"Dying, but not from making copies," he said. "Why make them go to all the work of hunting down *The Dark Lady*, then?"

"It's not the copies killing me," Hennessy said. "It's the dream itself."

"No," Ronan said.

"Yes, Ronan Lynch," Hennessy said. "You're gonna have to trust me on this one. This is the truth. If I could change my dream, I wouldn't be dying."

"It did change your dream, though. You dreamt an ocean."

"I dreamt that cursed ocean *and* the same dream I always do," she said. "And look at me: another step, step, step, waltzing toward death."

He puzzled this out. "But if the copies aren't killing you, how do you know how close you are?"

She gestured to that choker of flowers around her throat, careful not to touch it. "I've got my countdown, don't I?"

It is not as easy as you think, Bryde had said.

Ronan frowned at her. He tried to imagine if he could dream her something to conclusively alter her dreams. *The Dark Lady's* spell was strong, though, and if she'd managed to dream her recurring dream even over the top of *The Dark Lady's* seashore, she needed something incredibly powerful. And with space for only two more flowers around her neck, there wasn't room for error. Perhaps he could dream something that would eat her dreams as soon as she had them. It was hard once one got into the very abstract dreams; they sometimes had unexpected side effects, like a fairy bargain from an old story. He didn't want something that would eat all her dreams and her thoughts as well, or something that would eat all her dreams and then her living dreams, too. Perhaps—

"Ronan—it is Ronan, right? Lynch?" Hennessy broke into his thoughts. "Brother of Lynch, Declan, son of Lynch, Niall? Yeah, so I thought. I'm gonna give you a very solid piece of cheddar to chew. I can tell you're looking at me and thinking you can fix this. You're looking at me and thinking you're a big-shot dreamer"—she wiggled the palm cross at him—"and you can make this work. You're running those numbers of how to get it done before I die. But here's the thing, Ronan Lynch. I've killed so many people. You wouldn't believe how much blood these hands have on them. You've seen my girls. Their blood's on my hands, too, when I die. I can't change any of that. But I can stop you from being just more blood that won't wash out. Get out of this cursed place while you can."

"You don't care about me," Ronan said. "You just met me."

Her eyes glittered.

"So you don't care if I get dragged into something."

Her timer went off. Automatically, she thumbed it to begin counting down again. Twenty minutes. Who could live like that? She had to be tired every minute of every day of her life. It had to feel like she was sleepwalking. Nothing mattered to Ronan when he hadn't slept, because nothing felt true.

Every minute of every day of every week of every month of every year, that had been her life.

The girls said Hennessy didn't give a toss about anything. How could she?

"So sending me off is about you, not me," Ronan said. "What are you afraid of? What is this dream that's killing you?"

There was no trace of the spoiling, catty rock star the other girls had painted large in their stories. Whatever this thing was, it loomed over her, bigger than the need to impress him. She was hiding from it. He found that cowardice far more acceptable than the lying. Some things took time to look in the eye.

"If I haven't told them for a decade," Hennessy said, "I'm not sodding telling you."

51

Because Ronan wouldn't pick up his phone, because nothing had changed, because it was always Declan being responsible at the end of the day, Declan went to Great Falls himself.

It was a wide-awake day, too bright and too warm for a Virginia November, the cloudless sky a sick, hazed blue. Declan had to wind around strolling locals and foreign tourists as he made the familiar walk along the canal. His pockets were ten dollars lighter from the parking fee; how much money had he spent coming to this place on Matthew's behalf? Tourists glanced at him as he walked, and he knew he was conspicuous in his suit. It made him invisible downtown, but not here.

Matthew wasn't at the first viewing area, nor the second, nor the third. There were only old folks with their dogs and chattering tourists asking Declan to take a photo for them.

The canal walk was ever so long when one was looking for a brother who had to be caught somewhere along its length. On past visits, Declan had walked for nearly an hour before finding Matthew. He didn't have that kind of time today. His work might have been torpedoed, but he still had a chance of making his adviser meeting, and, after that, his volunteer hours at the gallery.

"Can you make a photo?" a lady asked Declan in accented English. "Of us?"

"I can't," Declan said. "I'm looking for my brother."

She became solicitous. "Do you have a photo?"

He did.

"Good-looking boy," said the woman's companion.

"I saw him," said the other woman. "Number one deck. Number one. He was looking at the falls so nice. Now can you make a photo?"

He did. He returned to the first observation deck. Matthew still wasn't there; no one was. Declan leaned on the railing long enough to text his adviser that he had to reschedule again. Rescheduling again wasn't good; it was not invisible. The falls roared. Dry leaves rattled. Voices lifted from the trail. He ate three antacids. He gave himself a little pep talk. So he was failing as a student and as an intern, he thought, but at least he had shepherded Ronan to another birthday alive. And in a month he would have managed to get Matthew to eighteen, all the Lynch brothers surviving to adulthood. Surely that was worth something.

Leaning on the edge of the observation deck, a dark assemblage in the nearby trees caught Declan's eye. He studied it for a long minute, trying to decide if it was a collection of dried leaves or something else, and then he climbed into the woods to get a closer look, the underbrush snarling at his suit pants.

It was Ronan's damn bird.

Chainsaw, the raven. It could have been another raven, of course, but what were the odds that another raven would be here where Ronan's other dream came to stare at the water? With a glance behind him to make sure he wasn't being observed by any tourists, he stepped closer, using trees to keep his footing; the ground sloped precipitously down to the river.

"Bird," he hissed. No response. "Chainsaw."

Now Declan saw something else on the branches around her:

several trembling blue moths, a handful of jet-black hornets, two mice, an improbably colored skunk, and one of those damned double-sided murder crabs that he'd had to haul out of Adam Parrish's dorm.

A confluence of Ronan's dreams at the riverside.

Declan narrowed his eyes. He tilted his head back to look at the other dreams. It was impossible to tell if the hornets or the moths or the murder crab were distressed, but the mice and the skunk looked as out of sorts as Chainsaw.

Which meant Matthew might be in the same condition.

Declan searched ever-widening circles, careful to not lose his footing on the steep hillside. The Potomac roared down below.

It didn't take him long to spy a splash of white: Matthew's school uniform shirt. He tried to move too fast, slid, and caught himself on a tree. He edged the last few feet more slowly.

Matthew sat on the jutted lip of a lichen-covered boulder with his arms wrapped around his legs. He stared at the water. His lips were parted a little, too, and his breathing was fast and shallow like Chainsaw's. He looked dreamy, feverish.

Declan thought, *Fuck you, Dad,* because he couldn't blame Ronan for Matthew—he loved Matthew too much. He had to blame Niall for keeping the dreaming so secret that he never taught them anything about the rules of it.

He knelt beside Matthew and laid his hand on his cheek. He wasn't actually feverish. "Matthew."

"I waited," Matthew said.

"They called me from the school."

"I felt tired," Matthew said.

"Tired people sleep."

"Hungry, then."

"Hungry people eat."

Matthew leaned heavily against Declan, like he would've when he was small. Declan wasn't a huggable Lynch, but Matthew had never cared. He'd hugged him anyway. Matthew murmured, "Hungry for this."

For the river. Always hungry for the river.

Fuck you, Declan thought prayerfully.

"Come on," he said, guiding Matthew up. "We have to meet Ronan for his birthday."

"I forgot," Matthew said, with a sort of awe. He muttered something else, but trailed off at the end.

On their way back up through the steep woods, Declan paused by Ronan's raven. It didn't feel right to just leave her, but he wasn't exactly sure how to handle her, either. She was a dustier, realer creature than he normally preferred to handle, particularly in his suit. Declan's annoyance at the raven's dirtiness and his annoyance at Ronan not picking up his phone battled with the knowledge of how Ronan would feel if something happened to this bird.

"I can't believe I forgot," Matthew said to himself. He was squeezing the thumb of one hand with the fingers of his other, absently swapping back from one to another, thoughtlessly self-soothing. "I can't believe anything would make me forget Ronan's *birthday.*"

Declan, finally resolved, stretched up and tapped on the raven's shaggy legs until she half-flapped, half-fell into his arms. She lay there, feathers askance, beak slightly parted.

"What's wrong with her?" Matthew asked.

Something about Matthew's voice made Declan look sharply to him.

His youngest brother's expression was very un-Matthew-like.

Eyes tight. Brows low. Intense. Pensive. His blue Lynch eyes were fixed at a point directly past Declan; he was looking right at the other limp dream creatures.

Shit, thought Declan. He'd never thought it would happen. He had no road map for the journey after this.

"Same thing as me," Matthew said flatly.

Fuck you, Declan thought miserably.

"If I was Dad's, I'd be asleep," Matthew said. "So I must be one of Ronan's."

52

St. Eithne was a weird little church, Ronan thought. Everything was small and green in it. Tiny green shutters on the tiny windows of the lobby, tiny green door to get in. Tiny green rugs on the worn old lobby floor. Tiny green banners that said ST. EITHNE 1924 hung on the walls. Tiny little pews with deep green pads on the kneelers. Tiny stained-glass windows acted out watery green Stations of the Cross around the church. A tiny Mary, tinted green by the stained-glass windows, a tiny Jesus behind the altar, colorless and sanguine except for his green thorn crown. A tiny green-painted ceiling that imposed itself from above.

Ronan was just dipping his fingers in a tiny font of greenish holy water when Declan grabbed his arm.

"Where were you?" Declan demanded.

"Hey now, psycho," Ronan said, catching a glimpse of Matthew's golden curls in the front row of the church right before Declan hauled him back on his heels into the lobby. "Someone didn't take their pills today. Happy birthday to you, too."

"Happy," spat Declan, "birthday."

At Declan's raised voice, Ronan glanced around, but the church seemed to be empty. Not much call for a church for tiny green mermaids on a weekday afternoon during prime rush hour, he guessed. When the boys came on Sunday, the building was always full of little old ladies and men with hair tinged green by the light through the stained-glass windows, all presided over by ancient Father O'Hanlon in deep green vestments that seemed so strengthened with body odor that they should've been able to stand up even without Father O'Hanlon inside them. Ronan spent most of confession warring over whether or not he should confess how odiferous the process was.

Declan asked again, "Where the hell were you?"

Ronan wouldn't lie, so he gave Declan a partial truth. "Adam came."

"Today?"

"He left today, yeah."

"I needed you," Declan said. "It was an emergency."

"A zoo emergency."

"Did you even read the texts I sent you? Did you listen to the voicemail?"

Ronan had read the texts. "It wasn't like it was a big surprise where he was going to end up. He always goes to the falls, to the exact same place at the falls. Overlook One, rinse, repeat. My phone was in the car, man, stand the fuck down."

"I had work," Declan said. "I had appointments. This created a situation that put me into a difficult place."

A prime Declanism.

"Created a situation," echoed Ronan.

"Where were you really?" Declan asked. When Ronan just raised an eyebrow, Declan said, "Fine, don't tell me. I assume you're just blowing off everything I told you about not chasing trouble, because that's what you do, isn't it? I keep my head down and you dream up a fucking skywriter that says *kill me please.*"

"Goes to show," Ronan said, "you don't need a priest in the house for a sermon. We still hitting the zoo?"

Declan, to Ronan's surprise, grabbed both of Ronan's arms and propelled him to the doorway of the nave via biceps. Ronan could feel his brother's fingers digging into him. It had been a long time since either of them had landed a fist on each other's faces, but Ronan remembered it in the pressure of those fingertips.

Declan hissed in his ear, "You see that kid there? Head down? You know him, right, your baby brother? I don't know where the hell you really were, but while you were there, that kid was putting the pieces together. While you were out doing *fuck all* with yourself, he figured out you dreamt him. So no, we are not. Still. Hitting. The. Zoo."

Declan released him with such force that it was as if he were throwing Ronan away from himself. "I'm going to the car to put out some fires. You can go look him in the eye now and be a fucking smartass if you want."

Ronan was left standing looking into the tiny green nave at his little brother. He could now see that he was seated in a very un-Matthew-like position. Head down. Hands folded over the back of his neck.

He looked over his shoulder, but Declan had already seen himself out.

Pacing quietly down to the front of the church, Ronan made the sign of the cross and slid into the pew beside Matthew.

"Hey, kid," he said.

Matthew didn't move.

Ronan put a hand in Matthew's thick golden curls and tousled them. "Do you want to talk or not?"

Matthew didn't say anything. Ronan leaned his shoulder against Matthew as he had many times before, trying to imagine what his brother needed from him in this moment. Probably a hug. Matthew nearly always wanted a hug.

Matthew remained motionless. He wasn't crying. He wasn't doing anything. Matthew was always doing something. Fidgeting. Talking. Laughing. Falling. Getting back up. Singing.

But he wasn't doing anything right now.

The church was quiet except for the dyspeptic sigh of the old heating system. It varied in tone like a human snoring, a phenomenon that had offered much mirth to the two younger Lynch brothers over the course of their Masses there.

Ronan caught a sudden whiff of incense, of salt water, the smell of a tiny green mermaid Mass coming to a close. *Go in peace*, but Matthew was far from peace.

"What do you need me to say, little man?" he asked.

Matthew said, "I don't want . . ." He didn't say anything else for a long moment. Then he added, "To hear you say anything—" He seemed to be measuring the words out, tipping them out of a jar and checking to be sure he still had enough to go on. "—because now I know—" He did not remotely sound like himself when he spoke that way. "—you're as big a liar as Declan."

Ronan's face felt hot. Stinging.

"Oh," he said.

He could feel the heat in his stomach, too, in his knees, his legs, a rush of it, something like adrenaline, familiar—

Shame.

Ronan sat back.

The two of them sat there for a long time as the light slowly changed through the tiny green windows.

They didn't say anything else.

53

Jordan thought that she might be furious with Hennessy. In her life, she hadn't been angry about many things, and she'd never been angry with Hennessy.

But she could feel it now.

It was as if hope were oxygen and anger the flame. It couldn't properly take hold while Hennessy was pitiable and recovering, but by the time she was well enough to go out with Jordan to Senko's that night, it was burning outrageously. It was burning down the whole place.

Ordinarily Jordan liked Senko's, even if it was associated with bad times. She'd been in more artist studios than most people would be in their entire life, and yet Senko's professional garage was one of the more satisfying creative spaces Jordan had ever been in. And in comparison to the space she shared with Hennessy and the other girls, it was positively zenlike. Inside, the space was bright and open, the ceiling high enough to accommodate three auto lifts. The lifts were stark, black, and purposeful, and the three of them always looked like a modern art installation, each holding a candy-colored automotive corpse with hood agape and dark innards dripping from beneath. The concrete floor was swept clean, but it was scarred with oil splatters, paint overspray, tire scrubs, and a blood-red stenciled logo. One wall of shelves held bright knobs and joints, metallic body parts waiting to be fitted into the Frankenstein's automotive monsters, it lives, it lives. A cheap but chic black vinyl sofa faced the dyno. One of the huge walls was covered with bright, modern automotive paintings, gifts from Hennessy and the girls over the months. There was a single space left on the wall. Waiting for Jordan's contribution.

She had always vowed she'd paint something original when she got to live as an original.

So, never.

She was *very* angry, she thought with some wonder. So this was how Madox felt all the time. How did she ever get anything done? There wasn't room inside Jordan for anything else.

In the place where an office should be, there was Senko's tattoo parlor, and that was where Hennessy and Jordan headed that evening. Jordan wasn't exactly sure how hygienic it was, but Senko didn't ask questions about the Supra's origin and he didn't ask questions about Jordan's, either. It wasn't the easiest thing to find five different tattoo parlors to do identical flowers on each of the girls each time Hennessy got a new one.

"Another flower," Senko said. "Two flowers this time, we're nearly done." He was the most compact man Jordan had ever met, both short and slight, like a taller person seen from far away. His densely curled hair was either dull brown or gray. She had no idea how old he was. Thirty? Fifty? Supposedly Hennessy had slept with him once, but for Senko's sake, Jordan hoped this wasn't true. "Pink this time."

Jordan was already situated in the chair as Senko examined the new flower on Hennessy's throat, making sure that the one he was about to put on Jordan matched precisely. He was taking his time. Senko was not the sort to do anything rash. He wasn't the sort to do anything at speed, really, which was ironic considering that his profession was making things go faster. Senko himself was the slowest driver Jordan had ever seen; she'd once encountered him in his GTR north of the city and had spent ten minutes trying to provoke him into exceeding the speed limit before realizing first that it was impossible and second that it was him.

"Pink is the oldest color on the planet, did you know that?" Hennessy said. She still sounded a little drugged, but she had stopped bleeding hours before. She lolled in a rolling desk chair, holding the shop dog, a tiny female Yorkie named Greg. The story was that Senko used to have a shop guy named Greg who'd botched a turbo swap years ago and been unable to pay for the fix, and Senko had taken his dog in reparation, but Jordan found the story suspect. Senko wouldn't let any of his shop guys touch a turbo. "According to fossil records. Cyanobacteria. I read that in *Smithsonian Magazine*. Ground 'em up, add them to solvent, it turns bright pink, making it one-billion-year-old pigment. I'd like to paint with that. Maybe a steak. A rare color for a rare food. Too on the nose?"

Jordan didn't answer.

Jordan didn't want this tattoo.

It seemed impossible how much she didn't want the tattoo.

A decade of matching tattoos, matching hair, matching clothing, matching lives. Matching hopes, matching dreams, matching expiration dates.

"I'm gonna piss first," Senko said, standing slowly. "Don't go away." He moved out of the room with slothlike intention.

The moment Jordan heard the shop bathroom door close, words blew out of her mouth; she couldn't even stop them. "What did you tell him?"

Hennessy and the dog looked up in surprise. "Steak? Pink? I didn't make him need to piss."

"Ronan Lynch," Jordan said. She didn't even fully recognize her tone. She sounded like Madox. The words were spat out. Hateful. Ronan. Lynch. "He was all ready to take us on and in he went to you and something *you* said sent him sodding right back out that door."

"He couldn't do anything for us."

"And how would you know? Did you see the painting he did? Out of his head? It took him no time at all, maybe even *better* than the original *Dark Lady*. He said he might be able to do something just for you. You didn't even let him try."

Hennessy said, "It'll just get the girls all strung out."

"On *hope*, is that what you mean? Are you saying they'd be all strung out on *hope*, like they might get excited about seeing the other side of twenty-one? You're right, that seems truly fucked up. What was I thinking."

Hennessy gave Jordan a fond look. "This doesn't look good on you, Jordan. Leave it to Mad."

This did nothing to quench Jordan's anger. If anything, it strengthened it.

"I spent every second of every day for months getting *The Dark Lady*," she said. "For you, so you wouldn't be like this. But also for them, because they needed it. Before this, Trinity was about ready to eat a bucket of pills, you and I both know that. Having an idea it might go somewhere kept her from going off her oats. For once it didn't just hang over us. All of us. And now you're saying that's not worth going after again?"

Now Hennessy looked angry right back. It was a version of Madox's anger, but a shade darker, more complicated. She put her finger on her temple. "You don't know what goes on in here, Jordan. I played along with you, I played along with *The Dark Lady*, even though I knew it would just fuck us up the arse. And here we are, fucked up the arse, as predicted."

"We never had another dreamer," Jordan said. "He knows what you can do. He knows what's possible."

And then she saw from Hennessy's face that this was exactly why she didn't want it. Jordan narrowed her eyes. "Is this a cry for help?"

Hennessy said, "Don't dig in this hole, Jordan. It's not what you think."

"I'm thinking about the others. You might try it."

Hennessy's eyes simmered. "As if I ever think about anything else."

Senko returned. He began to slowly assemble the alcohol and his gloves and his envelopes containing needles. The air crackled with tension, but he seemed oblivious.

"What is the closest you've ever come to death, Senko?" Hennessy asked, with aggressive carelessness, not meeting Jordan's eyes. "I don't mean a swerve in traffic. I mean a good, quality, brand-name near-death experience."

Senko's was generally a place of no-questions-asked-or-answered, so Jordan thought this one would be ignored. But Senko paused in the middle of examining his needles under a magnifying glass.

"Those bullet holes in the door," Senko said.

"Don't leave us hanging," Hennessy said.

Senko turned to Jordan and began to wipe her throat down with the alcohol.

"Better not be swallowing like that when I'm working or

you'll turn this thing into a lily," he told her. "Three guys came in here to rob us. Years ago. This wasn't my shop then. It was my boss's. Tubman. They were coming to rob Tubman. Nobody would rob me, I was an asshole. I had nothing. I was nothing. Tubman hired me to keep me off the street. Said I'd make an ugly corpse. I was an ugly tech, too. Good for nothing. I don't know why Tubman himself didn't kill me. These guys who broke in, they were tweaking. They got me down on the ground and they had a foot on my neck, a boot, just like this, and a gun right here, just like this, and they told me they were going to kill me. You know what I thought?"

I've never lived my own life, thought Jordan.

"This is the most boring thing to do on my back," guessed Hennessy.

Senko quirked an eyebrow. For Senko, this counted as intense humor. "I thought, 'I've never tried to fix anything.' Not a car, not my life, nothing. I just messed over it. I just turned a few bolts. I never saw it through. I was going to die, and I was going to leave all this broken shit laying around I never really even failed at fixing. I just didn't even try."

"I hope this story ends with you explaining this to them and you revealing to both of us that those three yobs were Eliot, Pratt, and Matt," Hennessy said. These were three of the other shop guys.

"I spat in the guy's eye and took his gun and pistol whipped him, then shot the other guy three times through the door. Served two years for it, which is where I got interested in tattooing . . . and here I am today," Senko said.

"Truly inspirational," Hennessy said.

Jordan could feel her pulse pounding in her neck, right

where Senko was about to place another flower, one step closer to choking the life out of her. She didn't *want* this, she thought. She wanted to stop being afraid, and she wanted to be able to call Declan Lynch and give him something she'd painted with Tyrian purple, and she wanted to have a future that didn't look exactly like her past.

There had to be something they could do.

This wasn't living, it was just giving up while still breathing.

"You ready to go?" Senko asked Jordan.

Jordan sat up. She locked eyes with Hennessy. "I'm not getting the tattoo."

"Oh, we're doing drama," remarked Hennessy.

Jumping up from the chair, Jordan thumbed a twenty out of her bra. "Buy yourself something pretty," she told Senko, who didn't look surprised, probably because he wouldn't be provoked into changing his expression that quickly. She headed for the door. She heard Hennessy murmuring something wry to him before scuffling after her.

"Jordan," Hennessy said, "you arse, come on."

Jordan pushed out into the cold night. It was ferocious, suddenly freezing her nose and throat and skin. She heard cars howling on the distant interstate, honking on the highway. Someone was shouting several blocks away. She felt more awake than she had in one thousand years.

The shop door slammed behind her.

"Don't be pissed at me," Hennessy said.

Jordan swiveled in the lot, still walking backward to where the Supra was parked. "Then say you'll ask him for help."

Hennessy bit her lip, sealing in the answer.

Jordan spread her arms to say *see?*

"Why don't you think of *me* for half a tick, then?" Hennessy snarled. "You aren't the one bleeding black shit and turning inside out. *You're* the dream. I'm the dreamer. I'm the one who has to live with this. I get to call the shots here."

Jordan's mouth hung open.

Hennessy didn't back down from her words. She meant for them to wound, but Jordan was too shocked for even that.

She opened the Supra door.

"Have fun with that," Jordan said. She got in, slammed the door, stared at Hennessy out the open window. "Get yourself a fucking Uber."

She tore out of the lot. Jordan didn't know how Hennessy felt about it, because she didn't look in the mirror as she left her behind.

For the first time, she was very, very sure that she and Hennessy were living two different lives.

54

It hadn't remotely occurred to Farooq-Lane that Parsifal Bauer might have lied about heading back to the hotel after he got out of the rental car. For all the many annoying facets of Parsifalness, untruthfulness didn't seem to be one of them. And yet he did not come back to the hotel, and he did not pick up his phone or answer texts, except for the first one she sent. He replied: *You are still talking.* Farooq-Lane waited for him in the room for hours, simmering.

Lock called and she, too, ignored it, like Parsifal's Parsifality was rubbing off on her. Really she couldn't stand telling Lock that she'd lost their Visionary. That she hadn't found anything this entire time but the old Zed. She felt as if she had been given a craft project without any tools, a puzzle without all its pieces. A quest with only Parsifal Bauer as her guide. It was unsolvable as currently structured, and yet she was being blamed for it.

For a few hours she tried to research Bryde on forums, looking for any clues that might be helpful beyond what a vision might offer. She made herself some bad coffee. She ate some of the apples Parsifal had found too flavorless.

Finally, she went through Parsifal's stuff.

This was very bad behavior and she knew it, but so was getting out of a car and walking away when the world was literally depending on you.

Parsifal's case was neatly packed, which was no surprise.

Three days of clothing folded, each day's outfit folded skillfully into each other so that he could simply remove it as one piece and apply it to his body. Toiletries tucked into a spotless canvas zipper pouch. Two Nicolas Mahler comics. A notebook with a single journal entry started in it. March 14: *Ich versucht so zu t.*

He'd drawn a very ugly, savage dog in the bottom corner, the lines rigid and unfriendly. She didn't care for it.

In the webbed flat pouch of the case, she found a chipped old CD case. Opera. It was Wagner's *Parsifal*. As she was sliding it back in, she noticed the name of the performers. JOANNA BAUER. Sister? Mother? She flipped it over, looking for a copyright date. It was all in German. She opened it up and inside was a CD and a photograph. It was a posed photograph, and although no one was laughing in it, it was easy to see from their faces they were all finding it hilarious nonetheless. A plump woman (mother?) and three girls (sisters?) all stood on one side of the shot, pointing dramatically at the other side of the photo, where a much younger Parsifal looked dramatically long-suffering, so dramatically long-suffering that it was obvious he was being a parody of himself. It was painterly in its compositions, the four arms all directing the viewer's attention from their shocked forms to his contrite one.

I killed them all, Parsifal had said.

Uncontrolled Visionaries were frightening in their destructive power, even to themselves. Lock said he'd never known one to come to them without a tragedy already packed in their suitcase.

Here was Parsifal's tragedy.

He didn't return.

A few hours into the night, Farooq-Lane's annoyance turned

to concern. He must be lost. Kidnapped. Hit by a car. Any number of things could befall a teen boy with poor social skills and a lack of appetite.

He wasn't picking up his phone.

She bundled up and packed a small bag of food for him, then went out, making sure the DO NOT DISTURB plaque was still in place.

She drove. She drove all night. She drove to where he'd gotten out of the car, pulling into every café and still-open shop, and then she tried the hotels that were anywhere close to the route, and then she tried the hospitals.

She dreaded telling Lock she'd lost him. She couldn't really believe that she had. What would Parsifal do if he wasn't being a Visionary, here in this strange country, no family, no friends? Farooq-Lane was starting to feel like she might have been unkind. If only he'd been easier to like.

The night stretched and pinched in changeable measure: minutes would drag as she coasted through neighborhoods she'd already checked, and then hours would fly by as she leaned on hotel desks asking, *Have you seen anyone who looks like this?*

It reminded her of the night Lock had found her, the first night she'd lived through after Nathan's murders. She'd gotten into her car that night, too, because what else was there to do? She wasn't going to sleep, or watch TV, or read, and the thing about a murder instead of an accident is that there's no hospital to sit vigil in. There's just the night, the night, the night. She'd circled and stopped and gone into every place that was open in Chicago in the middle of the night. She collected all the late-night artifacts one could collect: lottery tickets, frothed coffee, old corn dogs, cheap sunglasses like the pair Parsifal had been wearing in the bathtub. *Somewhere*, she thought, *Nathan is out there in this night*, and she didn't know what she would do if she saw him. When she finally got home to her crime-scene row house, Lock had been sitting on the steps waiting for her. *I think you need for this to mean something*, he'd rumbled.

She was going to find Parsifal. She was not going to have to tell Lock she had lost their only Visionary.

She drove.

55

It was in the middle of the night, and it woke them.

Mags Harmonhouse shared a bedroom with her sister, Olly, just as she had when they were girls: two twin beds a twin-bed width apart, close enough that they had jumped from bed to bed before their mother had put an end to it. There were a lot of years and three husbands between that time and now, but sometimes when Mags woke up she thought they were girls again. It wasn't a good thought, though. It always made her think, *Oh no, now I have to do it all again.*

She woke up now and clawed up her glasses. She heard Olly clawing up her glasses as well.

The sisters looked at each other in the dark. Olly's eyes were bright, glittering beads in the streetlights outside, nothing comforting about that, even knowing her for decades. Anything seemed possible on a night like this when you'd been woken by something and didn't know what the something had been.

Maybe it had been a thump. A thump was a good thing to wake you in the night, Mags thought, a solid choice, classical. Once Dabney had tried to get up to piss in the middle of the night when he was baked more than a potato, and he'd made a thump when he'd tried to go through the mirror in the hall instead of the kitchen doorway.

Olly blinked. Mags could tell she was listening, too. Deciding if it was a thump or a *commotion*. This neighborhood had never been *Leave It to Beaver*, as Olly sometimes said, but it was getting even rougher, and last year a *commotion* had preceded a robbery. The three young men had come in and taken the cash out of the dressers they tossed and the microwave out of the kitchen. They'd roughed Mags up a little bit when she'd tried to keep them from taking Olly's little television.

Maybe it was that new girl. Mags had been p.o.'d at Olly for the charity case—no point getting some runaway in here because the law would follow—but Liliana had already transformed the house. Mags wasn't sure how she had accomplished so much in so little time. She was always working, that was for sure, but one person shouldn't have been able to clean all the mold and repair the stair and find the good dark sheen of the wood floors beneath years of wear and dust in a day. Mags only saw her using Olly's water and vinegar, but the house even smelled different, like flowers, like summer. She'd had to examine the hallway walls to see if the girl had painted, because everything seemed brighter.

"The girl," Olly whispered. "She's crying."

And now that she said it, of course that was what it was. Low whimpering came from the room above them. Little moans, like a hurt animal. Subtle footfalls with it as well, as if she paced or moved about as she did. It was a sad sound, but also, for some reason—in this dark night, with Olly's eyes still gleaming white behind her glasses, with the trees shadowing the walls— unsettling.

The two sisters hesitated and then Mags grunted and threw off her covers. Olly followed suit. She'd always do something if Mags did it first. The two crones stood in the middle of their bedroom, shoulder to shoulder, listening. Had it stopped?

No, there it was again.

They put on their bathrobes and shuffled into the hall.

It was louder out here, the weeping. It was so sad. Particularly when one imagined it coming from that sweet-faced girl, her gentle eyes clouded with tears, soft mouth torn with despair.

They turned on the light, but it didn't do much. It was just a single bulb, and it was barely better than when the hallway was just illuminated by the tepid orange streetlights.

Mags was not fast to climb the stairs, and Olly was even slower. Mags kept pace with her. She still had that feeling of ants running over her arms, and she didn't like the idea of getting there before her sister.

Liliana's door was ajar. Through the crack, Mags could see something moving back and forth. A column of light and then dark. Then light. Then dark. It must have been Liliana's blouse, but it put Mags in mind of a spirit. Her mother said she'd seen one once; it had come up in a jet, she said, a beam from the floor in the old kitchen she'd been working in, gave her a scare that was still chewing her bones years later.

Mags and Olly were nearly to the top of the stairs. The final stair let out a splitting creak.

The column of white froze in the door and then vanished.

There was silence.

Mags hesitated. She wanted to go back down the stairs.

"Child?" Olly called out, which was the first time she'd been braver than Mags in her life.

Liliana sobbed, "Please go away."

They were both so relieved to hear her voice that they both let out a breath.

Mags said, "—"

But the words were lost because suddenly there was no sound.

It was as if the house had been paused. As if there had never been such a thing as sound. As if this thing they remembered as sound had always been a false memory.

Olly reached out and gripped her sister's hand tightly.

And then all the sound came back at once.

56

I like your place, mate," Jordan said. This was a joke, because it was not his place. It was a twenty-four-hour convenience store that Declan had been loitering in for the last fifteen minutes, staying out of the cold.

It was one o'clock in the morning. He was very awake. This was a side effect of not taking his sleeping pill. This was a side effect of Jordan Hennessy calling him at midnight. This was a side effect of him being a fool. The entire place had the feeling only achievable at one o'clock in the morning, when everyone has joined a club, the club of people who are not in bed. A club defined not by being *with* the other members of the club but rather against everyone else. Jordan Hennessy had just pulled up to the gas station in a red Toyota Supra, and she gazed past Declan to the glowing lights of the convenience store behind him with an approving nod. She didn't seem to mind that when she'd called thirty minutes before, he'd given her this address to pick him up at instead of his real address. He supposed she was a forger. She was hardwired for suspicion, for criminality, for covering one's tracks.

What are you doing here, Declan?

"I've fixed it up a lot," he said.

Jordan looked brighter than when he'd seen her in the museum, more alive here in this after-dark world, under glittering midnight fluorescents, behind the wheel of a car, unfettered by walls and opening and closing times and the wakeful expectations of other people.

"Well, it really shows," she said. She unlocked the car door. "Ready to roll?"

What are you doing here?

Getting into a car with a girl from the Fairy Market.

Just for tonight, he thought. He'd go back to being dull as soon as the sun came up.

When he opened the passenger side door, *The Dark Lady* looked back at him. The painting rested across the seat so that it would be the first thing he saw; it was meant to shock him. He stood there, the door in his hand. The Dark Lady's expression was bitter, wary, intense.

He knew at once that this was the real painting. The seething desire leaked from the brushstrokes in a way it hadn't for the one still hidden in the closet by his kitchen. This was why he had not dreamt of *The Dark Lady*'s shore these past nights.

"When?" he asked. He shook his head a little. He could figure that part out; he knew the last time he'd had *The Dark Lady*'s dream.

"We've both got things we can't say," Jordan said. "That's just who we are, isn't it? This was the only one that made me feel ugly to not say it."

He asked the question he couldn't guess. "Why did you do it?"

Jordan's expression was frank. "Here's the deal: You don't ask me why I had it, and I won't ask you about the man who made it. I can't do any better than that right now. It's all I got on a"—she looked at the car's clock, which was clearly wrong—"Friday night at four p.m."

He could feel his mouth quirking at the absurdity of it all.

He felt like laughing. He didn't know why. If it was because she was funny, or if it was because he was laughing at himself because he was an idiot, or if it was the way her wide grin was so infectious when she made a joke.

"So what I have is a fake," he said.

"*Fake* is a strong word. *Replica* is gentler, don't you think? Limited edition print, finished by hand?" Jordan said. She was not nearly as apologetic as one might expect in the circumstances. "You can take it back and walk away, no hard feelings. Or you can shove that old bag in the back and come with me for a little while."

If this was the real painting, that meant there was still backing paper to be pulled from the canvas, still swords to be pulled from stones. He wouldn't think about that. He was shivering there standing in that open door, though he didn't know if it was from the cool night, or the lateness of the hour, or the difficulty of the day, or the Dark Lady's scowl, or Jordan Hennessy's grin.

What are you doing here, Declan?

"Do you have a preference?" he asked.

Jordan said, "This car's a two-seater, Mr. Lynch."

He would be dull again tomorrow, he told himself again.

He maneuvered *The Dark Lady* into the back and slid into her place.

"Where are you taking me?" he asked.

She put the car into gear with the thoughtless certainty of someone who has been in cars so often they are just another part of their body. "How do you feel about being the first Jordan Hennessy original?"

They drove to Georgetown, which he wasn't expecting, to go with this wild girl to one of the most cultivated and comely neighborhoods in Washington, DC. Here, historic townhomes crowded like close friends behind mature trees, everything handsome and polite. He longed for a Georgetown town house like he longed for a *Senator* or *Congressman* before his name——he longed for it because he liked the look of them, but he also longed for it because he liked the look that followed when people heard that you were a congressman or lived in Georgetown.

Jordan parked along a quiet, dark street and got a bag from the back. "Sorry, it's a bit of a jog. I hope you have your Crocs."

Together the two of them walked a few quiet blocks to a neighborhood picturesque even in the middle of the night: warm streetlights, lacy dark leaves before them, gentle brick townhomes, wrought iron, ivy. Jordan sidled between two tall buildings, past parked bicycles and rubbish bins, to a low back garden gate. It had a small padlock. Jordan rested her bag on the other side of the gate, climbed, and then waited for him to climb after her.

Trespassing was not on Declan's ordinary menu.

He did it anyway.

At the back door, Jordan leaned into a keypad and punched a few digits. The door hummed and unlocked. She stepped inside, gestured for him to follow, and then closed the door behind him.

They stood in a dark hall that was nonetheless incompletely dark in the way of city darkness. The streetlights came in red-gold through the front windows and made big squares of comfortable city night light across the wood floor. The house smelled of lemon verbena and stale old house.

"It's empty?" he guessed.

"They rent it sometimes," Jordan replied. "You just have to gander the calendar online to make sure no one's coming. It's too spendy for the area, though, so mostly it's empty."

He didn't ask her how she'd gotten the keycode, and she didn't offer it. She gestured for him to follow her, and he did, moving quietly toward the staircase.

"You don't live here."

"No," she said, "but I gave it a look when we—I was finding a place in the city. And now I just come every so often to paint. Not as much as I used to."

They were climbing now, one flight, to a second floor that was mostly a single large room that must have been quite bright during the day, because it was quite bright during the night. The streetlight was looking right in the window at them, and its attention was illuminating. The room had a beautiful tattered Persian rug on the floor and a clawfoot desk that looked as if it would walk up for a pet and a biscuit. Easels were set up everywhere. A concrete greyhound sniffed the air. It was very chic and specific.

"I don't know who lives here," Jordan confessed, "but I love them. In my mind, they're old lovers who can't stand to live with each other but can't stand to live entirely without, and so they keep this place as a sort of pact to see each other for one week each season."

As she began to unpack her bag, Declan wandered from easel to easel, looking at the paintings on them. Landscapes, mostly, some fiddly cityscapes of DC-area landmarks. The walls behind them had photos of places all over the world in black and white. He looked for evidence of the old lovers who couldn't stand to live with or without each other but saw only one older woman smiling at the camera. She seemed in love with her surroundings, not with the picture-taker.

"I'm going to paint in the dark," Jordan said. "Even I don't want to see what I create left to my own devices."

He turned to find her standing at one of the easels, a blank prepared board propped up, her little paint palette open with eight colors squeezed on it within brush's reach on a spindly table beside her. The jar of Tyrian purple was there, too, unopened. He just looked at her there, standing with her things and her canvas waiting for his face, and he thought of the town house back in Alexandria with his brothers in it.

"You don't really mean that this is your first original," Declan said. "It can't possibly be." He remembered how quickly she had copied the Sargent at the Fairy Market. How thoroughly he'd been fooled by *The Dark Lady*. One didn't get that good at being other people without a lot of practice.

Jordan loaded her brush with paint. "I learned by copying. And then I copied for a living. I think some forgers would say their paintings 'in the style of' are originals, but they're telling themselves bedtime stories. So you're my first. Park your bum," she said, and gestured to the armchair opposite her.

"How?"

"With your arse and glutes."

He laughed, explosively, turning his face to do it, and she laughed, too.

He sat.

"How still do I have to be?"

"You can talk." She looked at the blank canvas. She let out a breath and shook out her hands.

"Whoo."

She began. He couldn't see what she was doing, but it was no hardship to sit quietly and watch her work. Her attention flicked from her canvas to him, checking reality against her creation and vice versa. It was a strange feeling to be studied after years of attempting to avoid it. He wasn't sure it was good for him. It was like dabbling in his father's criminal machinations; he could tell that there was a large part of him that secretly liked it.

"There are letters from Sargent's sitters," Declan said eventually.

The corners of her mouth rose, although her eyes stayed on the painting. "Tell me about them."

He did. He told her about how the people who would be the subjects of future Sargent paints wrote that they would come for sitting after sitting only to watch him face an empty canvas, doing nothing. Hours upon hours spent in the company of a painter who wasn't painting. Just facing down that empty canvas. Staring at them. A wizard without magic. An orchestra quiet in the pit. He told her about how they wrote that after a certain point, Sargent would suddenly attack the canvas, painting with ferocious energy, dashing at the canvas to slam paint down before retreating to eye it, circling for the next round. He told her how the letter-writers said he'd shout and curse at the canvas as he painted, how it was as if he was possessed, and they were half-frightened of him and his genius. He told her about how if he put down even a mark he didn't like on the subject's face, he would scrape the whole thing away and begin again. The only mark worth keeping was the spontaneous one.

"Is it really spontaneous, though, if you've done ten spontaneous marks and erased them before it?" Jordan asked. "I think that's just not showing people the work in the margins, isn't it? You've practiced spontaneity. You want the viewer to respond to the unfretful line, even though it took fretting to get there. You're making it about them instead of about you. True performance. What a master."

She was telling him something about herself.

"No one knew him," Declan said. He was telling her something about himself. "All those letters and all the records we have about him. He was such a public figure, he lived not long ago, but they still don't know for sure if he had any lovers."

Jordan put her brush into the turpentine and pressed the bristles against the side of the jar until the paint billowed dark.

"He had at least one," she said. "Because *I* love him. Here now. Come see yourself."

He got up, but before he got to the canvas, Jordan stood to interrupt him with a hand flat on his belly. He was very still. The room smelled of turpentine and the warm, productive scent of the paints; probably they should've cracked a window. The concrete greyhound kept sniffing the air and the friendly city night light kept sneaking in around the drapes and Jordan's palm stayed flat against his skin, not through his shirt.

He felt a bright humming energy all through him, something he hadn't felt in a very long time. His stomach was a ruin. His life in black and white; this moment in color.

Declan's phone buzzed.

He sighed.

Jordan stepped back, bowing a little, giving him permission, the moment instantly deflated by how little work the phone had had to do to capture his attention. He took his phone from his pocket and looked at it.

Matthew had sent a text: *please come home* ☹

It was the plaintive text of a child to a parent, sent to Declan because Matthew had no parent, and because it was the middle of the night, and he'd woken, if he had slept at all, and remembered that he was a dream.

"I . . ." he began.

Jordan smoothly anticipated the cue. She retreated another step back to her canvas, and there, with the side of one of her brushes, she scraped all of her work away.

"Why—?"

Jordan's slow smile spread once more. "You'll have to come back for another sitting."

He had told himself it would only be for that night, and he had meant it, he had, but he was a liar, even to himself, and so he said, "Yes."

57

Dabney Pitts had never done anything heroic in his life until that day. No one had really asked him to. No one had ever really asked him to do anything. He was twenty-eight years old and neither very clever nor very stupid. He was neither very handsome nor very ugly, tall nor short. He was just a guy, and before that, he'd been just a kid, and before that, he'd been just a baby. No one really asked him to do anything. They mostly didn't remember him. He didn't make waves.

But now he'd made waves.

He'd barricaded that strange woman in the freezer.

The old ladies looked pretty bad. When he'd come home from getting high with Welt, he'd found them careened across the stairs in an unnatural way. Mags's mouth was open, and there was a little bit of blood in it. On her tongue. Slicked, sort of. She didn't have as many teeth as he did. He wasn't sure if that was a new situation. Olly looked a little better, but one of her eyes looked wrong. *Collapsed* wasn't the word for it, but it was better than *crumpled*, because it was hard to crumple something as wet as an eyeball.

He'd found a woman who looked a lot like a more mature version of the old ladies' new tenant hiding in the bedroom with blood spattered on her. He'd forced her into the freezer with a kitchen knife. He had an idea that otherwise she might crawl out a window. The broom closet might have worked, but he didn't have a way to lock it, and in any case it was too much work to get all the stuff out of there she might use as a weapon. She was obviously dangerous.

Easier to put her in the empty chest freezer in the crawl space and set some shit on top of it.

She'd said, "Please don't do this."

"It's unplugged," he'd told her.

"Just let me go."

"Shut up," he'd replied, and the rush of bravery to his head had been nearly too much for Dabney Pitts. He wasn't entirely sure he was built for it. He'd been doing all right, he thought, until this recent downward turn had brought him to a spare room at Rider House after he used the last of his rent money for pot and a Redbox rental of that new comedy that involved a beach house and that one actress he thought was cute as a rabbit.

"Help's coming," he told Olly now. This probably wasn't true. This wasn't the kind of neighborhood and house that cops hurried to, not like nice white suburban neighborhoods where they didn't expect bad things to happen. People, cops included, expected bad things to happen at Rider House. It didn't make them less bad; it just seemed to make them less of an emergency.

He wasn't sure if Olly was even awake to hear him. He noticed Mags had a little bit of blood coming from her ears. That didn't seem good.

He guessed he could have marched the new woman at knifepoint to the cops. Maybe. Just the idea made him feel ill. Even if he hadn't had open warrants, his courage had already been overextended; he was starting to feel distinctly uneasy in this dark house with these two women who looked less alive than he would've liked, with a woman who had visited some kind of violence barricaded in a warm freezer downstairs.

He was going to be a braver person from now on, he thought. He was going to call his sister and tell her he was sorry about taking her cash out of the coffee can while she was out. He was going to swim upstream a little. Maybe he wasn't built for it, but he wasn't built for this, either. He could get muscles.

He sat down next to Olly and took her hand. It was very cold. He said, "Just hold on."

58

Ronan was a cloud, and he was raining.

"Everyone thinks their world is the only one. A flea believes a dog is the world. A dog believes the kennel is the world. The huntsman thinks his country is the world. The king believes the globe is the world. The farther out you get, the wider you get, the higher you get, the more you see you have misunderstood the bounds of what is possible. Of what is right and wrong. Of what you can truly do. Perspective, Ronan Lynch," Bryde said. "That is what we must teach you."

It was a confused dream, lacking all the clarity of his dream at the mansion. Within the dream, he couldn't remember what he'd successfully dreamt about, only that it had been sharper than this one. Mostly he remembered being a cloud. It was very peaceful. No one expected much from a cloud but for it to do what it was made to do. He could hear the little pattering of the precipitation down below.

"Are you going to do that all night?" Bryde asked.

Ronan didn't reply, because he was a cloud. He was glad to be spared the conversation, really. Words felt exhausting and he was relieved to find he didn't have the necessary parts to form them. He spread through the colorless sky and rained some more. He thundered a little.

Bryde's voice sounded a little annoyed. "You're not going anywhere, so I might as well tell you a story. Are you going to be quiet?"

Ronan did not entirely cease thundering, but he changed it to a low roar.

"Probably you've heard it before, your father from Belfast, your mother from a Belfast man's dreaming: the hawk of Achill," Bryde said. "The hawk of Achill was the oldest man in Ireland, so goes the story. He was born Fintan mac Bóchra in a place far away from Ireland, and when Noah's flood threatened, he fled to Ireland with two other men and fifty women. Noah's flood washed away his companions and the foolish world of men, but Fintan transformed himself into a salmon and lived."

Ronan saw vaguely, from above, his rain making interesting divots on a vast ocean's surface, and deeper, he glimpsed a salmon digging through the water. In the way of a dream, he could be above the water and below it at once, and he watched the salmon navigate through strange kelp forests and past frightening creatures of the open sea.

"Fintan coursed through the ocean and learned everything about that strange world that he couldn't have known as a man. After the flood receded, he could've become a man again, but he'd acquired a taste for worlds beside the one he'd been born into. Having learned the world of men and the world of fish, he transformed himself into a hawk, and he pitched through the skies for the next five thousand years, becoming the wisest man in Ireland."

Now Ronan saw this, too, the hawk with its crisp feathers wheeling through him, so deft and nimble with its flight the rain never touched it.

"You can learn a lot when you see something through someone else's eyes," Bryde said, and he sounded a little sad. "You can learn a lot when you see it from below, or from far above. You can learn a lot when you see generations live and die while you soar in slow, high circles in a changing sky."

The cloud that was Ronan had begun to rain on a pale beach beside turquoise water. He was starting to feel a little shitty again. He rumbled; words were coming back to him and he didn't want them.

Bryde said, "Some of the stories said Fintan finally turned back into a man, and finally died. But some of them say he's still up there, soaring far above the rest of the world, holding all the world's wisdom and secrets in that ancient mind. Five thousand years of knowledge, five thousand years of below and above. Imagine what you could learn if you put out that arm and the hawk of Achill landed on it."

The dream abruptly changed.

Ronan stood on a familiar cold shore. The cloud was gone; he had his human body back. The wind snagged his clothing and threw sand up against his skin as he faced a turquoise ocean before him. He knew without looking there would be black rocks tumbled up behind him.

The Dark Lady's ocean.

Ronan felt intensely present, there on *The Dark Lady*'s shore. The painting, he thought. The painting must be back under Declan's roof.

"There you are again," Bryde said wryly.

He was here, yes, and now that he wasn't Ronan-the-cloud, he had room in his mind for all the concerns of Ronan-the-boy. "Matthew hates me."

"Did you want him to be stupid forever?" Bryde asked. "Wisdom is hard. Do you think the hawk was always happy with what he learned?"

"He thinks I'm a liar."

"Then perhaps," Bryde said, "you shouldn't have lied."

Ronan put his hands behind his neck, just as Matthew had in the church. He closed his eyes.

"Perhaps the next creature you should turn yourself into in your dreams should be a dream," Bryde said. "What do you think a dream wants?"

"Fuck *everything*."

"What does a dream want?"

"I don't want to play right now."

"What does a dream want?"

Ronan opened his eyes. "To live without their dreamer."

"Look at me," Bryde said.

Ronan turned, shielding his eyes. High up on the black rocks, he saw a silhouette against the gray.

"You're ready for the next part of the game," Bryde called down. "I am, too. But I've been burned before. Wait, I tell myself, wait, slow, high circles, watching."

"Don't tell me I didn't save Hennessy," Ronan said. "I was there. I kept up my end."

Bryde said, "She is just afraid. She knows what dreams want, and she wants that for her dreams. Do you want that for Matthew?"

He already knew that Ronan wanted it for Matthew. It didn't even have to be said. Ronan had wanted that for as long as he knew Matthew was one of his.

Bryde said, "I want it, too."

"Do you know how to do it?"

The silhouette on the rocks scanned the sky as if looking for the hawk from the story. Then Ronan saw the silhouette visibly square its shoulders. Bracing. Preparing.

"Next box," Bryde said, "rabbits are coming to you. Next box. Are you ready?"

Ronan held out his arms on either side. *I'm here, aren't I?*

Bryde said, "You have been waiting for me; she has been waiting for you. When she stretches out her arm, answer the call. Remember that hawks have talons."

Ronan woke up.

It was early, early morning. The light through the blinds was still the ugly orange of the streetlights outside, fencing his vision in narrow slats. His phone was ringing on Declan's guest room nightstand.

He picked it up.

59

Ten years before, J. H. Hennessy had shot herself.

One shot, .45 caliber. The gun belonged to a friend of the family, reports said. It was registered, everything north of proper except for the part where it killed someone, and maybe even that, because isn't that every guy's fitful dream? There was music playing when it happened. An old jazz recording, some woman's voice pitching and lilting along as the sound fuzzed and popped. Jay was in a large closet. The lights were out. The only illumination came from a small, high window, and everything it touched was gray. She was dressed in a bra and underwear and a robe. Mascara was drawn down her face. She was holding a gun to her own head, and she was listening for the door to open.

This was not in the reports, but Hennessy knew it because she was the one who opened the door.

"Mum?" Hennessy said.

"You won't miss me," Hennessy's mother said.

"Wait," Hennessy said.

The gun barrel flashed.

It was also not in the reports that Jay had died disappointed. It was not supposed to be Jordan Hennessy, her daughter, who opened the closet door. It was supposed to be Bill Dower. All week long she had been courting his attention through a series of checks and balances, emotional outbursts and reticent withdrawals, and she had concluded the week's emotional roller coaster by putting herself in that closet with the gun. Hennessy understood now that Bill Dower was meant to feel sorry for her and find her; Bill Dower was meant to take the gun out of her hand. Hennessy understood now that she had not been important in the equation, which had always only ever had two variables: Jay, and Bill Dower. Hennessy was one of those inert bits in between, only important when she had to interact with a variable.

She was not supposed to open the closet door.

It was supposed to be Bill Dower.

It was supposed to be Bill Dower.

It was supposed to be Bill Dower.

But Hennessy ruined the setup, both by spoiling the surprise of her mother with the gun and also by proving that Bill Dower wasn't coming, the games were over.

And all she could say was—

Wait.

Later, therapists said she was taking it better than they had hoped.

Of course she was, Hennessy thought. She'd been expecting her mother to kill either herself or Hennessy for years.

She was a mess, Bill Dower said. What a beautiful mess.

Like mother, like daughter.

But Jordan wasn't a mess, Hennessy thought. Any mess in Jordan was from living with Hennessy. Hennessy, who'd said the worst possible thing to her in Senko's parking lot the night before. Where had that foulness even come from? Who was this person who would sneer that she was the dreamer, and Jordan only the dream, as if Jordan were not more competent at living in every single way?

A Hennessy, that was who.

She knew all the girls were disappointed with her. She saw it in their faces when she returned that night. Jordan was right. Something about Ronan Lynch, about another dreamer, had hopped them up on hope more than anything else she'd ever seen. They'd seen what he could do and they thought Hennessy, with a little help, could do the same. They didn't understand.

"Where's Jordan?" June asked.

"We had a row," Hennessy said. "She'll get over it."

And she could see in their faces that they were proud of Jordan.

She slunk off to the studio to chain-smoke. She hated that they were hopeful, but more than that, she hated that they were hopeful about *her*. She was going to let them down again. She always let them down. Her poor girls. What a mess.

Early that morning, her timer went off, and instead of resetting it, she called Ronan Lynch.

He met her at a place called the Shenandoah Café, near Gainesville, west of DC, a restaurant located the opposite direction of rush hour traffic and open at the absurdly early hour that she'd called him. It was not as empty as one would expect given the hour; the clientele had a vaguely truck-stop vibe although the café itself was far quainter than the typical interstate stop. Buckled wood floors, primitive shop shelves from floor to ceiling, booths huddled around glass-topped casement display tables, every cranny filled with hundreds—maybe thousands—of knickknacks. According to a sign by the register, these knickknacks had been donated by customers from all over the world. Some appeared valuable, like parchment-thin china cups, and others appeared worthless, like Dracula rubber ducks. It was an installation where noise, rather than worth, was the relevant measure of success.

The hostess had left them at a table that contained metal roses, golden bells, and etched ocarinas. The shelf beside it held hollow books and ships in bottles and Excalibur letter openers.

Ronan said, "My family used to come here."

"You and the big D. Declan." She tried out the word again as she picked up the laminated menu card. Everything you could want as long as what you wanted was breakfast food. "I don't know how you don't just say his name all the time. It's like chocolate in your mouth, isn't it?"

He regarded her with unimpressed silence. He had a judgmental silence that said far more than words. This particular silence conveyed that he thought it was stupid that she was blustering when he was being earnest, don't fucking waste his time.

Hennessy raised an eyebrow and shot back her own silence, which was less nuanced. It said something along the lines of *Sorry, man, bluster's all I got because I'm scared shitless and dying.*

Sad violins, said Ronan's silence.

I don't need your pity, said Hennessy's.

"Good morning, kids." The server had appeared and, without prompting, began disseminating coffee from an old metal carafe into the mugs already assembled on napkins before them. She was an older woman, plump and bright-eyed. Her name tag read *"Wendy,"* as if it might be an alias, her true identity hidden from the regular clientele of the Shenandoah Café. She leaned close to get their orders, confidentially, as if they were secret debriefings, then tapped her pencil against her pad and left.

Ronan waited.

Hennessy sighed and slid down into her side of the booth

with her mug of coffee. She wished she could have a cigarette. She wanted something more to do with her hands. "Okay then, what do you want to know? I've had the same dream since my mum died. Every time I close my eyes long enough to dream, it begins, always the same. Always the shit, always awful."

"What's the dream?"

"I read," Hennessy said, "that the most common recurring dream in America is falling. I would've guessed test-taking. I hear that one's common for perfectionists."

"What's the dream?"

"Supposedly, lovers can share the same dream if their heads are in close proximity," Hennessy added, a little desperately, holding her fingers up to demonstrate. "Not very peer-reviewed, though. At least the blog post I read said it wasn't."

"What's the dream?"

Wendy slid their food in front of them. She leaned in close, conspiratorially, and asked if she could get them any condiments. Ronan looked at her with his heavy silence. It said, *Get the fuck out of here we're having a private conversation.*

She patted his hand. "You remind me of my boy," she said fondly, and withdrew.

Ronan turned that silence on Hennessy, leveling it over the top of a waffle that Wendy had sprayed a whipped-cream smiley face on.

Hennessy looked down at her plate, which had four triangles of French toast, all pointing in the same direction, toward the door. She swallowed.

"It's," she said.

She tried to not even think about it while she was awake. It felt contagious. This was the closest she had gotten in a decade and it felt bad. Incredibly bad.

She didn't say anything else. She couldn't do it. She'd just have to let down Jordan and the other girls. Jordan didn't know what it was like.

Ronan turned his arms over so that his hands lay palm up on the table between them and for a moment, she thought he was making an elaborate gesture for *come on*. But instead he said, "Those are from nightmares."

She had to lean to look. Crazed white scars traveled up his forearms, carved by a sizeable weapon.

"Night horrors," he said. "Claws like this." He formed his fingers into talons, and then mimed them ripping him open, fingers skipping over the top of the leather bracelets that hid the worst of it and right up to his elbow. "Two days in the hospital."

He didn't add anything sentimental like *We'll beat this thing* or *I've been there, you can trust me.* He just withdrew his arms and smashed the whipped-cream smile on his waffles with the back of his fork. He said, "They all thought it was something easy as razor blades. And they couldn't fucking understand even that."

Ronan was not Jordan. Not a dream. He knew what it was like.

"The Lace," whispered Hennessy.

She could feel her ears ringing. Little sparks danced around the corners of her vision. She had to put down her coffee cup because her fingers couldn't hold it; they were weak and tingling. She was so afraid she thought she would pass out. She needed her timer—

Snap.

Ronan had snapped his fingers in front of her face. She focused acutely on his fingers, right in front of her.

"You're awake," he said. When she didn't say anything else, he handed her one of the overturned coffee cups and added, "Breathe into that."

While she breathed into the cold mug, he cut his waffle into four enormous bites and ate two of them.

"It's just me," Hennessy said. Her voice was very quiet. He had to lean on his elbows to hear her. "And it."

In her mind, it was unfolding, clear as the dream. Hennessy, small, insubstantial, fragile, every skill and power and cleverness she had ridiculous and human. *It*, however, was huge in ways her human mind couldn't fully understand. It was dark, but again, dark was an incomplete description of it. Shape and color were three-dimensional concepts and it was something beyond that. Where it was closest to her it looked like geometric slants and cutouts, through which she could see light behind it. Or perhaps included in it. It looked like a hectic, looming lace.

"It sees me," Hennessy said, in an even quieter voice. Her hands were shaking. God, it could see her *now*, she was sure of it, because she'd said it out loud, and that was enough to bring it into the waking world. "The dream begins, and it's there, and then it *sees* me—"

Her shoulders were quivering now, too. She could feel tears smarting in her eyes, but she couldn't quite convince them to go away.

Ronan was watching her closely, pensively.

"What does it look like?" he asked.

"The Lace," Hennessy whispered. "Like lace. It's huge. I can't explain it. It's something . . ."

Wendy reappeared. She was holding a coffee carafe, but she stood there with it hovered above the table, looking at Hennessy, with the tears caught in her lashes and her shaking hands and uneaten food.

Ronan eyed Wendy with his heavy silence, but it was not complex enough to offer an excuse for Hennessy.

"Honey, you okay?" asked Wendy comfortingly.

Through a hiccup of shaky tears, Hennessy managed to say, "I'm having his baby. Can I have an orange juice?"

Wendy shot Ronan a look that was less maternal before vanishing.

Ronan shook his head, with equal parts admiration and disbelief. "You're a real shithead. Look at you. You can't help it. You're out of your mind. You'll be a shithead on your deathbed."

Hennessy laughed shakily and stuffed French toast in her mouth. She wasn't bleeding. She had said it out loud, and she wasn't bleeding. She didn't have another tattoo choking her throat. Ronan was right. She was awake. She was awake. She was awake.

Her timer went off. She restarted it.

"My boyfriend saw something like that," Ronan said. "I don't know if it's the same thing you're seeing. But he's a psychic, and he described something similar to that. Scared the shit out of him, too."

"What'd he call it?"

Ronan stabbed his third waffle quarter. "Nothing. He screamed. Like he was dying. When I asked him why, he said it was because it saw him. Seemed like that was probably the worst thing he could imagine."

"Sounds like a match," Hennessy said. She was still shaking, but she could drink some coffee. Wendy brought her orange juice, patted her hand, and left again. "I like that old bag. She rolls with it."

"How does it hurt you? The Lace?"

This was harder to describe, not because it was any more fearful, but because it was not a process that followed waking logic. It was a process that followed dream logic, and waking language wasn't right for it. "It wants . . . it wants to come out. It wants me to *bring* it out. It knows I can. So I . . . fight it, I guess. I resist. And I know that when I do, the Lace will hurt me for it. It says if I don't let it out, it'll kill me."

"It speaks?"

"Not really. It's like . . . dream speech? I'm supposed to believe it's out loud, but it's not."

He nodded. He got it.

"It tells me it killed my mum and it will kill me, too."

This made Ronan look quite sharp-eyed, hawkish, all of a sudden. He said, "*Did* it kill her?"

"She shot herself in the face," Hennessy said.

"So it's lying. Or rather, your subconscious is lying."

Hennessy snapped, "What?"

He looked up, his final waffle quarter dropping from his fork. "It could be real, or it could be your subconscious, like my night horrors." He paused, though, frowning, as if something about his own words had puzzled him.

Hennessy said, "So is your Bryde your subconscious, then?"

"Bryde knows things I couldn't know, like you drowning," Ronan pointed out. "What does the Lace know?"

Hennessy thought, and then she said, "Your boyfriend."

That arrow neatly landed in its target.

"Bryde told me to stop saying that," Ronan said. "Asking if something in my dreams is real. He said for dreamers, it's always real, because we belong in both worlds. Waking and sleeping. One's not more true than the other."

"Do you believe that? When you dream of being naked in front of the class, that's real?"

Instead of answering, Ronan said, "There's a big part I'm not getting here, though. Where do the copies come in?"

"Well, I have to bring something back," Hennessy said. "And I can't bring the Lace."

His phone buzzed. A text from DBAG LYNCH. He ignored it. "Hold up. Why don't you just bring nothing back?"

She didn't understand.

"Are you telling me you don't know how to keep dreams in your head?"

Hennessy flicked her phone with irritation. "Why do you think I've set a timer for the last decade? Do you think I just enjoy it?"

"Before the Lace, though," Ronan said. "You didn't bring something back every time you dreamt then, surely." He saw the answer in her face. "Shit, man. You mean you've never been able to help it?"

"Are you taking the piss out of me?"

"I'm dead serious. You can't keep your dreams in your head?"

"I didn't know anyone could," Hennessy said. "I've tried. The girls are my best solution. There's only me and it in the dream, and I can't bring it, so I bring me—that's the copy—and it hurts me as I wake up. And gives me this classic little brand."

She pointed to the tattoo on her throat, careful not to touch it; it was still tender.

"And you've never told anyone this before," Ronan said. "All the girls think it's just the copies killing you. They don't know you're stopping yourself from manifesting a demon."

"When you put it that way."

Ronan let out a long breath. "Fuck, Bryde. What do you want me to do here?"

He took out his wallet and thumbed out some bills. He chucked them on the end of the table and rubbed a hand over his face several times.

"Now you know why I said you couldn't help me," Hennessy told him. But he sort of had already. It was a little less dreadful to have finally said it out loud.

"And I can't," Ronan said. "Not by myself. How do you feel about trees?"

60

Farooq-Lane finally found Parsifal because of the dogs.

Night had passed and morning had passed and it was well into day when she saw them. It was just three scruffy mutts of three scruffy sizes giving all their attention to a trash bin behind a strip mall, and there was no reason to stop except that she thought to herself, *Wouldn't it be awful if they were eating Parsifal?*

She had no reason to think they were, but it was such a gruesome idea that she pulled up beside the trash bin. She made an enormous amount of noise when she got out, clapping and stomping her feet, her heart thrumming unpleasantly. Because she was so keyed up, she thought they'd put up a fight, but they were just ordinary strays, not monsters, and they fled immediately with the guilty look of domesticated dogs caught in trash.

And then she saw Parsifal.

Or rather, she saw his legs sticking out from behind the trash bin.

Oh God.

With effort, she made herself take a step, and then another, and then another, stepping into the shadow of the strip mall.

He was not eaten.

It was worse.

Farooq-Lane often wondered if her brother had meant to kill her, too.

He'd clearly timed his attack around her visit to Chicago. According to various eyewitness reports, the weapon went off right as her taxi was seen pulling into the neighborhood. Hard to tell if he had timed it correctly for her to be the first to find the victims, or if he had timed it incorrectly and meant for her to have already been inside the house when it went off.

She'd tipped the taxi driver and rolled out her tiny, attractive suitcase and looked at her parents' home. It was magazine perfect: a brownstone with big stairs, old bushes and trees planted out front. What people wished city living looked like as they sighed and stacked themselves four deep with roommates in apartments. Her parents were moving to the suburbs at the end of the year, and this was going to be hers. She was the young professional who wanted the city life, they said, and could now take over the mortgage payments.

It was going to be such a handsome life, she thought.

She rolled up the walk, bumped her suitcase up the seven stairs, and found the door open.

As she did, she had three clear thoughts.

One: The cat was going to get out.

Two: There was a pair of open scissors resting directly on the inner floor mat. This was Nathan's symbol, his obsession. He hung scissors over his own bed as a child, and also over Farooq-Lane's until she made him take them down. He drew them in his notebooks and on the wall behind his bed. He collected old scissors in boxes.

Three: There were brains on the end table.

She didn't remember the day well after that. Everything she

thought she remembered always turned out to be something someone had explained to her afterward.

"Parsifal," Farooq-Lane said, and skidded to her knees beside him.

Her hands hovered over him, trying to decide what to do. It seemed foolish that she'd packed him a bag of food now. As if that would fix anything. As if that would ever fix anything. As if anything would ever be fixed again.

"I looked for you all night," she said. She was shivering, either because she was out of reach of the sun here, or from looking at him. She couldn't stand looking at him, but she couldn't stand to not.

His voice was very slight. "I would have killed you."

"What . . . what can I do?"

He said, "Could you fix my arms?"

Both arms rested at awkward angles, as if he had been thrown and then been unable to straighten then. Carefully Farooq-Lane put his pudgy young left hand on his chest, and then she put his angular, ordinary right hand over the top of it.

He was two ages at once, split more or less down the middle. His right side was the Parsifal she'd met, a teen, the oldest he'd ever get. And his left side was a much younger Parsifal, all of the right side twisted and warped to match up with how much smaller he was. It was impossible and yet there it was.

This was the first indication she'd seen of what must have been his truth before the Moderators found him and recruited him. Like all the Visionaries, he would have been caught shifting within his own timeline. From baby to child to teen to however old he would eventually get. Over and over he would swap from one age to another, bringing the sound of all those years lived between them with him as he did, killing everyone close enough to hear. Until the Moderators showed him how to turn the shifting inward, creating better visions . . . and eventually destroying him.

She had never seen it.

She didn't think this was what it was supposed to look like. This seemed like neither shifting nor having a deadly final vision.

"Can you change again?" Farooq-Lane asked. "Can you go all the way back to young if I leave?"

Parsifal's uneven, twisted chest rose and fell, rose and fell. With effort, he said, "I stopped it. The vision. Halfway. This is going to be the one to kill me and I . . ."

He had done this to himself?

He muttered something in German. Then he swallowed and finished: ". . . I need you to see the last vision when I do, so it hasn't been for nothing."

"Oh, *Parsifal.*"

Parsifal closed his eyes. It was a little easier to look at him that way. He'd lost his glasses somewhere and his eyes already looked strange and naked without them, even without them being two different sizes. "The vision will be important to you."

"To everyone," Farooq-Lane said.

"To *you,*" he said again. "Someone important to you. Oh— are—you—are—you—are—" His legs jerked.

Farooq-Lane took his right hand. "I'm here."

He whispered, "I am not tired of you."

Then he began to have the vision.

61

Farooq-Lane had seen the end of the world once before. It was after the Moderators had tracked Nathan to Ireland, but before they had organized the attack on his location. When the current Visionary found her, Farooq-Lane had been sitting in the tatty old hotel bar holding an untouched pint of beer a man had bought for her. She didn't know what her bene-factor looked like. He'd asked if she wanted a drink, and she'd looked right through him without answering, and he'd told the bartender: *Get this woman a drink and a priest* and left her to her own devices. Before they'd gotten into the car, though, the Visionary had come to her. Cormac was his name.

She was going to go kill Nathan. For what he had done: kill a lot of people. And for what he might do: kill a lot more.

The hotel was busy that night, she thought. There was a tele-vision playing sports, and men and women watched it and were rowdy. They moved around her like planets orbiting a burned-out sun.

They were going to kill Nathan.

Cormac had found her at the bar and asked her if she wanted to know why they were doing all this.

I can show you, he said. *You won't be able to forget it, though.*

Cormac had been the Moderators' Visionary for months by then, and he was well-practiced at it. If he had ever been an out-of-control Visionary, it was hard to imagine. He was a solid-looking middle-aged man with trustworthy crow's-feet around his dark eyes. She hadn't known then that was the oldest he would ever get.

Is it the truth? she'd asked.

Unless we stop it.

So she had let him show her. Life was already something she couldn't forget. She might as well *know*.

He'd drawn her into a side hall. The carpet was old green wool worn to nubbins and the wallpaper was scalloped brown and white worn to memory.

"Don't be afraid," he told her. "It's not real yet."

He put his arms around her. She could smell an unfamiliar shampoo, old perspiration, and a bit of onion. It was a hug with a stranger, which was always peculiar because unacquainted arms and ribs and hips don't fit together correctly.

And then she felt something else. Something . . . ephemeral. Something quite outside their bodies.

It was coming.

Her body hummed with strangeness.

She could tell it was coming.

Maybe I should change my mind, she thought.

But she couldn't change her mind.

It was coming.

Is this—

She only had time to wonder if it was already happening and she was missing it, and then the vision struck her.

Parsifal's vision hit her the same in that parking lot behind the strip mall.

The vision was like she was being dissolved from her feet up.

Her toes numbed, then her legs, then her body. There was no pain. There was no feeling.

There was nothing at all.

The cool dim of the parking lot melted into the glow of a different afternoon. Farooq-Lane and Parsifal walked beside an interstate packed slaughterhouse-full with cars. Everything shimmered with exhaust and smoke. She could tell from the signs that it was in the United States. From the trees it was probably east of the Mississippi. There was a city ahead of them, and the cars on both sides of the interstate were headed in the same direction: away from it.

It was on fire.

Everything that was not the interstate was on fire. A city, on fire; the world, on fire.

Her face burned with it.

It would never go out, the fire whispered. It would eat everything.

Devour, devour

The fire was doing what it promised. It was eating everything. This was the distant future. This part of the vision was always the same. Every Visionary experienced it the same way.

The vision changed. This part of the vision was the near future, and was always different. This was the part the Moderators chased. Follow this part of the vision to stop the rest of it.

This part of Parsifal's vision was fragmented. Breaking into bits. Jerking and stuttering, violently thrashing from image to image.

A battered old house. A silhouette of a person on a rearing horse. A strange, pointy, hat-shaped pile of bricks or stones. A staircase. Bodies. A little misshapen keyhole. A coffin, and in it, a mouth parted for air where there was none.

Everything was dying, including the vision.

Farooq-Lane found herself holding Parsifal's limp hand behind a featureless strip mall in the DC area. There was nothing gruesome outside his body, except that he had thrown up again, but nonetheless one could tell that everything inside his body had gone wrong-shaped, like he'd hosted a car crash inside himself. There were canyons in his form where there should not have been canyons. It seemed quite likely this was some of what he had thrown up. He was very dead.

No, he wasn't. Not quite.

"Hurry," croaked Parsifal.

Then he died.

62

Declan couldn't believe that Ronan had left him in the lurch again. His BMW had been parked in front of the town house when Jordan dropped Declan off (no point pretending she didn't know where he lived now), but by the time Declan got up a few hours later, it was gone. Declan texted him: *You leaving me to deal with Matthew today?* and Ronan answered with only *Dad's working, sweetie.*

Declan could've put his fist through the wall.

He didn't know what had come over him.

It felt like going out with Jordan the night before should've let off steam and made it easier to ease into another decade of dull hibernation, but it had had the opposite effect.

He made Matthew a weekend breakfast, sausages from the freezer, eggs, fat toast from the organic local bread the farmers' market people had sent to the senator's office. Matthew sat silently at the bar in the kitchen, not fidgeting, not kicking his legs, not laughing, not humming, doing absolutely nothing annoying at all. Since he'd moved in with Declan, Declan had often longed for Matthew to be quieter—less chewing with his mouth open, less prattling, fewer jokes read off websites, less dropping and knocking over of things with *ooops ha ha*, less thundering up and down the stairs as if he were seven instead of seventeen.

But now that he was quiet, Declan hated it.

Declan came to sit next to Matthew. "Are you angry?"

Matthew moved his food around his plate.

"Are you sad?"

Matthew lined up his sausages, then separated them with chunks of egg.

"I can't help you if you don't talk."

Matthew studied his breakfast as if it might wander off if he didn't. "This is the worst thing you've ever done to me."

It was an interesting way to frame it, but it wasn't wrong. It was a thing acted upon the creature that was Matthew Lynch. Ronan had imposed existence on him. Declan had decided for him how it would be easiest to bear it, knowing full well it would be disastrous if the truth came out. Yes, they had done it to him. Yes, Declan accepted blame for it.

Declan brushed his younger brother's curls back from his forehead. This motion was one he'd done so often—ever since Matthew was just a toddler—that sometimes he dreamt of it. His fingers had memorized the texture of his dense curls, his round forehead, the gentle warmth of him.

"Do I have a soul?" Matthew asked.

"I don't know."

"Do I have magic powers?"

"I don't think so."

"Am I invincible?"

"I wouldn't press it."

"Are *you* dreamed?"

Declan shook his head. No, he was human in a family that wasn't.

"Does this mean that if Ronan dies, I'm going to fall asleep like Dad's cows and Mom did?"

It was a rhetorical question. There was silence for several

minutes. Declan heard the neighbors talking on their phone in the next town house over. They were benevolent shouters. They wanted to cancel their premium stations, they told the phone, they just weren't home enough to justify it. This was untrue. They were home all the time.

Declan did his best to dispense comfort. "Matthew, everybody dies. We all have to come to grips with that. We all know that it's life-threatening for us to fall off a cliff or eat poison or step in front of a bus. You just have to also add that it's dangerous for you if something happens to Ronan. Nothing really has to change. You just know now that Dad bought your social security number on the black market."

"He did *what?*"

Declan went on, "And now we can be open with you about why you've never had a real school physical or anything."

"Wait, why?"

Declan regretted saying anything. "In case you don't have internal organs."

Matthew made a strangled noise. He dropped his head into his hands. Declan didn't know what was worse—being caught in the lie, or not knowing if it was even worth the lie all along. Would it have been easier for Matthew to grow up knowing he wasn't real? That he was a piece of Ronan's imagination, something so utterly dependent that if Ronan died, he couldn't go on? That his existence was so subservient that when an invisible external energy source fluctuated, he began to power down like a machine without fuel? Declan had thought he was giving him the gift of reality. Of believing he was true, whole, just as worthy of love as someone who had come into this world by more ordinary means. Not a thing. Not a creature. A human.

In a very small voice, Matthew said, "I'm the fake brother."

"What?" Declan, the true fake brother, asked.

"You two are real Lynches. You and Ronan. Real brothers. I'm just pretend. I'm just—"

This was awful.

"Matthew," Declan interrupted. "That's just not true."

Matthew's mouth was crumpled.

This was *awful*. Declan could feel the awfulness rising in him, combining with that desire to put his fist through the wall, combining with just plain *desire* for Jordan Hennessy and everything she represented, and he thought about diving deep into *The Dark Lady*'s turquoise ocean and disappearing and everything that meant.

And he broke. He broke for the second time that year, after being good and dull and invisible for so very long. He had broken the first time by dialing that phone number and asking for the key to Colin Greenmantle's collection. He broke on that Saturday morning by asking, "So you think Ronan and I are true Lynch brothers?"

"Don't be stupid," Matthew said. "Of course you are."

Declan's pulse slowly stepped up. "You sure of that?"

"You *are*."

"Get *The Dark Lady*," Declan said. "From the closet. The one closest to the front."

Matthew shot Declan a bemused look, but Declan could tell that the puzzle of it had shaken him from his stupor. He slid off the stool and opened the kitchen closet. Inside it were the two *Dark Ladies*: the original that Declan had just put away last night after returning with Jordan, and behind it, the copy that she had somehow managed to sneak in there.

"What is this?!" Matthew said, with a bit of his old rollicking tone.

"Front one," Declan said. "Put it on the dining room table."

He joined his brother at the table, swiping aside a pile of bills and newspapers so that there was room.

"Facedown," Declan said.

The two of them looked at the brown backing paper, the tiny printed words: *Mór Ó Corra.*

Matthew waited for Declan to explain. Declan put a box cutter into his hand instead.

"Cut the paper off," Declan said.

He crossed his arms tightly over his chest as his youngest brother leaned over the painting and began to cut with the precision of a surgeon, his face deep in concentration. The paper hissed and crackled as it fell away.

Declan realized he'd closed his eyes.

He opened them.

"What is this?" Matthew asked again.

There was a square dark card tucked between the canvas and the stretcher. Durable, rounded edges, printed with the image of a woman with a cross painted on her face. Matthew plucked it out and turned it over. On the back was an Irish telephone number and, in Niall's handwriting, *The New Fenian.*

"This painting isn't of Aurora," Declan said. "It's of Mór Ó Corra, and she is my mother."

63

urry, Parsifal had said. *Hurry.* There was no hurrying when it came to putting together fractured clues from a dying vision. There was no hurrying when it came to getting across Washington, DC. There was no hurrying when all you could think of was a ruined body behind a trash bin. There was no hurrying when you didn't know what you were hurrying *to*.

Farooq-Lane felt as if she had been staring at the same neighborhood for hours. They all had the same atmosphere. Tatty lawns, tired buildings joined at the hip, cars on blocks, heaving sidewalks, blistered asphalt.

None of them were the house Parsifal had shown her in his last vision. The problem with the vision was that it was like a dream—filled with emotional truths instead of actual truths. It conveyed the way a building felt rather than how it looked.

It was hard to focus on anything with Parsifal's body bundled tenderly in the Zed's rug in her trunk.

There was the End of the World, capital *E*, capital *W*, she knew. She knew she had to focus. She'd just *seen* why she had to focus. But Parsifal's world had ended, small *w*, small *e*, and it felt very bad, and it was hard to keep things in perspective.

Someone was tapping on her back window and she realized she had let the car drift to a stop in the middle of the road, staring off at the houses. It was an old man with no teeth and a walking stick. He seemed to want a conversation. He was chanting *pretty lady, pretty lady.*

"You lost, pretty lady?" the old man said. He tapped the walking stick against the side of her rental car. *Tap tap tap.*

Yes, thought Farooq-Lane. *Utterly.*

Tap tap tap. She suddenly realized that the top of the walking stick he was using to tap her window was a very familiar shape: a person on a rearing horse. Another piece of Parsifal's vision.

Rolling down the window, she held up the drawing she'd made of the pointy hat shape she'd seen in the vision. "Do you know what this is?"

He leaned in close. He smelled incredibly bad. "That's Fairmount Heights, there. That's that old World War II memorial." He said it like *ol whirr wah tuh morial,* but she got the gist.

"Is that close?" she asked.

"Just south, pretty lady," he said (*jussow, pree lady*).

She had no cash, so she gave him her unopened coffee beverage instead and he seemed content. Plugging the memorial into her GPS, she discovered it was just minutes away. She didn't feel like she was hurrying fast enough, but she was doing the best she could.

The memorial was exactly how it had appeared in the vision: a stone monument shaped a little like a witch's hat. As she drove around it in ever-widening circles, her adrenaline started to flare. She was thinking about what she was really hurrying *to.* The visions took her to other dreamers. Sometimes other Visionaries. Either way, it could be a dangerous situation, and she never had a very complete picture of what she was walking into. At least before she could have asked Parsifal if they were headed into peril. She wasn't asking him anything now.

For a fleeting moment, Farooq-Lane thought she heard opera. It was faint, as if from outside the car or as if the radio were turned down nearly all the way. But before she could reach to roll down a window or turn up the music, all at once she saw the old house from the vision. Like the other houses in this neighborhood, it was a run-down building that had probably been quite charming many decades before. There was a sink in the scrubby front yard. The walk was more split than not. It was a good enough place to hide.

At the door, she knocked. *Hurry.* She tried the knob. It gave way.

She stepped in. It smelled better than she'd expected. The sun was full on outside, but little of the light made its way into the house. There was an odor of old damp below, but overwhelmingly what she smelled was fresh flowers and summer. The lights were turned off. No. They were out of order. Thin lightbulb glass crunched beneath Farooq-Lane's boots.

Before her were stairs leading up into the gloomy dim. The stairs from the vision.

She went up.

At the top of them she discovered the bodies of two old women, and a note. The note said *I stayed untill I got to scared. Shes downstairs.* The old women had blood in their ears and their mouths. Their eyes had imploded.

So it wasn't a Zed who lived here.

It was a Visionary. Parsifal's last vision had taken her to his replacement.

She didn't know how she felt about this.

Hurry.

Farooq-Lane checked every room downstairs for evidence of

a Visionary. Cautiously at first, because she wasn't eager to share the fate of the old women on the stairs, and then more boldly, because every room she entered was empty.

Maybe it was like the time they'd followed Parsifal's vision to the cul-de-sac, looking for the gray BMW. Maybe she was too late. Perhaps she had not hurried enough.

Just as she was getting ready to give up and go back to the car, however, her attention was pulled to a tiny door in the stair-case that she'd missed when she'd come in. It had a keyhole. Misshapen. Another piece of Parsifal's vision.

Pulling it open, she saw that it led to a crawl space.

She clicked on her phone's flashlight and climbed down the few stairs. Then, bent over double, she peered. The last piece of Parsifal's vision was a coffin, which she didn't think was a thing she would find in a place like this. And she was right. She didn't find a coffin. But she did find a chest freezer. With bags of gravel piled on it to make sure the lid stayed closed. To make sure no one got out from inside it.

Not a coffin. But close enough.

Working fast, she shoved and kicked the gravel bags onto the floor. Dust from the floor and from the bags themselves clouded the air as they landed; her cell phone flashlight, on the floor, cast a searchlight through the billows. She couldn't see anything clearly.

Finally, Farooq-Lane cracked the lid.

She heard a convulsive gasp for air from the dark interior.

"Is it going to happen soon?" Farooq-Lane asked the unseen occupant.

Several more huge gasps for air, then: "No, not soon."

"I'm not in danger?"

"Not right now. Don't be afraid." This Visionary had just been suffocating in a chest freezer and *she* was reassuring Farooq-Lane. A limp hand stretched out, resting on the edge of the freezer. The skin was very pale and wrinkly—so completely opposite to what Farooq-Lane had been expecting that she flinched a little. Farooq-Lane got her cell phone and directed the light into the chest freezer. Inside, an old woman with long snow-white hair shielded her eyes with her other hand.

Farooq-Lane had never seen a Visionary so old before.

"What's your name?" Farooq-Lane asked.

"Liliana."

64

I had different intentions for our next d . . . get-together," Declan said, and Jordan heard him cautiously place his foot upon the word *date* before deciding it wouldn't hold him.

"Did you?" Jordan asked. "It seems about par for the course, if you ask me, old friend."

They were in her car again, through no particular discussion. She preferred driving to riding, and he seemed happier to be able to look out the window and in the rearview mirror in a paranoid way in between studying directions and texts on his phone. He looked handsomer than she remembered, with his good straight teeth and his dark curls and a nice sweater Hennessy would hate. Easy to imagine painting him again, framed as he was in the window, the fall colors rich and deep on this overcast day. Easy to imagine touching him again.

"You remind me," Jordan said, "of a dog."

He tapped away at his phone. He had a peculiar way of texting—he used his thumb on one hand, his index finger on the other. Odd. Charming. Without looking up, he murmured, "Thank you very much. Right at the next light."

"They look different when you know them," Jordan said. "You know when you see a dog on a street, and it's just some stray tosser, and when you see a dog on the street, and it's one you've met before?"

"I don't meet many dogs on the street."

"I'm saying you scrub up nice," she said, and he laughed his disbelieving laugh again, the head turned away to hide it.

They were going to see Boudicca.

"I'm looking for my birth mother," Declan had said, when he called her. "But the people I need to talk to won't talk to me unless I bring a woman."

And Jordan had known instantly that he was talking about Boudicca.

Boudicca. Jordan didn't know if the word itself sounded like a threat, or if she only thought it did because she knew what it stood for. *Boo-dih-kah.* The first time they'd approached Jordan it had been at a Fairy Market in London. The woman had been as mundane in appearance as one could possibly manage: straightened light-brown hair, wing eyeliner, blouse, blazer. Looking to partner with talented women like yourself, she'd said, as if she was pitching a job fair. Benefits to both parties. Lifelong investment. Taking care of business to allow your creative energies to be directed. Jordan had accepted her card, a durable little square with a logo of a woman with a cross on her face, but she hadn't really understood what was being offered.

At the next Fairy Market, Jordan saw a deal go down badly. She didn't see the fine details of it, but she heard the man shorting the woman for the price of her dyes. She saw the edge of the whispered conversation, the threats he made to keep the woman from making a fuss about it. Later, she saw the man being beaten by three women in the parking lot as other vendors walked by without turning their heads. They sliced a cross on his clothing that matched the squat, square one on the logo's face. Jordan understood a little better.

At the Market after that, Jordan saw another woman arguing

with the blazer-wearing woman from her first meeting. The blazer was saying it was time to pay what was owed; she had known it was a fair exchange. The woman said she didn't have it. Later, when Jordan and the girls had packed up, Hennessy said that she'd seen the arguing woman strung up in the elevator, half-dead, a cross marked on her face.

Jordan understood even more.

Boudicca offered protection, it seemed, opportunity, maybe. But Jordan was already tied to one group of women. She wasn't tempted to be tied to another. She wouldn't have ever called the number on the back of the card.

But she was willing to go with Declan Lynch to see what there was to see.

"Do you know what you're walking into?" Jordan asked, after she'd found parking on the congested streets. They were within walking distance from where they'd spent the night before, actually; they could've walked there without much trouble. Boudicca had arranged for the meeting to take place at the gardens at Dumbarton Oaks, at the edge of Georgetown. Jordan had been to Dumbarton Oaks, many times, more often to the museum than to the gardens, and she thought she understood their choice. The garden was a place that would be private but also a place where extreme violence would be noted. It was polite for both parties.

Declan said, "Not at all. All they said when I called the number was 'who?'"

"What'd you say?"

"I didn't know what to say. I just said 'the new Fenian.' That's what was written on the card. Then they asked 'where' and I said DC. They told me to call back in ten minutes, and I did, and they told me Dumbarton Oaks. I didn't expect it to happen so fast. Not the same day." He didn't sound pleased about this and Jordan understood; it would've made her a little nervous, too. One didn't like to be *too* wanted. As they turned to walk through the gates to the garden, he said, "So that we're on the same page, this is my understanding: Boudicca is the mob, right? They take a cut in exchange for protection?"

"I think so," Jordan said. "There might be a bit of marketing to it, too. Access to their client base and all that."

"You're not tempted?"

"Not a golden chance," Jordan said as the attendant waved them on; he recognized her.

"I was going to call you anyway," Declan said. "Not for this."

She grinned. "Crime syndicate today, maybe a steak dinner tomorrow."

Declan frowned, completely earnest. "Maybe not steak."

Now it was her turn to laugh outrageously.

They were to meet the Boudicca contact by the fountain terrace, so they made their way there. The surroundings were striking this time of year: the lawns were still bright, lush green, but the trees were moodily arrayed in autumn browns and reds. The winds and rains had not been strong enough here to strip them of their leaves. Everything smelled good—the damp released the scent of the oak leaves, a smell that couldn't help but be nostalgic. The gardens were impeccable, and so, too, she thought, was Declan Lynch among them in his good sweater and collared shirt, in his good shoes and his good watch. He was very good at being companionably quiet, and for ten or twenty strides, Jordan let herself imagine it was an ordinary date, an ordinary stroll, two people walking in companionship instead of the strange demands of a powerful secret group.

"Go on, tell it," she said eventually, as they moved through the dormant rose garden.

"Tell what?"

"I know you must have a story about this place you're dying to tell."

He smirked a little. "I don't know very much about it."

"Liar."

"That's what they tell me." But after a moment, he said, "All of this was created by the Blisses. What a name. The Blisses. Mildred and Robert. A couple notable for many things, including managing to make the ambitious move from stepsiblings to spouses."

"The scandal! How old were they when they met? Do you know? Of course you do."

"Teens, I think, I—" Declan broke off.

A figure was already standing at the fountain as they came down the stairs to the fountain terrace, clad in a dark jacket and dark slacks, a square gray bag by his shoes. Jordan turned Declan's wrist enough to look at his watch. The time was right, but she didn't think that could be the contact—it was a man.

The figure turned around, and both Declan and Jordan stopped in their tracks.

It was Ronan Lynch.

But then he stepped toward them and Jordan saw that it wasn't Ronan at all. The way he carried himself was all wrong, the way he wore his face was all wrong. His hair was curled like Declan's, but longer, chin-length. This man looked like a brother, perhaps, more like a brother to Ronan than Declan was.

"Look at you, Declan," the man said to Declan, and his face was delighted. "Look at yourself. What a handsome devil. You could knock me over with an eel. Declan himself, all grown."

Declan hung back.

All the handsomeness Jordan had seen in him had vanished, just like that, and suddenly he had become the bland and invisible Declan she had first met. *Young Man on a Terrace*, name unknown.

"Always the clever one," the man said. He had a bit of an Irish accent, mostly on the *R*s. "Slow to trust. That's all right. I won't ask you for trust. I might look like your dad, but I don't offer things I can't give."

Jordan looked from Declan to the man. *Dad?*

"Who are you?" she asked.

The man stuck out a hand, seeming relieved that she had spoken to him. He was jumpy, nervous, flighty in a way that Ronan wasn't. It was hard once he was moving to see how she'd ever mistaken him for Ronan. "The new Fenian is what they call me, and it's good enough for this."

"Hennessy."

He shook Jordan's hand, but he was still looking at Declan, his expression complicated. Longing. Proud. "Smart of you to be wary. This is nothing you want."

"What *is* it?" Jordan asked. "What is it we're talking about?"

"It's a box you get into and don't get out of. It's a bigger box than you're thinking. It's a stronger one. You came here thinking it's a racket, right? Maybe that it's a cult. You're thinking maybe it's a bunch of lady thugs and you might want in on that because things have been getting rough out there for you. I promise you, it's rougher in here for you." To Declan, he said, "And you don't want them finding out about Ronan, tomcat."

Declan physically flinched.

The man saw it, looked sorry. "I'm sorry, boy-o. I know I'm not a father to you, but you have to know that you're my kids to me. I remember you when you were this tall."

Declan finally said, "You're a copy."

It was an unsettling thing to hear. Jordan had gotten used to the idea of being an *I* to Declan instead of a *we*. He didn't know she was anything more than Jordan Hennessy, singular, and she liked it far more than she was allowed to.

This was a reminder that he was brother to a dreamer, son of a dreamer, and he knew what mysteries they were capable of.

Jordan expected the man to dislike being called such a thing, but he just laughed a little. "Maybe my face. But it's been nearly two decades; I've got different stories than Niall Lynch. But this head still loves you like you were mine. It's been watching when it can. And you can't get tied up in this; it'll be the end of you. They'll use him till you don't recognize him."

Declan swallowed. He was as dazed as she was during her episodes. But Jordan hadn't forgotten his task. "We're not here about that, though, friend."

Declan shot her a grateful glance and then said, "I didn't expect the number to bring me to you. I'm here about Mór Ó Corra?"

"That's a name you definitely don't want to be whispering," the man said.

"Is she in Boudicca?"

He inclined his head. "But forget it, forget Boudicca. Pretend you never met me. I'll tell them you didn't show. They'll leave it at that. Mór will make sure of it."

"This is very cryptic," Jordan said.

"And it has to be. Please go. It'd break my heart and not much breaks it anymore."

Declan said, in his most dull tone, "I don't owe you anything, though. I owe him nothing and you less. If I wanted to talk to her, what would I do next?"

"Ask someone else, boy, because I won't be the one to kill you."

"Does she not want to see me?"

This made Jordan look away, much to her own surprise. This felt a little too personal, like she wanted to give him privacy for it.

"I wouldn't answer for her," the man said. "She deserves that much. That's all I can say."

Declan's eyes narrowed just a hair, judging this, and then he nodded a little and pressed no more.

"You see, he knows," the man said, clearly relieved. "There's the one who knows how to stay alive. Can't trust Ronan to save himself. He throws his heart and then runs in after it."

Jordan knew someone like that.

"That's that, then," Declan said.

The man hesitated, then reached a hand out toward Declan. "Can I— I don't know if I'll see you again like this."

Declan didn't draw back, and so the man stepped forward and put his arms around Declan's neck. He hugged him, the simple, complete hug of a parent hugging a son, hand on the back of his neck, cheek rested against the back of his head.

Declan stood stiff as a middle-schooler hugged by a parent in front of school, but Jordan saw his nostrils flare and his eyes go terribly bright. He blinked, blinked, blinked, and then he had his usual bland expression by the time the man stepped back.

"I'm proud of you," he told Declan. Her dauntless Declan.

"Thanks for meeting us," Jordan said, because it felt like someone ought to say it.

The man leaned and picked up his bag. "Stay alive."

65

Hennessy had not had a dream that wasn't the Lace for so long that she'd forgotten what they could be like. Lindenmere was a dream.

It was worlds away from the café she'd met Ronan at that morning, both physically and spiritually. A two-hour drive had taken them to the base of the Blue Ridge Mountains, and then Ronan had navigated up increasingly smaller roads to an unpaved fire road, and then he'd told her they would have to walk.

They walked.

Neither of them looked particularly like the hiking sort—Hennessy in her leather and lace, and Ronan in his black boots and his shaggy raven on his shoulder. There was comfort in the absurdity of that, Hennessy thought.

Because she was getting afraid again.

Lindenmere is a dreamspace, Ronan had told her in the car. *So control your thoughts in it.*

Control had never been Hennessy's strong point.

She checked her timer on her phone. She'd just reset it. The odds of her slipping and knocking herself out while walking were low, but she couldn't bear living without the comfort of it counting down to waking her up before the dream.

Ronan texted someone as they were walking. Hennessy saw only that the contact was labeled MANAGEMENT.

"Who's that?"

"Adam," Ronan said. "I'm telling him I'm going in so that he'll know where to find me if days go by."

Days?

"We're here," Ronan said.

She didn't think she'd be able to tell, but she could tell. This far into the mountains, the ordinary trees were thinner, more slanted, striving for toehold among the granite and straining for the sun. But Lindenmere's supernatural trees obeyed different rules. They were broad and tall, watchful and lovely, unaffected by the paucity of resources on the mountaintop. Green mosses and lichens furred their northern sides, with small moss flowers trembling at the end of delicate stalks.

And the sky was different. It had turned gray. Not the dull gray of high fall cloud cover, but rather a turbulent, molten gray that was really blue and purple and flint, all of it shifting and moving and swirling like the undulations of a snake. It had no eyes and no heartbeat and no body, but nonetheless one got the sense that the sky itself was sentient, even if it did not notice them below it.

"Wait," Hennessy said. "I changed my mind."

Ronan turned to look at her. "Lindenmere won't hurt you unless you want it to. Not when you're with me. It only protects itself or manifests what you ask it to."

"But," Hennessy said. *I don't trust myself.*

She was trying not to shake again. For a decade she'd held herself together and now she was a ruin.

She couldn't bear the idea that she might have to see the Lace again so soon.

Ronan regarded her.

Then he cupped his hands over his mouth and said, *"Opal!"* He paused, listened. "Where are you, maggot?"

Hennessy asked, "What's Opal?"

An invisible bird let out an alarmed bark from somewhere overhead. Hennessy turned in time to see something dark move between the trees, or rather to experience the *feeling* that she'd just seen something dark.

"I told you, keep your thoughts steady," Ronan told Hennessy. "Lindenmere will give you what it thinks you want."

"They're like a fucking rock." They were not like a fucking rock.

"Chainsaw, go find Opal," Ronan told the raven. "She needs Opal."

Hennessy was not one hundred percent on bird body language, but she thought the raven nonetheless managed to look pouty. She hung her head and stepped from foot to foot on his shoulder, her neck feathers all ruffled up.

Ronan rummaged in his jacket pocket and removed a package of peanut butter crackers. He unwrapped one as the raven became suddenly attentive.

"Cracker," he said to her.

"Krek," she replied.

"Cracker," he repeated.

"Krek."

"Cracker."

"Kreker."

He gave her one. "The other's if you get Opal."

The raven took flight, her wings audible as they beat the air. Hennessy watched it all with some amazement. She and Ronan had been out of place while hiking, yes, but he was not out of place here. He belonged in this strange lush forest with his strange dark bird.

"You dreamt this place," Hennessy said.

"Sort of."

"Sort of?"

"I had a dream, and after it, Lindenmere was here," Ronan said. "But I think I might have just dreamt of it where it existed somewhere else, and then my dream was just the doorway for it. It's a forest because that's what my imagination could hold for it. It was limited by whatever my thoughts were. So, trees. Ish."

Hennessy shivered, both because it was cool in this lofty forest and also because this reminded her of the Lace and what it wanted her to do. "That doesn't bother you?"

She could see by his face that it didn't. He loved this place.

Another alarmed animal cry came from the underbrush, and something like a growl, either an animal or a motor.

"Steady," Ronan said, but she wasn't sure if he was talking to her or himself.

"If you made this place," Hennessy said, "why didn't you make it safer for you?"

He reached up to run his fingers along a low-hanging branch. "I had another forest before Lindenmere." He looked like he was going to confess something, but in the end, he just said, "Bad things happened to it. I made it too safe, because I was a chicken-shit. Made it more ordinary. So it had to rely on me to keep it safe and——" He did not finish this, but he did not have to. The girls relied on Hennessy to keep them alive, too, and she knew how it felt to let them down. "I let Lindenmere be more of itself, whatever it was in that other place."

"And what it is over there is dangerous."

"Dangerous things can protect themselves," Ronan said.

She could see he didn't judge Lindenmere for it. Ronan Lynch could be dangerous, too.

"It's not only dangerous," Ronan said. "Watch."

He held out his hands and said some words in an appropriately archaic-sounding language. Above him, small glowing lights winked into being among the fall leaves. They began to rain down around them. Ronan walked backward, admiring the lights, keeping his hands held out to let the lights sink into them.

Hennessy flinched as one sank into her skin with the slightest feeling of warmth. Not all of them dissolved. Some of them caught on her clothing, or in her hair. One caught in her eyelashes, and as she blink, blink, blinked, she found herself looking right into the light. It didn't burn her to look right into it as an ordinary light would have, and as she gazed into it, instead of a sensation of visual brightness, she felt brightness inside her. Like happiness, or optimism. As if she was gazing into a sun of actual bliss.

Ronan said, in a reverent voice quite unlike his usual, *"Gratias tibi ago."*

"What are you saying?" Hennessy said, finding her words only after the little light had finally dissolved from her eyelashes.

"That means 'thank you' in Latin," Ronan said, "and it's goddamn polite to say it when you like something. *Opal!* Come on, now! Here, come on, look over here."

It was like a devil's bargain, a fairy dance. Ronan Lynch stood there, dressed all in dark colors, only his eyes gleaming with color, his hand held out to her, glimmering lights drifting down around him. *Come away.* He didn't say it, but Lindenmere remembered the words for her, somehow, as if he had.

"Don't think, Hennessy," he said. "Just be."

She let herself be led.

They walked by an unforgiving field that grew only swords,

blade-down, the hilt two or ten or thirty inches above the ground. They walked by a cave entrance guarded by an enormous white stag with horns tipped with blood. They walked by a meadow that was actually a lake, and a pond that was actually flower petals.

Lindenmere was beautiful and complicated in ways that the real world was not. *Air* and *music* were two different things in the real world; in Lindenmere, they were not always. Water and flowers were similarly confused in this forest. Hennessy *felt* the truth of it as they walked. There were creatures you didn't want to meet in person if you weren't with Ronan Lynch. There were places you might get trapped forever if you weren't with Ronan Lynch. It was feral and confusing, but in the end, it followed one rule: Ronan Lynch. His safety, his desires, his thoughts. That was Lindenmere's only true north.

She could feel it: Lindenmere loved him.

"Kerah!"

"Opal, finally, you little puke," Ronan said.

A creature capered from between the woods, a scrawny, hollow-eyed child. She wore an oversized cable-knit sweater and a skullcap pulled down low over her short white-blond hair. Someone might have mistaken her for a human girl if not for her legs, which were densely furred and ended in hooves.

"I told you, that's Chainsaw's word. You have lips. Call me Ronan," he told her. The little creature threw her arms around his legs and then pranced around him in a hectic circle, her hooves leaving divots. He lifted a foot. "That was my foot, come on."

Hennessy sat down, hard. She was just staring at Opal's furry legs, the twinkling lights falling around her. All her bravado was quite stripped from her.

This immediately caught Opal's attention, and she spooked back behind Ronan.

"Easy, shithead," Ronan said. He wiped a little dirt off her cheek with a thumb. "That's Hennessy."

"Kruk?" Opal asked.

"I told you, stop using Chainsaw's words, you have English. She's a dreamer, like me."

No, Hennessy thought, feeling quite drunk. She was not a dreamer like this. Not at all.

Opal stalked over to Hennessy, who held quite still. She knelt beside her, her posture decidedly unlike Hennessy's, since her goat legs bent the opposite direction. She smelled quite wild and animally. She babbled in a language Hennessy didn't understand.

Ronan said, "You could say hello to her."

Opal asked Hennessy, "Do you eat meat?"

Ronan looked impatient. "She's not going to eat you. Don't be a coward."

"I'm not afraid," Opal said, but in a surly way that meant she had been.

Hennessy, who'd also been afraid, snapped her teeth at Opal.

Opal leapt back, catching herself on her hands, and then righted herself as Hennessy grinned at her.

"It's good," Opal decided inexplicably. With a sly look, she drew in close again and tried to pluck one of Hennessy's tattoos off. She was waiting to get in trouble.

"Slap her," Ronan advised. Hennessy didn't, but Opal skittered away as if she felt she might. "She's a psychopomp, like Chainsaw. She'll focus things, keep stuff from going to shit."

"Going to shit?"

"Usual dreamfuckery," Ronan said, as if that explained

anything. "Opal, we have an important task today—will you help us, or do I have to ask Chainsaw?"

Opal shot a suspicious look up at the sky and hurriedly began to shake her head. "Nope nope nope!"

"Okay," Ronan said. "Hennessy, are you ready?"

Hennessy blinked up. She was overwhelmed in a way she had no language for. "For what?"

He said, "To dream."

66

Ramsay was in town.

Farooq-Lane had just been up all night, had just dragged one dead body into a rental car and added another living one, and now, Ramsay was in town. *Ramsay* of all people.

Farooq-Lane's feelings on J. J. Ramsay were uncomplicated: She hated him. She thought he sounded like an overgrown frat boy. All the people who worked with Lock had their complicated reasons, but it was hard to imagine Ramsay having a complicated anything. Farooq-Lane had been disconcerted to learn that he had a really high-powered job. When he was not packing up a drone next to a dead body, he apparently consulted for corporations that had gotten themselves into trouble with other countries' governments. According to LinkedIn, he could sound like a frat boy in the five different languages most commonly used in the global business market. Farooq-Lane could also speak in the five different languages most commonly used in the global business market, but she suspected the two of them sounded very different when they did.

"Heyyy, I don't make the rules," Ramsay said, sounding Ramsayish over the rental car's speakers. Even Liliana, the new Visionary, frowned a little in the passenger seat. Douchebag was a universal language. Farooq-Lane hoped she wasn't going to regret picking up this phone over the Bluetooth. "Lock does."

He'd just told Farooq-Lane that he'd landed and that she needed to meet him, Lock's orders. *Now?* Farooq-Lane had asked, her fingers tight enough on the steering wheel that they felt wrapped around it a few times. *I have a new Visionary.* She hadn't added: *And I haven't slept all night, and I watched someone die, and I have already been across the greater DC area on a treasure hunt for someone who might explode into another age and kill me at any time.*

But she was thinking it.

"No time like the present," Ramsay said. "Lock 'n' load. And I hear you got a body to put in the back forty, so you need me anyway."

He hung up.

After he did, as they cruised southward toward Springfield, Farooq-Lane took just a few seconds to attempt a reconstruction of the Carmen Farooq-Lane who had originally joined the Moderators. That young woman had been a sea of calm. She had been the picturesque statue in the airport as chaos seethed around her. She had been the member of the meeting who sat elegantly on the other side of the table, listening to heightened voices and watching wringing hands, and then quietly broke in with a cool-headed solution. When she was a child, she'd once seen a feather drift down and touch lightly on the surface of a pond. The feather had not sunk, nor even really broken the surface tension. Instead, it had landed light as a butterfly, trembling just enough to look alive, and slowly turned end over end in the breeze. She'd recalled that image again and again and again in her teens. Farooq-Lane was that feather.

She was that feather.

She was. That. Feather.

Then she tried to explain to the ethereal old Visionary in

the passenger seat. "We're a task force. He's part of the task force. We . . ."

"I remember a little," Liliana said.

She was the opposite of Parsifal in many ways, and not just because she was very elderly, though she was. Once she'd been pulled free of the chest freezer, Farooq-Lane had seen that the Visionary was even older than she'd originally thought. She was agelessly old. Her long hair, now gathered back into two long braids, tricked one into thinking she was younger, but the depth of the wrinkles around her eyes and mouth spoke to many years behind her. She had a far-eyed look about her, as if she was seeing beyond the traffic and buildings to something more important. Farooq-Lane had immediately gotten her some chicken and rice and tea, and, in a low voice, Liliana had thanked the meat for feeding her before quietly and neatly eating the entire thing without comment. So unlike Parsifal.

I am that feather, Farooq-Lane told herself.

"You remember what?" Farooq-Lane asked. "A . . . vision?"

"No, just a memory," Liliana said. "It's been a very long time, though, so I don't remember it well. You are hunting dreamers?"

"Zeds. Yes."

"Right," Liliana said. "Yes, and you are Marchers. No. Moderators. Yes? See, it comes back to me. You are trying to stop that fire."

It still gave Farooq-Lane a jolt of adrenaline to hear it confirmed. Yes, the fire. The fire that would eat the world. She risked a glance over at her as she drove. "How does this work? What age are you really right now?"

Liliana rested her head back, stroking the ends of one braid absently. "At this age, I know that's not a useful question for

someone like me. I do so like being this age, it's very peaceful."
She sensed that Farooq-Lane wasn't satisfied, so she added, "I
think I must spend more of this year as one of the younger
ages, because my memories are very distant now. I remember the
moment we met well. I knew you were coming."

She set her hand on top of Farooq-Lane's with such fondness,
fingers slid familiarly through Farooq-Lane's, that Farooq-Lane
flinched.

"I forgot," Liliana said, going back to fussing with her braids
instead. "You're still very young. I'm grateful you rescued me."

It was too outside of Farooq-Lane's understanding of time
to make easy sense. For a few miles, she navigated traffic and
thought about it, and then she said, "So you know the future
right now."

"I suppose that is a way of looking at it. I remember my past,
which includes some of your future. I think I am very old right
now, though, so these are decades-old memories."

"If they're decades old," Farooq-Lane said, "that must mean
that we did it. That we stopped the end of the world. Isn't that
how it works? If you're looking back at this from someone who
becomes decades older than this memory? It means you are still
alive after all this."

Liliana frowned, and for the first time, something like distress flitted across her face. "I think I am harder to kill than
humans."

That completely silenced the car. Before Parsifal, Farooq-
Lane wouldn't have been shocked to hear this said out loud. She
would have completely cosigned the concept of Visionaries as
something human-shaped but not human. Their abilities, after
all, defied all understanding of life as everyone else understood

it; *human* seemed like an unuseful classification for them, just as it was dubiously useful for the Zeds. But then she'd spent time with Parsifal, aggravating, dead Parsifal, and he just seemed like a kid born under an unlucky star. She'd sort of begun to decide that the Moderators doubted the Visionaries' humanity in order to feel less bad about their deaths.

But Liliana's words reversed all that.

Liliana said in a soft voice, "It still troubles me how fragile you are."

"Badda boom, badda bing," J. J. Ramsay remarked, zipping the top of the drone's case, speaking loudly to be heard over the booming music, thundering tribal beats. "This puppy does it all."

Farooq-Lane should have recognized the address, but she supposed she had come to it by a very different way the last time she was here. Ramsay and Farooq-Lane stood just inside a familiar split-level house in Springfield, surrounded by colorful teapots and rugs.

The old Zed's house.

"You didn't wait for the others," Farooq-Lane told Ramsay.

Between them was the body of the old Zed who had given Parsifal three pieces of biscotti he'd actually liked. Ramsay had shot her before Farooq-Lane arrived. The body was laid out in a very undramatic way, on its stomach, arms by its side, head turned, as if the woman had decided to sleep in the middle of the floor. The only sign that she might not have opted voluntarily for this was that one of her ballet flats had come off and was parallel parked beside her foot instead. That, and she was missing the back of her head.

"Wait for the others?" he said. "You are the others."

Farooq-Lane crossed the carpet to turn down the speakers on the cheap boom box. It, too, had been painted, as if this Zed couldn't help but splash color on everything she saw. "And it was already done when I got here. Why did you even call me?"

Ramsay didn't hear the irritation in her voice. He was not particularly tuned to the subtleties of life. "Confirmation so that Lock doesn't get on my back."

"You didn't even confirm she was a Zed before you did this?" demanded Farooq-Lane.

This he heard. Hooking his thumbs in the belt loops of his khakis, he swiveled to her, pelvis first. "Gimme some credit, Carmen—"

"Ms. Farooq-Lane."

He grinned at her. "Some credit, *Carmen*. My drone friend and I caught her dreaming before I busted in. But I need you to do your little cataloguing job with everything else here. Lock said you found another Visionary? 'Bout damn time. Where's he at?"

"She's waiting in the car."

"Not a flight risk?"

"She's invested in our mission," Farooq-Lane said, even though she hadn't even begun to try to recruit Liliana. "Saving the world." She said this to remind him their mission was not *having a good time shooting people.*

"Saving the w-w-w-wonderful world!" trilled Ramsay, to a tune she was probably supposed to know. "Carmen, you're a gas."

The most infuriating thing about Ramsay was that he knew she hated the way he talked to her and didn't bother to alter it. It felt as if there should be consequences for being a boring, grown frat boy who enjoyed making people uncomfortable, and yet there did not seem to be. For a moment they stared at each other over the limp body, and then she told herself, *Just do your job so you can figure out someplace safe to house Liliana.*

Silently she catalogued all the dream objects in the Zed's home. They were similar to the crafts in the living room and the colorful thing she'd seen through the kitchen door. Brilliantly colored, confusing, fluid. There were not many. They were placed on the back of the toilet, on the windowsill by the cactus, the bedside table, the way you'd put pottery you'd done in college that you were proud of.

Parsifal had been right. This Zed was never going to be the kind of dreamer who dreamt the end of the world into being.

I am that feather, Farooq-Lane thought.

When she returned to the living area, Ramsay was sitting backward on a chair right next to the body, talking to Liliana, who stood in the doorway, her eyes gentle and regretful. He held up a finger as if Farooq-Lane had been about to interrupt him and finished his thought. "All these fuckers know each other, that's what we're learning, so it's best to hit them fast and close together, or they'll warn each other."

"I thought you were waiting in the car," Farooq-Lane said.

"I wanted to see if you were all right," Liliana said.

"Aw, honey," Ramsay said, "you want to help us out, you can get that next vision coming when you get a chance. World to save and all that."

I am that feather, Farooq-Lane thought.

She was not that feather.

She punched J. J. Ramsay hard enough that he fell ass over tits, chair wailing right over backward, depositing him flat on his back with his legs all tangled around the chair's legs.

There was complete silence. Ramsay had had his breath and

idiotic words knocked right out of him. His mouth moved as if he was trying out some of the idiotic words he was going to say when he got back enough breath to say them.

Farooq-Lane's fist smarted as if it had just been smashed against a douchebag's face, because it had just been smashed against a douchebag's face. Biting her lip, she risked a glance at the new Visionary, the Visionary she was, according to Moderator guidelines, trying to recruit to their noble cause.

Liliana looked from Ramsay to Farooq-Lane and said, "I'll follow you anywhere."

67

Because Hennessy was so clearly scared shitless, Ronan hadn't let on his reservations about his plan. Lindenmere, after all, was sensitive to all thoughts, and the last thing he wanted to do was give voice to something it would manifest for them.

But it was dangerous.

Opal and Hennessy sat cross-legged in the middle of a clearing in Lindenmere, on top of a pretty little hummock sprouting the kind of thin, hairy grass that grew in the shade. A fairy ring of dull white mushrooms encircled them. A little brook, dark with leaf tannin, mumbled by at the edge of the clearing. Opal sat behind Hennessy, back to back, looking self-important. Ronan was relying heavily on Opal's ability to act as intermediary between him and Lindenmere.

Because Ronan could accomplish what he needed in dreams back at the Barns, and because he preferred to have all dream consequences happen far away from his physical body, he didn't usually use Lindenmere like this. He came to Lindenmere to feel understood, to feel the power of the ley line rush over himself, to feel connected to something bigger, to make sure it did not need him, or vice versa.

He did not usually come here to dream.

Dreaming in Lindenmere meant making one's thoughts reality immediately. The monsters were there the moment you bid them.

The ocean rose around your very real waking body. The copies of yourself were fact until you or Lindenmere destroyed them.

But he didn't know how to show Hennessy how to dream otherwise.

The only other way might have been to meet her in dream-space as Bryde had met him, but he wouldn't have had the same kind of control. The consequences of Hennessy waking with another deadly tattoo were too dire to risk without the big guns.

"Lindenmere," Ronan said out loud, "I'm going to need every bit of you for this."

And Hennessy began to dream. Not truly dream, because she was awake. But rather, Lindenmere began to have her dream for her.

It was dark.

The light became dim in the clearing.

There was music playing. It was an old jazz recording, some woman's voice pitching and lilting along as the sound fuzzed and popped. Hennessy hadn't mentioned this to Ronan when she described the dream.

A woman stood in the glen, only it was no longer a glen. It was a closet. The lights were out. The only light came from a small, high window, and the light was gray. The woman was dressed in a bra and underwear and a robe. She did not look like Hennessy, but she didn't *not* look like her. Mascara was drawn down her face. She was holding a gun.

The woman in the bathrobe put the gun to her own head.

The door opened (there was now a door). Hennessy stood in it. Not the Hennessy who was dreaming, but another Hennessy. She was standing a little differently than Hennessy did now. A little more softly, her shoulders a little more sloped. She wore a white T-shirt, nice jeans, flowers embroidered on the butt pockets.

"Mum?" Hennessy said.

"You won't miss me," Hennessy's mother said.

"Wait," Hennessy said.

The gun barrel flashed.

The dream dissipated with the reverberation of the shot, and Hennessy came to with a second Hennessy staring at her from the edge of the fairy ring, the mushrooms trampled.

Ronan looked at that new Hennessy for a split second and then said, "Lindenmere, take her."

The forest dissolved the second Hennessy, incorporating her at once into the fine grass as if she had never been. The original Hennessy reeled, her hand pressed to her throat.

"That's not the dream you described to me," Ronan said.

Hennessy was breathing slow and hard, unfocused.

Ronan stalked over to her and pushed her shoulder with his boot. "That wasn't the dream you told me. Was that a memory? Did that happen?"

"Give—me—a—tick," Hennessy said.

"No," Ronan said simply. "You don't need a second. Lindenmere is dreaming for you. You aren't doing any heavy lifting here. Did that happen?"

When Hennessy didn't answer, Opal tenderly scrambled round into Hennessy's lap. She pulled Hennessy's hand away from her throat, kissed it, and hugged it.

"Did it?" Ronan asked.

Hennessy was as sullen as Opal when she didn't get her way. "I don't want to talk about it."

"Control your thoughts or we're getting the fuck out of

here," Ronan said. He stepped down to the edge of the clearing again. "We go again."

Rinse.

Repeat.

The glen dimmed. The music played. The woman lifted the gun.

"Don't let it open," Ronan said. "Don't let it play through."

The door opened.

"Mum?" said Hennessy.

"You won't miss me."

"Wait—"

Another Hennessy appeared again, splitting immediately off the first, as if she were peeling the memory like a skin.

"Lindenmere, take it away," Ronan said impatiently.

The dream fled; the extra Hennessy seeped into the soil.

Hennessy squeezed the heels of her hands against her eyes.

"Did that happen?" Ronan asked. "Or are we playing let's pretend?"

"I don't want to *talk* about this," Hennessy said.

"What are we even here for today? Are you even going to try?" Ronan strode to the center of the glen and cupped his hands over one of the knocked-over mushrooms until he felt it grow tall and sturdy beneath his palms. "Again. The actual dream this time."

Rinse.

Repeat.

The clearing went dark. Jazz filtered in. The gun, lifted. The doorknob, turning.

"Not you," Ronan said. "Anyone else. Santa Claus. A dog. No one at all; an empty room. You're not even trying to control it."

The door opened.

"Mum?" said Hennessy.

"You're not even fucking trying!" Ronan said, and shot the extra Hennessy.

The real Hennessy came to with a start, gasping, fingers clawing the grass. She stared at the gun in his hand.

"How did you get that?"

"Lindenmere is a dream," he snarled. "I told you. All you have to do is try. It's only doing what you ask it, and you're asking it for that. I asked it for a gun. Now I'm going to ask it to take it away. Lindenmere, take this shit away."

The gun and the dead copy melted away.

"Why are we doing this? Where's the dream?"

"I'm trying."

"I don't think you are."

Opal leaned against Hennessy, chewing on a watch Adam had given her long ago. She spoke around it. "She *is* trying." But she couldn't be trusted. She had a soft spot for the downtrodden, being one of them.

"Again," said Ronan. "At least have the guts to get rid of the other copy. This is everything, do you get that? We have all this, we can do so much. It means we have to be ready to do what we need to do to make sure we don't fuck everything up. No one else gets it. This is what we live with. *Again.*"

Rinse. Repeat.

Darkness, jazz, a gun, a trigger.

"Do not let a copy survive this," Ronan ordered. "If you won't change anything else—"

"Mum?" Hennessy said.

"You won't miss me."

"Wait—"

Hennessy gasped and curled on herself. Ronan knelt beside her, put his gun in her hand, pointed it at the newly formed copy. "This is what you do in the dream. No one's going to help you with this."

Hennessy made a helpless sound as he squeezed her finger on the trigger. She began to cry without tears, just the ragged, hopeless sobs.

"Lindenmere," Ronan said angrily, "take it away."

The duplicate copy seeped into the ground.

"I can't," Hennessy said.

"Did this really happen?" Ronan asked.

"I *can't.*"

Ronan sat back in the grass. "Fuck."

Opal whispered, "Bryde."

The name felt enormous spoken here in this place. It was the same word it always was, but here, in Lindenmere, it meant something different. Here in Lindenmere, he could say *Bryde* and possibly call the real Bryde, or he could say *Bryde* and invoke a copy, everything Ronan thought Bryde ought to be, like Hennessy and her copies.

He supposed Bryde would say that both versions were real.

Opal was still peering up at Ronan intently.

"Okay," he said. "Yes."

68

I had a dream last night," Bryde said. "That's what everyone says. I had a dream last night, and this is what it was about, it was crazy. It was about a hospital for zombies. It was about my fifth birthday party. It was about a space station but all the astronauts were actually you, isn't that crazy?"

His voice came from somewhere very close in the trees. He had not said *don't look for me* but the sense of it hung in the dark, shaggy mist that moved between the tree trunks of Lindenmere. Hennessy couldn't tell what kind of a person he was from his voice. It could be any age. It was sure of itself, though, calm. Wry. It had seen things, the voice implied.

"Everyone thinks their dream is about something else," Bryde said. "It's just you. You're not dreaming about your mother. You're dreaming about how you feel about your mother. Your mother's not there. You're not that powerful. You aren't pulling her from the afterlife to reenact her death scene for you. You're just up your own ass."

Hennessy didn't feel up her own ass. She really had been trying to think about the Lace. She didn't know why she had to keep looking at that shitty memory instead. "I'm not *trying* to do this. I'm trying to do my other dream."

"Are you?" Bryde asked. "Do you think this forest lies? Or does it just give you what you ask?"

"I wasn't asking for this," she said.

"Your mind wasn't," Bryde said. "Your heart, though."

She couldn't argue. She had been ignoring what her heart felt about things for too long to pretend to be an expert in it.

"We fool ourselves better than anyone when we're afraid," Bryde said.

"Can you help her?" Ronan asked.

Bryde sounded a little amused. "Haven't I been? Ah——" This was because Ronan tilted his head, as if to look around the trees in the direction of his voice. "That's a good way to get me to leave."

"I don't understand why you're still hiding," Ronan said. "You're here in my biggest secret. You know everything about me. I'm not asking for a birth certificate. Just a conversation with your face."

Bryde said, "That's because you don't know what you ask." He paused, and when he spoke again, his voice had changed a little. It was a little sad. "If you see me, it means everything's changed for you. You can't really go back from meeting me. I wouldn't take you from your life. And so, this close, no closer. That is the closest you can get without things changing."

"What happened to skip to the center?" But Ronan didn't try to look around the trees again.

"I don't know," Bryde said. "I don't know anymore. I don't know if I want your life to change."

It was clear from Ronan's face that he *did*. He was master of this tremendous place, dreamer of dreams, and still he wanted more.

Hennessy could understand that. She wished Jordan could have been here to see this place. All of them. Maybe she should have brought them all here with her instead of always feeling like she had to carry this by herself. What good had it done in the long run? It was *killing her as a secret*, anyway.

She spoke up. "I *need* mine to change."

There was a very long pause. Opal reached her fist into the air above her and opened it. A little light of joyfulness escaped out of her grip and, instead of raining down, drifted slowly up. They all watched it until it dissolved into the gray.

"Prove it," Bryde said. "Prove that you two can work together. And if you still want me, come for me together to tell me. But remember what I said. Oh—no. No. The world is going to shit."

The forest was silent.

He had not said goodbye, and he was not visible for them to see him go, but Hennessy could tell that he was gone. It was a disquieting send-off. She could tell from Ronan's face this wasn't how Bryde ordinarily vanished.

"I'm going to do it," Hennessy said. "Don't let me fall too hard, Lynch."

The clearing became dark.

This was how the dream began: in darkness.

There was no sound.

There was the vast movement of time and space, which had its own substance in the dream, but was not exactly sound. There was nothing in the dream you could really look at. There was nothing in the dream you could really put words to.

There was Hennessy, and in the dream, Hennessy knew she could manifest anything, if she really wanted to. It was limited only by her imagination—what an impossible, terrifying, brilliant truth. She'd been given this talent when born and not told how to use it. Given this talent and watched it kill her mother, or at least not save her.

She could do better with it.

If only she was dreamt of something besides . . .

It was there.

She felt it, and then she saw it. Dark and looming, the opposite of color and understanding.

Only its edges made any kind of sense. Slanted and hooked, checkered and geometric. Lacy, if they were anything at all.

Mostly it was bigger. It was bigger than anything she could understand. It was so enormous and old that age didn't apply to it. It had been there for so long that humans were bacteria to it. Infinitesimal. Irrelevant. It was so much more powerful than they that the only saving grace was that it had never noticed—

Its awareness became a thing in the dream.

It saw Hennessy.

She could feel how awful that weight was. How it changed everything. Now that she had been noticed, she could never be unseen. There were two Hennessys, the one who had lived without knowing this thing existed, and more importantly, without it knowing *she* existed, and the one who was seen.

Now that it had seen her, it hated her.

It was going to kill her. It was going to kill her like this: It was going to get inside her, it promised, and it was going to kill her just by existing there, because she was so small and porous, and it was everything. She couldn't hold it inside her.

Or she could let it out, and live.

She would never let it out. She was not strong enough to keep it from moving toward her now, but she was strong enough to never let it out. She wasn't so weak that she would let anyone else have to live with it looking, seeing, touching, invading—

69

Declan didn't ordinarily bring people home.

It wasn't that he hadn't gone on dates or hooked up, that unlovely euphemism for what was sometimes a perfectly nice time. It was that he didn't get too close. Intimacy was allowed as long as it revealed nothing truthful.

Which wasn't very intimate at all.

He'd had a few long-running relationships, three Ashleys in a row, much to his brothers' mirth, but they were like hobbies that never paid off. He didn't know why he was still going to film criticism club and he didn't know why he was still dating Ashleys. It was such a lot of his schedule for something that eventually cried bitterly that she could tell she didn't mean anything to him, or he'd have remembered *fill in the blank*. He got exhausted from carrying all their secrets and giving none of his away.

So he just didn't normally bring people home. He didn't really like people knowing where he lived anyway. Where his toothbrush was kept.

But he brought Jordan back home.

It wasn't exactly like going home with someone else after a date anyway. It was just that it seemed strange to part ways after they'd been told to forget everything they'd ever heard about a mysterious syndicate by a man who was a copy of Declan's young father.

So they went back to Declan's place.

He unlocked the door. "After you."

Jordan did as he asked, noting the town house as she stepped in. He saw it through her eyes: dull, predictable. Tastefully done, yes, expensively done, yes, but forgettably done. Gray sofa, white rugs, sleek contemporary paintings in dark frames. It wasn't a home, it was a lookbook. Handsome, neutral Declan was simply another accessory in his own house.

He checked his watch as he closed the door behind them. Matthew, to his great relief, had felt better enough to go to his weekend soccer practice. "My brother Matthew'll be here in about an hour."

"How many brothers do you have?" But she had already found a photo of them on the entry table. She compared it to him, the gesture similar to when she'd been studying him to paint him.

"Both younger," he said. "Matthew lives with me."

"Cute kid," she said. "Man. Boy. Whatever he is."

Yes. That was the crux of Matthew, he thought.

"This one looks like the new Fenian," Jordan said. "Crumbs, a lot like him."

"Ronan," Declan said. "Yes. He takes after my father." He did not want to think about his father. He didn't want to think about the new Fenian hugging him and telling him he was proud of him. It wasn't real. How typical of his father that he'd give Declan a puzzle that just led to another dream. "Coffee? Espresso? Latte?"

Jordan let him get away with the subject change. "I could worship a latte right now. Not in a truly devoted way but at the very least in the weekend, casual, sometimes-put-money-in-the-donation-tin way."

In the kitchen, he concocted a comely latte as she lifted herself up to sit on the counter. He hadn't turned on the lights, so the only illumination was from the living area and the last of the gray, late-afternoon light outside. It made everything in the little kitchen black and white and gray, a chic sensory deprivation.

When he brought her the coffee, she spread her knees so that he could stand close to her where she sat on the counter, effortlessly sensual, grinning lazily at him. She gestured with the mug around his dining room, toward the visible living area. "Why'd you do this? What a walking tragedy."

Declan said, "It's stylish and contemporary."

"It's invisible," she said. She put a hand under his sweater. "You can't love this stuff."

"It's ideal for entertaining."

"Entertaining robots." She teased his shirttail out in order to touch skin instead. "Where's the real you?"

Safely hidden. "How do you know it's not the real me?"

"Your shoes."

He studied her for a long moment, hard enough that she stopped teasing round his skin and instead pretended to pose, her chin adjusted artfully, coffee cup drawn close to her face as if for an advertising shot or a portrait. *Girl on Kitchen Counter. Still Life with a Past.*

He relented. "Upstairs."

She slid off the counter at once.

He led her upstairs. He saw it again as she must see it: more carpet. More forgettable framed prints and photographs. At the end of the carpeted hall was a modest master. This was slightly less anonymous; the prints on the wall were all black-and-white photographs of Ireland done in vaguely artistic and nostalgic ways. The bed was made as neatly as a hotel bed. Declan pulled a chair away from the corner of the room and stood on it. There was a door in the ceiling to an attic.

"Up *there*?" she said.

"You asked."

As he pulled down the ladder, she looked at the photographs. She put a hand against her temple as if it troubled her.

"Still up for this?" Declan asked.

She dropped her hand. "Beam me up."

"Hand up your coffee."

Once they were both up, he pulled a string to illuminate the space with a single lightbulb.

It was an attic crawl space, only tall enough to stand at its very tallest point. He'd put a shabby antique rug down on the floor and covered the unfinished plywood on the slanted ceiling with prints.

Declan leaned back to plug in an enormous sculptural stainless steel lamp in the shape of a violent, art deco angel. She was as tall as Jordan.

"Is that a—" He could see her thinking hard. "Stubenrauch? Right?"

"Reinhard Stubenrauch." He was absurdly pleased that she knew. He was absurdly pleased to be here with her. He was absurdly pleased. This entire day, this entire week, what a disaster . . . but he was absurdly pleased.

Jordan, her head ducked, examined one of the pieces carefully taped to the wall with hinges of tape to avoid damaging the front. Black bloomed at either end, and darker black stripes bisected it both violently and delicately, like bamboo leaves or handwriting or wounds. "Jesus, this is an original, Declan. I thought it was a print. Who is this?"

"Chu Teh-Chun," Declan said. "I know it deserves better; you don't have to say it."

"I wouldn't have said it," Jordan said. "And who's this?"

More black ink, rolled and splattered in pleasing, architectural shapes, like a creature flying or a sentence she couldn't quite read. She was touching her head again.

"Robert Motherwell."

She looked at another abstract print. This one was marked with jagged red and black exclamations like fire licking up the canvas. She guessed, "Still? Clyfford Still?"

Fuck, he told himself. *Do not fall in love with this girl.*

"Why isn't all this downstairs?" she asked. "Why do you have a hotel down there and Declan locked in the attic like a madwoman?"

He said, "Why do you paint other people and keep Jordan locked in your head like a madwoman?"

She was touching her temple again. Her throat. She looked at the Still for a long time, but she wasn't really looking at it. She put down her latte, trying to look casual about it, but he could see from the fumble that it was so she wouldn't spill it.

A sinking feeling was appearing inside Declan, invading in darkening blooms and jagged strokes, just like the paintings all around him.

"Why did you steal *The Dark Lady*?" he asked.

Jordan closed her eyes. Her voice was dreamy, dazed. "We said . . . we said we weren't going to talk about that or about . . . your dreamer father."

No, he thought. *Please no.*

"I don't think," Declan said, "I ever said the word *dreamer*."

Jordan's eyes were still closed. She was fighting valiantly. Harder than Matthew. But he thought he knew what it was anyway. She murmured, "No, probably . . . Crumbs . . . Come *on*."

But this last bit was to herself, not Declan.

He stood up and laid a hand on her forehead. Not hot. He

knew it wouldn't be, really. He was already touching her, so he used it as an excuse to slowly tuck a piece of hair behind her ear. She opened her eyes.

"You look so sad," she whispered.

"You're a dream."

"If I had a puppy for every time a man said that to me," Jordan said.

He didn't smile. "How long ago?"

"Decade. Give or take."

"Where's your dreamer?" He hated saying it. He hated everything. He couldn't take it anymore. He didn't have it in him to love another dream. It hurt too bad. Loving anything did.

It was not Niall Lynch's fault, but Declan wordlessly cursed him anyway, out of habit.

"Mm. I don't know. Getting pissed somewhere. How did you guess?"

"You aren't the first dream I've seen do this," Declan said. Then he told her a lot of truth, because he was too crushed to not say it out loud. "It's not just that. I grew up surrounded by them. You start to . . . feel them. Dreams."

He closed his eyes and shook his head.

"My feet keep bringing me back," he said.

Jordan swayed. She was as bad as Matthew at his worst. There was air in the room but not the right kind for her.

"I'll take you home," Declan said. "You can come back for your car later. Okay? Is that okay?"

It was hard to tell what she was thinking. Her eyes were glazed. She had gone far away to someplace that was for either dreamers or dreams, not for someone like Declan.

She nodded.

70

F arther," Liliana said. "There are houses there."

Farooq-Lane and Liliana had been flying down the highway for several miles now. Liliana gazed out the window, her eyes on the lights of houses in subdivisions and speckled across increasingly broad fields. They were nowhere near the hotel. After leaving Ramsay, Farooq-Lane had told Liliana that she'd get her an end suite at the hotel until they could find a more private vacation rental. Just give her until morning, Farooq-Lane promised, and she'd have it all sorted out. Could she have that long?

No.

No, she couldn't.

Liliana had not yet learned to turn her visions inside to make them harmless, but she promised Farooq-Lane that the episode would be productive regardless, as long as she was far enough away from other people.

So now they drove, and Farooq-Lane's phone rang and went unanswered. It pinged as voicemails came in. She didn't need to listen to them to know what they said; she had been on the other side of this part. Farooq-Lane had found a new Visionary and so now all over the world, planes were being boarded as Moderators got ready to mobilize according to the new visions.

She didn't need to pick up the phone to tell them where to

come or to give them the go-ahead. They knew where she was. They were coming no matter what.

Liliana was being very calm about the entire process, despite the fact that she had to have been as sleep-deprived and stressed as Farooq-Lane, despite the fact that she had just had to live through a conversation with Ramsay, despite the dead bodies in her past and probably her future. Despite the fact that she was about to blast into a completely different age, possibly taking Farooq-Lane with her.

Farooq-Lane wasn't sure if she would have preferred for her to be frantic or not. It felt like *someone* had to be frantic, so if it wasn't Liliana, it fell to Farooq-Lane.

"Don't wait too long," Farooq-Lane said.

"Soon," Liliana said.

"Soon we'll be to a place to stop, or soon you'll *need* to stop?"

Liliana smiled as if she found her anxiety familiar and amusing. "Both."

This was intensely discomforting. "What are you looking for?"

"What I remember," Liliana said. She tapped the fingers of one hand on the fingernails of her other thoughtfully.

The miles passed. The houses thinned. The night blackened. Farooq-Lane wondered how much trust she was willing to put in the hands of this stranger.

Liliana said, "Oh, there. Over there."

There was a dirt driveway that led a few feet to a metal farm gate before disappearing into field grass. A four-board fence on either side of the gate held back several drowsy cows.

Liliana clucked when she saw them.

"Pity," Liliana said, opening the door. She put her legs down, stiffly, and hefted herself out of the car.

Farooq-Lane looked from her to the cattle. Slowly, it dawned on her. "Are they going to—"

Liliana advised, "Don't follow me."

In the headlights, she stumped through the field grass. Farooq-Lane saw her fiddle with the gate before letting herself into the field. She did not bother to close it behind her; Farooq-Lane found this to be possibly the most troubling development in the past twenty-four hours, a complete subversion of what was right and true.

Liliana disappeared into the darkness.

Farooq-Lane sat there for a long moment, trying to decide if she should back out and put some more distance between herself and the field. Then she tried to decide how she would know when Liliana's episode was done. Then she tried to decide how she felt about anything at the moment. She'd punched Ramsay, and her hand still hurt, and Parsifal was dead, and her heart still hurt, but life went on.

She heard something hit the windshield. It was a small, odd sound, a feeling as much as a noise. It was a little like a strong gust of wind, or like the sound one got if you pushed a seashell over your ear. It lasted for less than a second. The entire car bucked a little, but only a very little.

Farooq-Lane realized the cows by the fence were no longer standing. They were dark lumps behind the four-board fence. One was keeled right against the post by the gate, its tongue lolling. Something dark oozed down the post.

She clapped her hands over her ears.

She knew it was a belated response, one that would do

nothing, but it was that or put them over her mouth or her eyes, and neither of those gestures made any more sense.

Those cows were dead. Liliana had just killed them. Farooq-Lane had only been fifteen feet out of the Visionary's range. Had Liliana known that? Had she remembered it that well, or had she just been willing to take a chance with Farooq-Lane's life?

Farooq-Lane had seen so many bodies today.

Movement caught her attention. Someone was letting themselves through the open gate and carefully shutting it behind themselves. The headlights illuminated Liliana's familiar dress for a moment and then she stepped out of the headlights to approach the car. She opened the passenger side door and let herself into the car.

Farooq-Lane's lips parted rudely.

Liliana was beautiful. She was still clearly the old woman who had just been there before, but she was also not. Her long pale braids had become long red hair instead, and the eyes that had before been full of calm were now full of tears.

She said, in a very small voice, "I hate killing things."

This version of her had not yet worked out how to like living in her own life.

"Me too," Farooq-Lane said.

Liliana sighed. "But there is more to come."

71

There was something strange about the house when Jordan returned.

She couldn't put her finger on it. Maybe, she thought, it was only that *she* was strange. The house loomed out of its atmospheric yard lighting and indulgent landscaping as it always did once the sun went down. The windows visible to the street were kept dark; the windows that weren't were squares of light. Brightness leaked out into the backyard through the big glass doors Hennessy had once opened to drive the Lexus through.

Declan opened the car door for her. They both stood by his dull Volvo and squinted at the house. If Declan thought it was an enormous house for her to live in, he didn't say it. He didn't say anything at all.

It looked as it always did, but—

Something's not right, her head said.

"You seem a little better," he said.

"They don't last long." She didn't look at him. He didn't look at her.

He peered around at the driveway as if it troubled him. His hand unconsciously rubbed his chest. Finally, he asked, "Are you okay to get in yourself?"

"Yeah, bruv," she said with a smile. "I left my coffee in your attic. I forgot it."

"I'll get it," he said.

If it was anyone else, she thought she might have gone in for a kiss. But something about the way his face had changed when he realized she was a dream had sort of cut the legs out from beneath her game. He'd known what she was, and it hadn't surprised him. It had disappointed him. She had been *Jordan Hennessy* to him and now she was something else. Less. She would feel something about it later. Right now everything just felt weird. So she just put out her knuckles for a fist bump. "Thanks for the ride."

"Oh," he said, and she didn't know what that meant, either. But he bumped knuckles. He got in the car and sat there. He was still sitting there when she got to the door.

She let herself in.

Inside, the feeling was stranger. The downstairs lights weren't turned on, which wasn't unusual at this time of night if Hennessy wasn't here—the other girls would be flung in other wings of the house. But she couldn't find the light switches right away.

She didn't know why she was so disoriented. Her dreaminess? Was that it? She ran her fingers along the wall for the switches.

There was music playing from farther in the house. The kitchen, or the living area. It thudded. Whoever it was had it cranked up.

She kept feeling for the switches.

An electric shock made her jerk her fingers away.

No.

Not a shock.

She thought about what she had felt a little harder. Not pain. Not electricity. Just the strange *ping* that comes when you feel dampness unexpectedly.

Dampness?

Jordan pulled her fingers close to her in the dark. The dreaminess broke through: trees, wings, fire, blackness. Was there something dark on her fingers?

No, she was confused.

The music was so loud. Why was the music so loud?

She ran her fingers across the wall as she headed down the hall and then stumbled. Someone had left their bag in the middle of the floor. It was heavy, warm.

It reached up and held her leg.

Jordan sucked in a breath of air, and then the bag resolved into not a bag, but Trinity.

She was twisted in the hall, a dark splatter the shape of one of Declan's abstract paintings up her front. She released Jordan's leg and instead put one finger against her lips. *Shhh.* Her hand slipped limply to the ground beside her.

Jordan's heart sped.

Now she looked behind her and saw that the dampness on the wall was another black abstract shape that smeared down to where Trinity lay.

Jordan crouched beside Trinity, but she was gone.

Just like that, she was gone.

Keep it together, Jordan.

She crept farther down the hall and into the great room. Although the lights weren't on in here, either, it was a little easier to see because the large windows let in the ambient light from outside. The enormous easel that had held *Madame X* was knocked over, legs akimbo like a downed giraffe. The music was louder in here, thumping bass going strong.

Oh God, oh God.

Here was Brooklyn. Fallen back over the sofa, bullet hole dark between her eyes and another in her throat.

Sickness and dreaminess washed over Jordan. She swayed, her hands reaching for balance and finding nothing.

Get

It

Together

She leaned against the couch until she felt steadier, and then she walked through the great room to the hall, past a study, and through the big, empty foyer.

She nearly walked past the door to the back staircase up to the bedrooms, but then she saw that the doorknob had been completely ripped out of it. Softly pushing the door open, she pressed the back of her hand to her mouth. Madox. It had to be Madox because she had natural hair, but her face was missing.

Jordan had to crouch then, stuffing her knuckles against her teeth to gasp silently against them, biting down until the pain focused her. She could tell she was getting light-headed, hyperventilating.

She made herself think about how Trinity had still been alive, and so maybe June still was, too. She made herself stand up. She made herself head down the hallway to the music, moving ever more cautiously.

It was coming from the kitchen, where lights were blazing. The entire house was fitted with a sound system and it could be adjusted by room. The kitchen had been adjusted to max.

So Jordan only barely heard June shout, *"Get down!"*

She rolled without question as a gunshot rang out. She just had time to glimpse an unfamiliar man as she scrambled behind the kitchen island.

The music blared. Every possible light was on; the shadows were confusing and didn't give away if someone was coming around the island.

Jordan shuffled to the end of the island—no point being quiet, nothing was audible over the railing music—and risked a peek.

A gun blast.

Nowhere near, went wide.

Jordan risked another look over the top. A man was reloading right next to her. She hurled herself over the counter, sliding down on top of him. She could see June fighting with another attacker.

She was in over her head. The man didn't need the gun to be a good fighter. He slickly flipped her onto her back and didn't even flinch when she kicked him in the nuts.

June screamed, high and light and airy.

"Stay down," the man said to Jordan, punching her. "Why won't you fucking stay down?"

Jordan elbowed him right in the nose and he swayed. Not enough to stop him, but enough for her to scramble out from under his weight. She felt her arms seized from behind. Her feet kick, kick, kicked on the tile. They had her by her biceps and she couldn't twist free. The guy was getting up. She was done, she could feel it.

Suddenly, she felt the hands holding her jerk. They jerked again, and then, just as the first man went for his gun, they fell away.

Jordan scrambled back, losing her balance, but an entirely different hand reached out to steady her. As this new person lifted her up instead of dragging her down, her gaze snagged on something familiar:

Beautiful shoes with exceptional tooling.

Declan released her in time to punch the man as he rose with his gun.

Jordan got her feet under her. There was a confusing number of people in the room. The stunned woman on the floor must have been who was holding Jordan before. Declan had landed another punch on the man. June was here, somewhere.

The man who Declan had punched staggered but didn't go down. He threw himself at both of them.

There was a professional precision to both his offense and his defense, a surgical and effortless way that he fought both Declan and Jordan, using the two of them against each other instead of regarding them as a double threat. When the other woman got up, the two of them quickly forced Declan and Jordan up against the walk-in pantry door. It flapped open behind them.

Jordan didn't want to think of how quickly it would be over in that small space.

Then the man violently spasmed back and the woman stumbled, unbalanced.

June, gasping blood, had shot the man.

She squeezed the trigger again, but the gun clicked, pointless, empty.

"Jordan," she rasped. Everything about her was ruined. Jordan couldn't bear it, but there was nothing to do but bear it. "Run. Go."

"June," Jordan said, "June, I can't."

The woman scrambled for one of the discarded guns.

"There's so . . . many . . . more . . ." June said. *"Go."* She told Declan, "They're looking . . . for Ronan, too. They know about his brother. Where he lives—"

Then she threw herself at the woman as the woman rose with the gun, wrapping herself around the woman's body even as the woman shot her.

"Matthew," Declan said.

They ran.

72

The Lace was killing Hennessy.

It was doing what it said, really, what it always did. It overlaid her, enveloped her, replaced her. Give in, it urged, and this will stop hurting.

It had been killing her for ever so much longer than it normally did. Normally she had hurled herself awake by now, arriving with a copy of herself, newly tattooed, a little closer to death.

But this wasn't a dream she could stop, this was Lindenmere, and the person who could stop it was—

"Lindenmere," bellowed Ronan, in a completely unfamiliar voice, light flashing all around her, *"take it away."*

And then the Lace had released her, and then it was simply gone, and Hennessy was lying in the middle of the clearing on her back. Opal was crying in a frightened way and petting Hennessy's sleeve carefully. Hennessy couldn't move because everything *hurt*. It hadn't been long enough since the last time to fully recover and now she just felt . . . extruded. Her throat stung and she knew without checking that the Lace had branded her with another tattoo. Room for just one more.

It was almost over.

It was almost a relief to let herself think it.

Ronan cussed under his breath as he knelt beside her. "I'm sorry, I wasn't fast enough. I didn't realize it was going to come for you like that, all of a sudden—" He cussed some more.

"The copy . . ." Hennessy said.

"There's no copy," Ronan said. "You didn't bring anything back because it wasn't your dream, you didn't wake up, you were never asleep. Lindenmere just stopped it. There's just you. Shit. Shit damn. Lindenmere, Opal, can you help her—"

So it really was true. The Lace really would kill her even without the copies. It *felt* true. It felt like she was almost dead now. It felt like if Opal touched her skin, it would just wipe away.

Opal laid something cool on Hennessy's forehead, then repeated her ministrations on the backs of Hennessy's hands, and then on her exposed ankles. She babbled soothingly in an unrealistic-sounding language. She was still snottily crying herself. Ronan stood and hugged Opal's head to his leg.

"I don't know," Ronan said. "You need something to drive it away from you, like my light did."

Hennessy was about to say she hadn't seen that, but it took too much work to talk, and anyway, she thought she had actually seen it, now that she thought about it. That flash of light. That momentary retreat of the Lace before Lindenmere had taken it away.

"Something already in place," Ronan continued. "Is that helping? What Opal's doing? Armor. Armor and then something else, like a shield, something you could bring back with you that's not yourself, until you learn how to not bring things back every time you dream."

"I can't do it," Hennessy croaked.

Opal made a sad noise and laid another cool thing on her throat. It felt good in the way that things only can when it was feeling very, very bad before. She could feel that whatever Opal was doing was working a little. She wasn't going to pass out.

"I could do it," Ronan said. "I could go to sleep at the same time as you, meet you in the dream, and manifest something right when I got there."

No idea sounded like a good idea when you had only one shot left.

"Just ask. It's easy," Opal said in what was probably supposed to be a soothing tone, but, because of her small, breathy child's voice, and her big black eyes, and her strange goat's legs, sounded a little creepy instead. "Shield."

And Hennessy had a shield on her chest, weighing her down. She let out a cry of distress.

"Opal," snapped Ronan. "Away."

The shield vanished. Hennessy gasped for a little bit, and Opal busied herself putting more cool things on Hennessy's exposed skin.

"You were only trying to help," Ronan said to Opal in a conciliatory way. "But it's true, it is easy here. You only have to ask for something. Try it."

Everything Hennessy ever asked for turned into a disaster. A cruel trick. A drowning instead of an ocean.

"Just a little thing," Opal said in a wheedly little voice, like a mother baby-talking to a child.

"Everything I dream turns to shit," Hennessy said.

Ronan looked at her, brows furrowed. His mouth was working like he very much disagreed but he couldn't quite work out how to mount a counterargument. She didn't think he could do it. He said, "Like Jordan?"

He could.

Because of course Jordan was good. Better than Hennessy. The best of all the girls. Hennessy's best friend.

Dreamt.

Opal knelt down very low to lay her cheek beside Hennessy's ear. She whispered sweetly, "Just a little thing."

Hennessy closed her eyes and drew her hands over her chest. She cupped them there, thinking of the lights that had rained down earlier. So kind and perfect and innocent and fine. Hennessy hadn't been any of those things for so long.

"Hennessy," Ronan said, "please don't let me be the only one."

This was the first gap she'd ever heard in Ronan's armor.

"Just a little thing," Hennessy said. She opened her hands.

A tiny golden light slowly lifted from her palms. Out of the corner of one's eye, it was just a light. But if you looked at it close enough, it burned with a tiny, almost-not-there emotion: hope.

She had done it. Ask, and ye shall receive.

Then Ronan's phone rang.

73

Phones didn't always work in Lindenmere. Lindenmere was a thing that both used energy—ley line energy—and oozed energy—dream energy—and that seemed to sometimes contribute to phone signal and sometimes rob from it. More often rob from it. It didn't help that Lindenmere seemed to use time differently than the rest of the world did; a minute in Lindenmere could be two hours outside it, or two hours could be a minute. Under those conditions, it was amazing a phone call ever made it through.

But this one did.

"I'm not in the mood for a fight," Ronan said to the phone.

"Ronan," Declan said. "Tell me you're in the city."

"I'm in Lindenmere."

The breath Declan released was a more terrible sound than Ronan had ever heard his brother make.

"Why?"

"People are coming for you," Declan said. "To the town house. To kill you. Matthew's not picking up his phone."

For a second, Ronan's brain provided no thoughts and no words, and then he said, "Where are you?"

"Stuck in traffic," Declan said miserably. "I'm trying. No shoulder. No room. I've called the cops."

Hennessy was struggling to sit up, weakly putting herself together. He could tell she'd heard Declan's side of the conversation. Lindenmere had, too, because fat raindrops were beginning to splatter the ground, distress weeping from the turbulent sky.

Ronan asked, "How far away are you?"

"I can't get out and run, if that's what you're asking," Declan snapped. "He's not picking *up*, Ronan. They might already be there. I . . . look, they already got . . . Jordan is . . ."

As he broke off, Ronan closed his eyes. Think. *Think.* He had so much power, especially standing right in Lindenmere, but all of it was useless. He couldn't teleport himself. He couldn't make his brother pick up his phone. He could manipulate anything he liked within Lindenmere, but nothing outside of it. Even if he was sleeping, what could he possibly do against an unknown attacker two hours to the east?

He could make baubles and gadgets. Useless. Useless.

Hennessy was staring at him. She had heard Declan say *Jordan*, but he didn't have time to deal with that.

"I'll try," Ronan said.

"Try *what*?" Declan asked.

"I don't know. I don't *know*." He hung up. He had to think—he had to—

Lindenmere was whispering all around him. The trees were muttering among themselves.

Greywaren, the trees said. *We will give you what you need.*

"I don't know what I need, Lindenmere," he said. He struggled to imagine a solution. "I can't get there in time. I need something that *will* get there. Something secret. I'm trusting you. *Give me what I need.*"

Something dangerous, like you, he thought.

And like you, the forest whispered back.

Hennessy's little glowing bauble of hope still remained in the clearing, suspended between raindrops.

Lindenmere began to work.

The rain sank into the ground.

Chainsaw reappeared with a wary cry, accompanied by the soft *whuff* of her wings through the air. She landed on his arm, her ruff hackled up. She chattered her beak. Her talons clung more tightly to his arm, and where his wrist wasn't protected by his leather bracelets, they drew blood.

Hennessy covered her head as leaves exploded from the ground. Birds swirled up around them, one and the same with the leaves. The ground rumbled, the dirt pulling loose from around the roots down below. That low booming growled through the earth, getting higher and louder until it was a pure and clarion note ringing through the air, a purposeful and clean version of Adam's scream— a sound that meant it was *alive, very alive,* not the reverse. The leaves were frozen in midfall. The birds were trapped in midflight. Everything was held in that note.

In this frozen moment, lights swirled and spiraled in between the trees. The lights spooled the darkness around themselves like they were twisting yarn onto a bobbin. The darkness had weight and mass and shape. This was what Lindenmere was making for Ronan, with Ronan.

The dark new shapes let out no sound except for the dry leaves rustling with the force of their movement as the darkness kept spooling new layers on top of the light, hiding the light away inside.

Then the trapped leaves fell; the birds flew away.

The pack was made.

They coursed toward Ronan and Hennessy, a pack of creatures without definition.

With a squeak, Opal begged to be picked up, and he did so just as the creatures reached them.

Ronan saw that they were dogs, or hounds, or wolves. They were sooty, dead black, all mingling into each other, less like distinct animals and more like smoke billowing. Their eyes gleamed white-orange, and when they panted, their mouths glowed and revealed the brilliant furnaces inside each of them.

Sundogs are as fast as sunbeams, the trees whispered. *They're hungry. Quench them with water.*

"They're frightening," wailed Opal.

"I think that's the idea," Ronan said.

Tell them what to do, the trees said. The sundogs milled before him, black tongues rolling over black teeth, smoke seeping from them.

Ronan told the pack, "Save my brother."

74

The Lynch brothers, the brothers Lynch. In a way, the Lynch brothers had always been the most important and truest definition of the Lynch family. Niall was often gone, and Aurora was present but amorphous. Childhood was the three of them tearing through the woods and fields around the Barns, setting things on fire and digging holes and wrestling. Secrets bound them together far more tightly than any friendship ever could, and so even when they went to school, they remained the Lynch brothers, the brothers Lynch. Even after Niall died and Ronan and Declan had fought for a year, they'd remained tangled together, because hate binds as strongly as love. The Lynch brothers, the brothers Lynch.

Ronan didn't know who he would be without them.

He drove like a demon.

It wasn't only in Lindenmere that time did funny things. It took Ronan and Hennessy one hour and thirty-eight minutes to get to Alexandria, a feat only made possible through a combination of illegal speeds and giving very few damns about the consequences of those speeds. But one hour and thirty-eight minutes had never taken up so much space before. Every second was a minute, a day, a week, a month, a year. Every mile took lifetimes to cover. He would not know if the sundogs had made it in time until he got there.

He called his brothers. They did not pick up.

"Pick up," Hennessy muttered, in the passenger seat.

Ronan was always the one to find his dead family members; it didn't seem fair. It wasn't that he wanted his brothers to be the ones to have to bear the emotional wound of discovering the bodies. He just didn't want it to be *him*. He had been the one to find his father's body in the driveway outside their farmhouse, skull, meet tire iron. He had been the one to find his mother's body in the dying ruins of Cabeswater, a dream, extruded. Those images were his forever now, to the victor the prize, to the discoverer the memory.

He called Adam. Adam didn't pick up.

"Pick *up*," Hennessy said.

Time stretched out long and weird and infinite, a night without end, a city no closer.

He tried calling his brothers again.

They still didn't pick up.

"Somebody *pick up*." Hennessy pressed her hands over her face.

Finally, they pulled into the sedate, sterile town house neighborhood Declan and Matthew lived in. It appeared quiet and ordinary, the cars sleeping in driveways, the streetlights humming to soothe themselves, the leafless decorative saplings shivering in their dreams.

The door to Declan's town house was cracked open.

Ronan discovered in himself not worry, nor sadness, nor adrenaline, but rather a dead, dull absence of feeling. *Of course*, he thought. He looked to the dark city street behind him, but it was empty. Then he pushed open the door, Hennessy limping in behind him.

Inside, the town house was trashed. Not just trashed, but

ruined, intentionally destroyed. He had to step over the microwave, which had been thrown into the middle of the entry. Art from the walls was cast onto the stairs, as if it had been shot fleeing. The drawers of the hallway table were pulled out and thrown against the wall. Every light was on.

Ronan examined himself for feeling again. It had not yet returned. He turned his head and told Chainsaw, "Find them."

Silently, the raven took wing, wheeling around a light fixture and swooping up the stairs.

The last thing Matthew had said to him was that he was a liar.

He pulled the front door closed and stalked through the first floor, Hennessy following him in a daze. The rooms were unrecognizable. It took him a moment to realize that some things were missing: lamps, statues, some of the furniture. And some things were like the microwave: hurled into a wrong place.

There were bullet holes in the sofa.

he

felt

nothing

"Matthew?" he said in a low voice. "Declan?"

The first floor was empty. He found he didn't want to climb the stairs. He still had that fuzzy noiselessness inside him, that lack of feeling, but he also sort of thought that if they were dead upstairs, this was the last minute he had before adding the memories of their bodies to his others.

"Kerah," Chainsaw called from the second or third floor.

Okay. Just do it.

Ronan climbed the stairs. At the top of them he found words painted across the wall that used to hold family photos.

STOP DREAMING

A pair of Matthew's novelty socks were inexplicably tossed in the center of the carpet. The beagles on them peered at Ronan, who peered back.

He heard a rustling from the master bedroom. It was impossible to place. It sounded busy.

"Ronan?" whispered Hennessy. She didn't sound like herself.

"Stay downstairs," he whispered back. He knew he didn't sound like himself, either.

"*Kerah,*" Chainsaw insisted, from the master.

Ronan risked it. "Declan? Matthew?"

"Ronan! We're up here!" Matthew's voice, and every feeling Ronan hadn't felt for the past five minutes returned all at once. He had to crouch for a second by the beagle socks, fingers pressed into Declan's carpet, normally perfect but now crunchy with paint splatters. *God, God, God.* It was both a prayer of gratitude and a plea.

"Did you send these damn monsters?" Declan called.

Yes, yes he had.

The mist had cleared; Ronan was able to straighten and continue to the master.

The sundogs filled it. Their omnipresence made no sense if one thought of them as a pack of dogs, but if one thought of them as a cloud of smoke, it made perfect sense. Like a gas, they expanded to fill the size of the container. They parted around Ronan, mouths gaping and fiery, as he looked in each room.

"Where are you guys?"

"Up here," Declan said in a sour voice.

Ronan looked up. The voice was coming behind the tiny panel in the ceiling that led to the attic space. "Why the hell are you still up there?"

"Your monsters are trying to kill us, too," Matthew's voice said, but it sounded cheery about it.

The attic door cracked. Instantly all the sundogs were at Ronan's feet, piling over one another, trying to get high enough to get in. They made a very good job of it in very short order.

"Whoa, whoa, shut it," Ronan said. "Get down!"

But the sundogs didn't attend.

"Ronan," Declan said, in a warning sort of way.

"Hold on, hold on," Ronan said, trying to work it out.

Lindenmere's words came back to him. He cast around the second floor until he found Matthew's sport water bottle rolled underneath his bed. *Quench them with water*, Lindenmere had said. There wasn't enough water in here to pour over all of them, but it was at least enough to test a theory.

But to his surprise, that wasn't how it happened.

He unscrewed the top.

Immediately, the sundogs poured into the bottle.

One moment the room was full of them, the floor covered by their milling, nebulous bodies. The next, the water in the bottle momentarily darkened and swirled and then went clear again. The only evidence that the sundogs were actually still in there, somehow, was a small wisp of darkness that wouldn't entirely melt away, like a strand of dark oil.

Ronan capped the bottle. "All clear. Hennessy, it's all clear!"

The attic door disgorged his brothers, first Matthew, then Declan, then Jordan.

Jordan rushed across the room and held Hennessy so fast that Hennessy stumbled and had to catch herself on the doorjamb.

"I thought you were dead," Hennessy said in a hollow voice.

"They're dead," Jordan whispered. "They're all dead."

Matthew went to Ronan to have his head embraced, like when he was younger, and Ronan hugged him tightly.

"I'm sorry I lied," he told Matthew. Declan and Ronan held gazes over the top of Matthew's golden curls. In that shared gaze Ronan saw what the destroyed town house already implied: It had been bad.

Declan said, "Without your monsters we'd be dead. Are they—"

Ronan shook the water bottle. "They're in here." He handed the bottle to Matthew, who pulled out of his embrace to sit on the bed and study it. "There you go, kid, don't say I never gave you anything."

Declan snatched the bottle away from Matthew. "It's like giving a gun to a toddler. Do you know what these things do? Did you see before you sent them?"

Ronan shook his head.

Declan put the water bottle firmly back in his hand. "I'd put this on a high shelf. Look on the other side of the bed."

A brief recce to the other side of the room revealed that there was an arm between the bed and the window, and a lot of blood that Ronan assumed used to be in the arm. He turned back in order to verify that it didn't belong to either Matthew or Declan. It didn't seem to. He searched inside himself for regret and couldn't find it. He looked for fear, too, but all he could find was incandescent rage.

"We need to talk," Declan said. He pulled his gaze from Jordan and Hennessy. "Because they'll be back."

75

The Visionaries never wanted to do it after seeing an attack. Lock had gotten used to it. They were gung ho ready to fight for the cause when they first met the Moderators, and then they saw how it really went down, and they all got cold feet. For a while Lock thought the answer was to keep them away from the attacks if at all possible, but then he realized that was futile, too. Eventually they saw the attacks in their visions, so one way or another the moment of reckoning was always coming.

Liliana was no different. He had checked into the same hotel as Farooq-Lane and Ramsay, and when he saw her with Carmen in the hotel lobby, he could tell that she wasn't going to be the sort with an iron stomach. She was more the gauzy, weeping, green peace type. People who looked like her wanted to do this to make the world a better place and people who looked like her rarely saw how shooting teenagers in the head and guts was making the world a better place.

So he already knew before they went out that it was going to require some negotiation after he returned.

And when it was all done with, he knew he was going to do whatever it took, because her intel was gold.

Sure, it had been a shit show. Bellos now had one arm. Ramsay had gotten shot in the same arm he'd gotten stabbed with a crucifix in, that was just his bum arm, but at least he still had it. Nikolenko had a motherfucking bite—a *bite!*—on her neck. Some odd number of dreams had gotten away. It was impossible to tell if any of those girls had been the original Jordan Hennessy. Ronan Lynch was nowhere to be found.

But that wasn't Liliana's fault. Her intel had been spectacular. Specific, brilliant, special information about two entirely separate Zeds in two entirely different locations. She was the Visionary they'd been absolutely waiting for. He'd never seen anything like it.

It looked like this thing might actually get fixed, where *this thing* was the apocalypse.

Good. He hadn't seen his dog in ages.

Many people wouldn't consider Lock's job a plum job; heading up a largely clandestine task force didn't allow for many public accolades and didn't pay as well as the private sector. But Lock didn't work for those things, he worked for the sense of purpose, for the acquisition of trust, for the eventual building of a pyramid of humans who assumed he would get the job done right the first time. He assumed that at the end of all this, assuming the world got saved, he could trade in this cache for fun and prizes of indeterminate nature.

Lock strode up to Farooq-Lane in the hotel bar. "How is she?"

"She wants to quit," Farooq-Lane hissed. He'd never seen her so angry. It was as unseemly as her grief had been when her brother had been shot. One wanted to give her something to put over her face until she could get her dignity back. "And why do you think that might be? Maybe put Ramsay on a *leash* or just put him down entirely."

"If we swapped Ramsay out, do you think that would be enough to change her mind?"

"It might not be enough to change *my* mind," Farooq-Lane said.

Lock gave her a look. He didn't say anything to her, but the look said it to her instead. The look said, remember that we talked about this. The look said, remember that we're not entirely sure you didn't know about all the shit your brother did before we caught him. The look said, remember that we could always begin a long and messy public investigation to find out if you were complicit. The look said, *you're not changing your mind.* The look said, *also by the way we're saving the world and who opts out of that?*

Farooq-Lane averted her eyes in the face of this look. She said, "I think it'll take more than that."

Lock said, "What's her room number?"

Farooq-Lane said, "Two fifteen. For now."

"Get some sleep, Carmen," Lock said. "We need your wonderful brain sharp. You've done very well this week."

He rode up the elevator to the second floor and walked down the hall. Liliana was in an end suite that Lock knew would still take out the occupants of at least ten other hotel rooms if she hadn't yet learned to turn the visions inward. God, he couldn't even imagine how good her intel would be if she learned to focus them in. This thing would be over before it began. The Zeds wouldn't have a chance.

Lock knocked on Liliana's door. Three authoritative knocks. The first said: answer. Second: the. Third: door.

She did.

"May I come in?" he asked.

Her nose and eyes were red from tears. She let him in.

He sat on the edge of her sofa and patted it to indicate she should balance out the other end. She did.

"I understand you found today very unpleasant," he said, "because it was very unpleasant." He had discovered there was no reason to beat around the bush. No point spinning such a gross truth into anything less gross; it was already emblazoned in their minds. "I don't have to tell you why we're doing it because you can see firsthand for yourself. It's an unpleasant task we simply can't do without you." The next step was always to remind them of why they had been willing to do it in the first place. "I completely understand if you have to leave us, but I'd ask that you'd please help us find another Visionary to take your place before you do." Then it was important, Lock found, to let them realize they weren't trapped. Trapped creatures did desperate things and so you wanted to remind them the window was open even if they could not fly through it immediately without being a bag of dicks. "But if you do stay with us, I promise you that we will do our best to make it worthwhile."

Finally, Lock had discovered it was important in the first few minutes of meeting a new Visionary to discover what it was they wanted most in the world, and see if it was at all within your power to offer it. People were straightforward. Girls, guns, gold, as the song went.

Lock looked at this crying redheaded girl, and he read her body language, and he guessed what she wanted. "If you stay on with us, I was thinking that what we could do is get you out of this hotel and we'd get you into a rental cottage you could return to between each trip and keep you in short-term rentals at each place we went to so you could feel more like you were at home.

You'd have a Moderator with you each place to help you get whatever you needed to eat or wear."

This Visionary wanted stability, he guessed. She wanted a place where she didn't have to worry about exploding innocents to bits. A place she didn't have to put her toothbrush back in her luggage each night. She didn't seem to have any luggage. Probably she wanted that, too, but he'd hold that for later.

Liliana lowered her eyelashes; they were as red as the hair on her head. She was truly lovely, but in such an extreme way that Lock realized it must be part of what made her a Visionary. They all had some strange attribute that worked upon the present in odd ways, and this must be part of hers.

She was thinking about it.

She chewed her lip, then made a decision. "Can Farooq-Lane stay with me?"

76

So the world had broken.

The world had broken, and in the end, Declan wasn't sure there was anything he could have done to stop it. He didn't know if the people who had busted into his town house had come because he hadn't been careful enough, or because he had called attention to himself, or because he had called a Boston number about *The Dark Lady*, or because he had called a number about Boudicca, or because of none of those things.

He just knew the world had broken and now neither of his brothers was safe.

STOP DREAMING.

They sat in the Shenandoah Café. It was quite some distance from the town house, which seemed important, and it was a public place, which seemed very important, and it was open twenty-four hours on weekends, which seemed very, very important.

They weren't really talking. They were supposed to be, but after some preliminary catch-up, they'd all fallen silent. Hennessy leaned her head on Jordan's shoulder, looking battered and exhausted and miserable and relieved that Jordan's shoulder was there to hold her up. Jordan stared off at some knickknacks on the wall. Not dreamy, but haunted. Matthew stared at Jordan, and why wouldn't he? The first living dream he'd seen since he'd learned he was one. Ronan clenched and unclenched his fist on the table, staring out the front door at their two cars parked in the lot. He kept looking at his phone: There was an unanswered text to Adam on it. Declan was waiting for his phone to attend to him, too. He had dictated emails and texts to Matthew as they drove here, put calls in and left voicemails, putting out all the feelers he dared to those who might know who was killing dreamers in DC.

Their server, Wendy, leaned in with a large platter.

"I brought you double apple fritters," she said. "You kids seem like you've had a rough night."

"I knew I liked her," Hennessy said after she'd gone, and put her head down on her arms. It was uncanny to see her beside Jordan. They were the same girl, but they were also very much not. They had the same face and used it entirely differently. It was hard to believe Hennessy was the dreamer. Jordan seemed like she should've come first. Hennessy was . . . less.

Don't think about it, Declan thought to himself. *Just stop.*

The phone rang.

But it was not Declan's; it was Ronan's. SARGENTO said the caller ID.

Ronan swept it up and put it to his ear. He put his head down and listened, saying very little. *What does Gansey say? No. But why . . . no. No, stay away. Have you heard from Ad— Have you heard from Parrish? Couple of hours. I know. I know.*

After he hung up, Ronan said, "They talked to Mr. Gray."

Both of the older Lynch brothers took a moment to square their jaws. Their relationship with Mr. Gray was complicated: He was the man who had been ordered to kill Niall Lynch. Niall was just one of the many people he had killed for his employer, Colin Greenmantle, who was blackmailing him. Did that make him

Niall's killer? Yes. Did that make him his murderer? Possibly. Or possibly Mr. Gray was the weapon in Greenmantle's hand.

Mr. Gray had spent much time since his freedom from Greenmantle trying to make it up to the Lynch brothers, although killing someone's parent just wasn't the kind of thing a relationship ever bounced back from. Regardless, it meant that he would always provide information if he could.

But the Lynches would never talk to him.

"He said all that's on the street is that a group is killing dreamers, and they have government backing. There's a lot of them."

"Why?" Matthew asked.

"They don't know why."

"How many is 'a lot'?" Declan asked.

"Enough that there was another attack going on in South Africa while they were attacking the town house tonight, apparently," Ronan said.

The world was broken, Declan thought. It was broken and could not be fixed.

He thought, *And I never actually lived, either.*

"How do they know, then, about the dreamers?" Jordan asked. "We didn't even know you existed until you showed up on our door, did we?"

Because dreamers were meant to be secret, Declan thought. Because they all knew secrecy was the only way to survive. Fuck, he thought helplessly. *What now?*

"And I didn't know about you until Bryde," Ronan said. "Oh. Do you remember what he said, Hennessy? When he left."

Hennessy turned her head so that her voice was audible. "'The world's going to shit.' He knew. It surprised him, but he knew."

"Declan," Ronan said, "don't tell me not to."

"What am I telling you not to?"

"Don't tell me not to chase Bryde," Ronan said. "Don't tell me to keep my head down."

Everything in Declan wanted to, though. The world could always be broken more. As long as his brothers were alive, there was always worse that could happen.

"Tell me some other way," Ronan went on. "Tell me something that's not asking Bryde for help and I'll do it."

Declan hated this. The old familiar twist of his stomach. The rank sourness of danger. It wasn't fear for himself, he realized. Because it had been dangerous to go see the new Fenian, but that hadn't felt like this. That had been illicit and thrilling, and not just because he had Jordan with him. Because his father's criminal blood pumped through him. No, Declan hated the idea of his brothers being in danger. "What good would he do? You don't know anything about him."

"We know he's powerful," Hennessy said. "We know they were talking about him at the Fairy Market."

"He knows about more dreamers than just us," Ronan added. "And he knows more about how it works than I do. We know the monster in Hennessy's head is afraid of him."

"But it will take both of you to convince him," Jordan said. "Isn't that what you said when we got here? You and Hennessy both. And she only has one more dream left."

Hennessy sat up. "I can do it."

Jordan said, "There's no fallback."

"I can do it," Hennessy said. "Or go out trying. It's this or the next time the black ooze—the nightwash—comes anyway."

Ronan said, "We can do it. I know it."

It was unlike Ronan to lie.

He cut his eyes away from Declan. "What about you guys?"

Matthew broke in, "I don't want to pretend."

Declan regarded his youngest brother. He looked different than he had just a few days before, because for the first time in several months, he'd lost sleep. He had dark circles beneath his pleasant eyes, and lines around his ordinarily smiling mouth.

He went on, "I went to soccer and all I could think about was how you said I might not have internal organs."

"M——" started Declan.

"It's just not real," Matthew said. "It's not real to pretend like any of the other guys are going to walk off campus and not remember why they did. It's not real to pretend they're all walking to Great Falls. It's not real, it's just not real. I want to be real. I want to know why it's happening. I want to know if I can stop it. There's no point otherwise, D, there's just no point."

"Okay," said Declan softly.

Everyone at the table looked at him.

Declan was powerless to deny Matthew a thing he wanted anyway, but it was more than that. It was that he'd given up everything and gotten nothing for it in return. It was that he wasn't a dreamer, and he wasn't a dream, and he couldn't be human; there was nothing left. Just a turquoise ocean with no sign that he'd ever been. Something had to change.

"We'll go to the Barns," he said. "It's hidden, right? We'll look for answers from there. We won't pretend anymore."

"And Ronan and I will contact Bryde," Hennessy said. "Jordan, I want you to go with Declan and Matthew."

Jordan sat by herself in the corner of the booth, one leg up on the booth beside her now that Hennessy had sat up. She some-how seemed more real than any of them. A dream, but more real than Declan. This was all so tangled.

"If she comes," Declan said, "I'll make sure she's taken care of if something happens to Hennessy."

Jordan eyed her dreamer, and then she eyed Declan, and then Ronan. She shook her head. "No. I'm coming to watch you sleep."

"Jordan," Hennessy said. "Please go with him. In case some-thing happens."

Jordan shook her head. "I'm not leaving you to do this alone."

"Jordan," Hennessy begged. "The others are all dead. They died thinking I just left them, that I wasn't even trying. I *saw* their faces. Please let me do this thing for you. Please. Please just be safe."

All of this was the opposite of safe, but Declan knew what she meant. She didn't really mean *safe*, any more than his life before this had been safe. She meant *something I can control*.

"Jordan," Declan said, "I'll let you drive."

77

Great Falls sounded wild at night. There were no tourists, no car sounds, no day birds calling. There was just the massive surge of millions of gallons of water rushing down from West Virginia toward the Atlantic, and the trees murmuring in sympathy.

It was cold, finally cold, properly November. They parked the car in a parking lot over a mile away from the falls; they planned to walk the rest of the way in since the park was closed from dusk until dawn. That was how they wanted it. Empty. Undisturbed.

It would have been better to dream closer to the ley line, but none of them felt like they had that kind of time. And they already well knew that Great Falls was the best source of alternate power close by.

Somewhere, the other two Lynch brothers were racing across the state toward the Barns. Hennessy had watched Ronan and Matthew hug, and then watched Ronan and Declan face each other. Ronan had kicked the ground like he was mad at it. Declan had said, *I'll see you at the Barns.*

And then Jordan and Hennessy had said goodbye. Maybe the last time they would ever see each other again, their faces that looked so like each other and yet were nothing alike. Jordan, who'd always believed in the world, and Hennessy, who'd always known it was waiting for her to die. The Hennessy who had never seen the Lace, and the Hennessy who had.

"Don't do anything I wouldn't do," Hennessy had said. It was a joke.

"Bring me back a T-shirt," said Jordan. Another joke.

Then they had hugged, tightly.

Hennessy didn't want Jordan to go to sleep forever.

And now they were at Great Falls. Hennessy and Ronan lay in the middle of Overlook I, looking up at the black leaves against the black sky, uncomfortably similar to the appearance of the Lace. The water sounded impossibly close when her head was resting on the boards, like it was just inches below the deck.

She was tired, because she was always tired, but she didn't know how she would ever sleep like this. Knowing it might be the last time she did.

After several minutes, she asked, "What do you think he'll be like?"

"Bryde? I don't know."

"What do you want him to be like?" Hennessy asked.

"Better at this than me," Ronan said.

"What's this?"

"Dreaming. Staying alive. Knowing what to do about the nightwash. Knowing what to do with Matthew. Knowing what to do with these dreamkillers. What do you want him to be like?"

She wanted him to tell her how to stay alive. She wanted him to tell her how to save Jordan for good, so that she no longer had to rely on Hennessy, who was always and ever unreliable. She wanted Jordan to have the life she deserved.

"Sexy as hell," Hennessy said.

They both laughed.

Every sound seemed amplified; their laugh boomed.

A bright square illuminated the night as Ronan checked his phone. He was looking for a response to his last text to MANAGEMENT. Hennessy could see a wall of text that Ronan had sent about Bryde, and then, on its own line, where Ronan had texted *Tamquam*. It was marked unread.

He put the phone away.

She could tell that he had been hoping for a reply before they did this.

"Okay. Okay," Ronan said. "You go to sleep first, because I know how to find you in dreamspace. But that means when you fall asleep, you *have* to make something to keep the Lace away from you. Immediately. You can't get shunted out of that dream before I get there to call Bryde, or you die, and the game's all up."

She didn't answer.

"You did it in Lindenmere. You saw how I did it."

She did. Not just with those little baubles of joy, but with those sundogs. The most incredible part of watching Ronan manifest them hadn't been the sundogs themselves. It had been when Ronan said to the vast dreamspace that knew every part of him: *I'm trusting you.* A savage fuckup like Ronan could trust his subconscious that deeply.

Could she?

"I'll make something, too," Ronan said. "As soon as I see you."

She was so afraid.

"Hennessy?" Ronan said, in a slightly different voice.

"Lynch."

"I've been alone a long time," he said.

Part of her thought that he hadn't, though. His brothers, his boyfriend, his friends who called him with information in the middle of the night.

But the bigger part of her understood it, because she'd been alone, too. Because at the end of the day, no one else could fathom what it was like living with these endless possibilities inside your head.

Hennessy had come tonight thinking she didn't want Jordan to sleep forever if this failed.

But now she knew this, too: She didn't want to die, either.

She reached between them and fumbled until she felt his leather wristbands, then found his hand. She held it. He held back tightly.

78

Ronan was in hell.

He was dreaming.

The Lace was everywhere; it was the entire dream. It was wrong to say it surrounded him, because that would imply that he still existed, and he wasn't sure of that. The dream was the Lace. He was the Lace.

It was hell.

It was the dreamt security system.

It was Adam's scream.

It was his last forest dying.

It was his father's battered body.

It was his mother's grave.

It was his friends leaving in Gansey's old Camaro for a year's trip without him.

It was Adam sitting with him in the labyrinth in Harvard telling him that it was never going to work.

It was *tamquam*, marked unread.

The Lace.

It would kill him, too, it said. You have nothing but yourself and what is that?

But then there was a furious flash of light, and in it, he felt a burst of hope.

He was part of something bigger.

He remembered what he had promised Hennessy. Something.

A weapon. Something. He felt it in his hand. He looked. It was no longer just him and the Lace. It was now his body, his hand, and in his hand, the hilt he'd woken with in the BMW after chasing Mór Ó Corra.

"Hennessy?" he shouted.

There was no answer.

Shit.

He had fallen asleep and come here.

And she had fallen asleep and gone where she always went. Into the Lace. Maybe already dead.

"*Hennessy!*" he shouted. "Lindenmere, are you here? Is she here?"

The Lace pressed in, hungry, dreadful.

If only Opal were here, or Chainsaw. He needed one of his psychopomps. He needed to have Adam strengthening the ley energy while he dreamt. He needed—

He needed another dreamer.

He shouted, "We're more than this, Hennessy!"

That slice of light came again, so brightly white that he couldn't look at it. He realized now it had been behind the Lace the entire time, and he'd glimpsed it before through one of the ragged holes. It was spinning in a massive circle, and it was getting closer.

Hennessy was behind it. She was spinning a strip of light around in front of her, and it was pressing the Lace away from her. Not vanquishing it, but not allowing it any closer.

It was a sword. Every time it cut the air it released pure white light like the moon and stars.

"Bryde gave this to me," Hennessy said. Her face was caught in wonder.

Ronan looked at the hilt in his hand. It now had a beautiful black blade to match the hilt. Ronan lifted it, and as he did, it carved a line of sun glow behind it.

The Lace fell back.

Together they might not be able to vanquish Hennessy's old dream, but they could hold it at bay.

Now they could get their breath. Now they could get their breath enough to say it together: "Bryde."

79

The very first dream Ronan had ever been truly proud of, truly euphoric over, had been a copy.

It had been in high school. Ronan wasn't good at surviving high school and he wasn't good at surviving friendship, and so while his friend Gansey's back was turned, he'd stolen Gansey's car. It was a beautiful car. A 1973 bright orange Camaro with stripes right up its hood and straight down its ass. Ronan had wanted to drive it for months, despite Gansey forbidding it.

Maybe because of him forbidding it.

Within hours of stealing it, Ronan had totaled it.

Gansey hadn't wanted him to drive it because he thought he'd grind the clutch, or curb it, or burn out the tires, or maybe, *maybe* blow the engine.

And here Ronan had totaled it.

Ronan had loved Richard C. Gansey III far more than he loved himself at that point, and he hadn't known how he was going to ever face him when he returned from out of town.

And then Joseph Kavinsky had taught him to dream a copy.

Before that, all of Ronan's dreams—that he knew about, Matthew didn't count—had been accidents and knickknacks, the bizarre and the useless. When he'd successfully copied a car, an entire car, he'd been out of his mind with glee. The dreamt car had been perfect down to the last detail. Exactly like the original. The pinnacle of dreaming.

Now a copy was the least impressive thing to him. He could copy anything he put his mind to. That just made him a very ethereal photocopier. A one-man 3-D printer.

The dreams he was proud of now were the dreams that were originals. Dreams that couldn't exist in any other way. Dreams that took full advantage of the impossibility of dreamspace in a way that was cunning or lovely or effective or all of the above. The sundogs. Lindenmere. Dreams that had to be dreams.

In the past, all his good dreams like this were gifts from Lindenmere or accidents rather than things he had consciously constructed. He was beginning to realize, after listening to Bryde, that this was because he'd been thinking too small. His consciousness was slowly becoming the shape of the concrete, waking world, and it was shrinking all his dreams to the probable. Bryde was right: He needed to start realizing that *possible* and *impossible* didn't mean the same thing for him as they did for other people. He needed to break himself of the habit of rules, of doubt, of physics. His *what if* had grown so tame.

You are made of dreams and this world is not for you.

He would not let the nightwash take him and Matthew.

He would not let this world kill him slowly.

He deserved a place here, too.

He woke.

Ronan saw himself from above. Strangely lit. Brightly lit. Hennessy lay opposite him, also motionless. A sword lay on each of their chests, a matching pair. Ronan's hands were clasped over the hilt that read VEXED TO NIGHTMARE and Hennessy's over a hilt that read FROM CHAOS. Both were sheathed in dark leather.

She'd done it.

They'd done it.

They'd held the Lace at bay, Hennessy had manifested something other than herself in the dream, and she'd come back to waking neither bleeding nor with a copy of herself. There was still a gap at her tattoo where another rose could fit.

Ronan heard voices; shouting.

This was wrong.

The lights striping across them were wrong. Headlights, or flashlights.

Move, he told his body.

But his body could not be hurried.

If those dreamkillers had tracked them here somehow, and if they found them before the paralysis wore off, it wouldn't matter if these swords performed as they did in the dream. They'd be shot where they lay.

Move, he told his body.

It was nowhere near movement. He was still looking at himself from above.

"Over here!" shouted one of the voices, drawing nearer to the observation deck.

No.

Now he could hear trees rustling, leaves being kicked up, boots on gravel. They were coming down to the viewing area. There'd be no time for negotiation, for threat, for anything but dying.

"Don't come any closer," said a very familiar voice.

It was calm, level, infinitely less surreal when spoken into a walking space instead of into Ronan's dreams.

The speaker was not visible from Ronan's limited vantage point, but Ronan knew who it was regardless.

Bryde.

"I suggest you stop right there, or I will be forced to detonate my weapon," Bryde said calmly. Nearby. Just out of sight. Ronan could only stare at himself and Hennessy from above.

"Show yourself!" called a rough voice.

Bryde, if anything, sounded amused. "I'd rather not. Let's have a bit more room. And in front, please put your guns down. This is uncivilized."

Finally, Ronan was getting a glimpse of the black sky above. He was returning to his body.

"Who are you?" demanded one of the other voices farther up the path.

"You already know me as Bryde."

"What do you want?"

"How about a conversation," Bryde said, "before you rush in here and shoot any more people in the head."

Ronan could move. Finally. He said, "I'm sitting up."

"Do you hear that?" Bryde called. "They're sitting up. Don't anyone do anything stupid. Like I said, let's not drive me to a massacre."

Ronan and Hennessy looked up the path. There were dozens of people. Probably sixty. Some of them were dressed in normal clothing, but plenty more were in uniform. Bulletproof vests.

Ronan squinted in the direction of Bryde's voice. He saw a figure among the trees, eyes glinting, cast in darkness. He could feel his pulse racing.

One of the dreamkillers shouted, "What do you want?"

"Why are you trying to kill us?"

"Not *trying*," Hennessy said. "Why are you killing us? You killed my entire family. We weren't doing shit to you."

"We have it on very good authority that one of you Zeds is going to end the world," rumbled one of the members of the party. "It's not personal. That's simply too much power for one person."

"What kind of authority?" sneered Ronan.

"Good," said the voice. "I thought I said that before."

"So you just want us to *die*?" Hennessy demanded.

"Or stop dreaming," suggested another one of the party.

Bryde broke in gently, "That's a little facetious, don't you think? We all know by now that dreamers must dream. So that's not truly a bargain any of you or us could strike. That's a thing you offer so that you can sleep at night. That's the story you tell your children when you call them. That's not a thing you tell another adult with a straight face."

"My girls were just trying to survive," said Hennessy. "You killed them for nothing. For nothing."

"Look," said a quiet voice. It belonged to a woman with dark hair and a very clean linen suit. "Maybe we can work with you if you give yourselves up. Do you want to work with us?"

"Carmen," said the rumbly voice. "That's not . . ."

"No," Hennessy said. "You gunned down my family. How about you just leave us alone and we leave you alone? Like you would anyone else in this country?"

"You're not anyone else," said the rumbly voice.

In a low voice, Bryde said to Ronan and Hennessy, "This isn't a negotiation, it's stalling. We're about to be shot at with some very large weapons. I told you what it meant if you called me."

"More hiding," Ronan said.

"Running and hiding are two different things."

"How long?" Ronan asked.

"As long as it takes."

His phone had still not buzzed; he had no answer from Adam. He wasn't going to get one before he had to make up his mind.

Ronan put his hand on the hilt of VEXED TO NIGHTMARE. If he pulled the sword from the scabbard, there'd be no denying what he was. Everyone here would know what he was capable of. This was not just a vendor at the Fairy Market and a few black market onlookers. This was a crowd of sixty, a good majority of whom would consider such proof of dreaming a definite death sentence.

Hennessy and Ronan looked at each other.

They pulled the swords free.

VEXED TO NIGHTMARE gleamed blindingly. The blade was made of the sky, and the sun blasted along every inch of it. As he swung it in an enormous arc over his head, it shimmered and dripped and blasted sunlight out from it, obscuring him. Beside him, Hennessy had unsheathed FROM CHAOS and now it gleamed with the cold, pure white of the full moon, and when she swung it, sparks and stars and fuming comet trail dripped and blasted out from it, hiding the rest of them from view.

It forced the dreamkillers back even more surely than it had forced back the Lace.

Bryde stepped into this furious light. He was older than Ronan and Hennessy, but hard to say by how much. His eyes were intense and clever over his hawkish nose. He was tawny-haired and tall, with an understated confidence to his movement, a tidy way of carrying his height. He looked like a man who didn't have to posture, who knew his strength. He looked like a man who didn't lose his temper very easily. He looked, Ronan thought, like a hero.

Bryde said, "Now we dream."

In his hands was a very familiar shape: a clone of the hoverboard that Ronan had dreamt back in Harvard.

He threw it down. It bobbed to Hennessy and Ronan and hovered just above the ground.

Ronan swirled VEXED TO NIGHTMARE one more time, creating a new shower of blinding light, and then Bryde, Ronan, and Hennessy climbed onto the hoverboard, gripping one another.

Bryde, in front, pitched the board over the surging and furious river.

When the light cleared, the dreamers were gone.

END OF BOOK ONE

ACKNOWLEDGMENTS

This book was a very long time coming, and for a nearly a year, I didn't believe in it. I was too ill for stories, which was not a kind of ill I thought was possible, but it turns out that one should avoid harboring parasites if at all possible because they never pay enough rent to justify their occupation. Because it took such a very long time to diagnose and then even longer to cure, the story of my illness would probably take more words to tell than this book, but it is not overstating to say that this book wouldn't exist without the medical team at Charlottesville's Resilient Roots Functional Medicine, Ryan Hall, and Robert Abbott, MD. I can't thank them enough in helping me stagger my way back to health.

My dear friends and longtime critique partners Brenna Yovanoff and Sarah Batista-Pereira were there every arduous step of the way, putting up with more bitching than any two humans should have to put up with, even when I was half-asleep. You've always been good at meeting me in my dreams anyway.

I'm intensely grateful to my editor, David Levithan, and my agent, Laura Rennert, for their forbearance. They saw many things in their inboxes that were not books before they finally got to see a book. Thank you for giving me time to blink awake.

Thanks also to Bridget and Victoria, for your reads of many ugly drafts without ends, and to Harvard Ryan, for late-night

Thayer adventures, and Will, for putting up with a dreamer for so long.

And thank you, as ever, to Ed. This was a long one, but we woke from the nightmare together, and I'm glad to find we're still holding hands tightly now that we're awake.